Bittersweet
Deceit

Bittersweet Deceit

Blakely Bennett

TandemWriters

Bittersweet Deceit

TandemWriters

Cover design by Clarissa Yeo
Logo design by Olivia E. Bennett
Edited by Read Owl Publishing

ISBN: 978-0-69226-201-6 (Trade Paperback)
ISBN: 978-1-63315-007-2 (eBook)

Bittersweet Deceit is dedicated to NC Simmons, a woman who stormed into my life with lots of love and passion. We initially connected over our erotic writing, and then found a friendship that defies the short time we have known each other. With all my heart, I wish you well and thank you for all your support.

Warmest hugs,
Blakely

AUTHOR'S NOTE

This is the second installment in the Bound by Your Love series, which centers on the romantic lives of a close-knit group of friends. It's not necessary to read the stories in order, but *Stuck in Between* is the first.

As you will see, each chapter is headed with a song title. The melody, title, and/or lyrics inspired me to choose each song for its corresponding chapters. If you're into music, like I am, I hope you enjoy the accompaniment.

Warning: This novel contains a marital affair, light BDSM (including, but not limited to, role-playing, bondage, spanking, and paddling), video watching of fisting, anal sex, and more.

You can't say I didn't warn you.

ACKNOWLEDGMENTS

So much goes into creating a novel. I have amassed the most amazing team of people who helped me with editing, cover art, beta/test reading, and moral support.

Much appreciation goes to April Duffy, my editor extraordinaire from Read Owl, Clarissa Yeo who continues to amaze me with her cover art talents, and Serena K., Ann P., Tami C., Kim L., Sara S., and Julie C. my wonderful beta/test readers.

The value of my moral support team can never be overstated. My family, friends, and fans keep me motivated to push forward and keep creating. A special acknowledgment goes out to my "street team". They show me love and support daily, and I feel incredibly blessed to be able to call each one my friend. I love you, babes!

Anyone who knows me at all knows I'm one of the lucky ones when it comes to love. Dana Bennett, fellow author (highly talented), husband, lover (very talented here as well), and best friend, continues to be my biggest fan, cheerleader, first reader, idea sounding board, and the best cuddlier the world has ever known. Thank you, my love, for the last nineteen years together and for being my strongest support in life and in writing.

CHAPTER ONE

Undertow

by Sara Bareilles

"**M**ason, get up," I said, jostling him. Underneath the gray sheet, his chest rose and fell slowly. It was a rare treat for him to spend the night.

"Hmm, Lainie come back to bed." He reached out from under the cover to pull me to him.

"Come on, I'm serious. It's already nine thirty and Jacqs will be here soon. Isn't Victoria expecting you home?"

"I told her my plane doesn't arrive until this afternoon." Mason looked up at me and pierced me with his ravishing, clear, blue eyes. "Can I come back after your brunch? I don't know when I'll be able to get away again." He scooted up against the headboard, which caused the sheet to fall to his waist.

The smattering of hair on his chest and taut lower abs made me groan.

"Come here, love. We still have a few minutes." He moved down on the mattress and held his arms out to me.

I climbed in and covered his body with mine. "We don't have much time."

"I love you, baby," he said just before his lips touched mine.

I wouldn't say I love you back, I couldn't. It was not that I didn't love him, I loved him so much it devastated me if I thought too far ahead, knowing that he would never truly be mine. I kissed him back hard, breathing him in, wanting to fuse our bodies together. My extra twenty-five pounds no longer deterred me with Mason. My full hips and soft belly seemed to inspire lust in him.

He flipped me over onto my back, spreading my long, smooth legs wide as he plunged in. "You're so ready, it won't take us long." He groaned once he gained full penetration and held himself still. Peering down into my eyes, he said, "I want to play the game again when I come back later."

I closed my eyes and shook my head no.

He shifted his weight to his right side and gripped my chin with his left hand so I was forced to look straight into his eyes. "You know you want to. I'm not sure why…" He said as he pulled his cock back slowly and rammed back into me, causing me to writhe. "you want to…" Then he leisurely stroked in and out of me. In his husky, deep voice he said, "pretend like you—ahhh yes I can feel you getting closer—pretend you don't love the game." He paused, but still held me in his gaze. "Come for me, baby. I want to feel your pussy grab onto my dick like only you can." He resumed his deep, frantic pace as I equally met his incursions. "Don't forget to breathe. Oh yeah, there you go, come for me."

"Please!" A squeak escaped from me followed by a low groan. I quickly gulped in air, spinning as my release erupted.

"I'm coming with you," Mason called out. He jerked rapidly and then held himself tightly against me.

The feel of his cock pulsing inside me almost got me off again. He rolled to the side, his chest rising and falling.

I nuzzled against his neck, breathing in his spicy aftershave and warm skin, a smell I would never forget. I glanced up at the clock and said, "Unless you want to meet Jacqs, we need to get the fuck up and get dressed."

He drew me close. "I love when you talk dirty, baby."

I tried to keep from laughing. "I'm serious."

"Are you aware you say that a lot?"

He tickled me until I pushed away from his chest and said, "Get dressed and skedaddle. I'm hopping in the shower."

"Text me when you're free. Should I pick the game or would you like to?"

"Out with you. Now! I need to take a really quick shower because she'll be here any minute." I threw him his pale-blue, dress shirt and turned before he could distract me again with his sexy good looks. He had this way of knocking me senseless with his steely smile and stellar physique. "What am I going to do with you?" I mumbled on my way out of the room.

I heard *bang, bang, bang* as I stepped out of the shower.

My robe hung from the hook on the back of the door so I quickly covered myself and stepped out of the bathroom. "I'm coming," I shouted.

I opened the door and Jacqueline blurred passed me in short, red shorts and a bright-orange top. She spun around to face me. Although short and petite, her personality gave the illusion of an Amazon. Her dark waves flowed to the middle of her back. Spring, or "flip-flop weather", was finally upon us in South Florida and the heat index had us wearing as little as possible. She kicked her shoes off by the door.

"Have you seen the new guy who lives in your building? I saw him strolling through the parking lot. His walk is almost feline but totally masculine," Jacqs said, placing her multicolored backpack on the table by the door. "I swear he looks like a tall Paul Newman—those light-blue eyes and gray hair at his temples. Swoon worthy." She glanced up at me and then squinted her blue-green eyes.

I folded my arms over my robe.

"Have you met him already?"

"Let me get changed," I said, turning away.

Jacqs followed me into the bedroom. "That's not your mystery man is it?"

I peered over my shoulder at her and then slipped into a beige T-shirt and navy shorts.

"Oh my god, it is! He is so—so—damn good looking." She stood there with her hands on her hips, staring as if to reassess me. Her mouth hung partially open.

"Don't you think you already have your hands full with Red and Bond?"

"Well, I don't mean for me. Damn, woman, I figured I must know him since you've been hiding him from me, but I don't recognize him. Should I?"

"No, you've never met him before. Should we go out or would you like to cook?"

"Let's stay in. You know I love cooking and this way you don't have any excuses not to answer my questions. You promised you would finally tell me everything."

I rolled my eyes, but Jacqs didn't see. She was too busy walking to the kitchen and checking out the contents of my refrigerator.

"So how old is he? I'm guessing mid-forties." She pulled out eggs, cheese, broccoli, a package of mixed, dark-green lettuces, and basil.

"Lettuce in eggs?"

"Have you ever not liked my cooking?" She didn't wait for my answer. "You're just stalling."

"Fine, he's forty-five," I said, sitting on the stool that

4

faced her across the wide granite countertop.

"Fifteen years older then. Kids?" She cracked an egg against the side of a bowl.

"Two: seven and ten."

After turning on the stovetop and pouring the oil into the pan, she cut up the broccoli like a veteran sous-chef. "So three kids? Wow."

"No, I meant two kids." I lowered my forehead into my palm, not wanting to have the conversation. Talking to Jacqs made it more real and took away my ability to rationalize the situation.

"Oh, okay." After spreading the oil around, she tossed in the broccoli and some basil leaves. "So how did you meet, and when did you find out he was married?"

"Do you remember the guy I sort of mentioned that I had two dates with?"

"Yes and you wouldn't tell me his name. Did you meet him online?" Stretching up to the cabinets behind her, she tried to reach the spices on the second shelf.

"Let me do that," I said, walking around to the other side of the island.

"Garlic salt and red pepper please."

After handing her the spices, I returned to my stool and continued, "I met him by accident."

The spatula paused in the pan. "What are you talking about, girl? Did you have a date or not?"

"Do you know GG's Waterfront Bar and Grill? It's much more upscale than it sounds."

"I don't think so. Anyway…" She resumed stirring the eggs.

"I was supposed to meet up at the bar with someone from one of my dating sites and he never showed."

Jacqs threw in a fistful of greens and stirred them into

the broccoli. "And Paul Newman's doppelgänger did?"

As I shared how we met, I became lost in the crystal clear memory:

I felt hopeful as I got out of my silver, two-seater, convertible Saturn Sky. I smoothed down my black fitted skirt and made sure my sheer blouse hung just right. I'd worn my three-inch heels, foregoing my favorite five-inch pumps so I wouldn't tower over my date.

I paused for a moment and watched Jacqs pour the eggs into the pan and sprinkle in cheese.

"According to my date's online profile," I said, "he also owned his own business, which you know is important to me."

"So you really thought he had potential. Go on."

I sat down at the bar, laying my small clutch in front of me.

"What would you like?" The bartender asked, tossing a square napkin on the bar. His crisp, white shirt and black vest suited the dark wood décor of the restaurant and bar.

"A Riesling and a glass of water would be nice."

"You got it."

Every time the door opened, I looked over my shoulder, expecting to see the guy from online. I lingered over my glass of wine, and once I had taken the last sip it was quickly replaced with another.

"I didn't order this," I said.

"Compliments of the gentleman," he said, pointing down the bar.

I bent forward, searching to my right and gasped when I saw him. Doing my best to recover quickly, I took a sip of water and waved. "Thanks."

"My pleasure," his deep, resonating voice answered. He lifted his drink and stalked toward me like a predator—confident and strong.

I would willingly let him catch and eat me for dinner. I shook the thought away.

Moving as though it took him little effort to command his body, he settled himself in the stool next to me. "You're waiting for someone." He said it as a statement, not a question.

His proximity unnerved me. I had always thought of myself as someone above being controlled by chemistry and attraction.

"You mean controlled by hormones like me," Jacqs said, holding out a plate with the omelet. "There's coffee too."

"Well, yes, if I'm being completely honest. It happens to be a first for me and part of the reason it's been so hard to talk about, notwithstanding the promise I made to him. I had been in judgment of your crazy libido. Something I thought you should have control over."

Jacqs burst out laughing and said, "Welcome to my world."

We sat down at the round, dinner table and I took a couple bites of the eggs. "Oh, this is delicious. The lettuce gives it an earthy taste, almost like spinach."

She gave me her I-told-you-so look and chewed a mouthful. She swallowed and said, "Well don't keep me in suspense."

"Okay…"

"Well, yes, I was waiting for someone," I said, adjusting my blouse and trying to hide the tremble in my hands. "However, if he'd planned to show, he would've been here by now."

"His loss is most definitely my gain." His eyebrows raised and his wicked smile sent heat over the surface of my skin.

He reached across the distance between us and caressed my shoulder. "He doesn't know what he's missing." His touch unleashed a frisson of excitement that caused me to shudder.

I stared at his fingers and then back into his eyes, not knowing what to make of the conversation or my body's outlandish response.

Seconds, minutes, hours, ticked by, or so it seemed as the silence enveloped us. I could no longer hear the clicking of glasses or silverware. The flare of his pupils and the red heat that crawled up his neck let me know I wasn't alone.

"Let's get out of here," he said, dropping his hand and pulling out his wallet.

"What? Wait! No," I said, swallowing hard to get my heartbeat to slow.

He chuckled slightly and said, "I just meant, let's go for a walk along the water. It's beautiful out."

"Oh, I..." I fumbled around for something plausible to say. I rested my hand on my upper chest, willing my pulse to settle down.

He smiled again and it devastated me.

In a daze, I watched him pay the bartender and leave a healthy tip. He took my hand in his and I let him lead me away from the bar and out of the restaurant. I kept a step behind him, my eyes trailing down to his small, round butt straining against his black slacks and then back up to the collar of his purple dress shirt that just skimmed the bottom of his salt-and-pepper hair. His strides were casual but strength infused each step.

"What's your name?" he asked once we reached the dock that ran along the back of the restaurant.

"Lainie, and yours?"

"Mason."

"Is that a family name?"

He stopped and casually leaned against the railing, looking out at the water with my hand still firmly in his. Lights refracted over the surface of the dark current of the Intracoastal.

"Like you can't imagine."

"What does that mean?" I asked.

"Would you believe me if I told you my name was Mason Mason?"

I laughed thinking he must be joking, but he didn't smile. "Not really? Oh my god, do your parents have an odd sense of humor?"

"It was my great, great grandfather who put it into motion, and the males in my family have carried it on."

"What does that make you?" I thought for a few seconds and said, "Mason Mason IV?"

"Only on my birth certificate." He lowered his head and kissed my hand.

I felt it way more than I wished to. The heat of his lips seared my skin and sent a throb between my thighs. "Why did you do that?"

"I would do more, if you'd let me. Your long, sexy legs, clear, green eyes, and conservative demeanor make my hands vibrate with the need to strip away the artifice..."

"I don't know what to say."

"I want to know everything about you. What do you do for work? What are your passions? Are you happy?"

I held onto the dock railing with my free hand and cleared my throat. "That's a lot all at once."

He stood up and we resumed our walk, "How about one at a time?"

I pursed my lips, trying to keep from smiling. I found it hard to contain the fluttering inside me when I looked into his eyes. His powerful gaze drew me in. I felt him rapping on the fortress I had built around my heart from years of disappointment in the dating arena.

He tucked my long, sandy-brown hair behind my right ear and said, "I want to see your face when you tell me."

I took a deep breath and plunged ahead into unchartered waters. "I own and manage a clothing boutique. I have now for five years or so."

"Do you enjoy it?"

"I love it. Once the place was mine, I changed the name and upgraded the curb appeal with large front windows."

We continued to stroll when he asked, "So you remodeled the store front?"

"Yes and reconfigured the floor plan."

"That's impressive."

"Thank you." I blushed. *Get your shit together, woman. You are not one to lose it over a man. The wine must have gone straight to your head.*

He led me over to a bench and we sat down. "How did you know what to do to the store?"

I adjusted my skirt and smoothed the fabric. Sitting down, he was a few inches taller than I. I looked up and said, "I studied business in college. Through high school and college I worked in clothing stores to help with expenses. The different shops helped me create the vision of what I thought would work best.

"To answer your second question, I'm passionate

about music. I love going to live concerts and Broadway shows and I'm always on the hunt for new songs. My taste in music is eclectic, as is my taste in friends. Other than working, my friends fill up most of my time. Your turn."

"You didn't answer my last question. Are you happy?"

His attention felt more like an indomitable gravitational pull than mere interest.

"Lainie?" he whispered too close to my ear.

"Let's save that one for another time," I said, looking at him through my mascara-laden eyelashes.

"Are you saying you will see me again?"

I bit my lower lip and said, "Are you always this forward?"

"In business, definitely."

"And otherwise?" I asked.

"When I meet a gorgeous woman who causes my heart to pound like you have, then yes."

He thinks I'm gorgeous? The man who might have walked straight off the pages of GQ? "Thank you. I'm flattered." Trying to deflect the emotions he stirred in me, I asked, "So what do you do?"

"I'm a CEO coach."

I turned my knees toward him and said, "What does that mean?"

"I'm a paid mentor to CEOs, business owners, and senior executives. I help them achieve their goals in business, and in their personal lives."

"I never knew that even existed. Do you enjoy it?"

"I love it. It's exciting to help other people manifest their dreams."

"Wow, I didn't know that job existed either," Jacqs said, pulling me out of my recollection.

"He has master's degrees in both business and psychology." I took a couple of bites of my omelet and followed it with a sip of coffee.

"That must mean he travels a lot."

I nodded. "He does, and that's how he was here today."

Her brows pulled together as she scrunched her nose.

"He flew in yesterday, but his wife expects him home this afternoon."

"Oh, so he's local. This seems so unlike you, girl."

I forced out a heavy sigh and said, "It's something I swore I'd never do. I don't have a good excuse other than he is simply every single fucking thing I've ever dreamt about."

"Other than being married with small children."

"Yes, other than that." I nodded.

"When did you know?"

"Please don't be mad at me, but he told me that very first night. He has been honest from the start. We were going to keep it at friendship level, but that flew out the window by the third time I saw him."

Jacqs wore a look of utter skepticism.

"I get that he is lying to other people. That's what kills me. I keep thinking I can stop it ... that I can end it. And I have tried. Remember the day when you came here, before we went to Red's together to hang out with everyone."

"How can I forget? That's the night Bond showed up drunk and outed Aidan and me to the whole gang."

"Yeah." I paused remembering that night and then asked, "So you're calling Red 'Aidan' now? Are you still the happy threesome?"

"Don't even try, girl. We aren't talking about me until you finish your story."

"Okay, fine. So where was I?"

"He told you what he does for a living and that he

12

loves his job." Jacqs cleared our plates so I had to project my voice to her in the kitchen.

The bench we sat on faced the dock, and I could see the current making ripples on the water. "It's great to love your job, isn't it?" I asked. I felt the overwhelming desire to run my hand up his neck and play with his hair. His manly scent inspired impulses I'd never considered, especially not with a stranger.

I felt his breath against my cheek and turned toward the warmth.

"Lainie," he said almost like a groan. His deep, gravelly voice caused my nipples to harden in pure lust.

I tried to force it aside. I drew my head back slightly and asked, "Are you happy?"

He winced. "In some ways I'm very happy. I'm fit—"

"Clearly," I said and clamped my mouth shut, wishing I could garner some self-control.

"Thank you." The sides of his mouth curved up, but the smile didn't reach his eyes. The soft lines in his forehead became more pronounced. His shift in energy placed a shroud over me, and I wanted to hug him to take away the pain.

"Tell me," I whispered.

"And he did," I said to Jacqs. "I'm not going to give you all the details because it's not for me to tell. What I will say is that he is dead in love with his kids and will never leave them. His marriage is very troubled, and they're working on finding a place of friendship. That doesn't mean she would be okay with what we're doing.

"We sat on that bench and talked for hours. I think I fell in love with him that very night."

"Are you sure you're not just hearing his side of things?" she asked.

"Do you trust Red and Bond?"

"With my life." She sat back down at the table.

"I feel the very same way about Mason. I shouldn't share this but I've heard some of his wife's phone messages and she is venomous."

"Look, Lainie, I don't want to be judgmental, but there are always at least two sides of the story and I don't want you to get hurt."

"That's unavoidable at this point. I'm in too deep. It will end someday and I try my best not to dwell on that. I have never loved like this before and I fear I might never again." I closed my eyes, pushing the thought away.

"Isn't this like me being stuck on Bond and hoping things will change?"

"Well, Jacqs, they have changed, but that's not the point. If nothing else, we are honest with each other."

"Will I get to meet him? I saw him, but I mean actually talk to him?"

"I don't think so," I said, shaking my head. "To him it's an even bigger deceit to his family to infiltrate my life, and he says it's worse for me too. He thinks I shouldn't have to miss him in the very places I go for friendship and support, and I can't argue with his logic."

"Well, girl, I think you are now the one mired in drama."

"It's never dramatic when we're together. It's waiting for the next time I get to see him that nearly kills me."

"I can imagine. Thank you for sharing with me." She reached out and touched my hand. "I love you, girl."

"I love you too."

Both Jacqs and I turned our heads to the sound coming from the back of the condo.

"That's my phone," I said. I scurried into my bedroom and over to the nightstand. I brought up the screen on my cell and saw Mason's text.

> **MM:** Your professor needs to discuss your bad grade and how you will make it up. Are you ready for me?

My body flushed in response, but our games still embarrassed me. Not when they were happening, never then. I enjoyed pleasing him, and had come to live for it. With Mason I had opened myself up to new sexual experiences I never imagined I would enjoy.

I texted him back.

> **Me:** Not yet. I'll text when she's gone.
> **MM:** Extra spanks with the paddle the longer you make me wait. I need to ravish your body again.
> **Me:** Yes, Professor Mason. :P
> **MM:** You better give me that tongue when I get home.

Home, how I wished.

"Him?" Jacqs asked when I sat back down at the table.

"Yeah. So how's your ménage à trois working out?"

Jacqs's face reddened and she wriggled in her seat. "It's wonderful, but I'm having a hard time really sinking into it. I'm expecting Bond to get bored at any moment and find someone more interesting. It's only been a few weeks, but he still hasn't dated anyone else. That must be some kind of record."

"I'd say! And Red?"

She sighed slowly and smiled. "He's amazing and I've

never felt so loved, cherished, and cared for. As Bond keeps saying, we're all taking it one day at a time."

"Well you sure do seem relaxed and content and it's a very nice change."

"Thanks." She paused and then I saw the wheels turning. "Have you heard from Stay?"

Stayman, or Stay as we all called him, was part of our group of friends, which met regularly at Red's house. Jacqs brought me into the fold via her alliance with Bond.

"Yes, Stay called me last night. Did you put that into motion?" I said my lips pursed in displeasure.

"Wipe that look off your face, Lainie. He had two tickets for Ed Sheeran, and you know you love him. I thought I was doing you a favor."

"Why, pray tell, does he have *two* tickets?" I folded my arms across my chest, feeling like I had been set up.

"I can only assume he bought them a while ago for him and his ex. Don't go if you don't want to. I thought you might enjoy it."

"I already told him I would," I said, shaking my head.

"Then what the fuck, girl?"

"You're pushing us together, and it's never going to happen."

She tapped my arm and said, "Never is a mighty long time and would that be such a bad thing?"

"Let's just drop it okay?"

She appeared to be considering it and then said, "Sure, back to the good stuff. I would guess he is just about your height?"

"Yeah, he's six foot one like me, so the few times we've gone out, I've left my expensive heels at home."

"Do you go out a lot?"

"Not at all anymore." Then I thought about our game

later and said, "He does love for me to wear them inside. That's a first for me."

"I'm sure your long legs look very sexy. Before I shove off I must know, is Mason a good lover?"

I blushed in mortification, like the young college student Mason wanted me to play.

"Boy, oh boy, that good?"

I just nodded.

She threw her head back and laughed. "And his cock? Tell me, is it stellar?"

"Jacqs!" I whined.

"Give it up, girl. You know all about my guys. Fess up."

"He's perfect for me," I sighed. "You know I hate when their cock is too long and bangs up against my cervix."

"I like that—"

"Yes, that has been well established."

She grinned and said, "And..."

"I'd guess six to six and a half inches, and average thickness, but he gets harder than anyone I've ever been with. Oh, and the stamina..."

Jacqs chuckled again and said, "On that note, I'm going to take off." She rubbed her thighs and stood. "Aidan wants to take Adjustable Bend into the open ocean today, and I think the boys have something planned for me."

I stood up and faced her as she threw her backpack over her shoulder. "Now who's blushing?" I asked.

"I think I have some idea of what they might have in mind." She twitched her eyebrows and made a funny face.

"I hope you're right."

After we hugged goodbye and I closed the door, I rested my back against it. After a moment, I took a deep breath, stood up, and went to the bedroom to text Mason. Another message waited for me.

MM: Wear the short black skirt you know I like with the white blouse. You know the rest.
Me: I need a few minutes to get ready.
MM: She's gone?
Me: Yes.
MM: On my way!

My pulse raced as I quickly disrobed and donned the schoolgirl outfit Mason had bought for me. He didn't care for the knee-high, white socks or the saddle shoes that usually went with the look. In his version, the naughty college student had stockings and garters with very high heels. I slipped into my favorite red, Manolo Blahnik five-inch heels that I only wear indoors, and shut the bedroom door to see myself in the full-length mirror. The short skirt barely covered my butt so the black straps of the garters could be seen. Without a bra, the thin, white blouse didn't hide much. My rosy areolas could be seen through it. I left the first three buttons undone so Mason could see some cleavage. My hair and makeup definitely needed some attention.

Dressing for the scenarios he created had an effect on me. Usually conservative, I was blossoming into a sexy, more confident version of myself.

I wasn't sure how much time I had to get ready, so I moved with haste. I flipped my thick hair over, which was still partially wet from the shower, blow-dried it, then teased it with a comb to give it volume. I used a black, coal liner around my eyes and a heavy layer of mascara. After putting on deep-red lipstick, I took in my reflection. *Perfectly slutty*, I thought.

I hurried to the second bedroom and pulled the desk away from the wall, angling it so the office chair faced the door. The second chair in the room, I set on the opposite side of the desk facing in. Several blank sheets of paper sat in the middle of the desktop and I left them there. I tidied the penholder and lined up the printer so it sat flush with the edge. When I yanked open the bottom drawer, I found it empty.

"Shit! Where did that damn paddle get off to?" I frantically looked around the room, checking near the blue, covered futon couch and the closet. Then I remember and laughed. I went back into the living room and opened the drawer of the end table. The heavy, shellacked, wood paddle had Mason's college fraternity's Greek letters along the handle.

My eyes swept the area to find places that needed attention. I pushed the chairs flush with the dinner table and put the spices back in the cabinet. While I rinsed the sink, I heard a knock. I ran on tiptoe back into the second bedroom and shoved the paddle into the drawer of the desk. Back at the front door, I said, "One sec." I tried to settle the excitement pounding in my chest by bouncing on my toes. Then I flipped the lock and opened the door.

He scanned me from head to toe and whistled. "You are stunning."

I erupted into laughter over his outfit: the tweed coat with oval patches on the elbows and the loafers were a nice touch, as was the pipe with a man's face carved in ivory in his hand, but the spectacles perched on the tip of his nose were what did it to me.

"Is that any way to greet your professor, the one who is willing to help out with your dismal grade in my class on the failure of American politics in the twenty-first century?"

"Well, no, um..." I tried to hold my breath so I wouldn't giggle. I stood up to my full height, which made me taller than him in my five-inch pumps. I waved him through the door.

Even in his silly costume, he looked overwhelmingly handsome.

He turned to face me and I could almost feel his hands on me, as if his light-blue eyes held the power to penetrate the surface of my skin. Simultaneously I loved and hated that someone could have that kind of sway over me.

"I'll be in my office," he said as he slipped off his shoes by the door. Over his shoulder, he said, "I expect you there in one minute. Do not keep me waiting."

"Yes, Professor Mason," I said, using a soft, demure tone and getting into character.

After ducking into the bathroom to check my appearance I knocked on the door to the second bedroom, which he had left partially ajar. I leaned my head in. "Excuse me, Professor, do you have a minute to discuss the grade I received on my paper?" I asked in a wispy voice trying to channel a mix of Betty Boop and Marilyn Monroe.

He beckoned me in with one hand while looking down at the papers in front of him, the pipe hanging from his mouth.

I suppressed a chuckle and pulled down on the hem of my skirt. My heels sunk into the thick, cream-colored carpet as I kept shifting my weight from one leg to the other.

"Stop fidgeting," he said, looking up over his glasses. "Sit."

Settling into the chair that faced him, I crossed my legs.

"Keep your legs open," he practically shouted.

"Yes, sir. Sorry, Professor."

He removed his glasses and the pipe and placed them on the desk. "Now about your grade..."

His eyes locked on mine and I felt myself leaning forward, being pulled into his orbital field of love and lust. Although I pissed and moaned about the games we played, I couldn't fail to recognize their purpose. If we made passionate, intimate love each time we came together, we would never part. This way we could still enjoy each other while creating a level of distance between us.

I believed, down to my soul, that he loved me. I couldn't deny it when he looked at me like he did in that moment. The intensity brought tears to my eyes, which I hurriedly blinked away. I cleared my throat and said, "Yes?"

"How do you intend to make up your grade?"

"Um..." I said, getting back into character. "I thought you might have some ideas." A coy smile played on my lips.

"I do. Fold your skirt up and spread your legs wide." He propped his elbow on the desk and rested his chin on his hand.

"Excuse me, Professor Mason, but—"

"There are no buts except what I plan to do to yours in a few minutes. Either do what I say, or get out." He leaned back in his chair and pointed to the door.

I looked to the door and then back to him, squirming in my chair. "But sir, what if someone comes in?"

"Well, I imagine they'll know what a poor student you are and that you're willing to pander to my whims to get better grades. I'm sure all the other professors will be thrilled to know."

I did my best to look embarrassed and ashamed, dipping my head down. My nipples had trouble cooperating, they flared hard and erect.

"Ahem," he muttered and pointed to my legs.

I stared directly at him, spread my legs wide, and slowly lifted the edge of my skirt. Moisture had already gathered between my thighs during the short scene.

"No panties and a smooth mound? I have to assume you've already met with Professor Charles." His brow creased and his jaw tightened.

"No, no. I have never had a class with him. I promise." I closed my thighs slightly.

"Keep your legs open. I can see you're already wet. I want to observe you while you make yourself come."

"Professor?"

"No ifs, ands, or buts. Get to it."

"Yes sir." I trembled slightly, I felt so turned on.

He circled around the desk and perched on the edge.

I snaked my right hand into my shirt and fondled my breast while my eyes took in his hard, cock straining against his pants. With my left hand, I caressed my thighs working slowly up towards the warm, wet cleft between my legs.

Spreading my knees even wider, I tickled around my aching pussy and delved my fingers into my wetness. Mason's eyes flared when I brought my fingers to my lips and coated them with my natural juices.

"Ohhh man," he groaned. "Oh sorry, fell out of character. Okay, I'm back."

I licked my lips and dipped my fingers back into my pussy. He loved watching me fuck myself with my hand, so I forced my fingers in deep. My eyes trailed away from his as I caught him rubbing his erection through his clothes. I wanted to unzip his pants and free his cock, but it was his game and I committed myself to playing it through.

I tweaked my small nipples, pulling and rolling them until they were longer and distended.

"Undo another button on your shirt and pull your breasts out," he ordered.

My tight, white shirt became more like a corset when I pulled it down around my breasts. Though still pert, my cleavage spilled over, and I could feel the cool air against my hardened peaks.

Scooting my ass forward in the chair, I trailed my right hand under the waist of my skirt, and found my already pulsing clit. I finger fucked myself with my left hand while I circled my arousal with my right.

He lowered his zipper and I looked up just in time to see him extract his cock and balls through the opening in his pants.

Masturbating for Mason coupled with watching him cup his testicles and draw a finger over the tip of his erection to coat the head with his pre-cum caused me to pant. "Oh god, I'm close."

"Stop!" he shouted.

"What?" I said, completely breaking character and yanking my hand out from under my skirt.

"You are forbidden to come before your punishment. Remove all of your clothes except for your garters, stockings, and heels."

"Yes, Professor Mason," I said, with a wispy voice, playing the naughty college student again.

"Come around the desk and lay face forward across it."

The cold air conditioning in the room along with the anticipation of the paddle had me shivering. I shifted into position, my arms folded under my chest, which allowed me to look over my shoulder. "What will you do to me?"

"Whatever I want, of course." He opened the lower drawer. "Stay still and this will be over quickly. Ten, plus two extra swats for making me wait so long, and I expect you to count." The punishment didn't start right away. Instead he ran the rope tassel that hung from the hole in the bottom of the handle across my back and over my full, round buttocks. Then he caressed each one and stepped back.

I felt the air move behind me before the first spank of the paddle landed on my right butt cheek. "Oof. Oh, one!"

"You have behaved well—so far—therefore your grade has moved up to a D. Let's see if we can improve on that."

The paddle hit my left cheek a bit harder and the heat quickly migrated to my pussy. "Two," I grunted, struggling to stay still.

The strikes landed faster as I called out, "Three, four, five, six."

He paused and said, "That's worth at least a C. I've always known that students could be quite trainable." He ran his hand over my tingling ass and trailed his fingers along my spine, up to my shoulders. He took me by surprise when he gripped my neck and held my head down, my cheek pressed to the desktop. I moved my arms to my side, my breasts sandwiched against the surface. "Let's see if we can get that grade up even more. Take six straight thwacks in a row and I can safely bump you up to a solid B. Are you ready?"

"Yes, Professor."

The strength of the punishment increased as did the wetness gathering between my legs. I yelled out each of the remaining swats, grunting and groaning, unable to move away.

"Very good," the professor said. "Shall we shoot for an A?"

"Oh, sir," I panted, "what would I have to do for that?"

"Spread your legs wide and find out." He let go of my neck and situated himself behind me. I felt the swollen head of his cock rubbing at the entrance to my pussy.

"Oh yes," I moaned as I felt him penetrate me. Already so turned on, I knew it wouldn't take me long.

He stroked deep and long, using my shoulders for leverage. "Such a nice and tight pussy. I think your pussy deserves an A."

Although the room was cool, all I felt was the warmth of his body and the intensity of being taken from behind and truly owned. I hissed and moaned as my first orgasm began to contract and spread the heat that caused me to combust.

A layer of perspiration began to form between us.

He continued his long thrusts while my contractions began to subside and I floated in the ethers of my release. Still rock-hard inside me, I knew I would have another explosive climax before he finished.

A melody interrupted the play and Mason said, "Shit."

I recognized the ring tone.

"I have to take it," he said, pulling out of me.

"I know." I wavered out of the room and into the bathroom. I struggled to focus on the mundane actions required to clean up instead of on the harsh reality that had just interrupted my time with Mason. From the wicker top shelf, I retrieved a washcloth. I turned on the hot water and waited for it to warm up while I removed my heels, the garter belt, and stockings. After cleaning my saturated labia, I rinsed out the washcloth and then sat on the toilet with my head in my hands. Ragged breathing in my throat and chest signaled the impending breakdown. "No!" I said out loud.

As I washed my hands in the sink, I shook my head at my reflection. *What the fuck are you doing?* I grabbed another washcloth and removed the smudged makeup from my eyes. I wrapped my robe around me, sighed, and went out into the hall.

Mason waited for me on the overstuffed, beige couch in the living room. "I'm sorry, Lainie."

"Yes, I know. Please, just go."

"I'll let you know when I can get away again. It sucks that we were interrupted but damn, baby, you were sexy as hell." He held his arms out to me and said, "Come give me a kiss goodbye."

Unable to resist him, I complied. I fell against him, his kiss confounding me. My heart broke with every departure, fracturing into a million pieces until he returned and his presence slowly re-glued each tiny piece together again. Every time my heart went through its demise and resurrection, the more fragile it became. Melting into his embrace, I thought, *If I could just stay right here.*

When we broke apart, he said, "I have to go. I'm already running late. I left the jacket and the other props in the closet."

I looked away and said, "Okay." I held open the door for him and watched him walk out of my life once again.

CHAPTER TWO

Waiting...

by City and Colour

Music from my iPod alarm clock rocked me awake Monday morning. My journal and favorite pen lay on the nightstand. I had struggled to fall asleep the night before, berating myself for doing the same thing over and over and hoping for a different outcome. If I didn't write down all my thoughts and feelings, extracting them from my mind, I may not have slept.

As always, after seeing Mason a low-grade anxiety had taken hold of me, and I had wondered how long I'd have to wait to hear from him again.

But today was another day, and I would focus on my work. I turned on the coffee maker and headed for the shower. Once out, I tied my sandy-brown hair back in a twisted up ponytail and put on an outfit that I sold at the shop at the time: loose fitting, crepe, white shorts with a wide cuff, and a sheer, long-sleeved, thin-collared white blouse that matched perfectly. The shorts had long ties that hung to my knees. I slipped on a pair of high, navy platform shoes and a pair of hoop earrings. I would accessorize more once I got to the shop, adding a bangle or two.

After applying a thin layer of mascara that highlighted my hazel-green eyes, I finished off the look with a lilac lipstick. The coffee maker had finished its job so I poured the dark liquid and creamer into a to-go cup. I grabbed my purse, a yogurt, and a banana and left for work.

Bella Boutique didn't open until ten o'clock that day, but I always like to get there at least an hour before. I enjoy having time alone to check on the inventory and eat my breakfast before I unlock the front door.

The entrance to the back of the store opens right into the storage room, which is also my office. A few boxes that needed to be sorted and tagged waited for me that morning.

I sat at the desk and checked my email and Facebook on my laptop. No messages from Mason. I refused to be the first to reach out. It was easier on my heart to wait for a message instead of waiting for a response back. I turned on the store stereo system to help drown out my thoughts.

After finalizing an ad to be placed in the newspaper and online and finishing my breakfast, I turned the sign around on the front door and unlocked it.

The morning breezed by and at 11:25 a.m., Samantha arrived to start her shift with lunch in hand for us both. It had become our ritual. She placed the food in the back for later. She towered over Jacqs even though she was the younger sister, and where Jacqs got the curves, Samantha had a slight frame. Her shape and her long, flowing, white-blonde hair made her look younger than her twenty-five years.

She performed miracles on the front window displays, so I gave her the freedom to work her magic. At first I worried about her slipping back into her drinking and drugging ways. According to Jacqs, Sam had never properly mourned the death of their father and once she became a teenager, alcohol and drugs had become her salve. But I no longer had any concerns. She really seemed to have turned her life around.

She opened and started unloading the boxes I had placed

behind the checkout counter. "Hey, Lainie," Sam said, she leaned over and kissed my cheek when I approached.

Although I hugged Jacqueline and Mason often, I had personal space issues. It took me a long time to get close enough to a person to want to press my body and heart against them. The only other exception was Catherine, whom we called Cat. Bond also brought Cat into our circle of friends. Neither Cat, nor Sam knew about Mason.

"How was your weekend?" she asked over her shoulder as she folded the new designer T-shirts she pulled from the first box.

"It was great to see Jacqs yesterday. You?"

"Oh yeah? I've been meaning to call her. Mom plans to invite her to dinner sometime this week, but I'll probably see her on Wednesday at Red's. You're going, right?"

I nodded.

"The weekend was good," Sam continued. "After I left here on Saturday, I spent the rest of the evening chasing Sarah around the park. That daughter of mine has enough energy to power three people."

We laughed together and then I said, "I love the new window display. Where did you find the headless mannequins?"

"Have you been in the attic lately?"

"I avoid hot, enclosed, spider-laden places."

"Lainie"—she laughed, doubling over—"you are an interesting bird. You come across so put together and confident, and now I find out you're afraid of spiders?"

She continued to crack up until I shot her a dirty look that just made her laugh harder.

"I never said I was afraid of them, I just choose to reduce the chance that I will have to take one out."

"Uh-huh," she said, giggling.

"Was there anything else of interest up there?"

"Besides spiders the size of your hand?" She raised her eyebrows and smiled. "Actually there is this white, wire mannequin. Circles of wire form this cool-looking, off-the-shoulder dress with a diagonal hem. It's hard to explain, but I think it has a lot of potential."

"That sounds interesting, can't wait to see it."

"I need some help getting it down. No, I'm not asking you to help." She shook her head. "We need a strong guy to move it. You would think wire would be light, but it's large, and the base is really heavy."

"What will you use it for?"

"I'm not one hundred percent certain yet," she said while opening another box that contained short leather skirts. "It's pretty cool as an art piece, but I was thinking we might try hanging beach wraps in such a way that it makes a multicolor skirt on the bottom. For the fall and winter, I was thinking we would use it to feature scarves."

"I trust your judgment. When do you need it by?"

"No rush. Do you have a price list for the skirts or is it the same as last time?"

"Same." The door chimed, signaling a customer, so I went to the front of the store to offer my assistance.

Samantha and I rotated nights that we stayed until closing. She mostly manned Saturdays on her own since Mason's wife expected him to be "golfing" unless he had plans to take his kids to the beach or some other activity. Sunday the store remained closed. On a rare occasion, I had taken a spontaneous "lunch" away from the boutique at a moment's notice, leaving Sam to man the fort and eat on her own. No such call came that day.

After I locked up for the night, I heard my cellphone

ring and ran into the storage room hoping to see MM across my screen.

"Hi, Dad," I said, slumping in my desk chair.

"Don't sound so disappointed," he said. His voice was kind and concerned.

"No, I'm happy to hear from you... I was just expecting another call."

"Mason?"

"Yes," I said, with a sigh.

"How's that going?" I heard him clear his throat.

"Same. I know ... I know I should move on, but I haven't summoned the courage yet."

"I understand."

"You do? Why are you always so sweet to me? Shouldn't you be giving me a hard time for my stupid choices? You know Mom would if she knew."

"Love can be complicated and of course, I'm worried for you. These things never seem to end well."

"Are you speaking from experience?" A knot tightened in my gut over the thought of my father cheating on my mother. Not that I would have a hard time understanding it. My mother wasn't someone you could easily connect with or become attached to. I never understood my father's loyalty to their marriage. As horrible as it is to say, I have long wanted something better for him.

"I was in love once, before I met your mother, and it wasn't an affair per se, but I would have moved heaven and earth to be with her. She had other priorities, or at least her family did and she went along with them."

"Do I know her?" I couldn't fathom my father being passionately in love.

"No, honey. Unfortunately she died many years ago."

"Oh, Dad, I'm so sorry."

"My point is that sometimes love takes us places we never thought we'd go. I've heard enough stories from friends over the years to know affairs often have tragic endings and it's usually the person in your position that suffers the most."

I knew he was right, but how do you let go of the greatest love of your life, knowing you might spend the rest of it in search of something even remotely close? Or even worse, settle like my father must have. "Where's Mom?" I knew Dad would never be talking to me this openly if she was home.

"She's out with Maxine helping her coordinate her latest fundraiser."

Maxine was my mother's best friend who she had known since her dorm days in college.

"Water towers for drought areas in Africa," he continued.

"Well, at least it's a good cause this time around."

"It seems to keep your mother busy and we know how your mother despises idleness."

"Oh, yes, that she does. How is she handling your retirement?"

"I make sure to be out of her hair as much as possible. George and I meet at the park next to Hollywood Beach to play chess and cribbage. I guess it's where all the *alter cockers* go to live out their remaining days."

"Dad! You're not that old."

"I've taken up walking along the beach too and I've dropped five pounds. Think I might be down to a beer belly instead of a full keg."

I laughed and said, "That's excellent. Maybe we can meet up at some point for a walk."

"I would love that. So listen, baby girl, your aunt is

coming to town in a few weeks and your mom is planning one of her soirees. Please tell me you'll come."

Both my father and I hated her parties, and I avoided them as often as I could. However, I couldn't say no to my dad. "Okay, let me know the date and I'll show up."

"Feel free to drag Jacqs along or—"

I cut him off before he had a chance to say the M word. "I love you, Dad."

"You know you are the world to me, Lainie. Stay in touch and let's plan a walk soon."

"Love you lots."

"Love you more."

"Bye-bye, daddio."

Once I arrived home, I stripped out of my work clothes and threw on a pair of boy shorts and a T-shirt. Although I enjoyed dressing up for work or when going out on a date, my daily wear was far more casual.

The wonderful spring weather beckoned me so I brought my cellphone, ashtray and a cigarette with me to sit outside my back slider overlooking the pool and Intracoastal Waterway. I never smoked around anyone and had cut back to one or two a day. The disgusting habit and I had yet to completely part ways.

Using my phone, I checked my email and responded to one of my wholesalers. I tapped out the cigarette and went back inside to watch *The Voice*. I hoped Shakira would win this time around, but it seemed that Blake had amassed another winning team.

Once in bed, I picked up my journal and wrote for a bit.

My father is such a warm man. I wonder why I didn't end up more like him. My reserve, my discomfort being touched by people I don't know well must be thanks to my mother. I can't remember the last time my mother hugged me or offered me any affection. Thankfully my father filled that role. Why can't I be more normal, and put together like everyone assumes I am?

Why did I let Mason in so quickly? What is it about him that caused my guard to lower in a way I have never done before with anyone other than Jacqs? Certainly never with another man. I didn't hear from Mason today. I tried not to think about him during work, but when Sam brought up cleaning out the extra storage room to use as floor space to sell lingerie to our customers, I couldn't help thinking about the garters and stockings he likes for me to wear.

I still can't believe Jacqs set me up with Stayman. I know it can't be a coincidence and I'm not even sure why I said yes. Maybe I just wanted to have something else to do for a change.

I always swore I would never live my life on someone else's terms like Jacqs did with Bond for so long. But now, isn't that exactly what I am doing? I keep thinking that I'll say no to Mason one of these times, but when he calls all I want to do is see him. Making either of us wait becomes a moot point.

Enough about him!

Remember to call Dad and schedule a walk and see if Jacqs will go to Mom's party.

CHAPTER THREE

A Drop in the Ocean

by Ron Pope

At work on Tuesday, I looked into some lingerie wholesalers before the start of the day. I still wasn't sure Bella Boutique had the right cliental to make selling lingerie profitable, however Samantha felt it might draw in a younger crowd.

"There is no place close by that sells sexy bras and panties and forget about garters or a bustier," Sam said, with her hands on her hips, looking very much like Jacqs, albeit much taller than my pint-sized best friend. "And it's not like I'm suggesting we carry sex toys or anything like that."

"Good, because that would be a definite no. When I place the next order, we will go through and choose a few items to start with. I thought maybe the right kind of bras for some of the more revealing dresses with matching panties."

"Perfect," she said, clapping her hands. "Clothing discount, here I come!"

"Very funny," I said, smiling at her enthusiasm.

We had a busy Tuesday, which I chalked up to the impending Easter holiday.

"I'll close up tonight," I said, "if you don't mind closing tomorrow. I'm planning to go to Red's a bit early and maybe go for a swim with Jacqs."

"That's fine," Sam said, printing out the credit card

purchases for the day. "I'll stop home, tuck in Sarah, and head over myself. Lainie, I think I hear your phone."

I hurried to the back and when I saw I had a text from Jacqs, I lowered my shoulders.

> **Jacqueline:** Still on for tomorrow? Please tell Sam I'll see her at Mom's house in a few. Did she forget to turn her phone back on?
> **Me:** Definitely on for tomorrow. Sam will close up. I'll tell her and remind her.
> **Jacqueline:** Later, girl.
> **Me:** Later.

"That was your sister," I said, taking the daily printout from Samantha. "She will see you at Mom's. She says to turn your phone back on."

"Thanks. She knows she can call the shop if she needs me, especially after hours."

"I'll leave that for you to remind her. You were great today, Sam. I can't believe you talked that husband into buying his wife the ruched, one-piece bathing suit in three colors."

"Well, I only told the truth. It fit her body perfectly, accentuating her gifts and hiding the flaws."

"Thank you for doing such a great job. It's a pleasure having you here."

"Lainie, this job has really saved me and you know that. I will be forever grateful."

I felt awkward standing there with my arms at my sides. "Hey, why don't you take off and I'll finish up and please tell your mother hello from me."

"Okay cool. I'll definitely tell her. Thanks a million."

As Samantha gathered her belongings and headed out

the back, I heard a familiar voice greet her. They exchanged hellos.

"Look at you, woman!" Cat said when she blew around the corner, reaching her arms out for a hug as she approached the counter.

She had a lithe body and blue-black hair cut in a long, angled bob. Her dark-black eyeliner came to a point, and her smoky eye shadow and pink lipstick finished off the look—a mix of fashion forward and punk girl. That night she showed up in her gothic garb: a black, cut and tied T-shirt she had altered herself, a short, plaid skirt, and her crazy knee-high boots with all the buckles. She percolated with energy and seemed to be in constant motion, as was her usual way, unless she's had a couple of drinks.

"If I didn't know any better, I'd think you had gotten laid recently," Cat said, scanning me up and down. "You're looking sexy today."

"Um, thanks?"

"You have the best clothes here, Lane. Love the red leather skirt you're wearing. Have it in my size?"

"Of course I do. We just got an order in yesterday. However, if you're dropping in out of the blue ... something's up."

She sighed heavily and followed me to the back.

"Did you and Kev have another fight?" I sat down in front of my computer to input the numbers for the day.

She perched on the side of the desk and bounced her right knee. "No, it's just that he wants me to give up my apartment. I mean, I'm never there and we could use the extra money but..."

"But?" I said, raising my eyebrow and peering up.

"Sometimes I think he's just too nice."

"What the hell does that mean? Not aggressive

enough sexually or he always lets you have your way?"

"Well ... I don't know. No to either, really. Sexually, we switch and that works for both of us."

"Oh, really now?"

She smacked my arm and we both laughed.

"Come on, Cat. You are the most feminine Domme I have ever known. Actually, you are the only Domme I know." I chuckled. "I guess I just imagine the women to be bigger and tougher."

"Don't kid yourself, I can be tough." She stood and paced a few steps.

I shook my head and said, "No doubt. So if it's not the sex and getting your way— I just had a thought."

"What?" She stepped around to the other side of the desk, and ran her fingers along the papers in stacks upon the shelf. "Are you always this neat?"

"Clutter drives me crazy and I like to be able to find what I'm looking for quickly."

"You should come over to my place and help me get organized. That's part of why I like having my place. I have my own space for my clutter."

"Could it be that you think you don't deserve Kevin's love?"

"Now you're sounding like Jacqs." Cat crossed her arms and leaned back against the wall by the desk.

"Jacqs has a good sense of these things. I know what your mother is like, and I can relate. Don't let her judgment of you impact your relationship with Kev. Here's my advice. Let his love in. Stop fighting against it. The man's devoted to you and lets you be you. What more do you want?" *And he's not married,* I thought.

"But I can be a cranky bitch sometimes. And he still—"

"Loves you? We all have our moods." I stopped

typing and caught her eye, "You have that look Cat. Don't do something stupid."

"Yeah, I know, I know. Thanks, Lainie. I won't." She pushed off the wall and perch on the corner of the desk again.

"Good. Is the atmosphere at Babes in Tattooland any better?"

She rose again and strolled around touching different items in the office. "The owner finally had the good sense to hire a female manager named Dallas. I never could understand having an all-female tattoo shop with a male manager? Dallas is great. Tracy on the other hand continues to be a raving bitch. At least her station isn't right next to mine anymore. However she still tries to pilfer the walk-ins when it's my turn."

She turned back, faced me, and continued, "Oh yeah get this, I overheard her complain to Dallas that I shouldn't be allowed to work there because I don't have a single tattoo." Cat laughed and said, "Dallas said to her that having tattoos on your body doesn't make you a good artist. If it did, Tracy would be the best. She didn't say that last part." She sat in the extra chair, crossed her legs, and shook her right foot.

"How do you manage to sit still for so long while you're working?" I asked, watching her bounce around.

"It calms me."

"That's good. I'm with you on needles as I avoid pain at all costs. I'm happy to hear the new manager's on your side."

"Yeah. You know, Lane, I love the work. I get paid well and I still get to do my art. Kev's not into tattoos anyway. I mean I'm not saying that would necessarily stop me, but the pain certainly does." She hopped out of the chair and said, "I know you're closed out for the night, but can I shop and you charge my card tomorrow?"

"Of course."

After my nightly ritual of a cigarette and TV, I debated emailing Mason. I never knew if a text or call might show up at the wrong time so I stuck to email while he was in town. I decided to hold out and instead I wrote in my journal for a while and crashed for the night.

My phone sounded, jarring me awake from a deep sleep.

> **MM:** I'm sorry you haven't heard from me sooner. You know how Victoria can be once I get back from a trip. I miss you so much. I need to hear your voice. Can I call you?

I stared at the message, willing myself to deny him. No such discipline.

> **Me:** Okay.

A couple of heartbeats past and then my phone rang.

"Hunan Chinese takeout, what is your order please," I said, pinching off my nose and using my best Chinese accent.

"Very funny, silly woman," he whispered. "Damn it's good to be able to talk to you."

"Where are you calling from?"

"The bathroom downstairs. I've missed you so much. I can't believe it's only been two days. Please tell me you're free tomorrow evening."

"Well, I ... when were you thinking?"

"Six or Seven. I already told Victoria I have a client meeting. Please let me come over."

I sat up in the bed and hung my legs over the side. "Fuck," I breathed out silently. "I'm supposed to be meeting up with Jacqs and then hanging out with the gang."

"Baby, please consider rescheduling. This weekend might be crazy, and I have long days with a new CEO Thursday and Friday."

"I'll talk to Jacqs tomorrow. It's already late."

"Thank you, babe. I *need* to see you tomorrow."

"I'll think about it. It's good to hear from you, but I would have appreciated a text, a note, something from you yesterday. I felt like a stupid woman checking her phone and email obsessively."

"I'm sorry it took so long. I promise you were on my mind every second of the day." The tenor of his voice became deeper when he asked, "What are you wearing?"

"Mason," I stammered.

"Come on, baby, help me out here."

"Boy shorts and a T-shirt."

"I bet your long legs look amazing. Why don't you lay back for me and get comfortable."

"Shouldn't you be getting back upstairs?"

"Shh. Just listen to my voice and do what I say," he said in a gentle whisper that still conveyed his authority.

"Okay..." I put his call on speaker and set it down on the end table. I pulled off my top and shorts, folded them neatly, and set them to the side. Just resting back against my pillow and waiting for his instructions stimulated my body. Mason always seemed to be pushing me to try something new and although I resisted at first, I always ended up experiencing abundant pleasure. What had happened to the woman who would have picked missionary sex every time? He had somehow eradicated her.

"Close your eyes ... imagine that your hand is mine

and follow my voice."

"Mmmhmm," I muttered as my eyes shut.

"Imagine me cuddling you in close and hearing your soft moans and sighs as I trail my hand across your cheek just before I devour your lip, sucking it into my mouth."

I bit my lower lip without thinking, listening as his gravely masculine voice washed over me as if caressing my naked body.

"Feel my hand tickle down your neck followed by nips of my teeth. You pull away and laugh, like you always do and say, 'that tickles.'"

I could almost feel him there, breathing against my neck, surrounding me in the warmth of his body and love. As he continued to serenade me with his voice, my hands massaged the swell of my breasts working toward the taut peaks.

"Wet the very tips of your nipples and breathe across them," he whispered, making his voice all the more seductive.

I groaned softly at his command.

"Good girl, I bet your pussy is already dripping for me. Let's tease it a little longer, shall we?"

I grunted and he chuckled.

"Don't worry, love, I plan to allow you to come in due time. Is that phallic vibrator still in your nightstand?"

My eyes flew open and the heat of embarrassment shot across my skin. "How did you—"

"I bet you're as red as a beet right now." I could hear the mirth in his voice. "I was looking for tissues one evening and saw it. It's impressive. Does the curved end hit your G-spot just right?"

I didn't respond right away.

"Lainie? Come on, baby, don't be shy with me."

"Yesss," I practically hissed out. Why my mortification

twisted in such a way to turn me on, continued to baffle me. Mason seemed to have found that trigger and use it to his advantage.

"Now be a good girl and tease around your pussy. Once you are sufficiently excited and on edge, I'll let you stick the purple dick in the space that was created solely for my cock."

I closed my eyes again and sunk into the arousal that Mason had stirred within me. My nipples continued to stretch toward the ceiling and I could feel the wetness gathering in the folds of my pussy. I tracked my hands across my nipples, down my stomach, skimming across my naked mound. My knees fell open as I tickled around my smooth labia.

"Let's make sure you're ready for your bad boy vibrator and delve two fingers into what must already be a puddle of come."

"Ohhh," I moaned as I plunged two fingers inside. My aroma filled the air around me and caused a longing for the mixture of Mason's scent with mine.

"That's it, baby. I'm fingering your tight pussy, making sure you're ready ... for my hard cock. I'm going to slide in right now," he said with a slight pant.

Hearing my cue, I opened the side drawer and picked up the dildo. Setting the vibration to low, I pushed the end inside me, using the angled, ribbed knob to rub against my G-spot.

"Come on, baby, breathe."

I laughed and took in a gulp of air. My unconscious habit of holding my breath was noticeable even over the phone.

"Feel me stroking you, bringing you ever closer to coming for me. I want to hear you this time."

My purple friend vibrated perfectly as I pushed the dildo in deeper, each time pulling it out far enough to hit all the right spots. "I'm almost there," I whispered.

"Come for me, baby."

"Uh ... uh ... hmmmm," I moaned as my pussy pulsed against the toy. Breathing in and out, I basked in my orgasm, letting myself sink down into it. Although the release wasn't as intense as having Mason there with me, I still enjoyed it.

Once I fully recovered, I said, "Did you come?"

"No, I'm still raging hard and plan to save it for tomorrow night."

"Don't hurt yourself," I said, laughing.

"Oh, do not worry, I plan to take it out—I think I heard someone moving upstairs. I should head up before Victoria wonders where I got off to. Sweet dreams, love. Got to go."

"Sweet dreams to you too," I said automatically, but the click of the phone left me unsure if he even heard me. The quick cut off left me stunned. "Fuck, fuck, fuck on a stick!" I yelled after putting the cell phone back into its charging station. Part of me wanted to see him, needed to see him, like an addiction without its fix. Another part wished I had the gumption to tell him to go to hell.

I lay in bed thinking of what I would say to Jacqs about cancelling plans and wondering if I was more like my father than I originally thought. My dad seemed to put up with whatever my mother tossed his way, like I did with Mason.

CHAPTER FOUR

Starting Now

by Ingrid Michaelson

At work on Wednesday, I sat in front of the computer staring at nothing. I had awoke in a fog that morning and had yet to clear the clouds. I was tempted to steal out before opening time to get a second cup of coffee and forgo the breakfast I'd brought with me. My disrupted sleep and anxiety over my relationship with Mason left my stomach in a state of unrest. I decided to text Jacqs to hopefully reduce the knot in my gut. I hated cancelling on her, but I figured she would understand.

> **Me:** Hey, Jacqs, let me know when you have minute to talk.

I wouldn't be a wimp and cancel plans over text. My phone rang a few seconds later.

"If you're calling me first thing in the morning, it can't be good," Jacqs said. "Is everything okay?"

"I'm not going to make it tonight because—"

"Because Mason's free," she said and in the background I could hear water running.

"Yes, girl. I'm sorry for cancelling at the last minute. Can we reschedule for next week?"

"You know I'm going to say yes, Lainie, but now I'm

the one worrying. Do you know what you're doing, because this doesn't seem like you? Hang on a second." Jacqs must have been in the bathroom, because the sound of paper towel ripping filled the silence. She continued, "You hate it when other people try to control your life and you're letting Mason."

"You're not saying anything I'm not saying to myself. You know how you would go running every time Bond would call?"

"Yes, of course. It hasn't been that long."

"I finally understand." I paused for a second and drank the last sip of coffee. "It's like part of me wants to say no, to stand strong, but I have no idea when I'll see him again and I have no say in it at all. I give in every time because when we're together, the rest of the world falls away and there's no other place I'd rather be."

"Oh, trust me, girl, I get it. I also know what the down times are like and I promise you, it will keep wearing at you. You've seen *me* go through it enough times. You already seem different and I don't think it's healthy for you. Having said that, you know I'll be here for you, no matter what."

"Thank you. Life is strange, isn't it?" I asked as I walked to the sink and rinsed out my to-go cup.

"It sure the fuck is."

"Did you get what you were expecting on the boat outing?" I sat back in my chair and spun it away from the desk.

"Aidan would correct you and say yacht, but to answer your question, yes. It was really great, but this week I'm starting to feel that twist in my stomach again. Something is up with Bond and I'm sure it will be showing up soon."

46

"It or her?"

"Yes."

I shook my head. "I hope you're wrong."

"So do I."

"I have to open the shop soon, but if you—"

"Yeah, I have to go too. I'm supposed to be meeting with my boss shortly."

"Is that still going well?" I asked. I stood up, smoothed out my dress, and headed toward the front door.

"Oh, I don't miss my old job at all. Ted's great and I get to see Aidan often."

"That's a very nice perk." I unlocked the door and turned the sign around.

"Like you can't imagine. I've got to run, but I might be by your way around lunchtime. Shall I bring a bite?"

"I'd love to see you today since I won't be going to Red's later. Let Sam know you're bringing the food. Love you, girl."

"Love you too and see you soon."

It was a slow business day, but we kept busy anyway. After our lunch with Jacqs, Samantha helped me place the new purchase order and switch around a couple of clothing displays. It was time to have all the shorts and bathing suits close to the front and the dresses, pants, and jeans toward the back.

"Hey, Sam, do you mind if I skip out a bit early," I said, scanning around the shop and loving how everything seemed to be in perfect order. It was only five o'clock, but I wanted to give myself plenty of time to shower before Mason's arrival.

"Oh, no problem at all. See you at Red's?"

"Sorry, I meant to tell you earlier, I won't be able to make it tonight. Have fun and please tell the gang I said hi and that I'll see them next week."

She looked perplexed and said, "Yeah, okay. Have a good night and see you tomorrow."

I tossed her the extra set of keys and headed out the back.

Mason and I alternated between role playing and intimate sex so I knew tonight would be special. I laid out the cheese, grapes, and crackers I had purchased on the way home so we had something to snack on after we worked up an appetite. I also had a few bottles of his favorite red wine open to breathe and extra food in the refrigerator in case he missed dinner altogether.

I slipped into his favorite lingerie including garters and stockings and as the time drew closer to his arrival, my excitement grew. I had sufficiently rationalized away all my angst as I got ready for him. He had made every effort to spend time with me, even staying over Saturday night, which was a special treat. Down to the bone I believed he loved me and even though I knew it wouldn't be forever, I would try to be happy in the now and not think about the future.

By 7:15 p.m. he hadn't showed and I received no text, message, or email. I scrolled through my memory and felt certain that he said he would arrive between six and seven o'clock. *He is probably just running a bit behind,* I told myself. I sent a quick email asking if he was on his way.

At seven thirty I wrapped myself in my robe, grabbed a cold hard apple cider in one hand and my cell phone in the other, and went out on the back balcony. I left the sliding glass door open so I would hear if he arrived. It was a beautiful, temperate night in Fort Lauderdale. Below, a young couple sat on the edge of the pool, dangling their legs in the water. I watched them for a few minutes as I twisted off the top of the bottle and took a few sips.

Leaning over the railing, I smoked one of my Natural American Spirit cigarettes. I planned to gargle quickly before opening the front door so he wouldn't smell the smoke on me. I still expected him to arrive any minute.

When 7:40 p.m. rolled around, I rested my drink on the ground and debated about texting Mason, something I never did while he was in town. *Fuck it!*

> **Me:** Where are you? Are you still coming? Are you okay?

By eight o'clock, I still hadn't heard from him and I steamed with anger. I didn't bother trying to reach him again. Leaving the food and wine where it sat, I changed out of my lingerie and into jeans, a black top, and flip-flops. I ran a brush through my light-brown hair, grabbed my purse, and headed to Red's house.

On the way, I picked up a six-pack of Angry Orchard Hard Cider and then parked my silver two-seater along the road just past the house. Red's large cream-colored home with a red barrel tile roof, had tall palms out front with multiple arching windows.

I let myself in, and found the front of the house quiet. As always, his place was immaculately clean, something I really respected about him. The hardwood floors sparkled as I strolled through the wide doors under the high ceilings. The large, bright kitchen was equally devoid of human life, but I could see a few of our group out back. I left my purse on the counter and put five of the hard apple ciders in the side door of the fridge, twisting the cap off of the sixth.

Jacqs wasn't out back so I went looking for her in

Red's game room. The warm wood-paneled room held two pool tables, a dart board, a couch, a bench, and two high-top tables. Stayman, Kevin, and Catherine were each holding a cue stick, talking. They turned to face me as I entered.

Kev, like Cat, dressed fashionably punk, and seemed partial to skinny jeans or baggy pants but nothing in between. However he wore attire utterly different from his usual garb and his spiked, short, blonde hair lay flat.

"We thought you weren't going to make it tonight. Jacqs said—" Kev started.

"Yeah, my plans changed." Ignoring Stay's half-cocked smile, I said, "Dude, what's up with the do and the clothes?"

"The principal at the high school wants me to take over managing the other counselors and in his not so humble opinion, toning down my look will help me garner respect. Of course my students are having a good laugh at my *normal* clothes."

"When does that job start?"

"Next school year. It's a pretty good bump in pay and gives me a little more control over the department. I'll still dress like me when we go out, of course." His dark-blue jeans and a button-down, short-sleeved, black shirt seemed a vast departure, but not a bad one to me.

"Sounds great. Plus, I like this look on you," I said.

"You mean when we all get used to it," Cat said as she twitched her nose.

Quickly changing the subject, I said, "Nice skirt Cat."

"You like?" she said, swaying from left to right. She wore the red leather skirt she just purchased from my store along with a black leather vest I'd seen her wear before.

"Definitely. It looks much better on you." I could feel Stay's stare, but I had yet to make eye contact with him.

"You're crazy, Lane," Cat said, leaning against her

pool stick and rocking back and forth from her heels to her toes. "With those long legs? Not a chance. I'd flip you if you were into that sort of thing."

I shoved her shoulder and whispered, "I'm all about the cock."

So the guys could hear her, she said, "It's a stellar apparatus, but you don't know what you're missing."

"Cut it out!" I said as I chuckled.

"I have to agree with Cat," Stay said. "I bet you look very sexy in that skirt."

I turned to face him and said, "Several sizes larger and—"

"Some men like curves." Stay raised his eyebrows.

He stood about an inch or so taller than me and had a smaller build than Red. He projected an understated sexuality, but mischief often showed in his bright, blue eyes and crooked smile. Mason's blue eyes were much lighter in comparison, but Stay's held a fierce intensity, at least when he looked at me. Like I possessed something only I could give to him, although we didn't know each other well. He had been absent from the get togethers for a while and only recently began attending again. He seemed closest to Bond out of our group.

He frequently dressed in blue jeans and a plaid, long-sleeved shirt with the sleeves rolled up. Although thirty-five, like Bond and Red, his smooth complexion made him look younger. He usually shaved his head bald, but his golden brown hair had started growing back in.

When my eyes finally met Stay's, I could feel the energy in his intention. The words got caught in my throat for a second and then I managed to get out, "Where's Jacqs? I didn't see her outside."

"She wasn't feeling well and went upstairs. She wasn't sure if she ate some bad food at lunch or is coming down with something."

Ugh, I thought. I took another sip of my drink and licked my lips, trying to decide whether to go home or finish my drink.

"You're debating something in your head," Stay said as he placed his cue stick on the wall rack. "I wanted to talk about Friday night. Care to go for a walk outside?"

Cat and Kev started setting up the pool balls for another game as Stay stepped closer to me.

"How long has Jacqs been upstairs?" I said, taking a step back.

"She was already upstairs when we arrived. You can check with Red to see—"

"That's okay. I don't want to bother her if she's not feeling well. I'll call her tomorrow."

"Let's get that walk."

I stood there trying to find a polite way to brush him off, but I didn't have it in me. Instead I finished my drink and walked out into the main part of the house heading for the kitchen. I put the empty bottle in the recycling bin and grabbed another.

Stay reached around me and took a chilled bottle of water off the shelf and held it in the crook of his arm. Then, before I could say otherwise, he took the apple cider out of my hands and opened it for me.

"I can do that myself," I said.

"I'm certain you can do all sorts of things for yourself." The way he said it sounded sexually provocative.

I glanced up at him and paused. Shaking my head, I thought, *I must have sex on the brain, because he seems like the perfect gentlemen.*

"Shall we?" he said, extending his hand in front of him, beckoning me to go first.

We exited the front door and walked side by side

down the street. I didn't know what to say, so I took another sip of the cider. My stomach roiled for a second and then it quickly past.

"Why don't we catch some dinner before the concert?" Stay asked as our arms swung in unison.

I almost expected him to grab my hand, which was crazy. Mason standing me up clearly had muddled my sense of reason.

"I can pick you up from the boutique at five-thirty and that should give us plenty of time."

"Well, I—oh!" I yelled, bending over at the waist.

He took the cider out of my hand and laid his large, warm palm on my back. "Are you okay?"

I shook my head, wishing I stood anywhere other than the side of the road getting ready to wretch in the bushes with an audience.

Stay set the cider and water bottle down on the street, and then gently lifted my hair off my shoulders, holding it in his right hand. With his other, he made soft circles on my back.

Tears poured down my cheeks and I couldn't do anything to stop them. I hiccupped once just before I divested myself of the contents in my stomach. When I stood and stepped back, I wiped my mouth on the back of my hand and said, "I'm not drunk."

Stay pulled a blue, woven handkerchief out of his back pocket and handed it to me. "I know you're not. It must be the lunch you had with Jacqs. I wonder how Sam's feeling."

I stared up at him and it was almost like seeing him for the first time. Who was the man standing in front of me? I knew nothing of importance about him. Who carries a handkerchief anymore? "Um, thank you. I'm sorry you had to see that."

"Not at all," he said, still holding my hair back. He pressed the cold water bottle against my neck.

I sighed and wiped my eyes and then my mouth with the cloth. Whether it was the food poising, or Stay being nice to me, or Mason standing me up, I felt at the very edge of a major breakdown. Too shaky to drive, I tried to mull over my choices. My head hurt and my stomach roiled again.

"Are you feeling any better? Do you want some water?"

"I'm scared if I ... oh shit." I gulped trying to force down the emotions threatening to erupt.

"Do you need to throw up again?"

I shook my head. His look held such compassion that my tears mutinied against my will. I only ever let myself fall apart when alone, or in my father's arms when I was a little girl. I felt so exposed and embarrassed.

Stay took the cap off the water bottle and handed it to me and then walked me back toward the house.

I sipped the water slowly as I continued to cry, using the hanky to wipe my tears.

"I'll drive you home. Where's your bag?"

"No," I said, my lower lip trembling. "I don't cry in front of people."

"I won't tell a soul." He smiled.

His expression triggered another wave of grief, causing my shoulders to shake as I tried to keep the sound in. Instead, funny noises came out and I started laughing through the tears.

"It's going to be okay, Lane." He helped me over to his blue Prius and we stood by the passenger door.

I took a few deep breaths and said, "I have to be at the store early tomorrow and I'm worried I might—"

"We can worry about the logistics in the morning and

I'll grab a plastic shopping bag just in case you get sick again. You might want to keep the door open until—"

"I promise not to throw up in your car."

He winked and took off toward the house.

CHAPTER FIVE

I Know You Care

by Ellie Goulding

I took a shuddering breath and looked around the interior of the car to distract myself from all the emotion and nausea that threatened to spill out. A stack of library books and a crumpled shirt sat on the backseat, a pressed white Polo shirt with long sleeves hung from the handrail, and a paper shopping bag full of trash rested on the floor between the two front seats. The outside of the car looked clean, but the inside needed a good vacuuming.

The driver's side door opened and Stay managed to get his long body inside. "Your coloring looks much better," he said, handing me my purse and a plastic bag. "I have good news and bad news."

"Ugh. Give me the good news first."

"Sam says she feels fine and has an iron stomach. She still has the keys and will open the shop at ten and said not to rush in. The bad news came from Red who said that Jacqs threw up a few times before she finally fell asleep."

"Great," I mumbled.

He touched my thigh and said, "Are you feeling okay enough to shut the car door?"

"Oh, yeah, yes." I took a deep breath and sunk into the seat.

"I've never been to your place so you'll have to

direct me," he said as he drove down the road away from Red's house.

"It's two exits up from here."

"Is it easier to take US1 or hop on the highway?"

"Either works." I lay back and closed my eyes. "This car is so quiet and smooth."

"Yes it is. It took some getting used to when I first got her."

"Her?" I said, opening my eyes and slanting my head in his direction.

"Of course," he said, shooting me a quick glance. "All cars are female."

"Even a Mustang GT with a V8 engine?"

His deep laugh filled the car. "Most definitely a Mustang, but she's more like a dominatrix wearing red leather and holding a bullwhip."

I laughed with him that time. "Such imagery. Well, your girl could use a good vacuuming."

While we were stopped at a light, he looked around the car. He shrugged and said, "I guess. I usually wait until there's an inch of sand."

My mouth dropped open and then I realized he was kidding me.

"Are you a clean freak?" he asked as he drove up the north ramp to I-95.

"I do like things clean and organized. Are you a messy pers—" I closed my eyes and leaned back against the headrest.

"Are you okay? Should I pull off the next exit?"

"Why don't you. That way if I have to, you know, you can pull over."

"Toss your cookies?"

I put the cold water bottle to my head and said, "That's one way of saying it."

"Should I come up with some others?"

"Uh, I think I'll take a pass."

He reached over and touched my hand. "Should I head toward US1?"

Somehow, he had made it through my bubble of self-protection, because I didn't flinch or feel inclined to swat his hand away. It actually felt kind of nice, as if he projected calming energy. "Yes and make a left on Seventh Street." I sighed and said, "Thank you for taking me home. Between the alcohol and throwing up I don't think I could have made it there myself."

"Yeah and staying at someone else's house when you're feeling sick is the worst. I always want my own bed."

"And my own clean bathroom."

"Do you like everything to be lined up neatly too?"

"Yes, I don't feel comfortable with a lot of chaos around me. I don't see anything wrong with that."

He flashed his crooked smile. "Nothing wrong at all."

I pointed to the right and said, "You can park in my spot."

He turned off the engine and came around to my side to help me up. I felt unsteady on my feet. Having consumed two and a half hard apple ciders and no dinner wasn't helping matters. After I got my keys from my bag, Stay held his hand out for my purse and swung it over his shoulder.

"I can carry you up," he said, reaching out to pick me up.

"Absolutely not! I can walk. I doubt you could lift me anyway."

"Then you would be surprised." He placed my arm over his shoulder and wrapped his arm around my waist. "Come on, OCDC, let's get you upstairs."

"OCDC?" I peered up just as he inclined his head to the side. His mouth hovered too close to mine and I quickly looked away.

"OCD is self-explanatory, the extra C is for cute."

"I should smack you, but I don't have the strength."

"You can owe me one," he said and winked.

"Oh, is it like that for you?" I asked as he helped me hobble to the stairs.

"My grandmother had to resort to it a time to two."

"Your grandmother?" I grabbed the railing with my free hand as a wave of nausea swept through.

He scanned my face and I knew he could tell. "Let's get you inside and we can talk about it later."

"Okay."

We climbed the first set of steps and paused on the landing.

"Do you need to sit down for a minute? You look pale."

"I'd like to make it to my bathroom as soon as possible."

He pleaded with his eyes. "Then let me carry you."

"Absolutely not. I don't let men lift me."

"Okay, we'll do it your way."

"Fast this time, I'm feeling—"

"I get it," he said, shouldering most of my weight.

We moved up the next set of steps at a hurried pace and once we rounded the corner I saw Mason hovering near my apartment. My intense nausea suddenly had a partner in crime: panic.

I started shaking and hoped Stay just thought it was from feeling ill, which I did in abundance. Mason's sad expression pulled at my heart, but at that moment, I couldn't worry about him. I needed to get to my bathroom quickly. He moved away before we got to my door. Stay took the keys and then held the door open for me.

I scurried into the kitchen and vomited into the sink. I didn't have the time to make it all the way to the bathroom.

Sound became acute. I heard Stay shut the front door,

remove his shoes, his soft footsteps on my white, tile floor, my phone going off in my purse, which he set on the counter causing the contents to ding against each other. His steps trailed away and then came back. He brought me a warm washcloth to wipe my mouth.

I started rinsing the sink until he said, "Leave it. Let's get you into something comfortable and in bed."

I stopped by the bathroom and said, "I have to wash my face and brush my teeth first."

"Okay, tell me where to get your bed clothes."

I held myself up against the door jam and said, "Go to the farthest panel of the closet and in there you will see a chest of drawers. Second one has shorts and the third T-shirts."

I made quick work of washing my face, brushing my teeth, and urinating.

He tapped on the bathroom door and passed the clothes to me. "Where in the kitchen would I find a large bowl?"

"Lower left cabinet if you're facing the stove." I sat on the toilet and undressed. Food poising had drained every bit of my energy and lifting my arms over my head was a struggle. I managed to get my dirty clothes into the wicker laundry basket.

"You okay in there?"

"One more sec." I scanned the bathroom and opened the door. "I think you're right."

"What about?" he asked as he helped me to my bed.

"I sleep on the far side." He had placed a glass of water and the bowl next to the bed with a wet washcloth hanging over the side.

"Let's get you settled and I'll bring the stuff around."

"Thank you, Stay. This is beyond the call of duty," I said as I lowered down onto the bed with my back against the headboard.

"Not at all. So tell me..."

"Oh, I must have OCD because as sick as I feel I still made sure the bathroom looked clean and neat."

He laughed and I could see the amusement shining in his eyes. "Accepting who we are is the first step."

"First step to?"

"Living in peace. Hey, Lainie, maybe you want to answer your phone? It keeps going off."

"I don't know."

"Who's the guy?"

"What guy?"

"Lainie, don't. I'm not blind. The man waiting for you outside. I imagine he is also the one who keeps calling. You should know—"

"I should know?" I didn't like the change to the tenor of his voice.

"I'm as easy going as they come, except for one thing: lying. Partly because of my belief in karma, but also because I always know when it's happening and then if I don't confront it, I'm put in the position of lying myself."

"I'm sorry. I didn't mean to offend you. You've been incredible to me. It's hard for me to let strangers in."

"I'm not a stranger."

"Well, I mean, oh damn." The faucet of my tears resumed and I again felt mortified.

"I'll get the phone," he said when it rang again, seemingly to let me get my emotions under control. "Here," he said when he came back into the room. "I'll give you some privacy." He shut the door on his way out.

I held the phone, not doing anything right away. *Should I check the messages or just call?* I opted to call him.

Before I had a chance to say anything, a torrent of words spewed out of Mason. "Damn, Lainie, I didn't think you were ever going to call me back. Are you okay? Who's that guy? Why is he in your apartment? Why hasn't he left yet?"

"That's a lot all at once. Give me a second."

It's humiliating to admit but at that moment, nauseous and all, I reveled in the fact that for once, the shoe was on the other foot and Mason got to experience some of the angst I lived with on a daily basis.

I took a deep breath and said, "I apparently ate some bad food at lunch. No, I'm not okay. I'm sick *and* I'm sick and tired of being an afterthought for you. The guy is Stay who is a friend and had the unfortunate luck to be with me when my lunch decided to relinquish its residency from my stomach. Where the hell were you?"

"Baby, I'm sorry. Victoria had one of her meltdowns and I couldn't get away."

"How convenient. And when exactly did you know you would be late? You couldn't steal to the bathroom and text me, email me, something? Do you think I'm just willing to suspend my life for you?"

"Of course not. Let me in and I can make it up to you. Send your friend away and let me come up and take care of you."

"I don't have my car. Stay is my way to work tom— Oh god," I groaned and dropped the phone. I grabbed for the bowl, pulled it into my lap and began rocking.

I could hear Mason say, "I'm coming now."

A tap sounded on the door and Stay poked his head in. "Are you—you're not. Do you want to try to get to the bathroom?"

"Yes, please." His kindness made me break again. "Oh, geeze," I muttered.

The front door flung opened as Stay helped me to the

bathroom. The men assessed each other as I stepped through the jamb and away from drama playing out in my living room.

Stay glanced back at me as I started to close the door and I didn't care for the forlorn expression on his face. I wobbled my head and shrugged my shoulders in apology.

After being sick yet again, I flushed the toilet and rinsed my mouth. The cold tile floor called to me so I lay down and rested my cheek against it. I couldn't decide which side of the door I wanted to be on. Did Mason tell Stay to leave? Would he listen? Stay didn't strike me as the kind of man who took direction well. I had come to understand that his laid back demeanor didn't mean passivity.

"Lane, are you okay in there?"

I heard Stay's voice. For some unknown reason I felt relief. As much as I loved Mason, I didn't want him to see me in my current state. We never had that kind of relationship, just two independent ships that crossed in the night.

"Come on, OCDC, say something or I'm kicking the door down." He sounded like he meant it.

"Sorry, I'm okay." I struggled to sit up, reaching for the knob.

"You're horribly pale again. Are you ready to get back in bed?"

"Where's Mason?"

"He's in the living room. He has to leave shortly."

"You talked to him?"

"I usually introduce myself to new people. Let's get you up," he said, reaching out to help me. He easily lifted me to stand.

"Thank you," I said, still shaky on my feet.

Once we stepped out into the hall, I saw Mason sitting on the couch with his head in his hands. "Mason? Give me a minute to get settled and then come see me." He didn't look well himself. When he glanced up I noticed the pronounced lines on his forehead and his five o'clock shadow. He just nodded.

Stayman continued to baffle me with his kindness. He helped me get into bed and placed the cool washcloth on my forehead. I had never let a man take care of me before. Stay seemed so natural at it.

"Try to drink a few sips of water," he said, holding out the glass to me. "You don't want to get dehydrated."

I did as directed and then asked Stay to go get Mason. Feeling ill, exposed, and vulnerable, I willed myself to keep it together. *No more tears, girl.*

Mason came into the room, shoulders down, looking dejected. "Baby, I'm so sorry I wasn't here. I'd be the one caring for you instead of..." He paused momentarily and then said, "...the boy."

"I don't know what to say. You hurt me, Mason. It's bad enough I have to deal with canceled plans, rescheduling, waiting, but not even calling to let me know? What the hell?"

"I won't let it happen again," he said, taking my hand in his and kissing it like he did that first night.

"Make sure it doesn't." I didn't have the energy to fight so I let it go. Brushing my hand across his cheek, I said, "I like you needing a shave."

"I'll have to remember that." He gave me a slight smile and it boosted my energy. "I have to go soon. I wish I could stay and spoon you to sleep with my hand across your belly."

We stared at each other in silence and I could see the pain underneath. He had placed himself between two women he could never fully satisfy. My heart thawed a bit.

"Let me make it up to you on Friday." Mason took a strand of my hair and looped it behind my ear.

"I thought you had a long day with a new CEO."

"I'll leave earlier than I originally planned." He came onto the bed and cuddled me against him.

"I can't—" I shifted uncomfortably, trying to sit up.

"What do you mean you can't?" He increased the space between us.

"I have plans and they can't be changed. How about Saturday?"

"With who? The boy?"

"His name is Stayman and the answer is yes. He had an extra ticket to see Ed Sheeran and I said I'd go. Of course that assumes I stop throwing up and feel well enough to go into work tomorrow and Friday."

"Baby going with him isn't a good idea. He already likes you. Do you really want to lead him on?"

I sat for a moment with my brow scrunched together, feeling the tension in my forehead. I tried to wrap my head around what he said. Not about the part that Stay was interested, I'd have to be dead not to realize that, but because Mason had an expectation of monogamy from me.

What came out of my mouth was, "What makes you think he likes me?"

"Aside from the fact that he blatantly told me that he does? What man takes care of woman he's not into?"

"Uh, how about a friend? What did he say?"

"Really, Lainie? I have to run and that's what you want to talk about?"

"No, you're right." I lay back and he hugged me to him. I tilted my head up and said, "Let me know about Saturday."

"What time do you think you'll be home Friday?"

"Late, I have to assume. The show doesn't start until eight and it's in West Palm Beach."

"What about before that?" He sat up and moved toward the edge of the bed.

"We're going to dinner."

He stood up and said, "I'm not happy about this."

"Don't expect me to stay at home being a hermit between our visits."

"Clearly. I've got to go." His stare seared my skin, as did his displeasure.

"Mason," I said, holding out my hand to him.

He took my hand and said, "Don't have sex with him."

I peered up at him and said, "I don't plan to."

"I love you, Lainie. Don't forget that," he said and then he left.

Holy mother of god, what the hell? I took a few sips of water and then rested my head down on the pillow. That lasted a few seconds until my stomach protested. I pulled myself back up into a sitting position.

"He didn't look happy," Stay said as he entered my bedroom carrying two plates. "Do you think you could handle eating a cracker? By the way this is a very ingenious way, albeit unconventional, to woo a man to your place. The smoked Gouda is excellent on the rosemary crackers."

"Very funny. I'm scared to eat anything at the moment."

"I'll put this on your side table in case you change your mind. Here, put this on your forehead," he said, handing me the washcloth. "Do you want to be alone?"

"No. I can't sleep yet. My stomach is still too upset, but if you need to get up early for work—"

"I work freelance and set my own schedule," he said as he settled himself on the bed facing me.

"Must be nice. I think I recall you saying something about working with computers?"

"Game animation." He placed a slice of cheese on top of a cracker and tossed it into his mouth.

"Get the fuck out of town, really?"

"Really, really."

"Well that's cool. Not that I'm into gaming but I'm awed by the creativity. Probably because I don't have a lick of it myself."

"Oh, I'm sure that's not true." The way he said it made me blush.

"Well, all creativity should have its admirers."

"Most definitely," he said and winked.

"Stop that."

"Stop what?" he asked, affecting an innocent expression.

"Flirting."

"That's an impossible request when I'm around you so you'll just have to learn to tolerate it."

"You come across as this mild mannered man, but I can tell you're a handful."

"You think so?"

"A very caring handful, but yes."

"Hopefully you'll find out." And he winked again.

I laughed. I practically wanted to hug him for taking my mind off my nausea.

"So Mason's an interesting man. Clearly married."

"How would you know that?" I asked my volume louder than normal.

"I don't think it makes me a genius to pick up the signs. I didn't even have to use my stellar intuition to deduce that. For one, you never bring him to Red's. Two, he hovered at your door but didn't want me to see him. And three, he didn't stay to take care of you. So he's either an asshole or married. I went with married."

"Well, I—"

"He wasn't at all happy about my presence." He coupled another slice of cheese between two crackers.

"He made that abundantly clear." I took another small sip of water.

"Did he? What else did he say?"

"That you professed your love for me and I was forbidden to have sex with you." I pursed my lips, holding back a laugh. "I exaggerate but that was the general gist. What did you actually say? He wouldn't tell me."

"You asked him?" A bright smile lit up his face. "He must have loved that."

"Don't go puffing out your chest or anything. I'm ill and not thinking clearly. So..."

"I said that I'm very interested in getting to know you better, and now I know what's been getting in the way. I told him I planned to pursue you." He ate more of his snack and washed it down with sweet tea that he must have found in the back of the refrigerator.

"You said that?"

"I'm not into men, but he certainly has it in the looks department. Even at his age, he's genetically gifted. So instead of dazzling you with my good looks, I'll have to win you over with my incredible wit and intelligence. If that fails, I'll have to pull out my tantric tricks."

"And if I said I wasn't interested?"

"I would know you're lying. You're just distracted at the moment. I'm a patient man."

"I love him," I said and sighed.

"I believe you, but you're not happy."

"That's a bit presumptuous."

He shrugged. "Maybe it is, but it's still true."

"Are you always this way?"

"What way?" Stay took the washcloth off my forehead and shook it out, letting it get cool.

"So confident of your own ideas?"

"Not ideas, perceptions and yes." He refolded the cloth.

"Well add this to your perceptions then, I'm open for friendship and nothing more. I know my relationship with Mason won't last forever, but I'm monogamous."

"Even if he's not?"

"Even."

He slanted his head and raised an eyebrow.

"Well that's not exactly true. If I found out he was sleeping with his wife or anyone else, I'd be livid."

"Well then, I hope you don't find out." He replaced the washcloth on my forehead.

"Are you saying—never mind." I didn't want to know. "Why do you carry a handkerchief?"

"My grandmother said that all gentlemen used to carry them, and it's a shame that my generation didn't. I started keeping one in my back pocket when I was eleven years old to please her. I found it very useful and never stopped. How often do you use a restroom that's out of paper towels? Or have a flat tire that needs to be fixed but have nothing to wipe your hands on. Or to give to a damsel in distress, like yourself. I could go on listing examples, but I'll spare you. I'm a handkerchief zealot."

"That's funny." When I fished out an ice chip from the water, the washcloth fell off in the process.

Stay shook it out again and said, "It feels really good on the back of the neck too." I leaned forward and he wrapped it around the nape of my neck.

"Thank you," I said, making eye contact. I felt the positive, sexual energy he projected my way, but I dismissed it, convinced that being sick had made me unusually vulnerable. "Did your grandmother raise you?"

"Yes, from eleven on. My folks weren't the reliable sort. Alcohol was their poison, still is from what I've heard. Even before I lived with Granny permanently, I spent a lot of my time at her house."

"Jacqs told me that you don't drink alcohol. Is that because of your parents?"

"Yes and no. It was poison for me too. I didn't like the person I was when I drank and neither would've you. Bond and Red stuck by me. Especially Bond. He picked me up off the ground many a time and tried to talk sense into me, still loving me even when I was a flaming dick. Red stopped me from getting my ass kicked on several occasions."

"What made you stop?"

"My grandmother. She had really sacrificed a lot to raise me, even her marriage with my grandfather. That's a long story for another time. I was a real handful in my teens and early twenties. One night she needed me and I told her I would come and I didn't show. I got shitfaced and passed out at Bond's old apartment. It's not like I hadn't disappointed my grandmother before but that last time, I could literally feel her pain. She thought she'd failed again and that I had become another lost cause. She didn't say those things, she didn't need to. She was my only family and she loved me unconditionally for years. That night broke me, and I thank the universe every day for it. I never had a drink again."

"I'm sorry."

"Don't be. I believe that everything in life shapes us into the people we are and I'm happy with myself. My grandmother is a truly wonderful woman and my parents are just people. They have a harder time coping with life

70

than most."

"That's a healthy attitude. You seem at ease with yourself. I'm definitely not there yet."

"You're also not as far away as you think."

"Thanks for your vote of confidence."

"Anytime. Ready to try to sleep?" He stood already expecting my answer.

"Yes. Stay, I ... I can't thank you enough. How will I ever repay you?" I lay down and he pulled the sheet and blanket around me.

"I have several things in mind, but you need to rest up first," he said with his cheeky smile.

I chuckled and tried not to show my real reaction. "Seriously, thank you for being such a good friend."

"You're welcome. Where should I sleep?" he said, stepping away from the side of the bed.

"The couch in the second bedroom becomes a bed. The sheets are in the closet."

"I could sleep in here with you, just in case you need me during the night."

"Tempting as it may be, I think it might be better if you take the couch."

"See, you do like me more than you let on."

"Good night Stayman."

"Good night, OCDC."

CHAPTER SIX

Heal Over

by KT Tunstall

Thursday morning showed up way too soon. The light coming in through the blinds quickly made me aware of a slight headache. I moved around in bed and felt relatively normal. Then I looked at the time. *Shit!* 10:35 a.m. In all that had happened the night before, I hadn't set or charged my phone. I'd have to plug it in once I got to Bella Boutique.

I stumbled to the bathroom, finding my land legs. After freshening up and taking two Tylenol tablets, I headed into the kitchen and almost collided with Stay. "Fuck, you scared the hell out of me!"

Stay, in boxers and a white T-shirt, was scrambling eggs. "I thought you might be hungry after last night."

I stood there staring at him, trying to wrap my head around having him in my apartment. Although thin, his legs and arms were far more defined than I imagined. *Maybe he could have carried me*, I thought. I also couldn't help noticing that his bulge strained the opening on his shorts. Our group had gone skinny-dipping before, but I hadn't taken notice of him then. It was hard not to while he occupied my kitchen. He needed to shave and it gave him a harder edged sexy appearance.

"Are you okay?" he said, reaching out to touch my shoulder.

"Oh, yeah ... just waking up. I came in here to start the coffee, but I can see you have it going already. Thanks. I'm starving."

"No problem. Do you mind if I cut up some of the cooked chicken from the fridge and toss it in the eggs?"

"Use whatever you'd like."

"Wheat or raisin toast?"

"Raisin," I said, finally noticing the kitchen. "You cleaned up?"

"Yeah, last night. I corked the red wine and put the bottles in the cabinet with the others."

"Thank you so much Stay, for taking care of me, cleaning up, and for feeding me too. I ... well ... I'm going to shower quickly and get dressed for work." As I walked away, I thought, *I need to get this man out of my home and fast or I'll end up adopting him and having him live in my second bedroom.*

As I showered, I wondered if I would hear from Mason. He looked so hurt when he left. I hope I hadn't screwed things up for us. His jealousy did something strange to me. Instead of angering me, it actually turned me on. We had never discussed exclusivity, but last night he had made it clear. I just wondered if he had the same expectations of himself.

My hair would have to air dry, however, I took extra care with my makeup and it irritated me. *You don't care what Stay think*s, I reminded myself.

I quickly jetted across from the bathroom to my bedroom, and found my bed made and the evidence of last night gone. Maybe Cat was right and a man could be *too* nice. Of course I couldn't ignore the fact that I told her that was ridiculous.

I dressed in a more casual outfit of crisp, pressed,

designer jeans and a nice, sheer blouse in the hue of blue that we currently had on sale. After pulling on my high heeled sandals, I called Sam.

"Bella Boutique, how can I help you?" Her chipper voice helped me to relax a bit. The store was in good hands.

"Oh my god, you are a godsend, thank you, Sam. How's it going?"

"Oh, it's going great. I've made a few sales already. It's quiet here at the moment. Oh, and I didn't have a chance to grab food on the way in."

"We can order something in at lunchtime."

"Great. Hey, the bell on the door just rang so I have to go."

"See you soon."

I checked my reflection one last time and decided to braid my hair into a ponytail. Once done, I thought I looked presentable. "Please let him be dressed," I said to myself before venturing out of the bedroom. To my relief, he was.

He had set the table for two. The cloth napkins that I rarely used were folded under the flatware. Eggs, toast, and sliced strawberries filled the table along with coffee and water.

I smiled, truly grateful that the night was over and that Stay had made it far less unpleasant than it could have been. "Wow, this looks great! And I owe you another thank you for straightening up my bedroom." I took in his warm easy smile.

The hair growing in on his head and face really altered his appearance. He looked older and more dangerous. "As long as you're impressed."

"How could I not be? This looks delicious."

We both sat down and I sighed internally that he not

only acted like a gentleman, he ate like one too.

"Oh yum. The eggs are delicious with the spicy chicken. Do you cook a lot?" I asked, buttering the raisin bread.

"I mostly do the expedient thing, like roasting a chicken or making a sandwich when I'm on my own. I did spend a lot of time in the kitchen with my grandmother and know how to make several dishes and desserts. I think I heard you say that you don't cook?"

"Cooking isn't my thing, but I can get by in the kitchen. I never do anything elaborate, but like you, I rely on the basics. Hot premade meals from the deli at Publix or Trader Joe's plus restaurant food make up a lot of my diet."

"Same. There's a Trader Joe's not far from my place."

We ate in comfortable silence for the rest of the meal and quickly cleaned up. We found an easy rhythm working side by side.

Once in his car, he said, "So are we on for dinner Friday night?"

"Only if you let me pay, to repay you for taking care of me."

"A definitely no to that one. A man always pays according to Granny and as I already explained, I have other ideas on how you can repay me."

"Stop it," I said, mostly because my body responded to his sexual innuendo against my will.

"I thought we already settled this. You're heavily in my debt and I'll accept payment at a later date. I told you, I'm patient."

"You're going to have to be because it's going to be a long time before hell freezes over."

"My intuition says otherwise."

Thankfully my phone rang and interrupted us.

"Hey, Lainie. Sorry about the food fiasco," Jacqs said

when I answer the call.

"At least you weren't the one who cooked it."

"Very funny. It figures my sister would be immune."

"How are you, girl?" I asked.

"Oh me, I'm fine, but Red insisted I take the day off. You know how stubborn he can be. He's also insisted on taking care of me," she said, chuckling.

"Sounds like he just wanted an excuse to stay in bed and ditch the office."

"That's exactly what I said. You can't argue with the head of the company. Plus there are plenty of perks right here."

"Oh, I can only imagine," I said.

"Is it true Stay took you home last night?"

"Yes, and he's driving me to Red's right now to get my car." I glanced over at him and he shot me a sexy look. I almost smacked his leg, but decided against it.

"He spent the night? You have to come in and tell me everything!"

"I have to get to the store. Sam opened for me and is there by herself."

"What happened to Mason last night?" she asked.

"Long story." I glanced at Stay.

"Fine. Call me as soon as you get into your car. I want to hear all of it."

"Isn't Red beside you, wanting your full attention?"

"We took a break from other activities, to do some work. He's on a conference call."

"Well, my insatiable friend, I'll call you in a few."

Stayed pulled up beside my car and said, "Five-thirty on Friday."

"Yes, okay." I turned in my seat to face him and said, "Listen Stay, all kidding aside, you made last night and this morning so much easier for me and I'm forever grateful."

He touched my cheek. "Thank you for letting me."

How do you respond to something like that? I had no idea what to say. My eyes started to close and my head rested into his warm palm. When I realized what I had done, I blinked my eyes and shook my head. "I've got to go. See you Friday."

Once in my car, I dialed Jacqs.

"I've been chomping at the bit here," she said when she picked up.

"All of three minutes?"

"It was a long three minutes. Tell me everything!"

"There's not much to—"

"Bullshit! This isn't the time to hold out on me."

"Fine, give me a second." I pulled into traffic and stopped at a red light. "Stay stayed the night because he's the one who drove me home and I didn't have my car."

"That was nice of him. Did he sleep in your room?"

I thought I heard her whisper something. "Of course not. Is Red with you now?"

"Yes, go on."

"He was an incredible gentleman and after I got over being mortified to be "tossing my cookies" as he called it, in front of him, and crying like a blubbering idiot, I found out that he's a decent guy. That is, when he's not being a complete flirt."

"That's what I've been trying to tell you. So he flirted with you. Excellent!"

"Well, let me tell you this. Mason was there waiting for me."

"At your place?" she asked and then she mumbled something to Red.

"If you're going to tell him everything, you might as well put me on speaker phone."

"Great!" she said and then I heard the click.

"I was kidding."

"I'm not. Go on. Did Stay meet him?"

"Yes and it was no love affair."

"Oh, I see what you did there," she said and giggled. "I'm so jealous that he got to meet him. Boy that must have been exciting."

"That's not what I would call it."

"Did Stay and, um, the other man talk?"

At least she had some boundaries. "Yes. When I was busy in the bathroom divesting myself of lunch."

"To be a fly on the wall in that room... What did they talk about? Hang on a second." Then I heard her say, "Stop it," to Red, but her voice sounded playful. "Red says I'm being too nosy. Please tell him this is how we talk."

"She's right, but she is excessively nosy too," I said, laughing.

"Thanks for throwing me under the bus. So go on..."

"There's not much else to tell other than Stay really saved me from what could have been a horrible night. He even made me breakfast this morning and it wasn't half bad."

"So wait a second. If you ended up at our place, that had to be because..."

"Yes, Mason stood me up, but then showed."

"Wow. You certainly had an interesting night."

"Listen, I've just pulled into the back of Bella's and I need to run. Oh, before I forget again, my mother is having one of her horrible parties in a few weeks and I was hoping I could drag you along."

"Just let me know when. I would love to see your father, and the food is always amazing. Plus, you have to admit, the people watching potential is just excellent."

"That's only because you and my father make up fake

conversations that are hysterical."

"Your dad is a kick. Tell him I said hi next time you talk to him."

"I will. Hi and bye Red."

"Hey, Lane. Glad to know you're better. Has Jacqs told you we are planning a dinner party soon?"

"Honey, I wasn't planning on inviting her. Just kidding! No, I totally forgot," Jacqs said before I could respond.

"A week from Saturday," Red said.

"Sounds good."

"Talk soon," Jacqs said.

"Bye guys."

After placing my purse down on my desk, I lifted an unopened box and carried it out into the shop. Sam stood behind the counter.

"Love the flowers," I said to Sam as I placed the box down. "They look great on the counter. Where'd you get them? I can reimburse you the cost."

"They were delivered. Who's MM?" Samantha said with an assessing look that reminded me of Jacqs.

The multicolored, gerbera daisy bouquet filled a clear rounded vase. I plucked the envelope off the plastic holder and opened it.

Lainie,
I hope you're feeling better.
I need to see you tonight.
Call me.
MM

A mix of conflicting emotions took hold. I wanted to see him and I loved the flowers. Gerbera daisies had always been my favorite. However, at that moment I was in an awkward position with Sam. She stared at me and I had no idea how to respond. Instead I said, "I have to make a call. I'll be in the back."

I pulled in air and pushed it out with force. *Be happy,* I told myself. You're going to have him in your bed tonight. At least for a little while, anyway. I dialed his number and held my breath as it rang through. No answer. I shook my head at myself and began to stand. The phone rang in my hand.

"Hey, baby, I've been waiting for your call. I had to step out of the office."

"Hi, Mason. The flowers are gorgeous. Thank you."

"Not nearly as gorgeous as you. I have to have you in my arms ... under me ... right away. I'm getting hard just thinking about it."

When he said things like that, a line of fire hit squarely on my clit. How could I fight against that? "You have a way with words."

"Just with you, love. Your condo at six?"

"I have to close tonight. I can't be there until—"

"Have Samantha close."

"No, I can't. She opened for me this morning and I'm not going to take her away from her daughter in the morning and at night."

He sighed. "I'll meet you at your place at seven."

"I won't be there until seven-thirty at the earliest. The store closes at seven."

"That won't give us much time." He sounded frustrated.

"It'll have to do."

"I miss you."

His declaration warmed my heart. "I miss you too."

"Are you feeling better?"

"Much. Thanks for asking."

"I'm sorry yesterday was such a clusterfuck. I really

wanted to be there with you."

"It's okay."

"I know it's not, but I promise to make it up to you."

"The flowers were a nice touch. I have no idea what to say to Sam about them."

"Secret admirer?"

"I don't feel comfortable lying to her or sharing the truth." Stay crashed to the fore in my mind and I recalled what he'd said about lying. "I'll sort it out."

"Baby?"

"Yes?"

"You know I love you, don't you."

"Yes, Mason, I do." *I love you too,* I said silently.

"I have to get back in there. See you tonight."

"Okay."

Back out front, Sam had opened the box and started to hang up a very attractive beach maxi dress in black and white. The sleeveless top had broad horizontal strips and a little above the waist the stripes went vertical to the floor.

"Oh, I hope that's one of the dresses that come in my size," I said as I approached.

She sorted through the dresses she had hung and asked, "Extra large or 1X?"

"I'll start with the 1X. I want to make sure it's long enough for me."

She handed it over and then said, "I'm not going to mess in your business, but from my experience if you have to keep a relationship hidden it's not a good sign."

"Do you know this from experience?"

"Too many of them."

"It's still new."

"Is it?" It didn't sound like she believed me and I didn't know if I even believed myself.

"I'm going to try this on."

"I'll go check on the customers in the front and see if they've decided on anything."

"Thanks Sam."

She looked back at me, and then walked off.

I went into the changing room and tried on the dress. When I came out, Sam stood back at the counter.

"What do you think?" I asked as I stared at my reflection in the mirror. "Do you think it makes my hips look large?"

She approached me and said, "Not at all. The vertical lines going down are very slimming. And it's long enough."

My cell phone rang. I picked it up and saw a number I didn't recognize. "Lainie Simmons speaking."

"Hi, Lane," Stay said and I felt my heart start to race. "How are you feeling?"

"Hey Stay. I'm feeling okay other than a little sleepy. You?" In my free hand, I fingered the bottom of my braid.

"I'm feeling great. It's hard to feel otherwise on such a beautiful day. How's Sam doing?"

"She seems fine and no worse for the wear." I leaned against the checkout counter, trying to suppress my grin.

Sam helped a new customer toward the front of the shop and sent me an inquisitive look.

"I know I've already said this," I said, "but I can't tell you how much I appreciate last night."

"Of course you can. Give it shot."

It took me a second to realize what he had said, and then I laughed.

"Glad to add some humor to your day. I wanted to let you know that the restaurant we're going to tomorrow night is a bit upscale. I plan to bring a change of clothing for the concert."

"Thank you for checking in on me and letting me know."

"See you tomorrow?"

"I'm looking forward to it."

"Me too."

"Bye."

"Bye."

I saved Stay's number into the phonebook on my cell. As soon as Sam made it back to me she asked, "MM?"

I shook my head.

"Oh really? Aren't we the popular one?"

"It was just Stay checking to see how we were doing."

"Uh-huh."

"Cut it out," I said, shoving her shoulder.

She stared down to where I touched her and then looked back up at me with a huge smile. "Should I call in lunch?"

"No Mexican food."

"Yeah, that's off my list for a while too."

I let Samantha leave at four and had the shop to myself for most of the evening. After closing out the register and locking up, I picked up two chicken Caesar salads on the way home.

Climbing up the stairs to my apartment, I found Mason sitting on the top step.

"I hope you haven't been waiting long," I said.

He held out his hand to me and I pulled him up. His lips immediately touched mine and I sighed against him. Once we broke apart from a steamy kiss he took the bag of food and held my hand as we walked to my place.

"I like your hair like this," he said. He let go of my hand and flipped the bottom of my braid.

"Thank you." I smiled. As I unlocked the door, I asked, "How's the new client working out?"

"He's a stubborn one, but I'm used to dealing with that."

"How so?" I asked as I slipped my shoes off by the door and Mason followed suit.

"He's paying me big bucks to help get his business to the next level, but he thinks he's the expert," he said, placing the bag of food on the island. "I have to keep reminding him of why he called me in. CEO's tend to be alpha men that don't like to follow the ideas of others. I finally got his buy in to try a few of my suggestions. I guess we will see how it goes."

"That sounds frustrating."

"It's better when they're more desperate than he is." He sat down on the edge of the couch and watched me pour him a glass of red wine.

"How so?" I asked, coming around to hand him his drink.

He took the glass and wrapped both arms around my waist, pulling me to him. Speaking against my stomach he said, "They listen far better when they're desperate and are open to new ideas."

"I see." I took his head into my hands and closed my eyes. "Food first or—"

"Bed, definitely."

"I should shower first."

"No way. I love your natural smell." He placed the wine glass on the end table and pulled up on my blouse, unbuttoning it from the bottom. He stood to finish. The blouse fell open and he pushed it off my shoulders, letting it fall to the ground. He unfastened my jeans and pulled them down around my full hips.

I stepped on the bottom hem of the opposite leg of the pants and pulled one side off and then the other. Fortunately, I wore to work a matching set of a white, lace bra and panties.

"Let's get you in bed," he said, tugging me along.

I quickly picked up my shirt and jeans with my free hand, tossed them over the couch, and then followed him in. I turned my iPod station on and set it to my favorite list. *Jericho* by Weekend Players started to play.

He hurriedly stripped off his clothes and had me lay down with my bra and underwear still on.

"Damn, baby, you are a sight for sore eyes." He climbed onto the bed, his cock already straining to fullness.

Having a man like Mason being turned on by my body changed my perception of myself. How could it not? I no longer felt like hiding in the dark during sex. Missionary had always been the most comfortable position because my body lay covered under my partner. For once in my life, I didn't feel like my lover sacrificed to be with me.

He further illustrated this when he lowered his head and kissed my belly. "This is my favorite part," he said, kissing me there again. "Other than your tight pussy, of course."

"Of course," I said, joy infusing my words.

I spread my arms out wide as he smelled and nipped his way up my body, finally tickling my neck with his wet kisses.

"Stop squirming you silly woman."

"Then stop making me!" I laughed.

"That's the most wonderful sound in the world," he said, just before he swallowed the chuckle with his kiss. With his body on top of me, his tongue wooed me as his hard cock swelled against my stomach. Using his arm to prop himself up, he stared down into my soul. "I live for the time I get to spend with you, Lainie. I wish it could be every day."

"So do I," I said and I meant it. I dreamt about it constantly, what it might be like if we lived together.

Mason rolled to the side and trailed his hand down my

neck, just like he described on the phone. He loved to tease me while I still wore my bra and panties. He pulled on the strap, fingered the side of the bra, slipping in but not yet touching my nipple. Then he brushed over it, the cloth separating the heat of his hand from my skin. My nipples became erect as he played, which also sent a throbbing to my pussy. He loved when my wetness saturated my bottoms, knowing how badly I craved his penetration.

Oh Home by Cathy Battistessa swirled around us, wrapping us in sensual music.

Through the bra, he clasped my right nipple, rubbing and twisting until my tiny bud stuck out, yearning for his warm, wet mouth. He gave the other side the same treatment, just before he lowered the straps and gifted me with his kisses between my cleavage.

"Oh, you smell so good," he moaned. He licked his way around my areola and I strained up, wanting, needing him to suck my tit into his mouth. He knew what I wanted, but made me wait. He slowly pulled the straps down my arms and lowered the cups of the bra. His eyes met mine, just before he lowered his mouth and sucked on my nipple.

"Ohhh," I moaned, my hips rising up.

"Not yet," he said, breathing out against my reddened peak. He moved to the other side, flicking his tongue and tugging and sucking with his mouth just hard enough to make me yelp.

It felt so damn good.

As he continued to draw me into his mouth, his hand tracked down my belly, his fingers teasing the elastic waist of my panties. Then he strayed down the side between my thighs, keeping my right nipple in a constant state of arousal.

My hips bucked beyond my control. So turned on, my

clit poked out for attention from under cover.

On the side of my panties the tip of his finger found its way under the elastic, and discovered just what he hoped: a pool of wetness. "Damn, Lainie." His cock twitched against my leg. Two fingers wiggled their way toward my labia, dipping into my natural juices. He groaned and that turned me on even more.

By that point, all I wanted was his cock deep in me.

He apparently felt the same. He removed his hand and unexpectedly flipped me on top of him.

I couldn't wait any longer. Not taking the time to rid myself of my panties, I pulled them to the side, and positioned my cleft above Mason's mushroom headed cock.

He took hold of my hips and lowered me down onto him.

Nothing in my life ever felt better. Down I sunk until he filled me not just with his cock, but his love too. His eyes told me there was no other place he'd rather be. All the disappointments washed away in the pleasure of our coupling.

We moved in unison, first slowly as I rocked my hips back and forth. I spread my legs wider, hitching my hips forward and gliding in a circular motion.

"Oh, baby, that feels so good." He relinquished his hold on my waist and tugged on my nipples.

I arched my back as he thrust into me from below. My braid swung back and forth as we increased the pace, crashing into each other in our frantic pursuit to merge our bodies. I no longer heard the music playing, so lost in love. The place we occupied together felt transcendent. Back and forth we danced to our own song.

"Mason," I whispered just before my climax fired. In the ecstasy of our love making, all the problems in our relationship no longer existed. "Ahhh," I cried out, tears pooling in my eyes from the intensity. I dropped my upper body against him as my pussy continued to squeeze against his cock.

He wrapped his arms around my back and waited for me to recover.

The music flowed back into my consciousness and I laughed.

"What's so funny?"

"The song. It's by Texas called *Inner Smile*. It just seems very appropriate."

We listened to the words for a bit and then he smiled up to me. "You are totally right. Ready to go again?"

"Yes, please."

"Good girl." He took the tie off the bottom of my braid and slowly unfurled my hair as he sensuously pulsed his hips under me.

"So good," I moaned.

He held me against him, with one arm wrapped around my back, perspiration building between us. With his other hand he gathered my hair in his fist and raised my head up to him. I felt captured and controlled in such a delicious way. We kissed deeply as he sashayed under me, holding on tight.

His erection grew thicker and harder and I knew it wouldn't be much longer. "How close," he muttered.

"Take me."

He groaned into my mouth and I grunted back as we climaxed together.

Breathing heavily, we lay in each other's arms, gazing at each other.

"That was amazing," he said, running his fingers through my hair.

"Beyond," I said, snuggling against his neck. I started to doze and he shook me awake.

"I don't have much more time."

My eyes blinked rapidly. "Shall we eat?" I asked.

"I really should get going soon. Let's dress and talk for a bit."

"Okay," I said lazily. Pushing myself up, I stood and retrieved my clothes from the living room. I walked to the bathroom and deposited them into the laundry basket along with my bra and underwear. After using the toilet, I threw my robe around me and waited for Mason on the couch.

He looked a bit sad when he settled next to me. "I hate to leave you, especially knowing you're going out tomorrow night. I would like to see you on Saturday." He paused for a moment and then said, "Will you be available?"

"I would love to. What time are you thinking?"

"I usually tee off at nine. Are you sure you'll be home."

"Of course I will be, where else would I be."

He tilted his head down and looked up at me through his pale eyelashes.

I got the gist. I shrugged my shoulders.

"I have a new game in mind."

"Oh?"

"Bra, garters, stockings, and a trench coat. Along with the highest heels you have. All black."

"Trench coat in black too? I have a gray one."

"That's perfect. I really need to go. I don't want to give Victoria a reason to give me a hard time about golfing Saturday." He pulled me onto his lap and hugged me close. He kissed my head and rocked me. "Thank you for tonight. I really needed it."

"Me too," I said and stood up.

"Love you babe."

"See you Saturday."

He kissed me briefly and then left.

My heart sunk as it always did when he closed the

door. I shook it off and went into the kitchen. I transferred my salad into a bowl and placed the other in the refrigerator. Taking water and my food, I sat down in front of the TV and watched *The Big Bang Theory* while I ate.

I cleaned up the kitchen and swept by the front door. Even though people took their shoes off, dirt still managed to be tracked in. In the bathroom, I got ready for bed.

Exhaustion had set in, but my mind continued to race. In bed, I pulled my journal onto my lap and clicked my pen.

Mason seemed different tonight. The sex was otherworldly and we were more connected than ever, but it was almost as if he is afraid of losing me. Saturday will be the fourth time in a week that I'll be seeing him, and that has never happened before. I am lucky if I get to see him twice a week and when he travels even less.

I don't even know what to write about Stay. He seems like a good guy but I'm not interested in the push and pull Jacqs put herself through being sandwiched between two men. It was painful just to watch it from the sidelines. I sure hope Bond isn't back to his usual ways or if he is, he is upfront and allows Jacqs to be free. She and Red seem to be the perfect couple and I could see her marrying and having a family once Bond lets go.

Mason and Stay are so different. Mason is far more self-contained like me. Stay just lays it all out there. I'm flattered but I really need to keep my guard up around Stay. It would be nice if we could just be friends but he doesn't seem like the type to back down from a challenge. I won't complain that Stay has seemed to spur Mason on to spend more time with me. That's a definite improvement. Now if I could just get Mason to open up more.

I wonder what he has in mind for Saturday. Who

wears a trench coat? I have to assume I won't be a flasher. Maybe a detective like Sherlock Holmes, or a spy?

I'm totally excited to see Ed Sheeran tomorrow night. Dinner I'm not so sure about. I think I'm going to wear the new dress I grabbed from the shop. I hope it's dressy enough. I have to remember to pack jeans and a T-shirt for the concert. Boots, definitely. Maybe the ankle high ones with the small heel.

I still need to call dad. Maybe he'll be up for a walk Sunday afternoon. I just don't want to chance that Mom will tag along. I'm sure he'll understand. Call him from work tomorrow!

I closed my journal and set it back on my nightstand. With my alarm set, I changed my playlist to my mellow music and closed my eyes.

CHAPTER SEVEN

Suit & Tie

by Justin Timberlake (ft. Jay Z)

As soon as I arrived at work, with my bag of clothes and the maxi dress on a hanger, I put my stuff aside and called my dad.

"Hey, sweetie."

"Hi, Dad, I'm calling about the walk. Are you free Sunday afternoon? I'd rather avoid Mom if possible."

"I sure am and you mother will be gone midday for one of her reading groups. Want to meet at Hollywood Beach, or would you like me to come to you?"

"Hollywood Beach is great. Let's say one o'clock?"

"Can't wait to see you."

"Me too, Dad. Love you lots."

"Love you more."

"Bye-bye, daddio."

❀ ❀ ❀ ❀ ❀

Friday turned into another busy day at Bella and the time sped by quickly. By five o'clock the butterflies were fluttering in my stomach. "I'm going to get ready for the concert," I said to Samantha.

"Okay," she said, refolding a pile of jeans that a customer had recently tried on.

In the bathroom I freshened up and washed my face.

After applying mascara and a burgundy lipstick, I brushed my hair smooth. I changed into my new Maxi dress, black sandals, and silver dangling earrings.

Back out in the shop, Sam said, "What if you get cold?"

"I hadn't thought to bring a jacket. The temp has been fairly warm out the last few days."

"Give me a second," she said and strolled toward a rack on the wall of the shop. Quickly returning, she held a short gray leather jacket. "Try this on."

"I don't think it will fit—"

"Give it a shot and this silver bracelet too," she said, plucking one off the display carousel on the shelf next to the register.

I slipped into the jacket and latched the repeating circles onto my wrist. The bottom of the coat stopped just where the broad lines of the dress changed from horizontal to vertical. "What do you think?" I asked Samantha.

"You look stunning," a deep male voice responded. I turned around and found Stay smiling at me.

"Wow Stay," Sam said before I could respond. "Looking mighty handsome. If I didn't know any better, I'd think this is a date."

Stayman looked sharp in his black dress pants, matching coat, and dark-gray dress shirt. I gazed at him but was at a loss for words. We stared at each other for a second.

Sam saved me by saying, "Stay, there's a wire mannequin in the attic that I'd like brought down, and Lane and I can't lift it. I wondered if you could do that for us. Not now. I wouldn't want you to mess up your clothes, but—"

As he removed his coat, he said, "It shouldn't take long and I'll just take off my shirt." He started unbuttoning as both Samantha and I watched as he slowly revealed his chest. Stay slipped out of his shirt and laid it neatly on top of his jacket.

His smooth, lean torso was highly defined and I got caught staring at his chest. He winked at me and then said to Sam, "Come on and show me the way."

Once they walked away, I glared into the mirror and said, "Don't even think about it."

Minutes later, he had managed to carry the mannequin down.

"Let's put it in the back," I said, leading the way. "It needs to be cleaned up before it can be out on the floor." I showed him where to put it. Scanning his physique from his head to his shoes, I noticed that he continued to let his golden-brown hair grow in and chose to wear black boots instead of dress shoes. To make matters worse, his five o'clock shadow was incredibly sexy. *Damn, he looks hot. Look away, girl, just look away!*

"Here," I said, holding out a lint roller, but not making eye contact.

Some dust had settled on the front of his pants just over the zipper area. "You don't want to help?"

I turned away and said, "Go get dressed."

"Are you sure that's your final decision?"

"Very sure." My rapidly beating heart settled down once his clothing was back on.

"Are you ready to go?" he asked.

"Let me go grab my clothes bag and my clutch and I will be." Sam followed me into my office.

"He looks hot!" she exclaimed. "He must really like you. I've never seen him dressed up before."

"Stop it," I said, making sure my dress lay straight.

"Forget about MM for the night," she said to me with a serious expression. She pulled the tag off my jacket.

"That's not possible. Thanks for closing up and

helping with the outfit."

"No problem."

We walked back into the shop and said our goodbyes. Stay followed me out the front door.

"Where's the Prius?" I asked, scanning around the parking lot.

"I left her home. I thought I might introduce you to my other girl. She's a 1956 Corvette convertible."

"Wow, she's a beaut. The white side coves look great against the shiny, red paint job. Have you had her long?"

"About five years now." He walked me around the car and opened the door for me.

"Thank you," I said, settling into the red leather seat.

"My pleasure," he said, moving around the car and getting in. "Is the top down okay?"

"Definitely," I said, finding a hair tie in my purse and pulling my hair back into a ponytail.

"You look amazing, Lainie." He gazed at me with his bright crooked smile that lit up his face.

I stole a quick glance and said, "Thank you. That's a nice look on you too. Are you going to behave tonight?"

"Not a chance."

I shook my head. "I don't even know what to say to that." *I think I'm in trouble,* I thought to myself.

"Let's just go and have a good time," he said, as he drove out of the parking lot.

"I'll try my best," I closed my eyes against the cool wind flowing around us. I felt grateful to have the jacket Samantha had suggested. "Where are we going for dinner?"

"50 Ocean in Delray Beach. Have you ever been there?"

"No, but I've wanted to try it. We should go dutch. That place is expensive."

"Not a chance."

"You're pushy you know."

"Wait until you really find out." He listed his head and popped his eyebrows.

I decided to just shut up. Somehow he made everything sound sexual and my body seemed more than happy to be a puppet to his advances. My mind however, thought of Mason and what tomorrow would bring.

I turned on the stereo in the car and found it set to 88.5, my favorite alternative rock radio station. *Too Close* by Alex Clare was playing.

"Have you seen him in concert?" Stay asked as he drove down the highway.

"No, although I definitely would love to see him live."

"You should. His show was excellent."

Once we arrived and parked, I helped Stay close the convertible top and then shook my hair free. We waited for a break in traffic to cross the street to the restaurant.

"This place is extraordinary," I said when we walked inside.

"Name please," the young blonde hostess asked when we approached the podium.

"Stills for two," Stay said.

Stayman Stills? I thought.

"Follow me," she said.

The room we entered had floor to ceiling windows, deep-blue patterned carpet below and wood paneling with tropical, palm leaf fans above. We were sat at a dark, wood table against the window that gave us a nice view of lush trees and the ocean in the distance. Stay helped me out of my jacket and pushed the chair in behind me just before the hostess handed me a menu. He removed his own coat and sat across from me, taking the menu from the girl.

"Your server should be with you shortly," she said

and then departed.

"Did you see the bar when we came in?" I asked.

"Yep, the blue, geode bar top is a real art piece, huh? Would you like to start with an appetizer?"

I lifted my silverware out of the folded napkin and spread it across my lap. "Do we have enough time?"

"Plenty."

I glanced up and asked, "What shall we start with?"

"You strike me as a woman who knows what she likes. Ladies choice."

"Let's see..." I said as I pursued the menu. "Rock shrimp pot pie, or mussels?"

"Mussels. There's more to share. I have a hearty appetite."

The double entendre wasn't lost on me, but I chose to ignore it. "So do I."

The busboy filled our water glasses, and the waiter came to our table just after him. "What can I get you two to drink?"

"A cola for me," Stay said.

"Water's good for me."

"I don't mind if you have a drink." He reached out, touching my hand.

I smiled at him and said, "Water's fine."

"Can we get the mussels to start with?" His hand remained on my mine and once again his peaceful energy radiated from his palm.

When the waiter moved away, I slipped my hand out from under his and placed it in my lap.

"What are you leaning towards for your main course?" He looked up from the menu. "I love the color of your hair. What do they call it? Wheat?"

"Thank you. Light-brown or dirty-blonde usually. It gets lighter in the summer." I smiled and looked back down at the menu. "It all looks so good. What do you recommend?"

"The scallops or snapper. If you don't want another seafood course, the freebird chicken dish is another good one."

"They all look delicious. How to choose?"

"Shall we share two?"

I smiled. "Sure. I'll order the chicken and you pick one of the others."

"Scallops. Now that that is settled, tell me something about you, Lainie." He leaned in over the table. "Are your parents still together?"

"Yes, but I don't understand why my father stays with my mother."

"What are they like?" I felt like his deep-blue eyes were busy trying to assess what went on behind my hazel green orbs.

"My father is warm and non-judgmental. I wish I was more like him. We are close."

"Does he know about Mason?"

If felt strange that yet another person knew about Mason, especially Stay, but it was also sort of nice. "Yes, he knows about him."

"What does he say about it?"

The busboy returned with Stay's drink and I waited for him to walk away before responding.

"My father's worried for me. He says the person in my position is usually the one left devastated."

"He sounds like a wise man."

I took a sip of my water and said, "He's like a big teddy bear and I can always count on him. He helped me afford the shop in the beginning."

"And your mother?"

"If you ever met her, one of the first things out of her mouth would be how she had the perfect figure until she had me. She loves that story and several others that are very unflattering to me."

"She sounds like a gem."

"A deep black onyx—maybe—letting in very little light. Her girlfriends love her though. She's quite popular. To me, she's always been cold."

"Brothers or sisters?"

"No, you?"

"No, thankfully. I was plenty enough for my grandmother."

"Is she still alive?"

"Oh, very much so. I'd love you to meet her. She's in an assisted living home, not that she needs the assistance. She just loves all the activities and socializing opportunities. She's eighty-three and you would never guess it."

"I can tell you really love her."

"She's my only blood I consider family. Bond is like a brother to me, though. I know you don't care much for him—"

"I'm sure he's an incredible friend, but when you watch your best friend's heart ripped out repeatedly, all of his best intentions are lost."

"I understand," he said and I believed he did. His eye contact became too intense and I looked away.

Smoothing out the napkin on my lap, I asked, "So tell me, is he about to stray again? Will he be upfront about it?"

"I can't answer that. Anything Bond tells me is in confidence."

I angled my head back up. "You just answered my question. I hope when the shit hits the fan, Jacqs can finally mourn the relationship and move on with Red."

"I hope that for both of them. I'm guessing it will be harder for Bond in the long run. He has to see Red with his girl or that's at least how he sees it. I'm not telling you anything you don't already know."

"Yes, that's true."

The server placed the appetizer, two small bowls, and bread between us. The aroma of the broth surrounding the mussels made my mouth water. Stay spooned some into a bowl for me and handed it across the table.

I took a bite and said, "Hmm, delicious. That chili broth has some kick."

"I'm glad you like it." He served himself and watched me for a few minutes.

"Aren't you going to eat?"

He flashed me a smile and took a bite.

"I have a question for you," I said after I drank some water.

"Shoot."

"Why did you have two tickets to the concert? Were you planning to take your ex?"

"No, Karen and I didn't have the same taste in music."

Pointing my fork at him, I said, "Wait, was Bond supposed to go with you?"

"No, OCDC, I bought the ticket for you."

"Shit."

"What shit?"

"I thought you had an extra ticket and I was doing you a favor." I placed my fork down and bit my bottom lip.

"Oh, Lainie," he said with his impish grin, "you are doing me a huge favor. You're letting me win you over."

"Why, Stay? Why me?"

"I'm not sure I can give you a satisfactory answer that would match up with the order you like to have in your life. I've been interested since before Karen but I didn't do anything about it."

"Why not and why now?"

100

He rested his fork in the bowl and said, "You had an impenetrable wall up when you first started hanging out with the group. You would come with Jacqs, but it took you a long while to get comfortable."

"Why now?"

"Even though you probably won't let yourself believe it, you're far more receptive now, even with Mason struggling to hold onto your attention."

"There is no struggle," I said emphatically.

"Okay, okay." He held his hands out in submission.

"Your turn. So what happened with Karen?"

"I have a loyalty problem."

"A loyalty problem? What does that mean?"

He took a noticeable breath and said, "I have a hard time giving up on people even in light of evidence that should have me running for the hills."

"Given your history, that makes so much sense."

"How so?" He removed another mussel from its shell and dipped it into the broth before popping it into his mouth.

"From what you've told me, your parents were only loyal to alcohol and your grandmother was exactly the opposite. She stuck by you no matter what and that's love to you. Damn, Jacqs would be proud. She's the psychoanalytical one."

"Yes, I've pieced that together for myself. Karen was amazing in the beginning. Laid back, breezy, spontaneous, easy going, but it all turned out to be a mirage."

After chewing a piece of bread, I wiped my mouth on the napkin. "I'm none of those things. I don't see what you see in me. I'm at a loss."

"I think you have a value problem." He set his fork aside and leaned back in his seat.

The waiter returned and removed the appetizer.

"Would you like another soda?" he asked.

"No, thank you," Stay responded.

"More like a mother problem," I said, lifting my clutch.

"Yes, they are one in the same."

"Indeed. I'll be right back."

Stay stood as I did.

I made my way to the bathroom. After using the toilet, I refreshed my lipstick and checked my appearance.

Since the first night I met Mason, we had lunch out once and have not gone out since. My apartment had become our sole enclave. I enjoyed being taken to dinner.

"You're not doing anything wrong," I said to my reflection before departing the bathroom.

When I returned our entrees had been served and Stay had move to my side of the table. He stood and held out my chair. "I thought it would be easier to share if we sat on the same side."

His energy surrounded me and I found his proximity unnerving. I decided to focus on the meal. "The food looks amazing."

"So do you, Lainie. Is the dress one of yours from the shop?"

"Thank you again. It is. We just got it in a few days ago." I tasted the chicken dish in front of me. "Oh, that's good. What about your suit?"

"I save it for special occasions and for wooing the ladies."

I laughed and shook my head. "You can be quite amusing when you want to be."

"Why thank you very much."

We sat in silence as I accepted a bite of the scallops that Stay held out to me.

"Ohhh," I moaned, "That's divine."

I did something I had never done before. We ate off

each other's plate and I immensely enjoyed myself.

"I'm full," I said, scooting my chair back from the table.

Stay took me completely by surprise when he asked, "What is it about Mason?" His golden-brown eyebrows clinched in the middle, altering his usually playful demeanor.

"Well, um, truthfully, I've never been so drawn in by a person in my life."

He shifted his chair to the side. "Great chemistry doesn't always mean a great match. Sometimes it's the exact opposite."

"I don't see how talking about Mason is going to get us anywhere."

"Maybe not, but you're worth more, Lainie. A lot more. Are you ready to get out of here?"

"I still need to change and my clothes are in the car."

"We can do it on the way."

"Okay."

"Thank you very much for dinner," I said, after Stay paid the bill.

"It's truly been my pleasure." He held out my short-cropped, leather jacket and helped me into it. He folded his coat over his arm and took my hand.

And I let him.

When our hands clasped, his larger palm fit perfectly against mine. We ran across the street back to the car. The night had chilled so we left the convertible top up.

Once on the highway, heading north again, I asked, "Where are we going to stop to change?"

"We aren't stopping."

"What do you mean?" I turned in the seat to face him.

"I figured you could change in the car."

"You must be joking."

He glanced over at me and said, "Not at all."

"I guess I can leave the dress on. Is this your attempt to see me naked?"

"When I'm ready to have you naked underneath me, you'll know it."

My clit twitched and I wanted to smack him and myself.

"Come on, OCDC, what's the big deal? Shimmy your jeans up under your dress. I'm sure I'll see less of your nipples under your bra than I saw in the little shirt you wore to bed the other night."

"Stayman, you're incorrigible!"

"I want you, Lainie. I'm half hard every time you are even in the same room with me and it's not just sex I want. I want to peel away the layers all the way down to your soul. Just give me the chance."

I didn't respond to him, instead I grabbed my bag from the back seat and pulled out my jeans. After taking off my jacket, I lifted up my long dress until the hem was mid-thigh. Scooting my butt to the edge of the seat, I yanked on the pant loops until my stretch jeans were at my hips. Then I bounced until I brought them up to my waist. When finally zipped and buttoned, I took out my T-shirt, which had a steampunk, geisha graphic.

I peeked over at Stay and then quickly pulled my dress over my head and the T-shirt on. Changing out of my sandals into my boots presented no problem. Happy with myself, I rested back and pulled the seat belt across me again.

"See how easy that was?" he said, driving down the ramp off of I-95. "Sexy bra, by the way."

Ignoring him, I said, "When are you going to change?"

"In the parking lot. We should be there soon and have plenty of time to make it to our seats."

CHAPTER EIGHT

Give Me Love

by Ed Sheeran

After shoving some cash into my pocket, I placed my clutch in the glove box and waited outside the car while Stay changed into jeans. The solid green T-shirt he put on made the blue of his eyes even more intense. The boots he wore with the suit, worked with the jeans too.

As we strolled toward the Cruzan Amphitheatre entrance to see Ed Sheeran, his hand slipped into mine, his fingers curling around my hand.

"That T-shirt is killer. Do you sell that in your boutique too?"

"Yes, I get most of my clothes from there. The owner gives me a good deal."

"Very funny."

"I'm terribly funny. Terribly really."

He laughed with me and handed over the tickets to the concert staff guy.

We checked out the T-shirts and I bought a plum color one with a photograph of Ed Sheeran, filling up most the front. His hands covered the bottom portion of his face, fingers spread on either sides of his eyes.

"I would have gotten that for you," Stay said as he pulled me along to the front of the arena.

"I know but I didn't want you to. Tenth row? You got

tickets for seats in the tenth row? How? I can never manage anything on the floor."

"I'm resourceful."

"Huh." I scanned around and watched all the fans finding their seats or spreading out their blankets on the lawn past the overhang and main seating. Had I expressed what I felt in that moment, I would have thrown my arms out and spun around like a little kid. I loved concerts and had never been so close to the stage at such a large venue. I couldn't suppress my smile.

"Damn, Lainie, when you smile like that I can barely resist taking you into my arms and ravishing your mouth."

"Well, I don't—" I started to say.

The announcer introduced the opening band and I squealed. "You didn't tell me Passenger was opening! They do one of my favorite songs."

"I love this side of you, OCDC. I might have to change your nickname. I can see how you must have looked as a young kid, full of joy and sharing it out with the world. It's my new goal in life to help you feel like this often."

I looked over at Stay and wondered what the hell he saw in me, but I started to be glad he did. "Thank you," I said and then jumped up and cheered when Passenger came on stage.

The concert passed in a blur and when Ed began to play *Drunk in Love* we hopped up and danced. Surprisingly Stay had great rhythm and some moves too. I knew my cheeks would be sore the next day from all the smiling.

For his encore, Ed Sheeran played the song everyone waited for, *Give Me Love*. The audience stood, arms in the air, swaying back and forth.

The moving moment caused my eyes to fill with tears.

When I looked over at Stay, I caught him watching me. He touched my cheek and we stared at each other for a moment. When it became too acute, I broke away and continued to sway to the music.

Once the song ended, we made our way out of the arena.

"That was incredible," I said as we walked to Stay's antique Corvette. I spun around and walked backward a few steps. "Thank you so much, I had a blast. I could see the stage so well and the music was just incredible."

"It was my pleasure."

"Let's take down the top for the drive home," I said once we had gotten to the car.

We drove in silence for part of the way and I let myself bask in the music playing on the stereo and wind blowing through my hair. It was almost like after an orgasm and not wanting the feeling to leave too soon. I didn't think about Mason or even Stay per se but just the incredible night. I hadn't had so much fun in a long time.

Before I could stop myself, I reached out and brushed my hand over Stay's head. I could see by the expression on his face that I'd taken him by surprise.

"Are you letting your hair grow back in?"

"I'm thinking about it. What do you think? Oh, no, don't stop," he said when I pulled my hand back.

"It's a gorgeous golden brown and so soft like this. I've been wondering what it felt like."

"It feels incredible."

His damn smile just about rendered me speechless. I turned back to face the front and watched the night pass us by. After we were about halfway back to my shop, I said, "I need to pee."

He turned down the radio and said, "Want me to pull off the highway?"

"I hate gas station bathrooms. I'd use one in a restaurant, but I don't know what's still open around here."

"Me either. Let's go to my place and you can go there."

"That's a really bad idea. I'll just hold it."

"Don't be ridiculous, OC, I'll behave this one time."

"If you promise."

"I promise."

He drove into a garage under a nine-story, multilevel, modern condominium with blue, tinted windows and balcony railings.

"Holy shit, you live here?"

"Yes. I don't take to driving into random buildings and parking." He laughed.

He pushed seven when we got to the elevator.

When he let us into his place, I forgot about peeing. "Holy shit."

"You said that already. Would you mind taking your shoes off by the door?"

I took in the shoe shelf by the entrance. "You do that too?"

"I'm not sure we do it for the same reason."

"Oh?" I said and bent over to remove my ankle boots.

"I assume you have people remove their shoes to keep your place clean, right?"

I nodded.

"For me it is more symbolic of leaving the outside energy at the door."

"That's interesting." My eyes scanned the place and I said, "I really didn't know you at all, did I?" I glanced over to him and he gave me a sheepish grin.

The main space had cream color walls and big, square, beige, speckled tiles covering the floor. A four piece set of comfortable looking, plush, dark brown couches sat around a large, square coffee table. Shelving filled with books, lined the right wall. No TV. On the left sat a four-top glass table. I walked toward the big sliding glass doors and could make out a large balcony and a view of the water below.

"Bathroom?" he asked.

"Oh, yes please."

He led me to a half bath near the front door.

"Thanks," I said and closed the door behind me. *Who the hell is this guy?* I would have never guessed he had money. *Could his grandmother be rich?* I didn't get that impression. After washing my hands, I tried my best to smooth out my wild hair, an after effect of driving with the top down.

When I emerged from the bathroom, Stay asked, "Want to see the rest of the place or should we get going?"

"I'd love to see the rest. You must make a fortune on designing virtual games." I followed him into the kitchen and whistled. "Jacqs would be in heaven." Granite countertops, wood cabinets with long stainless steel handles, and ultra-modern appliances.

"Game animation is now more of a hobby to keep me busy. About ten years ago, a buddy of mine and I designed a game that got purchased by a large gaming company." He led me to what had to be the master bedroom and continued, "I sunk a bunch of the money into this place and my retirement. The condo's not nearly worth what I paid for it."

"Must be nice to have such an incredible view of the Intracoastal."

A large window filled up half of the outside wall in his bedroom. He had a king size bed, a small end table next to it, matching chest of drawers, and a dresser.

Against the opposite wall sat a light gray couch/chair that looked more like a wave, higher at one end, swooping down, and then slightly curved up on the other end. The thin couch seemed to be designed to hold a single person lounging in the concave middle.

"I like the dark gray walls. And what's this?" I asked, sitting down on the very cushioned furniture too narrow to be a couch.

"I hope I get to show you and soon."

"Excuse me?" I said but I assumed it had something to do with sex because of his comment. "And who is this big boy?" I reached down to pick up a very large cat that rubbed up against my legs.

"That's Rusty. He's a Burmese and quite the talker. Isn't that true," he said to the cat that meowed in response.

"I've never seen this rust color fur before, and the yellow eyes. He's gorgeous." I rubbed behind his ears and then placed him back down on the floor.

Next he showed me a guest room that contained a murphy bed. "Bond crashes here sometimes."

I nodded as we moved along.

"I should probably prepare you—"

"To see a room?"

He opened it and I understood.

The largest bedroom contained three distinct spaces. On the right stood a large, wooden desk with a hutch, which held two computers: a laptop and a large desktop screen. The back left corner held an altar with a Buddha effigy in the lotus position, candles, various stones, and a matt laying in front of it. Two posters framed in black hung above the altar: a poster illustrating the seven chakras and another showing the sun salutation yoga poses. My eyes shot across to the last area where he had two guitars, a keyboard, and a stereo system. A comfy looking chair sat between the altar and the music area.

Papers littered his desk and stacks of books lined the wall near the altar. Like his Prius, this room needed a good vacuuming.

"I don't let the cleaners in here."

I could tell and didn't say anything about it.

"Well?"

"You meditate and do yoga? You play guitar and keyboards?"

"Yes, I started meditating when I got sober and have been doing yoga for a few years now. It beats lifting weights."

"You look like that from yoga? Dude, yoga does the body good," I said and I meant it.

"I also run a few times a week."

"Huh," I said, nodding. I followed him into the living room and we sat on a couch facing each other.

"Can I get you something to drink?"

"I would love a glass of water. Thanks."

He returned with two waters and handed me one.

After taking a sip, I placed my glass on the coffee table. "And the instruments?"

"When I hear a song I love, I like to learn how to play it. I'm not great on either but I can get by. Do you play any instruments?"

"Not unless you count singing in the shower or in the car with the music blaring. Sam and I occasionally sing at work when there are no customers."

He reached out and touched my knee.

His warmth invaded my senses. I didn't ask him to move his palm. I stared down at the veins on the back of his masculine hand, wanting to trace the lines they made. Instead, I swallowed hard and said, "This was a great night. Thank you so much for dinner and the concert."

"And my good company?" His deep voice didn't sound mocking or joking, it was sincere.

"Yes." I knew we should head back to the shop so I could drive home but I didn't want the night to end. "I'm sure I'll regret admitting this but it's really easy to be with you. I don't feel that way with many people."

He didn't smile. Instead he held out his arms and I moved into his embrace.

We sat quietly like that for a while, his energy wrapped around me.

I sighed into his chest, not wanting to move.

He wore no cologne that I could detect and his masculine scent was as stimulating and calming as his energy. Somehow he managed to relax me and turn me on at the same time. He had slipped under my wall of self-protection like a mist through the cracks in the foundation.

He ran his hand over my hair and down my back and I felt as safe as I did in my father's arms. Stay would never hurt me, of that I felt convinced. I wasn't sure I could say that about myself in his case.

"I have to get home," I whispered.

"I don't want you to go. Spend the night in my arms."

I slanted my head up, still in his embrace and said, "Stay, I don't want to hurt you. I'm in love with someone else. As much as I would enjoy what you're offering, I can't."

"He won't be there for you the way I can."

"I know. Love isn't always logical as you yourself know. I don't know what else to say."

"Spend the night anyway. Just sleeping and I'll take you back to your car in the morning."

"I have plans tomorrow at nine."

"I see."

The silence and his energy shift made me want to cry. I had never known any person whose energy felt so full and all encompassing. I believed he could actually sense information from people because his heart was so open, like a conduit and a receptor.

"I'm sorry," I said, sadness casting a shadow over us both. I pulled away and he let me go.

We drove to the boutique in silence, the distance between us palpable.

My heart ached for Stay and yet I wanted to be with Mason. Why I felt so committed to a relationship that had no future made no sense. I could see that, but couldn't stop it, and I really didn't want to. Mason lived as an enigma, so worldly, and sexy, and not like anyone I ever thought I would get the chance to be with. He rocked my world and I had accepted what came with that, all the costs.

Along with the pleasures Mason had brought to me, it was a lonely relationship. It's not like I'd had blinders on. I could see it for what it was and that it had a short shelf life. *Why couldn't have Stay waited? Why now? Maybe we could have been something to each other if he had only waited.* I had never seen the potential between us before, but I clearly hadn't known him.

"I'm sorry," I said again silently.

Once he parked in the back of the shop, I gathered my belongings and walked around to his side of the car. He stepped out and stood in front of me.

"Thank you again," I said, searching his eyes, hoping that friendship still existed for us. "I had a wonderful time."

"I did too."

The awkward silence made me uncomfortable. I put my stuff on the front of the car and stepped closer to him.

"You're a great guy, Stay. Really."

"I know my worth. Someday I hope you know your own."

I searched his eyes and saw heaviness there, the same feeling that overwhelmed my heart. It felt like a final goodbye, not like 'see you soon'.

He took me into his arms and I melded against him. We rocked for a moment and then he whispered, "I hope you change your mind."

I stepped back and collected my stuff. My eyes filled as I walked to my car.

My empty apartment exacerbated my bittersweet emotions. Instead of having one maddening relationship, I now had two.

I stripped out of my clothing and tossed them into the laundry basket. Sleep seemed far away yet so I got ready for bed and pulled my journal onto my lap.

I need to let my feelings for Stay find their rightful place. Friendship. He is a great man, just like I said to him. I'm just not the woman for him. Maybe he and Samantha could date. They both have beaten their addictions and she was definitely attracted to him. Sam is gorgeous in her own right. Her long straight blonde hair and white skin with those blue-green eyes attract all the men. She might be young, but caring for Sarah has matured her. Maybe I'll drop a hint or two.

Ugh! Why does that idea make my stomach hurt?

I wonder what it would've been like on Wednesday had Mason shown up on time. Would he have taken care of me like Stay did? He says he would have. I wonder if I would have been as comfortable with him. I never let people see me when I'm down or going through something, other than Jacqs and my dad. How would have Mason dealt with me breaking down?

I sighed deeply and then started again.

Tomorrow should be fun. I have no idea what to expect and he didn't give me any instructions of how to set up for it, like the time he rented a massage table, which showed up unexpectedly. Masseuse/client was very fun. VERY!

I need to stop thinking about Stay and the incredible night and focus on my time with Mason. I hope he doesn't ask me about tonight. Please don't let him ask me about tonight.

I closed the journal, turned on the soft mix on the iPod station, and rested my head on the pillow. Both men swirled in my mind until I finally fell asleep.

CHAPTER NINE

Spies

by Coldplay

I awoke on Saturday resolved to focus on the upcoming time with Mason.

After having a cup of coffee and a cigarette on the balcony, I took a long, hot shower, giving my under arms, legs, and lady parts a smooth shave. I took extra time on my hair, curling up the bottom of it, working to recreate the look of a French spy from a 1960s film I'd seen years ago. If I had to be a detective or something else, I'd pull my hair up into a twist before we started. I used black liquid eyeliner to create a cat like effect on my eyes and chose a blood-red lipstick. Cat would be proud of me.

Just as requested, I donned a black bra, garters, stockings and the highest black heels I owned. I didn't recall him mentioning panties, so I left them off. I slipped into my gray trench coat and tried to relax on the couch. I felt anxious to see Mason again. Fear and excitement mixed an odd cocktail with arousal as the garnish. I desperately wanted to reaffirm my connection with him.

At nine o'clock sharp, I heard a rapping at the door, like the police do in movies.

"Open up."

Getting into character I deepened my voice. "Who is it?"

"It's the FBI and I have some questions for you."

"One minute please." I made him wait for a couple moments.

"Open up! What are you hiding in there?" he said, his voice gruff.

I unlocked the deadbolt and cracked the door open. "Officer, what do you want so early in the morning? I've barely had the chance to dress."

"I'm not an officer, I'm FBI. Now let me in."

"Do I have choice?"

He pushed the door open and I stepped back. While he scanned the apartment, I took in his outfit. He certainly looked the part and sexy as ever in his black suit, white shirt, and black tie. He also had on reflective sunglasses and carried a black briefcase. His five o'clock shadow was obvious. I held back my smile.

"What can I do for you officer?" I said as I closed the door behind him.

"I already told you I'm not an officer, I'm an agent. Are you Natalia Bancroft?"

I threw my head back and laugh. "You've got the wrong girl."

"I don't think so. Do you know this man?" Agent Mason asked, holding up a picture of a half-naked Jake Gyllenhaal.

I struggled to hold in my laughter. I shook my head and said, "No, but I might like too. Sorry I can't help you."

"Well hopefully you will help yourself." He spun me around and pushed my upper body over the couch, handcuffing my arms behind me.

My clit was already coming out of hiding. It pulsed and tingled. Trying to focus on the game instead of my amped up arousal, I said, "Like I said, you've got the wrong girl. I'm not Natalie something or other, and I've never seen that man before."

"We will see about that." He yanked me up to stand, led me to the second bedroom, and placed the extra chair in the middle of the room. Forcefully, he sat me down, my arms over the back.

"This isn't very comfortable and I'm not who you think I am."

"Where were you on Friday between the hours of six and one a.m.?"

I sputtered in response, his question throwing me completely out of character.

He stomped back and forth in front of me and said, "If you won't talk, I'll have to torture it out of you."

Realizing that not talking was an option, I regained my composure. "I have nothing to say," I said with a sexy, deep voice.

"We will see about that." He placed the briefcase down on the couch and opened it. He then retrieved a black strip of material, which I hoped would replace the handcuffs. Instead, he tied it around my eyes. Everything went black and my breathing accelerated.

I had never been blindfolded before and I wasn't yet sure how I felt about it. My nipples were certainly on board because I could feel them straining against the material of my bra. He past behind me and chills rushed over the surface of my skin. Not knowing what he might do had me on edge and highly aroused.

"First question, young lady and I highly recommend you answer. What is your connection to *Stas*, the known Russian spy?"

"I have no connection to him," I asserted.

His hands grasped my left leg and I yelped. He pulled my knee out wide and tied my ankle to the leg of the chair. On the other side, he applied the same treatment.

Although the trench coat had me covered, I felt wetness gather on my thighs.

"You would do yourself a favor to stop lying. This is your last chance. Answer carefully. You were seen with him last night. What is your connection to him?"

"For the last time, I have no connection to a Russian spy and I don't have the slightest idea who you're talking about."

"Have it your way," he said.

I felt his hands unbuttoning my coat as I imagined his hard cock straining against his black slacks. Trembling, I wondered what he would do to me next.

"It's time. I have my ways to make you talk." He spread the coat wide and fondled my breast over the lace, black bra, making my nipples full and hard. Air then hit my chest as he pulled down the straps freeing my breasts. The warmth of him, which had loomed over me, left and I could hear him rummaging for something in his briefcase. "This will make you talk."

I shivered in excitation and trepidation. He had never hurt me before, but I couldn't fathom what he had in mind. "Oh fuck, what is that," I yelled when I felt something sharp and cold clamp down on my nipple. It hurt initially, but then I adjusted to the pressure and started panting. "Oh god. I'm telling the truth. I ... don't ... know—oh fuck!" He clamped my other nipple and I could hear a chain jiggle between my breasts. The pressure on my swollen buds accelerated my titillation and caused a deep yearning to be fucked and fucked hard.

"Are you ready to confess?" He aggressively grabbed my face and moved my head up and down in a nod.

I pulled my head back and shook it. "No!" I heard him walk away and out of the room. *What the hell is he doing now?*

He quickly returned and moved in front of me. "If you are unwilling to confess I will have to up the ante." A buzzing sound filled the room as I felt the pressure of his finger against my labia.

I heard him grunt and knew he must be as turned on as I.

Hands on either side of my ass made me jump. He drew my lower body forward to the edge of the chair and then inserted a vibrator into my vagina.

It felt so good, I just wanted to moan. Instead I said, "I swear I'm not Natalie and I don't know anyone with ties to the Russians. You ... oh god ... have me confused with ... with ... with someone else."

He pushed the vibrator deep inside of me and drew it out slowly, making sure the vibrating head grazed my G-spot. He grunted again when I moaned out loud. Keeping in character, he said, "Our agents saw you out last night with the known suspect. Explain yourself."

"I can't, oh, I don't know. There were a lot of people around ... I ... I ... ohhh."

Then the real torture began. He removed the vibrator, denying me the orgasm that hovered close. "My agents saw you talking to *Stas* and we won't let you go until you tell us how to find him."

"Please. There is nothing I can tell you," I cried.

"Can't or won't." His angry voice was quite convincing.

"Is there a difference?"

"We're about to find out."

I felt a soft pressure against my lips and Mason's salty smell filled my senses. My lips parted and I licked the head of his cock.

"If you don't tell me how to find our man, I will have to give you my truth serum."

"No, please, not that ... anything but that."

He reached behind me and untied the blindfold, letting the material fall to the floor.

He stepped back and what a sight to see. He had removed his jacket and sunglasses. The tie around his neck had been loosened. Through the opening in his pants, he held his smooth cock, slowly stroking it from the base to the tip.

There was a new intensity in his expression. Whether it was acting or something else, I didn't care. I wanted whatever he planned to give me.

Coming closer, he ran the tip of his hard-on around my lips. I strained forward to try to get more of him in my mouth, but he pulled back allowing only the head to float in and out past my lips.

His pale blue eyes blazed down on me and held my stare. "What is your connection with *Stas* and don't lie to me?" He continued to jerk his cock right in front of my face.

Peering up at him, I said, "None." But I wasn't sure that was true anymore.

He seemed to see the waver in my expression and said, "We are going to forgo the truth serum treatment and escalate the interrogation."

Jumping back into character, I said, "Please! I'm not sure I can take much more."

"Then tell me what I want to know."

"No," I said, shaking my head. "I can't give you the information you want."

He removed his pants and his whitey-tighties. It felt as if he tried to possess me with his stare, like he could lasso my heart with it. The tie came off next and then he unbuttoned his shirt revealing the hottest chest I have ever had the pleasure of seeing or touching. The smattering of hair highlighted his well-defined pecks.

"This is going to cost you," he said, kneeling down in front of me.

I wasn't sure if he was playing the game or talking about my time with Stay. Hoping it was role playing, I said, "I'm not a Russian spy and you have me confused with someone else."

He untied my ankles from the chair and lifted me, leaving the nipple clamps in place. After shoving the briefcase away, he grabbed hold of the handcuffs and manhandled me over to the couch, onto my knees. He pushed the trench coat to the side, exposing my ass.

I started to shake in desire and apprehension. I desperately wanted him to fill me, but I didn't want it to be out of anger.

Not waiting for me to catch my breath, he lifted his arm and spanked my ass with strength. "I will make you talk if it's the last thing I do," he grunted.

My arousal grew with each subsequent thrashing until he stopped.

Behind me, I felt his weight settle against me, his hard cock poised at my entrance. "This will make you more pliable," he groaned as he thrust deeply into me.

"Oh god, anything you want," I cried when he finally took possession of me.

Using my cuffed arms as leverage, he repeatedly crashed into me with full force.

I was so wet that the juices inside me made a swashing sound each time he withdrew and recurred. Incredibly turned on by the foreplay, I quickly reached the precipice of a riotous orgasm.

He must have known because he slowed down, letting my climb fall off. "Are you ready to talk?"

"No!" I grunted, grinding my ass against him, trying to find fulfillment.

"Prison is not a fun place for strumpets like you," he said and resumed his hard fucking.

"Oh, Agent Mason," I emitted as my orgasm began.

He reached under me and tugged on the chain between the nipple clamps, accelerating the violent explosion.

Grunts, groans, and moans escaped as I struggled to catch my breath.

"I'm not done with you," he said not giving me any time to recover. He clutched my shoulders and upped the pace and intensity. He rammed against me, over and over, until I hung at the edge of another huge release. As the girth of his cock expanded he slowed down the strokes, making it last longer for both of us. "You're mine, Lainie, don't forget it."

But are you mine? I wondered just before my orgasm obliterated the thought. We cried out together, coming in unison.

I fell forward onto the couch, my heart trying to pound its way out of my chest.

Mason pulled me up and unlocked the cuffs behind me, the trench coat sliding down my arms.

"This is going to hurt," he said just before he removed the nipple clamps.

I yelped at the sensation. I had become used to the pressure, and had to adjust to their absence.

He held my nipples tight, slowing letting the blood back in. His hands then massage my shoulders that had grown sore and tight in their bound position. After the tension in my shoulders relaxed, we lay down side by side and spooned together.

I floated in our afterglow, trying to ignore the implication of the game.

Too soon he sat up and I followed suit. "That was hot," I said, breaking the silence that hung between us.

"Are you hungry or would you like something to drink?"

"No, I'd rather talk first."

My heart lodged itself in my throat and I thought, *Be calm, girl, you haven't done anything wrong.* The summersaults in my stomach weren't listening. "Okay..."

"How was your *date*?" he asked, his chest still rising and falling from the exertion of our sex.

I knew the question was coming, but it didn't make it any easier to deal with. "Dinner was good and the concert was fun."

"Come on, Lainie."

I didn't care for the disapproving expression on his face. "What do you want me to say?" I shrugged.

"Did he kiss you?" he asked, probing me with his eyes.

"No, and it wasn't a date." I pulled in my knee and repositioned to face him.

"Wasn't it?"

"Mason, I've made it very clear I'm not available." I slipped off my heels and lined them up against the edge of the couch.

"What time did you get home?"

Given the role playing, that questions shouldn't have surprised me, but it still did. "How is that even relevant?"

"I want to know."

I started to get pissed. "Where were you last night, huh? What did you do?"

"That's not the same thing."

"In what universe is it not the same? I was *not* out on a date. I already told you and until you're ready to leave your wife, it's none of your fucking damn business anyway."

"I thought so." He sounded bothered and at the same time sedate.

"What's that supposed to mean?" I clinched my jaw

and narrowed my eyes.

He stayed calm to the point that it further incensed me and said, "If it meant nothing to you, you wouldn't be arguing with me about it."

"Jesus Christ! Are you trying to set me up? Do you want to have a fight?"

Mason and I had never had a disagreement before, let alone an argument.

He held my angry stare. "I don't want you to see him anymore."

"That's ridiculous. He's my friend and our paths *will* cross." I slowly let out a long breath and struggled to get my emotions under control. "You have nothing to worry about," I said, reaching out and touching his forearm.

"I'm not so sure about that."

"I don't understand what this is about, Mason," I said, pulling my arm back.

"You put me off to go out with him."

"There were tickets involved and I said I would go. It's not like I broke plans with you to go out with him. You aren't being reasonable."

"Love is never reasonable, Lainie. He's young, available, and around way too much for my liking."

"What do you want me to say?" I shifted uncomfortably.

"That you don't care about him. However, it's clear to me that you already do."

"He's my friend. He knows it can't be more than that."

"But do you?" he asked, tilting his head.

I sat with my mouth open, not knowing how to respond. I ended up saying, "I feel like we're talking in circles. I'm here, with you, because I want to be. Are you?"

"I'd be with you every day if I could." He took my hand into his.

I frowned, hearing his words but not believing them. "If that were really true, you would leave your wife."

"I will never put my children in jeopardy."

"Of what? People get divorced all the time."

"Is that what you want?"

I answered before really thinking about it. "To spend my life with you? Yes. To not have to wait for your calls or have such little time with you? Of course. To know I'm coming home and you'll be in my bed. Definitely." *To take care of two kids I do not know?* And *have to deal with an ex-wife who hates me? Not so much.* I didn't say that part.

"You've never told me that you love me, Lainie."

"And I won't. Not until you're truly mine."

"I wish things could be different but I was clear with you from the first day we met. I will not divorce and have my kids going back and forth."

"I understand. I really do. What you don't seem to get is how it is for me. You expect loyalty and fidelity without giving it in return." My gut dropped when I thought of the real question I wanted to ask. However the potential fallout from his answer scourged me to even think about. *Do you still have sex with your wife?*

"I'm completely loyal to you. From the first day we met."

Before I could stop myself, I said, "But not faithful."

"Lainie, don't."

"Don't what? You started this Mason, not me."

He stood up and started to dress.

There were so many questions I still had like: Have you had other affairs? Am I your only indiscretion or just another in a line of them. Sometimes, not always, but sometimes, ignorance is truly bliss. I felt more knowledgeable now and I didn't like it one bit.

"Victoria and I have a very complicated relationship."

I abruptly stood up and said, "Right and so do we. I'm ready for you to leave and take your complications with you." I pointed to the door.

"Lainie, come on," he said, closing the gap between us.

"You aren't being fair to me," I said, fighting to keep my tears from falling.

I let him take me in his arms. He kissed my head and said, "I know. You're right. I just got scared that I'm losing you. I need you, Lainie. So much. You make my life worth living."

I wrapped my arms around his waist and allowed myself the dangerous luxury of melting into him. I didn't want to lose him, even given what it cost me.

"I love you so much and it nearly killed me to know you were out with another man."

I lifted my head from his chest and said, "I can't talk about this anymore. This isn't good for me and it's not good for us. Do you want something to eat or not."

"No. I think we both need time."

"Wait, Mason, I don't want us to part this way."

"It's going to be okay, baby. I just need some time." He retrieved his briefcase, kissed me goodbye but melancholy hung in the air between us.

And out of my life he went once again.

I collapsed on the couch as grief overwhelmed me. I didn't want to give into the tears. I didn't want to become one of those women who cried all the time. I punched the cushion a few times and lay on the couch in a daze of my circumstance. I ran over the argument in my head, trying to fix and alter the outcome.

"Enough!" I finally yelled. I pushed myself up and entered the bathroom. Avoiding the mirror, I splashed water on my face.

I lumbered to the second bedroom, setting everything back in place. With the trench coat and heels in hand, I trudged to my bedroom and put the items away. I rid myself of my bra, garters, and stockings and climbed under the covers, falling into a deep sleep. I dreamt of Mason and Stay only remembering snippets when I awoke.

I'd like to be able to say that the pain in my heart had lessened while I slept. However, when I checked my phone and saw no message or email from Mason I had to consider that I might never see him again. The date with Stay swelled in importance. Not because of the connection that we forged, but what it might ultimately cost me.

Everything.

CHAPTER TEN

Use Somebody

by Kings of Leon

I spent the rest of the afternoon catching up on my TV shows, noshing on whatever was expedient, and smoking more cigarettes than I normally allotted myself.

My phone rang and I darted to the bedroom to answer it.

"Hey, girl, are you free tonight?" Jacqs said, sounding out of breath.

"Are you running?"

"No, I just jogged up the stairs to call you. Bond invited me to come by the club and I hoped you'd come with."

"That hasn't worked out well in the past," I said, sitting down on the edge of the bed.

"He promised not to give or get phone numbers or flirt. I told him to forget about the flirting, which would be impossible for him to stop. It's like breathing to him."

"Good thinking." I stood, slid open my closet door, and perused my clothing choices.

"So please tell me you'll come. I hate sitting around like I'm one of his groupies."

"Will Stay be there?" I slid a few of the hanging clothes to the side to better see a top.

"Not that I know of. Does that matter?"

"Yes ... no ... I don't know. What are you wearing and what time?"

"Something cool, it's so hot out. Skirt and colorful shirt probably. How about nine-thirty? That way we can get a good spot at the bar before the place fills up."

I thought about it for a moment. Remaining home with all my confused thoughts seemed the worse of the two evils.

"Lainie?"

"Yeah, I'll come. See you soon."

"Thanks. Love you, girl."

"Bye." I hoped I wouldn't regret it. Being sandwiched between Jacqs and Bond's potential drama might shove me over the edge.

❋ ❋ ❋ ❋ ❋

I arrived at the CroBar Club a few minutes early and looked around trying to spot Jacqs. My shoulders lowered when I saw that she picked a place away from Bond's deejay booth. A few people surrounded the long central bar and littered the dance floor. *Gonna Make You Sweat* played through the massive speakers. Lights bounced off the dancers, floor, and walls.

"Hey, girl," I said as I bumped her with my hip.

"You're here!" She bounced up to give me a hug. I bent down to return it.

I pulled my cell phone out of my pocket, set it on the bar, and took the stool next to Jacqs.

"Cute look," I said, recognizing the navy/purple batik top from my shop. Her short, purple, pleated skirt and sandals spoke to the temperature outside.

"Going casual today, I see," she said, looking me over. "Damn those black shorts make your legs look a mile long."

"Yeah, I didn't feel like dressing up and geeze they

have a dress code here?" I kidded, looking around and seeing a wide range of outfits.

She laughed. "What do you want to drink? I was waiting on you."

"Something different for a change. Tequila sunrise?" I asked, feeling like I needed something to shut my mind off. I wanted to stop waiting to hear from Mason.

"Joe Nichols sings, *Tequila Makes Her Clothes Fall Off.* Should I be worried about you?"

"I'm definitely leaving mine on," I said, I flipped my cell phone over so I couldn't see the screen. "I need a drink though and something strong."

Jacqs raised her hand and Frank, their regular bartender said, "What can I get for you, half-pint?"

"Two tequila sunrises please and water for us both. Thanks."

He stepped away and spun a basket of pretzels along the bar that landed right in front of us.

We both smiled.

"A strong drink? Are you okay?" Jacqs asked, popping a pretzel into her mouth.

"I've been better. Mason and I had our first fight and it was a doozy. He wasn't happy about me going out with Stay."

She touched my shoulder and said, "Anything I can do?"

"Nah, I just needed to get out of the house. We can talk about it tomorrow."

"About that, I'm spending the night with Bond at his place."

I raised my eyebrows and said, "And Red's okay with that?"

"He has plans with his sister tonight. He isn't thrilled about it, but he understands."

"He's a keeper, Bond on the other hand—"

"Let's not, okay?"

"Yeah, sorry. Really. I'm just in a strange headspace."

"Stay or Mason?" she asked just as a chill ran up my back.

"Did I hear my name?" Stay said from behind me.

I jumped and said, "How long have you been there?"

"I just walked up. I'm going to go talk to Bond, I'll be right back."

"Do you want something to drink?" Jacqs asked.

"A club soda with lime would be great, thanks."

I followed him with my eyes as he walked away. No plaid shirt again. I had the sneaking suspicion he knew I'd be at the club. He had on jeans but instead of his usual blues, he had on black pants with a deep-blue, dress shirt that he wore out. He had shaved his face but the hair on his head was still growing in.

"You like him," Jacqs said, watching me watch him.

I shook my head.

"It's clearly written all over you face. That and your nipples got hard when he walked up behind you."

"If this is what it's going to be like tonight, I might move over to the other side of the bar."

Frank interrupted our conversation when he set our drinks on top of the round coasters. "Bond said the drinks are on him."

"I'll have to thank him," I said. "Can we get a club soda with lime when you get a chance?"

"Coming up," he said and tapped the bar as he moved away.

"So sorry, girl. You're worried Mason won't call?"

"Yeah, I am." I took a long slip of my drink and almost spit it out. Frank had been very generous with the tequila.

"I'm sure you'll hear from him. In the meantime, let us distract you."

"What are we distracting you from?" Stay said as he occupied the stool next to me.

"You have a bad habit of sneaking up on people," I said in a tone a bit more angry than I meant.

"Oops. Should I move over a few stools?"

"No, I..." I took another sip of my drink and shut up.

"She's just having a rough night," Jacqs said. "We're going to cheer her up."

He looked at me like he wanted to wrap me up in his arms and I almost wished he would. Instead he rubbed my back and said, "Let's dance when the next fast song comes on. That'll take your mind off of things."

"That's a great idea," Jacqs said. "Shall we toast?"

Frank slid the club soda to Stay and we all lifted our drinks.

"What are we toasting to?" Stay asked.

"To complicated relationships," I said, holding my glass out.

"I think you're supposed to toast to something good," Jacqs said.

"Let's toast to budding friendships," Stay said, suppressing a smile that showed in his eyes.

I gave him a dirty look and he laughed.

"That seems like a safe bet," Jacqs said.

Stay and I knew better. Jacqs probably did too.

"Cheers," I said.

Jacqs said, "Salute."

"Down the hatch," Stay said.

We took sips from our drink and then Stay said, "I have another toast.

May you never lie, steal, cheat or drink.
But if you must lie, lie in each other's arms.

If you must steal, steal kisses.
If you must cheat, cheat death.
And if you must drink, drink with us, your friends."

We all drank to that.

"Nice," I said, setting my drink down on the bar. "It sounds familiar. Have I seen it in a movie?"

"It's an old Irish toast that was used in *Hitch*."

"Right," I said.

His rapt attention caused the butterflies in my stomach to morph into humming birds. Truthfully, it was nice to see him again, but it just embrangled everything. In an attempt to deflect myself from my bodily responses, I leaned over my glass and sipped my drink through the tiny straw.

Blurred Lines began to blast out of the surround sound system.

Stay clasped my hands and pulled me to my feet. "Coming?" he asked Jacqs.

"Later," she said and waved us off.

He bobbed to the music, walking in front me and holding my hands behind his back. Once we made it to the middle of the dance floor, he flipped around to face me. His smile radiated and between him and the drink, I was feeling considerably better. We had more room to move around than at the concert. Stay could really move and our dancing styles suited each other.

He clasped my hand and spun me around. Then he sashayed toward me and hooked his arm around my waist. We swayed back and forth in unison and rocked incrementally lower, my knee between his legs until we were squatting. When we swung back up, and he pressed himself against me, I felt his prominent erection. His mouth hovered near mine until I pushed away from him.

BITTERSWEET DECEIT

We broke apart and danced around. When I braved to look up, the lust on his face hit me like a stone from a slingshot, directly on my clit. I closed my eyes, allowing the sensation to run its course.

Stay had a not so subtle way of stoking my arousal. Even though I had sex earlier, he made me horny as hell.

He swayed his hips back and forth and approached me again, his crooked smile gleaming in the flashing lights. He gathered my hair behind my head and then wrapped his arms tightly around me. We dipped to the right and then left, our pelvises locked tightly together. Stay could rival Patrick Swayze in *Dirty Dancing*.

The song quickly came to an end as another one started up.

"I'm going to say hi to Bond," I said, needing a few minutes away from Stay to get myself under control.

When he flipped my hair over my shoulder, his mouth was set in such a way, which made me think he held secrets in there that he intended to share with me later. He said, "Okay, I'll see you at the bar."

I approached the deejay booth and waited until a cute woman finished asking for her song request.

"Hey, Lane, how's it going?" Bond asked, standing up from behind the console that had many slide pulls and nobs.

"It's going okay. I wanted to thank you for covering our drinks." I had to shout to be heard.

He inclined his head forward and said, "No problem. I'm happy to do it. You and Stay looked great out there."

"Uh, yeah, it was fun."

"He's into you, Lainie," he said, resting his shoulder against the door jam.

"He's made that abundantly clear. He's great Bond, but I'm not available."

135

"That's what Jacqs said."

My eyes opened wide and I could feel my face get hot.

"Lane, relax, she wouldn't tell me anything about the dude. She said she wasn't free to talk and I respect that. She's concerned though. I know she wishes you would give Stay a chance. She's thought you two would make a good match for a while now. I told her we just have to let you two figure it out."

I stared at Bond for a moment and had to acknowledge the difference in him. Jacqs's recent car accident really seemed to shake him up and cause him to reevaluate his relationship with her and his choices.

"You and Jacqs doing okay?"

"Never better. One second." He inclined into the booth and flipped a switch. "Okay," he said when he faced me again.

"Do me a favor," I said loudly over the new song that began to play.

"Sure."

"If you're in the processes of starting up a new relationship with someone else, please be upfront with Jacqs."

"Has she said something?" he asked, crossing his arms in front of him.

"Yes."

"But you're not going tell me?"

I shook my head. "No."

"We have agreements and I plan to keep them."

"Okay, that's good to hear. I'm going to head back to the bar. It's good to see you and thanks again for the drinks." Amazingly, I meant it. He seemed like a better man and I would hold out hope that he would take care of Jacqs's heart this time around.

He took hold of my upper arm and said, "Thank you for being there for her and for taking on Sam. I never did thank you for that."

"No problem. Be good to her."

"You got it."

Back at the bar, I reached for my phone.

Stay touched my back. "You want another drink? Frank came by and asked."

"Uh, no, that's okay." I felt uncomfortable drinking around Stay now that I knew he abstained.

As if he read my energy or expression, he said, "I don't care if you drink, Lainie. I know a lot of alcoholics who live with the constant craving. I'm not the same person I was when I was drinking and I don't miss it. It's not an issue for me. If I thought you had a drinking problem, then it would be."

"Okay then, I'll have another. I'll be right back." I swallowed the last of my cocktail and then turned to leave.

"Where you going, *chica*?" Jacqs asked.

"Got to pee. I'll be right back." I strolled to the bathroom and got in line behind the other women. My phone vibrated in my hand and I clicked on the screen. "Shit."

The woman in front of me turned and glared, then did a one-eighty. Apparently I had offended her.

I stepped forward, looking down at my phone and saw that Mason had texted me.

> **MM:** I'm sorry about my abrupt departure. I didn't really want to leave you and yet I felt like I had to. We've never argued before and I was at a loss. It was
> **MM:** entirely my fault. I know our situation isn't fair for you. I'm not blind. Even if you won't tell me, I know you love me. I see it in your eyes every time

MM: we're together. It kills me to know I can't give you want you need. Meeting Stay just made it clear to me what I'm taking away from you and I became defensive

MM: and as I already stated, scared of losing you. I'm sure you're upset with me. You have every right to be. I'm sorry, baby. Although I know I should, I don't

MM: think I could ever let you go.

MM: Are you there?

MM: Please give me another chance.

MM: Text back, please. Want us to make plans for next week. I don't have much time before I have to turn off my phone.

"Fuck, shit, fuck," I muttered.

The woman in front of me turned around again.

"What?" I said, throwing up my hands.

Two stalls became available at once and I quickly slipped into the middle one. There were no covers so I lay out toilet paper to cover the seat. After peeing, I washed my hands. I tried to quickly pass the bar where Jacqs and Stay sat.

Stay caught my arm and said, "Where are you going?"

"I have to make a call. I'll be right back." I raced out the front of the club and texted Mason, hoping it wasn't too late.

Me: Are you still there? I'm sorry I haven't responded sooner. I was in a loud club and I didn't hear my phone. Please still be there.

I tromped back and forth in front of the door to

CroBar, waiting. I should have stayed home. Now I couldn't be sure when I'd hear from him again. *He probably thinks I don't want him anymore*. Panic and fear washed over me and I wanted to run. To where, I had no idea. Away from the club maybe or away from myself and the feelings that threatened to do me under.

"Come on, call me. Please call." So intent on watching the screen on my phone, I almost walked into someone who had opened the door to club.

I paced away from the entrance and when I circled back it opened again. Stay came out.

I lurched my head back, breathed out heavily, and faltered over to him.

He held out his hands as if to ward off an assault. "Jacqs sent me to check on you." His compassionate eyes scanned my expression. "What is it?"

"You don't want to know." I could feel the corners of my mouth turning down. When he looked at me like that, it was if all the barriers around my heart fell away and I stood there in front of him unprotected. "Stop it."

"Stop what?"

"Whatever it is that you're doing to me, and stop looking at me like that." I felt young and vulnerable standing in front of him.

"Like what?"

"Like you want to hold me in your arms and make me better."

He stepped closer and said, "Just let me be your friend, Lainie. That's all I'm asking."

"No, it's not. I thought you didn't lie. Just tell Jacqs I'm fine and I'll be in, in a minute."

He didn't listen to me. Not at all. He wrapped his strong arms around me and I gave in.

"I'm not going to cry," I said.

"Shh," he whispered. He held me against him and stroked my hair.

Resting my head against his chest, I asked, "Why can't you stop being so nice to me?"

"I don't know," he said, tightening his hold on me.

"I'm just going to break your heart."

He rocked us and said, "I know."

That caused me to cry, and I wasn't sure who I was crying for. Myself? Mason? Stay? How could my heart be breaking for a man I had never loved? Something was really wrong with me. I used to think the one thing that would truly make me happy in life was a relationship with a man, but now look at me. I'm a fucked up mess. Maybe I'm better off abstaining from love like Stay abstained from alcohol.

My phone chirped and I looked up into Stay's deep-blue eyes. "I need to take this."

"I'll see you in side," he said, but he didn't let go of me right away.

"I really need—"

"Okay." When he walked away my heart wrenched but I still hurriedly checked my messages.

MM: He's there, isn't he?

I texted back:

Me: I came out as a favor to Jacqs.
MM: I'll take that as a yes.
Me: Please Mason, don't do that.
MM: I'm going out of town and leaving Sunday night. If you still want to see me, I'm coming in

Tuesday around midnight and I'm not expected
home until the evening. Can you make time for me?
Me: Of course I want to see you. I miss you
already. I hate how today went and I wish we
could do it over.
MM: Let's just try to move forward from here. I
have to go in a minute. Victoria thinks I'm on a
work call.

He wrote *try*, as if there might be some doubt.

Me: Will I hear from you before Tuesday?
MM: I'll stay in touch. Lainie?
Me: What?
MM: Don't do anything with the boy. I don't think
I could get past that.
Me: I won't.
MM: Love you, baby.
Me: Bye, Mason.

"Holy fucking piss shit goddamn hell," I mumbled.
Apparently I'd come down with Tourette syndrome on top
of everything else. I circled around a couple of times and
finally pulled the door open and headed back to my seat.

The new tequila sunrise sat on the bar sweating and
calling my name. Stay, who sat next to Jacqs, shifted off
my stool onto his. I took a long drink before
acknowledging either of them.

The music lowered and Bond's voice came over the
microphone. "This next song, *Feel So Close* by Calvin
Harris, is by request for my good man, Stayman. Bring me
a beer dude!" And then he laughed and so did everyone
else in the bar.

"Go dance," Jacqs said. "I'll take care of his drink."

"Come on, OCDC, we need to boogie off some of the stress."

I let Stay lead me out on the dance floor and said, "Why this song?"

"You know why."

"You're going to keep wooing me even though I don't want you to?"

"Yes. Just shut up and dance."

"Excuse me?" I yelped but then he swept me up in his arms, and led me around the dance floor, making me forget my indignation.

When the song finally ended, I said, "You're in denial, you know."

"How do you mean?" he said, taking my hand in his.

"The lyrics to the song." I tried to pull my hand free, but he wouldn't let me. I didn't try very hard.

"I told you, OC, I have a loyalty problem."

"And I told you, I have a Mason problem. Well, not a problem but my heart is wrapped up elsewhere."

"That's just a matter of untangling and it's already begun."

I pushed against him and said, "It seems to me that you are fascinated with your bittersweet deceit."

"And who am I deceiving?"

"Yourself."

He caught me in his arms and then took me completely by surprise. His mouth descended on mine and instead of ravishing my lips, he lightly kissed them.

And I let him. I cleared my throat when he pulled away. *What the hell is wrong with me?*

"Don't do that OC. I can see that look. It's not wrong."

"You don't know what you're saying. Our friendship

is already hurting my relationship. We had our first fight ever over you." Then I really shoved him. "Get that self-satisfied look off your face!"

"Whoa, Lane, settle down," he said, waving his hands in a downward motion. His cheeky smile gave him away.

When we walked back to the bar, we found Jacqs's chair empty.

Most of the ice in my drink had already melted, but I didn't care. I took the last swallow of the cocktail. When Stay sat next to me I said, "I'm going to see Mason again."

"I'm sure you are," he said. There was no smile left on his lips or in his eyes.

"I feel like I'm using you and I don't like it. I don't like how it makes me feel. I don't want to hurt you. I don't want to hurt anyone." I held up my hand and Frank held up one finger in question. I looked at Jacqs empty glass and gave him the peace sign. Frank nodded.

Stay squeezed the lime into his club soda and then looked at me. "Let me worry about me. Trust me ... I know what I'm doing. I know what I'm getting myself into and I'm willing to take the risk."

"And if it all turns to hell? Then what? It's awkward each time we cross paths?" I lay my head in my hand and continued, "I don't think I have ever understood Jacqs better than I do right at this moment."

His big warm hand touched my back and I flinched. He kept it there and said, "Let me in. Give me a chance. That's all I'm asking."

"Do you know how much that is? It's too much. I can't. I'm in love." I glanced up and saw sadness in his eyes. "God, Stay, stop making me hurt you. I can't stand it."

He stood up behind me and gathered my hair onto my back. His strong hands began kneading my shoulders.

"The only thing that will hurt me is if you don't give us a chance," he said close to my ear. His breath tickled my neck and when my body responded, I silently cursed myself.

He continued, "There's something intense and powerful between us. I know you know it. I know you feel it. I won't dismiss it." He circled my stool toward him and stood over me. His hands cupped my face and tilted my head up. The ferocity in his blue eyes stole my breath.

"Stay I..." My pussy throbbed and my breathing deepened. I wanted to look away, I couldn't look away. Then I didn't want to. "Please," I pleaded, only I didn't know what I was asking for.

That time when he lowered his lips to mine, all the sexual tension that had been building between us exploded in the most infernal kiss of my life. At first he leaned over me but then he lifted me to him and I let him. Our bodies melded together perfectly, his hands cupping my ass and pulling me tightly against his aroused body.

When we briefly broke for air, I mumbled, "Oh."

He said nothing at first, but his face spoke volumes. He looked high and crazed, his eyes bouncing around, scanning my face. "Oh, OC, I can't stop." And he didn't.

With an audience of the whole bar, I gave myself over to Stay, not thinking about the consequences that would befall me. His energy captivated me so fully, I forgot about everything but the feel of his lips on mine, his tongue taking me on a journey of sensation. He shifted his hands to my head and angled my face so he could deepen the kiss further.

I felt wetness gathering in my panties and on my cheeks. It didn't stop or deter me. Instead, I pushed myself into him, as if our bodies could merge. In his arms, overcome by his kiss, there was no other place I wanted to be.

We might have remained glued together for the rest of the night if it wasn't for Jacqs tugging on my sleeve.

"Lainie, so sorry to interrupt, truly, but Frank has been trying to break you apart for a few minutes. You're creating quite the scene plus you're blocking the way by."

I looked around and several people stared back including the couple that was waiting to get past us. "I'm sorry," I mumbled, both Stay and I shifting out of their way.

They quickly passed by.

Stay still held me as I started to shake. "I have to go, I need to leave."

In a soft voice he said, "It's okay, Lane."

"It's not," I said, pulling away. "It really isn't. Jacqs, come outside with me?"

"Yes, girl, of course." As soon as we stepped outside, she said, "Boy, Lainie you took me by surprise. From the looks of it, you took Stay by surprise too."

"He started it." I rested against the concrete wall and rubbed my forehead.

She peered up at me and said, "I thought tequila might be a dangerous choice."

"It wouldn't have been if you hadn't invited Stay."

"I didn't. Bond did." She looked away.

"Uh-huh and you didn't know about it."

She made eye contact again and said, "Well, I ... I want you to be happy. Doesn't that sound familiar?"

"Oh great, throw my words back at me."

"Stay's a great guy, Lainie."

"Yeah and thanks to your handy work, I'm going to end up hurting him. Is that what you want?" I asked, my palms out in question. I sighed. "I already am. That dude is a glutton for punishment and he doesn't take no for an answer. He's persistent and stubborn and has a way of making me..."

"Well if he was smitten before, I think he must have moved on to full blown infatuation after that kiss. That was hot, girl. You like him too, Lane. It's so easy to see and I mean aside from that smoking hot, grinding kiss you gave him. I'm surprised the bar didn't clap when you guys finally parted."

"I was too shocked over my own behavior to be mortified by the people watching."

"I'm sure Jose Cuervo helped give you the nerve."

"I can't blame everything on the drinks. He does something to me. He strips away my armor and I love it and hate it at the same time. I especially hate it when I end up doing stupid, stupid things. What the hell am I supposed to say to Stay now?"

"The truth."

"I don't even know what that is anymore."

"Start with that." She waved me to follow. "Come on, girl. I'll leave you two alone and go visit with Bond. He likes having me on his lap in the booth."

We parted company at the door. She traveled around the right side of the bar toward Bond, and I trudged back to my seat.

"I wasn't sure you were coming back," Stay said, when I sat back down. "Are you okay?"

"No, not in the least."

"I can't say I'm sorry about that kiss. That was ... it was..." He laughed. "Indescribable. You ... damn, OCDC, I didn't know you had it in you."

"You're gloating."

"This isn't a contest. It's not like that for me. Before our date—"

"It was not a date," I shouted and hit my hand on the side of the bar. Fortunately the music was so loud that it covered my noise.

"I guess I'm not the only one in denial. Call it what you'd like: dinner and a concert. My point is that before that night, what I thought we had between us, the potential that existed was just in the realm of speculation and hope. You and me, we have an intangible between us."

"I don't even know what that means."

"It's that unnamable quality that allows two people to connect in a rare and deep way. Red and Jacqs have it."

"But not Bond and Jacqs?"

"Maybe they do. It's just very apparent between Red and Jacqs. There's a flow, a dance, and you can almost see the connection between them even when they are across the room from each other. Like an energy trail of love that links them together."

"That's beautiful. I think I get what you're saying. I just don't see how it applies to us."

He raised his eyebrow and I knew he was questioning my honesty.

"I don't know what this is between us. I just know it's messing with my head and confusing the hell out of me."

"Had I not spent the night at your place taking care of you, I might have been able to move slower, but when you're around me, my energy shifts and my usual calm, centered, patient manner morphs into a crazed, pressing need to have you in my arms. Sometimes the desire feels soft and sweet and I just want to bury my face in your silky hair and hold you. Other times I want you on your knees before me, your green-hazel eyes peering up into mine, opening your mouth for my hard cock."

He placed my hand over his pants and I closed my eyes. His erection excited and scared me. He was significantly thicker than Mason and longer too. Gazing up, our eyes locked and I couldn't be sure what I wanted anymore.

He pushed his hand down over mine and continued, "Sometimes it's so strong I think if I don't get to fuck you hard and fast I just might expire on the spot." A warm, bright smile transformed his face when he said, "Then I think about taking you very slowly, teaching you my tantric ways, making you come harder than you ever have before.

"That kiss, Lainie, it changed everything for me. You might regret it, but I never will, even if you never again give me the privilege. Because now I know what we really can be. It's left in your hands." He looked down at his hand on top of mine.

I sat up straight, pulling my hand away.

He lifted my head up. "Lainie, please don't shut me out."

"I think it would be best for me to leave. My mind is racing"—*and my body,* I thought, but I left that out—"and I can't think straight. I ... I ... please don't look at me like that." I felt young, and raw, and really scared. I wished I could crawl into my father's lap and hide there like I had done as a little girl.

Stay rested his hand on my knee as if he couldn't bear to be near me without touching me. "Are you okay to drive?"

"I'll have Frank call me a cab. You can stay and keep Jacqs company."

"Lainie, let me drive you home. We can talk on the way. If you go, I'm leaving anyway and it's on the way to my place."

I gave in. "I'll go say goodbye to Jacqs and Bond."

"I'll just wait for you here. Tell Bond, I'll talk to him tomorrow."

Once at the deejay booth, I said, "We're taking off."

Jacqs jumped off of Bond and said, "Is everything okay? Did you guys talk?"

"Yes, and it definitely did not help. I need to get home and journal and try to wrap my mind around what I'm feeling and what I want. Why couldn't he have waited?"

Bond answered, "According to Red, there comes a point where it's out of your hands. It's not like you can set love on pause forever."

"Stay doesn't love me," I practically yelled.

They both gave me a questioning look.

"I'm in love with someone else! Why can't you all understand that?"

Jacqs touched my arm. "We get it. Me better than anyone else. Let me know if you want to get together after your walk with your dad and please give him a big hug from me." Then she stretched up on her tiptoes and embraced me. She whispered, "Trust yourself, girl. I'm here if you need me."

"Thanks," I mumbled, and took a step away. Then I turned back around. "Oh, Bond, Stay said he'll talk to you tomorrow."

Jacqs was already back in his lap. Bond waved.

CHAPTER ELEVEN

These Eyes

by The Guess Who

I ambled through the CroBar not really seeing the flashing lights or the crowd of people that had gathered since I arrived. In a daze, I headed back to Stay feeling one step removed from my emotions. A dark cloud of depression hovered way too close.

"Ready?" Stay asked as I approached.

"Yeah."

"Do you have a purse or anything?"

"No."

"Try not to look so sad," he said, taking my hand and leading me around the other patrons, out of the club to his Prius. He opened the passenger side door for me.

I slid in and pulled the seat belt across my chest as he closed the door. I watched as he made his way around the car and got in. "I'm not sure what I'm experiencing," I said.

"What does it feel like?" he asked as he started the car.

I closed my eyes and said, "Pain, anguish, confusion, euphoria, fear, lots of fear. I feel stupid and out of control. I'm responsible for hurting you and hurting Mason too. He specifically said that if I did anything with you, he didn't think he could get past it."

Stay pulled out of the parking lot. "Will you be honest with him?" he asked, resting his arm across the bucket seats and touching my elbow.

Opening my eyes, I watched the familiar scenery pass by. "If he asks me, yes and I'm sure he will. Will I offer the information? I don't know. Until recently, we didn't have that kind of relationship. He never asked me and I never asked him either."

"What changed that?"

"You. You've blown in like a hurricane, shattering all the existing structures, and leaving fresh air and wreckage behind in your wake."

He glanced over at me and his doleful expression shot through my heart. "That wasn't my intention," he said.

"I'm sorry. I don't know what I'm saying." I lay my head against the headrest and closed my watery eyes.

He squeezed my arm and said, "I can understand your mixed emotions. It makes sense. I didn't set out to make your life more complicated, but I can see that's exactly what I've done. I didn't know you were dating anyone. Jacqs never mentioned it. I didn't know until I saw Mason hovering outside of your apartment. If I had thought you were happy with him, I wouldn't have continued pursuing you. Now it's just too late."

My heart dropped into my gut thinking Stay had changed his mind and yet that was exactly what I wanted. I needed the clock to turn back to when we were just friends. So why did the thought hurt so much? "Too late for what?"

"Too late for us to stop." He drove onto the highway and continued, "I desire you like I have never wanted another soul in my life. And I've tried to get your attention before but back then, you looked right past me. My chance is now."

"What are you talking about? We've hung out at Red's together and even played darts and pool a few times."

"Come on Lainie. Are you telling me you didn't notice my interest?"

"It was too late by then. I already had Mason in my life." I suddenly became so tired. I wanted to be home, in my own bed, alone.

"It's not too late for us."

I turned my head toward him and said, "I'm seeing Mason on Tuesday and if he doesn't end it because of my indiscretion with you, I'm going to continue to see him until the time comes that we need to go our separate ways."

"The time has already come and even he knows it."

"I don't want to talk anymore, Stay. You seem to think I can just flip a switch and turn off how I feel about Mason and then direct it to you. It doesn't work that way."

"Why do you love him, Lainie? Help me understand. He can't give you want you need."

I paused and couldn't come up with a reasonable response so I said, "What do you mean why?"

"It's a simple question." He pulled down the ramp from the highway and stopped at the red light.

I uttered in sheer exhaustion, "It's an emotion without logic."

"Love is an emotion *and* a verb. What is there besides amazing sex? I mean I'm assuming it must be amazing to keep you."

"Friendship, comfort, attention."

He made a left turn and asked, "Does he take you out?"

"No, not since the beginning."

"I see," he said, nodding.

"What?"

"You are worth more. Way more." He pulled into my parking spot and turned off the engine.

"And if I don't want more."

"I call bullshit."

I turned in my seat to face him on the verge of an angry outburst or a meltdown. Anger seemed the better option. "You are probably one of the nicest, sweetest, most considerate, sexy men I have ever met and please don't take this the wrong way, but fuck off." I opened the car door and got out. "Thanks for the ride."

His mouth hung open in shock. "Whoa, wait a minute." He scrambled out of the car.

"I should have taken the cab home. I can't give you what you want or need. I'm sorry, probably sorrier than you know, but the timing is all wrong. I have to assume that Mason will again ask me to avoid seeing you after he knows about the kiss, and I don't see how I can argue with him. I can't trust myself to be in your vicinity."

He moved closer to me. "I don't know how long I'll wait for you."

"I understand. I don't think you should," I said, wrapping my arms around myself.

"Please at least let me say goodbye."

I shook my head knowing if I let him touch me again all might be lost.

"Please," he pleaded, closing the distance between us. "A hug only." He didn't wait for me to answer and enclosed me in his arms.

At first I kept my arms between us and then rationalized that it was just a hug. Embracing him back, our hearts lining up together, I felt the annihilating loss of what had started to grow between us. I had to say goodbye. It was the right thing to do for everyone. It was, wasn't it? If it was so right, why did it hurt so much? Tears ran down my cheeks as I quietly cried.

We hugged each other for a long while, knowing that

once we separated it really was goodbye.

He finally stepped back and I saw a single tear escape and roll down his cheek. That caused the dam on my emotions to break.

"I'm so sorry," I said and then ran up the stairs to my place. With shaking hands, I retrieved the keys from my pocket and struggled to unlock the door.

Inside I kicked off my shoes and ran to my bed, not taking the time to undress. I sobbed like the teary eyed wretch I had recently turned into. I lay there in a daze of my own making. Why had I allowed Stay in? Maybe because he took care of me when Mason wasn't there for me? Regardless, I had to rein in my ill-conceived actions.

After the pain eased enough, I got ready for bed, avoiding looking in the mirror. I suspected I might breakdown again if I saw my own refection.

With my journal on my lap, I clicked my pen.

In the past few days I've cried more than in the past ten years. If this is what love does to a person, I don't want it! Maybe I should tell them both to go to hell.

Stay and his stupid questions about love. Love isn't something easily definable or explainable to someone else. I love Mason because he is, because he is the one man in the world I want to spend my time with. Is it an easy love? No. I'd be kidding myself if I said it was, but that doesn't make it any less real.

Just because Stay wants to have a relationship with me doesn't mean he gets to. Even if I want a relationship with him too. And maybe I would've if I hadn't already given my heart away. I'm not like Jacqs. I can't split my loyalties down the middle. I'm a one man woman.

I've never been this way before, all confused and

emotional and struggling to make concrete choice, allowing chemistry and seduction to influence me. Decisions have always been clear-cut and straightforward. Now it all seems muddled.

Part of me wants to punch out Stay for messing with me in the first place. He seems so nice but he has his own agenda and pushes for it even when I say NO. Why couldn't he just leave me alone? He's like an infection that just takes over without your permission, spreading out to all the nooks and crannies. He's a sickness I just need to get over.

The Kiss. It seemed liked more than a kiss. It felt more like alchemy, our energies merging and swirling around us in a whirlwind. I wonder if it was part of the tantric stuff he keeps hinting about.

Stay and Mason are so different. In some ways my relationship with Mason is much simpler. We come together and share love and passion, and have our own independent lives. Stay seems all consuming, like I might not have room to breathe with him. How the hell Jacqs juggles two men is beyond me. How does she have any time for herself?

I know Mason is going to ask about Stay. I can just feel it and I'm not sure if I should just bite the bullet and confess or wait. I'll probably take the chicken shit way out and wait. Hopefully we will have an opportunity to reconnect before it comes out. I have no idea what to say if he asks me how the kiss was. I don't think saying, "epic" will go over well. It was though. Epic, astonishing, awe-inspiring, unfathomable too. FUCK YOU Stay for kissing me like that. He doesn't fight fair.

Yes, I know, I kissed him back. I know, I know, I know. UGH!

I bet Mason is going to be so hurt. It's the only thing he asked of me and I couldn't even do it. STAY AWAY FROM THE BOY!!!!

I'm so happy I will be seeing Dad tomorrow. Maybe he will knock some sense into me. Probably not. He will probably just listen and be non-judgmental. I could use some of that because I have all sorts of judgment of myself. Stupid, stupid, stupid.

I hope I can sleep. I need some mindless oblivion.

With my alarm set, I scooted down in the bed, rolled on my side, and pulled a pillow between my knees. Luckily, the exhaustion from the day and my emotions made sleep come easy.

CHAPTER TWELVE

The Deep End

by Crossfade

My dry mouth woke me up before my alarm was set to go off. I hadn't consumed enough water the night before. After downing two Tylenol tablets and a full glass of water, I decided to knock out some chores before meeting up with my dad. I started the coffee pot and gathered the supplies I needed from under the kitchen sink. I planned to start in the bathroom. My basket of laundry was getting full but I didn't have enough time for the wash and a dry.

I flipped on the stereo in the living room and got busy. I sang while I cleaned to drown out the thoughts threatening to surface. Bed made, bathroom scrubbed, carpet vacuumed, floors swept, refrigerator wiped out, order and cleanliness was once restored, at least externally.

I ate a quick breakfast, called the cab company for a ride to my car, took a brief shower and dressed for my walk with my dad.

I parked near the racket ball courts and searched for my father. Gathered around a grouping of tables set nearby, I found him playing chess.

He was a big guy in height and in girth. I got his

genetic code instead of my mother's petite stature. The similarities between Dad and me seemed to bother my mother early on. I often wondered if that fueled my mother's disenchantment with me.

Dad wore long, beige shorts and a large, brown T-shirt. He stood up and embraced me in a warm bear hug, lifting my feet off the ground. "Gentleman, let me introduce you to my daughter, Lainie," he said as he lowered me down. "She owns her own clothing boutique."

After shaking several hands I asked, "Would you like to finish the game?"

"No, honey. They knew I'd be leaving soon. Catch you next time Sal and count on me winning."

"Whatever gets you through the day." He laughed.

My dad patted him on the back and waved to his friend George. Then we walked over to the boardwalk along Hollywood Beach.

Spending time with my father worked as an elixir, which cured most of my ills, at least while I was in his presence.

"How's my favorite daughter?" he said, taking hold of my hand.

"I'm your only daughter, Dad."

"That doesn't make you any less my favorite. Thanks for making time for your old man."

I touched his belly and said, "You're right, you're looking good, Dad."

"You, my love, look stressed. Are you sleeping okay?"

I looked out over the ocean and then shielded my eyes from the sun to make eye contact with him. "I'm sleeping but I'm not okay."

"Is this about Mason?"

"Mason and Stay."

As we strolled side by side he said, "Stay, I think you've

mentioned him before. He's part of your group, right?"

"Yes, Papa, he is."

"And you like him?"

"I don't know. I mean I do but I'm already involved in a relationship. I love Mason, even though I know it's not ideal. My emotions are not like a faucet I can turn off."

He stopped and turned to face me. "You're in a relationship. You can't just exchange one for the other."

"Exactly. I just wish Stay and Jacqs understood that."

He started walking again and said, "I'm sure Jacqs wants what she thinks is best for you. What's this Stay fellow like?"

"He's a good guy. I realized recently that I really didn't know him well before. He's interesting, self-made, has overcome a bad past and is a gentleman for the most part. He's also very pushy and assertive and thinks I should stop seeing Mason to see him."

"Does Mason know about Stay?" he asked.

"Unfortunately. They crossed paths and Stay stated his intention to pursue me."

My father smiled. "That's ballsy. You have to give him credit for that."

"I give him credit for causing problems in my relationship with Mason."

"Honey, you know I love you and you know I'll always be on your side, but Stay can't cause problems where there are none."

We walked silently for a few steps and then I said, "But if Stay hadn't decided to chase me now, Mason and I wouldn't have had our first fight. And before then we hadn't even argued."

"Maybe that's true, but if after all this time you've never had a disagreement, one or both of you aren't being honest."

"How do you mean?" I said, sidestepping a runner who passed by.

"No two people live so in sync that there aren't issues to work out along the way, especially when one holds all the cards."

"You mean Mason," I said, biting my lower lip.

"Of course."

I thought about seeing Mason on Tuesday and the minefield we still needed to cross. "I don't know if Mason will even see me anymore."

Looking surprised, he said, "Why? What happened?"

"I let Stay kiss me."

"Really?" he asked as if processing my new disclosure. "What kind of kiss?"

"Does it matter?"

"Of course it does, Lainie. And by the look on your face, it was definitely the kind that matters."

We walked onto the sand to avoid the people gathered on Johnson Street in front of the stage.

Once back on the boardwalk on the other side, I asked, "Oh Dad, why couldn't Stay have waited until I was free? This all could have been so different."

"I can't fault Stay for his good taste. Why would he wait, honey? Men tend to go after what they want and damn the obstacles."

I furrowed my brow. "Well, he didn't know about Mason at first but he did before we went out together."

"Interesting. So you had a date with Stay?" he asked with no judgment in the question.

"It wasn't a date!" I said, vehemently.

He chuckled and said, "Baby, did you go out with Stay, just the two of you?"

"Yes, to dinner and a concert." I shrugged my shoulders.

"How is that not a date?"

"Because we're just friends. You wouldn't assume it was a date if I did the same with Jacqs."

He turned me to face him and asked, "Did you know he was interested in you at that point?"

"Well ... I, yes, but he had purchased tickets and I had already agreed to go."

"Before you knew he was interested in you?" he asked.

"Well, no, I knew, but I made it clear I was interested in just friendship."

He paused before responding as we continued to stroll. "How do you feel about Stay now?"

I have never lied to my father, even if I sometimes lied to myself. I told him the truth. "I like him and maybe if the timing was different, it might have worked out. I don't know. He's all consuming and I feel stripped bare and naked in front of him and I don't particularly care for the sensation. I don't know how he managed to make it happen but I feel connected to him in a way I haven't felt before."

"And with Mason?"

"It's completely different. It feels more staid and adult. I love him and I miss him every second we're apart."

"Even when Stay kissed you?" he asked as we turned back the other way.

"Dad!" I said, smacking his shoulder.

"Baby, I'm just trying to help you to see what's in front of you so you can make your choices clean and clear."

I gave in and answered him. "No, I didn't think about anyone or anything while we were kissing."

"So what do you plan to do now?"

"Beg Mason to forgive me for the kiss. The plus side of Stay's pronouncement to Mason is that I have seen him more in the last week or so than ever before."

"So he feels threatened."

"Very."

"How does that make you feel?"

I thought about it for a minute before responding. "Honestly, I like that he's worried about losing me but I also don't like the double standard."

"Which is?"

"He goes home to his wife and yet he expects me to be monogamous."

"Do you think he's still having sex with his wife?" He held his arm out toward a bench facing the ocean.

After sitting down, I said, "He won't answer the question directly. He makes it sound like he and his wife are barely getting along. He said they are working on finding a place of friendship and will raise the kids together."

"And divorce?"

"Not an option."

He gazed out at the ocean and then looked back at me. "I hate to be the one to state the obvious and I understand completely that you are in love with him, but you're thirty years old and I know you want a family. There is no future with him."

"I know, Dad, truly I do. It's just, I can't let go. He's so intelligent and worldly and frankly stunning."

"And good in bed, I imagine."

"Dad!" I pushed into him with my shoulder.

He chuckled. "So what are you going to do about Stay?"

"I told him not to wait for me."

"So you've decided."

"Yes. Now I just have to wait to see if Mason will forgive me."

Dad threw his arm over my shoulder and held me against him. We sat quietly, watching the waves roll in.

Surrounded by his warm, caring energy, I couldn't help being reminded of Stay.

My phone going off thankfully knocked the thought out of my head.

"Hey, girl, can you come by?" Jacqs asked.

"Are you still at Bond's?"

"No, my apartment." Her voice wavered.

"Are you okay?"

"No."

"I'm on my way." I stood up and said, "That was Jacqs."

My Dad took my hand and we headed back toward my car. "Thank you for the lovely walk, baby girl."

"Thank you for listening to me."

"And for my sage advice," he said with a warm smile.

"Yes, that too," I said, peering up and smiling back.

"Your mother and I will be out of town next weekend for a wedding of one of her friend's son. Be happy you're not being dragged along."

"Hang in there, daddio. I'm sure it won't be too bad. Shall we shoot for a walk the week after that?"

"Yes, lets."

We embraced and he rocked me back and forth before letting me go. "Please stay in touch. You know where to reach me."

"I know, Dad. I love you lots."

"I love you more."

It took me about seven minutes to get to Jacqs from Hollywood Beach.

"Hey, girl," I said, knocking on her apartment door.

She pulled the door open, tears pouring down her cheeks.

Her cute one bedroom apartment had a different warm color on each of the walls in the combined kitchen living room. Her pictures and paintings were no longer displayed. I followed her over to her comfy brown couch and sat down.

"What going on?" I asked. "I thought you were staying over Bond's last night."

"It's stupid."

"Tell me anyway," I said, patting the cushion next to me.

She plopped down and said, "Last night was great at first. I loved being with Bond. He was very attentive and I didn't feel jealous once, which is some kind of miracle for being at the club."

"Totally. So what changed?"

"After he got off work, we went up to his place and had amazing sex. Some hardcore stuff he's wanted to try. I'll spare you the details."

"Thank you. It's appreciated. Go on."

She shifted and pulled her legs in, wrapping her arms around them. "I swear I felt closer to him than I ever have, even more so than in the very beginning of our relationship. When I got ready for bed, my toothbrush wasn't there and another hung in its place."

"Oh fuck," I said. "Seems we're both swimming in the deep end."

"Totally and I know I have no right to be mad or hurt. He's followed our agreements. He hasn't brought anyone over to Red's and keeps his dalliances to his place. However, to me a toothbrush means more than a one night stand."

"Right. So did you ask him?"

"I came out of the bathroom waving the toothbrush and said, 'What the fuck is this?' He said, 'I'm sorry, I forgot to put yours back out,' all nice and calm. Then my anger spewed out, 'Who the fuck is she?' and he tried to hold me and calm me down but I'd have none of it."

"Why did you come here and not go home to Red's?"

"Because I didn't want to hurt Red in the process and I needed to sort out how I feel."

"And have you?"

"No, I mean yes, I don't know girl. I feel all torn up inside and I really don't want to care. Bond and I have been in an excellent place and I've enjoyed my time with him lately more than I ever thought possible. I felt so close to him and now I don't know."

"Have you talked to him since?"

"No."

"I'm surprised he didn't follow you."

"You know he won't drive if he's had anything to drink."

After years of not driving because of a past automobile accident, Bond had recently gotten his driver's license and purchased a car.

"It's still crazy for me to think he's driving at all," I said.

"Yeah."

"Has he called?"

"He's at Red's now and they've both called me and texted. I told them to give me space."

"What are you going to do?" I asked.

"I don't know. I just know I don't want to feel this way. It brings up all the feelings of not being good enough or being enough for him."

"But—" I started.

"I know what you're going to say. I have Red too so I'm sharing Bond as much as he has to share me. I don't want to feel this way. I just don't know how to make it stop."

A knock sounded on the door and we both jumped.

"Apparently they're done giving you space."

She frowned and didn't move.

"I'll get it," I said. I opened the door and Red stood before me, his massive frame filling the doorway. His green eyes held a look of worry and his red clinched eyebrows bid me to let him pass.

"Bond's in the car," he said.

"She worried about hurting you," I said softly.

"The only thing hurting me is her not letting me comfort her."

Moving out of his way, I let him pass. I turned and watched him pull Jacqs up and settle on the couch with her on his lap. He wrapped her up in his arms as she cried. He smoothed her hair and held her tight.

Watching them did something to me that I didn't like at all. She had a man who loved her more than life itself and would always be there for her no matter what. I didn't see that in my future for myself.

After closing the door behind me, I made a beeline to Red's SUV. I climbed into the driver's seat next to Bond. He looked wretched.

"Fuck, Lainie. I can't seem to ever get it right with her."

"All I can tell you is that she wishes she felt different than she does."

"It was a stupid oversight on my part." He ran his fingers over his long, dark hair.

"Is it serious?"

"It's convenient. She's a nice gal, but it's not love. I needed a balance away from Jacqs and Red. I doubt you can understand but watching their—"

"Oh, no, I get it. I was wondering all this time how you were going to cope. It makes sense to me. Maybe if you can explain it to Jacqs, she won't feel so hurt. I think it might help."

His light-brown eyes searched my faced. "Thank you,

Lane. I never thought you and I would ever be on the same page."

"Yeah. Who would've thunk it?"

"Not me." He chuckled. "Have you talked to Stay?"

I shifted uncomfortably and said, "No and I don't see that happening for a while."

"Relationships are complicated aren't they?"

"Very," I said and meant it.

"Will you check to see if she's ready to talk to me?"

"Yes, of course." He looked so bereft, I reached out to him and he hugged me back.

When we broke apart, he sighed heavily.

I climbed down out of the ridiculously high SUV and knocked on Jacqs's door, praying I wasn't interrupting.

"Come in," Red said.

"Are you ready to talk to Bond?" I asked Jacqs.

"Yes, and Lane?"

"Yeah?"

"Thanks." She held her hand out and I grabbed it.

"I'll go get Bond," Red said.

"I'm coming with you," I said to Red. "Call me if you need me, girl."

"You too."

When Red and I exited the apartment, I waved Bond over.

Bond passed us and slipped into Jacqs's old place.

"Are you okay?" I asked Red.

"I just hate to see her in pain. My heart hurts for her." He rubbed his red, short-cropped beard and asked, "How are you doing? I've heard you're dealing with your own drama."

"It's a right mess but I hope to sort it out soon. I'm not sure I'll make it to your place on Wednesday. I think it's best if Stay and I avoid—"

"He's not planning to be there. He said the same thing

so you're free to come."

Red's words were like a sharp knife stabbed straight through my heart. Stay didn't want to see me.

"It's going to be okay, Lane. These things have their way of working out."

"I hope you're right."

Back at my condo, I looked around at my clean home feeling more alone than ever. Even though Jacqs's relationships held challenges, she shared her life with another—two others currently. I had been solitary for so long. Until recently it hadn't bother me. I would even say I had preferred it that way. I did not welcome all the complications that came along with love, but at some point we all wanted to find our one and only. Why I stayed with someone I had to share, made no real sense to me. But when does love make sense? If it did, would Jacqs have hung in there so long with Bond? Would Red have been okay or even suggest that Jacqs see both he and Bond? What about my father staying with my mother? And Stay and his loyalty?

Fuck Stay. Fuck him. He doesn't want to see me? Well I don't want to see him either. Good riddance!

I didn't want to think about him anymore. Instead I did something I rarely do. Out on the balcony, with a cigarette in hand, I typed out an email on my phone to Mason.

To: MMontheLam@gmail.com
From: Lainie.Simmons@gmail.com
Hi Mason,
I know you're probably getting ready for your flight out. I

just wanted you to know that I'm thinking about you and looking forward to our time together on Tuesday.

I'll make arrangements with Samantha to cover for me. What time should I be home? Is there anything special you would like to eat?

I hope your trip goes well and I'd love to hear from you when you have the time.

Yours,

Lainie

I hit send before I had the chance to change my mind. I tamped out my cigarette and headed in to strip my bed and then tackle the laundry.

By bed time and no email back from Mason, the last thing I wanted to do was to peruse anymore of my thoughts. I had sufficiently exhausted them and dissecting each one hadn't helped to lessen the tight knot in my gut. Two more days until I had to confront the inevitable, whatever that turned out to be. At least for tomorrow, I could count on my job and the start of my weekly routine. I welcomed the normality.

I set my alarm and turned on my music, letting the sound lull me to sleep.

CHAPTER THIRTEEN

Lovesong

by The Cure

Monday breezed by with the exception of me obsessively checking my email. If Stay managed to weasel his way into my thoughts, I shut them down before they could make any headway. Samantha was a doll about covering for me and as always, we worked well side by side. Although Mondays tended to be slow, we managed to move a good bit of merchandise. Having a restaurant a few doors down provided traffic we might not otherwise have caught.

I worried about hearing from Mason and whether or not we were still on for Tuesday.

After closing the shop, I stopped by Publix and picked up food for dinner and the next day. At home, I followed my usual routine, trying to drown out the growing feeling of dread. I ate the chicken lo mein I bought from the deli counter and watched *The Voice* on TV.

My phone finally chirped so I paused the show. Bringing up the screen on my cell phone, I saw a message from Mason. His long text came in all at once, blowing up my phone.

> **MM:** Sorry it's taken me so long to respond. I
> don't often check that email address and as you

know, I don't have it set on my phone. The meeting has gone well, which

MM: will mean a lot of traveling. This CEO has three different locations he wants me to check out once we get started. I still have the last local job to finish up

MM: this week so the new job won't start until next week or the following. Don't worry about anything special to eat. I miss you too. It kills me to be away from

MM: you for so long. I hope you've been a good girl. I'd hate to have to punish you over my knee. Well, no, I wouldn't. I think we need to start with that and

MM: we'll both feel better. I need to be inside you. Be ready for me.

My pussy clinched over his comments about the spanking. I texted back:

Me: I'm already more than ready. What time? Any special instructions?

MM: Be ready, willing, and naked. Let's say one to be on the safe side. That should give us a few hours to ourselves. Again, I'm sorry about Saturday and let me

MM: make it up to you.

Me: You already have. I know I'll feel better when I'm back in your arms and can see your love shining back to me. The spanking too. :*

MM: I'm wiped out from the day and will be going to sleep shortly. See you soon.

Me: Bye Mason.

I hopped up and danced the jig around the living room. *He still loves me!* "Woohoo!" I whooped. Once I expended my excited energy, I collapsed down on the couch and finished the show. Setting off to bed, I checked and noted that everything was in place. Stay, a distant memory.

❀ ❀ ❀ ❀ ❀

Tuesday dragged by painfully. Every minute felt like ten. Samantha stared at me on a few occasions seeming to assess my crazy, frenetic mood. I left Bella just before noon, and waited in my robe for Mason to show. I felt jittery and alive, like I was on a precipice looking down. I craved his reassurance as if it was the very air I needed to breathe.

I heard his footsteps before he arrived at my door and scurried to hold it open for him.

We stared at each other for a moment before we clasped onto one another, our lips connecting in a fiery kiss. He pushed the door shut with his foot and kicked off his shoes while we continued to kiss, not wanting to spend a second disconnected. He walked me backward into the bedroom, until the edge of the mattress hit the back of my knees. I fell and he came down on top of me.

Still lip locked, I pulled on the buttons of his shirt as he tugged my robe out from between us. I needed his skin next to mine and I knew he felt the same way. As I worked on the last button, he unbuckled his belt and pants and kicked them off.

"Lainie, I can't wait."

"Oh god, please don't!"

When he slid inside, I felt vindication and exaltation. He was the man I wanted and I would hold on for as long as I could.

"Oh, baby, you feel so good," he said, pausing mid thrust. The lust and love in his eyes told me everything.

"Mason, don't stop moving, I need you to take me. Please," I gasped in desperation.

He propped himself on his arms and held my legs against his shoulders, bending me over and taking everything I had to give. The deep penetration of his hard cock and passionate stare consumed me.

We writhed together, my hips meeting each incursion with equal zeal.

"This is ... where I'm ... oh baby ... meant to be. I love you ... I love you ... I love you!" he grunted.

"Mason, oh Mason, please!"

"You're getting close ... your tight pussy, oh yes, baby, you can do it, you're clutching my dick. Come for me my love."

I flew to the edge of my release, so full of my love for him. I could no longer hold it back. "Oh, Mason, I ... I."

"Give it to me, baby!"

"I love you ... oh god ... I love you," I screamed as my climax fired and my pussy began to spasm against him.

"Lainie." He lowered down so he could kiss me as my aftershocks continued to fire.

I spread my legs out to the side and wrapped them around his back.

He placed his hands on either side of my head, his elbows into the mattress for leverage. He danced his hips, rubbing his pelvis against my swollen entrance. "You've made me the happiest man on the planet," he whispered. His lips lowered to mine and he kissed me again with slow soft caresses.

"I love you," I said again. "I have since that very first night."

He held his hips still and said, "I've known for a long time, baby, but hearing you saying it, giving that part of you to me—I understand what that means to you—I will never take it for granted."

"I believe you." I stared back into his pale-blue eyes.

"Before I come, I want something from you."

"Anything."

When he rolled off of me I cried out. "I'll be back there very soon," he said, chuckling. "Let's move into the living room."

My robe fell off when I sat up. I grabbed a towel from the bathroom on our way and spread it over the bottom cushion of the couch.

"Over my lap," he said, pointing down. His prominent erection stood at attention and I couldn't help noticing. "I wish I could spank you over my lap with my cock inside but that tight glove will have to wait."

I complied, most of my body across the couch, my hips over his lap.

He rubbed and squeezed my globes. "I think about this ass often. So full and round. I've been fantasizing about make it rosy pink to remind you that you're mine."

I swallowed hard. Stay was brought into our scenario and I didn't want him there. I wanted him as far away as possible.

"I do acknowledge that I was an ass about it, especially leaving so abruptly," he continued.

"Please stop, please stop," I said silently.

"Shall we begin?" he asked.

"Yes."

He spanked my right butt cheek and then asked, "Who does this buttock belong to?"

Heat rushed to my hard nipples and my already throbbing, wet pussy. "You," I grunted.

He hit the other side and his cock twitched against me. "And this warm, round globe."

"You ... only you."

Then he escalated the speed and intensity of the spanking.

I panted heavily, groaning and squirming as my natural juices dripped down onto his legs below.

"So rosy and inviting." He bent over, and to my surprise bit either side of my ass.

"Hey," I giggled, placing my hands over my butt to protect it.

"Stop wiggling all around or I'll come against your stomach." He kissed each globe and said, "Come to me."

Without hesitation I straddled his lap, slowly easing down over his steely erection.

"You make me so hard, love. I only get this hard for you."

Oh how I wished that was true, with every fiber of my being.

Facing each other, he held my head in his hands and kissed me like his life depended on it. When our lips broke apart, he said, "The thought of losing you—"

"You won't, you can't. I'm exactly where I want to be." I rose and fell over his lap, floating in the exquisiteness of our connection. I felt the love he freely expressed, our linked stare, and our bodies colliding together.

He gripped my waist, controlling the pace and angle, circling my hips over him. The friction inside and out caused a light-headed euphoria. I grasped his shoulders, lifting and dropping, as he thrust up to meet me.

"Baby, lean back and play with your tits for me. Pull and tug on your nipples. Oh yes ... so womanly ... so hot. I want to see your face when you come. There you go. Oh, I can feel you getting close. Take me with you, milk me. Oh, Lainie!" His orgasm exploded as I pulsed around his invasion.

I didn't stop moving, I couldn't. I held my breath and rode out the torrent of waves crashing inside my pussy and my heart. I'd never before given of myself so fully to another. Whether ill-conceived or not, I took the risk with Mason. I wanted it to be him and I had come to need his love as the nutrition to sustain me. In that moment, I didn't give a flying fucking shit what anyone else thought.

I collapsed against him, my heart pounding and my breathing erratic. "I love you, Mason. Please take care of my heart."

"No question. I always will. I've never loved like this before Lainie, and I can't let you go."

"Good."

He soothed my back and held me close, as he softened inside me. I didn't want to move off of him, because I knew what it meant. He would have to go soon. I wanted him for a week, all to myself and yet I knew he would be traveling soon and I would have to live on this moment alone.

As if he heard me, he said, "I need to get going soon."

"I don't want you to leave," I said, never before uttering such sentiments to him.

"And I don't want to go, love, but I must."

"I know it's just—" A ripple of guilt overcame my bliss as I struggled to swallow away the lump that had lodged in my throat. I shifted off of his lap and sat next to him on the towel covering the couch. Our joined aroma filled my senses and I no longer wanted to deal with my indiscretion. It really wasn't important anymore? Was it?

"Just what?"

"Oh, never mind," I said, lightly. I lay my head on his shoulder.

He pulled me away from him and asked, "Is this about the other night?"

"Yes, I mean, you have nothing to worry about. I've decided to avoid seeing Stay."

"Why? I thought it wasn't an issue." He shifted to face me.

Heat crawled up my neck to my ears. "I thought that's what you wanted."

"If you need to avoid seeing him, something's happened. What did you do Lainie?" His deep voice of disapproval frightened me.

I started shaking, believing I had screwed up the best thing in my life. Why couldn't I just keep my mouth shut? "Before I explain, please promise me something."

"What?" he said calmly, which scared me even more.

"You'll hear me out."

He breathed out heavily and said, "Lainie, just say it because you are making it worse by making me wait."

"I let him kiss me," I forced out.

"Were you drinking?"

"Yes, but..."

"But what?"

I shook my head. "Nothing. Listen, I'm not interested in Stay and I've made that crystal clear to him."

"And it didn't go further than that?" He touched my thigh and it was as if the light had risen just slightly over the horizon.

"No. I felt horrible afterwards." I rested my hand on top of his.

"Okay, just don't let it happen again."

"I won't," I said, climbing back onto his lap. "I promise you. I love you Mason. I want you in my life and will be grateful for any time we can be together."

"I'm going to be away a lot for the next few weeks. Can I steal you away on Friday around lunchtime?"

"Meet at my place?"

"No, I won't have that much time. We'll meet up at a friend's place."

I paused, not liking that idea at all. "Have you taken other women there?"

"No love, of course not," he said with conviction.

"Yeah, okay. Call or text when you know the time." I threw my arms over his shoulders and said, "Thank you so much for today. I needed to know we're going to be okay."

"We're more than okay love." He glanced at the time on the DVD player. "I have to get going."

"Okay. Let's say goodbye now," I said, hating to watch him dress and walk out my door.

He gave me a passionate kiss goodbye, and I went to the bathroom to shower as he left.

I contemplated going back to Bella but decided against it. Instead, I enjoyed the downtime, catching up on TV and recalling my time with Mason.

My phone chimed while I was in the bathroom getting ready for bed. I brought up the screen.

> **MM:** I was lying in bed and couldn't get you off of my mind. Your tight pussy and huge heart have me completely captivated. Please don't text back. I just wanted to
> **MM:** say again how much I love you and need you in my life. Thank you for today and I can't wait to see you on Friday.

I practically skipped my way into bed. I pulled my journal onto my lap and clicked my pen.

He loves me! He really loves me. I'm going to save

that message forever and ever.

Today was amazing! I loved my time with Mason and he totally forgave me for the kiss with Stay. Now I can put all that awful business behind me.

I can't believe I told Mason I love him, but I don't regret it at all. He treasured it more than I could have hoped. AND he wants to see my again on Friday!

I know he'll be going away for a while and that's always hard to face, but being confident in his love for me will make the waiting far easier. Maybe we will do phone sex again. That wasn't so bad. Not at all.

I should make a point to call Dad and let him know how things are going. I hate to think he's worried for me.

I'm a bit behind at work and need to check the numbers and work on the next ad for publication. Get on it, girl!

Tomorrow should be fun at Red's. It will be nice to see everyone. I haven't talked to Blue in a while so it'll be good to catch up with her. Hopefully Cat is doing better and not having any more crazy ideas. I can't wait to hear from Jacqs. It certainly seemed like she, Bond, and Red would resolve their issues.

Wow, I don't have much to say tonight. It must be because I'm so happy. Just two more days to go before I get to see Mason again! Life is good.

Once under the covers, I fell asleep fantasizing about Mason and our upcoming quickie.

CHAPTER FOURTEEN

You've Got a Friend in Me

by Lyle Lovett & Randy Newman

On Wednesday evening, I closed up Bella Boutique after another great day at work. My good mood seemed to translate into abundant sales. Sam said, on three separate occasions, that I must have gotten laid because of my huge grin. *Oh that and so much more,* I thought but kept it to myself.

At Red's for our weekly gathering, all the regulars were there with the exception of Doug aka Dawg who recently had been travelling a lot between South Florida and Canada.

Jacqs pulled me outside to sit on the couch glider before I had the chance to greet everyone.

"You look happy," I said, sitting down and stretching out my legs. "I have to assume everything worked out."

"Red has been amazing as always and Bond understands my insecurities. Thank you for being so nice to Bond. I think you surprised him. He told me about the woman and what kind of friendship they have. I can't say all of my jealousy has evaporated, but it doesn't hurt nearly as much."

"I'm very happy to hear it," I said, patting her knee.

"And you? Where do things stand with Mason and Stay?"

I crossed my legs and said, "Mason and I are better

than ever. I'm so happy. I think Sam had a hard time dealing with me today at the shop."

"And Stay?"

"We haven't spoken since Saturday night, but I can promise you, I'm not a bit conflicted anymore." And I wasn't.

"I'm happy to hear that because I want both of you at the dinner party on Saturday."

"It might be a bit awkward, but that's fine with me." I thought it would be good to get past that hurdle since we couldn't avoid seeing each other forever.

"Oh good! I'm so glad you feel that way. I spoke to Stay and he said he was staying away today because he didn't want to make you uncomfortable."

"No need at this point. I'm so in love, Jacqs, I think I might burst at the seams."

"If you're happy, I'm happy for you."

"Thanks, girl. That means a lot to me."

The French doors opened to our right and Blue approached us.

She said, "You can't hog Lainie all night. I haven't seen her in a while."

"Take my spot and I'll go check on the others."

"Thanks," Blue said, sitting down next to me.

Judy, Blue's real name, had been in the group much longer than I, and even dated Red briefly years ago. She had the hardest time coming to terms with Jacqs having a relationship with both Red and Bond, more because of Bond than Red. Sweet Judy Blue Eyes had been dubbed Blue by Bond. She had the brightest and lightest blue eyes I had ever seen until I met Mason. She had large eyes, full lips, and a body to envy. Petite like Jacqs, but a few inches taller, her large breasts gave her a much more voluptuous appearance.

"How've you been?" I asked. I knew she struggled in relationship and valuing herself for more than her sexy looks.

"Mostly the same," she said, brushing her auburn bangs out of her eyes. "I'm still waiting tables, but I've started bartending too, which is going well."

"Are you still writing?"

"Yeah, when I can find the time but I don't know if I'll ever do anything with it. It's a fun hobby and takes me out of my crazy mind for a bit."

"I'm still open to reading as I know Jacqs is too when you're ready," I said, noting that Kevin and Catherine had strolled outside.

"I might not ever get there," she said, adjusting her bra and the straps of her tank top. "Will you be here for the dinner on Saturday night? It's a dinner party. Do we need to dress up for it?"

"Yeah, I'll be here. I imagine the dress is casual."

She glanced over at Kev and Cat and then quietly said, "I heard things are precarious between you and Stay. I didn't know you liked him."

"Who said that?"

"Bond mentioned it. Was it supposed to be a secret? I asked why Stay wasn't here tonight."

"No, I guess not."

"Are you into him? I mean, he and I are just friends but..."

"But?"

"Nothing. All's good."

The conversation made me a bit uncomfortable. I should be used to no secrets in this group, and Blue's possible interest in Stay shouldn't have bothered me. "I'm going to grab a drink. Do you want anything?"

"I'm good."

"Hey you guys," I said as I approached Kev and Cat.

"I was hoping you were going to make it," Cat said, holding her arms out for a hug.

Hugging back, I whispered, "Is everything okay?"

Kev walked over to the glider couch and sat next to Blue.

"Yeah, I'm hanging in there. Still haven't let go of my place."

"But you're behaving, right?" I asked, leading her back into the house.

"Well there's this new girl at the coffee shop we go to a lot..."

"Don't do anything stupid, okay?"

"You know me, all talk and no action."

I stared with clear skepticism. "Let's keep it that way." My hypocritical stance on her potential behavior had more to do with the incredible love Kev held for her and less about the morality of it. I also knew it was her way of keeping distance between her and Kev. Knowing Kevin, bringing a woman home to share would be most welcomed.

I really enjoyed my time at Red's. Although it had taken me a while to forge connections with each person in the group, I had come to love each and every one of them. They had taught me a lot about love and friendship. Although I didn't share my most personal life with all of them, I knew in a pinch, I could rely on any of them in a crisis.

We played pool, laughed a lot, shared stories and affection. It was a joy to see Jacqs so happy and in love. Of all of my friends, she was the one who taught me the most. I envied her ability to grow and change through her experiences.

She walked me out at the end of the night. "Blue and I were talking about going to Delray Affair art and music festival on Sunday. I was thinking we could go in place of our brunch. What do you think?"

"That sounds like fun," I said, excited to see the artwork and hear the music.

"We can firm up plans on Saturday."

"Great. Hey, are we supposed to dress up for the dinner party?"

"Not at all."

"I love you, girl," I said, hugging her goodbye.

"You too. Talk soon."

CHAPTER FIFTEEN

Un-thinkable (I'm Ready)

by Alicia Keys

Thursday breezed by in normal fashion and on Friday morning I chose a sexy slip with garters that I wore under a mid-thigh, spring dress that synched at the waist, my brown high heels completed the look. Mason had texted the time and address where we were to meet, which was only a few minutes away from Bella Boutique.

Sam eyed me when she arrived at work just before I had to leave.

"Sexy dress, Lane," she said. "Hot date, huh?"

"Something like that," I said, rehanging a dress a customer had tried on. "I shouldn't be gone long."

"I understand," she said, her tone indicating she understood more than I would have liked.

To deflect her curiosity, I asked, "Are you seeing anyone these days?"

"Between working here, Sarah, and the online class I'm taking, there isn't time. Plus, I tend to pick the wrong guys, or truthfully, let them pick me. I think taking a break from dating and working on myself is good for me and my daughter." She stepped closer and said, "I'm sorry things didn't work out for you with Stayman. He's a really good guy."

"Yeah, he is," I said, straightening the objects on the counter. "You should consider someone like him when you're ready to date again."

"Guys like him don't really notice me."

Her assertion shocked me. "Don't be ridiculous Sam, every man from here to Mars notices you."

"That's not how I see it, but thanks for the compliment."

After checking the time on my cell phone, I said, "Listen, I need to take off. Call me if you need me."

"Don't forget the condoms," she said as I passed by.

I shot her a look and headed out back.

As instructed, I parked in a guest spot and made my way to apartment 305. I knocked tentatively on the door and Mason quickly pulled me inside, wrapping me up in his arms before I could catch my breath.

"I have to be back for a meeting soon, love," he said, rubbing his hard cock against me.

"Slow down for a second," I said, pushing away from his chest and scanning the small space, which held little furniture. His jacket lay over the kitchen table.

"I'm sorry. I just got so excited waiting for you to show up. Let me see what you have on." He whistled as he circled around me. "Just for me?"

"Especially for you. Now kiss me like you mean it."

"Oh, baby, I always mean it," he said, stepping toward me and lifting me onto the yellow laminate countertop. "Just as I thought."

"Oh?"

"Perfect height," he purred against my mouth. Then his kiss overtook me, hot and insistent. He slid the skirt of my dress over my thighs and groaned, feeling the garters underneath. "Do you have panties on?"

"No Mason. I thought they would just get in the way," I said coyly.

"You make my cock so hard it hurts."

I reached down and caressed his erection through his slacks. "Kiss me again," I said, my arousal sparking.

"Let me remove my pants. Walking into the meeting with your juices all over me might not go over well."

"They might give you a high five or think you're a sloppy eater."

He chuckled as he kicked off his shoes and unzipped his pants. "What's gotten into you?"

"You, definitely you, but not often enough."

"Let's remedy that."

"Should I take my dress off?"

"Leave it on but lift the bottom so I can see your incredible legs. Oh, yeah, you look so damn sexy that way. Spread your thighs and scoot to the edge for me." He jutted straight out, but didn't penetrate me right away. As he ravened my lips with his, he circled around my labia and clit, making sure I was ready."

And I was.

Hands on my ass, he pulled me forward and impaled my pussy tightly against him. "Right here," he said, "this is where I need to be."

"Won't get any ... ahhh ... arguments from me. So good, Mason. Fill me."

Stroking slowly, he said, "You need to come for me first. I'm in a hurry but not in that big of a rush. I have to feel you clamp down on me, baby. It's what I live for."

I placed my arms behind me with my wrists turned out and pushed my pelvis into his.

His hands threaded under the back garter straps and squeezed my ass in his palms. "Lainie, honey, breathe for me."

I laughed. "I can't ... help it. It feels so ... so fucking good."

"I'm getting closer," he said, increasing the pace. His light-blue eyes held me imprisoned in his love and devotion, his eye contact absolute.

Each stroke of his cock roused my sensitive G-spot and rubbed all the right places. I lived and died in his orbit, but this time it felt different. I had given him my heart and it left me feeling powerful.

The building eruption hovered close, my nipples straining against my bra, the friction tremendous.

"There you go ... so close. Your pussy opens just before you're... Come for me. Take me with you!"

Making sure to take deep breaths, I grunted out my orgasm, still grinding my hips onto his cock.

As my contractions slowed, he held me tightly against him, filling me with his come. "Oh yes, my sexy love."

"Yesss," I said, feeling the heat of his release. "Don't forget me while you're gone."

"Not a chance. Never. Let me grab you a towel."

I watched him stalk away, naked from the waist down. *That sexy man's heart belongs to me,* I thought.

We quickly cleaned up and fixed our clothing. I straightened his tie for him and smoothed down his hair. "No worse for the wear," I said.

"But you, love, look absolutely radiant."

"Thank you," I said, blushing over his remark.

"If we can manage it, I'd like to see you before I fly out on Sunday."

"Oh really," I said, jumping toward him and hugging him tight.

"Yes, really. I'm going to miss you as much, if not more, than you'll miss me. We'll talk a lot while I'm gone. You can text or call me anytime. If I'm free to take the call, I will."

"Excellent."

"I hate to make love and run, but I do need to go."

"Of course, I understand. Let me know when you know what time on Sunday. We've never had this much time together and I truly appreciate the effort. Even if it's a quickie."

"Kiss me, and then out with you. You go first and I'll lock up."

We shared a short passionate kiss and then I left the apartment and headed to the boutique.

As soon as I parked in the back of the shop, I noticed something attached to the door. I found an envelope with my name on it and yanked it off. After running my finger along the flap, I pulled out a card. The front simply said, "Thought I'd send a recent photo of myself." When I opened it, I laughed so hard, I stumbled on my heels. Inside was a very scenic picture with a horse's ass taking up most of the space on the right. Next to it read, "Sorry." The left side was filled with handwriting I didn't recognize.

Dear OCDC,

I missed seeing your beautiful face on Wednesday. I know my behavior has been appalling. My only defense is how I feel when we're spending time together. Regardless, I've been a horse's ass and should have respected your boundaries.

Jacqs tells me things with Mason are going well. I promise to stand down if you promise we can still remain friends. I might flirt here or there, but I promise to be the pillar of respect.

Our peeps are having a dinner party and I want you to come and feel comfortable there.

*Let me be the friend I should have been before.
I'm good at it and you'll see if you give me the chance
to redeem myself.*

*See you at dinner? If you want to talk, you have
my number.*

*Begging at your feet and NOT looking up your
dress,*
Stayman

It was hard not to forgive the boy when he was being
so utterly adorable. Everything in my life was lining up
well for me. Mason and I were in the best place in our
relationship and Stay and I would be the friends we were
meant to be. What could be better?

Samantha and I shared lunch and thankfully she didn't
grill me about my whereabouts and I didn't tell her about
the card. The day sailed by as I floated high on a cloud of
love. Mason even texted me to say he misses me already
and can't wait until Sunday. Life was more than good, it
was great!

I closed up for the night since Samantha would be
opening in the morning. I tried to reach my father and then
remembered he went out of town for a wedding my mother
dragged him along to. I didn't bother leaving a message.

Back at my condo, it no longer felt like a lonely place.
I could envisage Mason in every space in the apartment.
In the kitchen leaning against the island as I fixed us a
plate of food, snuggling on the couch or making love
there, our games in the second bedroom and most
definitely sex in my bed.

The bliss I felt stayed with me through the night. I
didn't feel like smoking my nightly cigarette so I climbed
into bed to write my thoughts down.

Jacqs has wanted to have a dinner party for a while now. She and Red planned the menu and will be cooking for us. Jacqs and Red have cooking in common and I wonder who cooks the most at their house. I would guess Jacqs. Definitely not Bond. I think she missed her calling as a chef instead of an executive assistant. I wonder if Bond will be helping or if he'll be at work.

I'm no longer worried about seeing Stay and am kind of looking forward to it too. He seems to have gotten the message and I do like him. He's a great guy, just not the one for me.

I'm super excited about the art and music festival in Delray. Jacqs and I have gone before. The huge event offers people watching in every direction. I can't wait. Maybe I'll find a new fruit bowl for the counter. I hate that my current one has a chip on the rim. I'll probably check out the music more than anything. I'm happy Blue is coming too. That will give me more freedom to wander.

On top of that, I get to see Mason one more time on Sunday before he leaves town. I definitely need to drive myself to the Delray Affair so I can leave when I need to.

He loves me. I wasn't as sure as I am now. I think Stay turned out to be good for us. It clarified things for Mason and me. Here I have been busy telling Cat to let Kev's love in and yet I wasn't really letting all of Mason's love in. I was scared it wasn't real that I was a passing fancy and he would quickly move on.

I'm walking on a cloud of hope and love. It still amazes me that he finds me so attractive and sexy. He is by far the best looking man I have ever seen. His body is hard and fit where my body is soft and fuller in places more than I would like. I hate my ass and yet he loves it. Who am I to argue? He loves my stomach too which means he must love me because he is completely blind.

I might not get to have him all the time, but I know his heart belongs to me. And for now, that's enough.

Settling under the covers, I found myself genuinely looking forward to the dinner party and seeing Stayman again.

CHAPTER SIXTEEN

Starry Eyed

by Ellie Goulding

S aturday morning at home, I worked on a new ad and did some research on a new sign for the front of the shop. I reconciled the debits and credits for most of April and even took a nap, which was a rare event for me.

I threw on my most comfortable jeans and T-shirt for Jacqs's and Red's dinner party. Standing by the front door, I chose a pair of black flip-flops and on the way out, I grabbed my purse and the wine I left on the entrance table.

As soon as I opened the door to Red's house, the aroma of the upcoming dinner wooed me to the kitchen.

"Oh, what smells so good?" I said, taking in Red's and Jacqs's attire. They wore matching aprons and I almost cracked up laughing but held it back. Stay didn't make it easy, raising his eyebrow as if he knew exactly what I thought about it.

"It's a surprise," Jacqs said, hugging me with her hands out to the side.

"The rest of the gang is out back," Red said, taking the wine from my hand. "I can open this or you can help yourself to something in the fridge."

"Thanks."

Stay walked to the refrigerator and said, "What will

it be?"

"Hard lemonade or cider." I crossed my arms and rested back against the counter.

Stay dressed in his usual relaxed blue jeans and plaid shirt with the sleeves rolled to his upper forearms.

I could feel him watching me watch him. "Thanks," I said when he handed me the bottle of cider.

"Can I steal you for a minute?" he asked.

I glanced at Jacqs who waved me off with her head, her hands busy mixing a dressing for the salad.

"Okay." I let him lead me to the front sitting room.

Red's decor reminded me of an upscale bed and breakfast. He must have used an interior designer because everything coordinated together. The loveseat we sat on matched the area rug below our feet.

"How are you?" Stay asked. He seemed relaxed and at ease, the way I'd always known him to be until recently.

"I'm good ... really good. Thanks for the card. You made me laugh so hard, I nearly fell off my feet."

"I'm happy to be of service."

"It's good to see you," I said before I thought better of it.

"You too. I've missed you." He stretched his arm along the back of couch, behind me.

"Um, thanks."

"Don't get weird on my OC. I get it. We're just friends. I'm a reformed alcoholic and now a reformed 'Lainieaholic'." Then he flashed me his dangerous, crooked smile and chuckled. "We good?" He scooted forward to stand and laid his hand on my thigh.

An electric current pulsed through me, taking me completely by surprise. My body felt aroused, and singed.

"You did that on purpose." I shifted away from his touch.

He frowned and said, "I didn't intend for that to

happen. It's never happened before."

"Did you feel it too?" I asked, believing that he spoke the truth.

"I'm still feeling it."

"Maybe we should refrain from touching each other."

"Yeah," he said, but he seemed shaken.

"I'm going to go say hi to everyone," I said, standing.

"I'll see you outside in a minute." He seemed to be mulling over something.

Stay, don't make too much of it, I thought.

I stopped in the bathroom along the way and when I sat down to pee, I found my pussy wet. I had to wipe a few times to dry the moisture that had settled there. It didn't worry me at all. My body might still respond to him but my heart definitely resided elsewhere.

Outside I ran into Cat and Blue. "Hey girls," I said. "How's it going?"

"I'm happy to have the night off," Blue said.

"I bet," I said, raising my chin and letting the warm wind hit my face.

Cat had the good sense not to hug me in front of Blue and said, "Anything new at the shop I should come by and check out?"

"Sam talked me into getting some matching bra sets. They should be in mid-week."

"Oh great! It's really getting warm out, isn't it? I'm kind of glad I'll be working in the AC for the rest of the weekend."

"Yeah. It could be really hot tomorrow at the fair," Blue said. She stepped over to the pool and dipped her toe in.

"I'll have to remember to bring along a hat to the fair," I said. "I'm going to go back in and see if Jacqs needs any help."

I saw Sam on the couch with Stay when I made my

way back inside. They seemed deep in conversation.

Once we all sat down to dinner, Stay sat in the seat farthest from me and barely made eye contact the entire night.

The dinner was ridiculously yummy and I'm sure I gained a few extra pounds from all the delicious food. They started with lobster bisque, which they made from scratch. It was so creamy and delicious, I could have licked the bowl. Then they served a small Caesar salad with fresh parmesan shavings, followed by lemon-garlic shrimp and grits with a pinch of red pepper for heat. Already full, Jacqs insisted I try her freshly baked strawberry tart. Who was I to deny her?

"Someone needs to roll me out to my car. That is if I still fit in it," I said.

Everyone laughed, although Stay seemed subdued.

"I know what you mean," Bond said, rubbing his stomach.

Like that man spent a day in his life being fat. I shook my head. I gathered the plates around me and carried them into the kitchen. Once I rinsed a plate from the stack, I handed it over to Jacqs.

"Did you do something to Stay? He's been quiet all night," she said, loading another plate into the dishwasher.

I looked over my shoulder and saw we were alone in the kitchen. "I thought we were fine but then he touched my leg and..."

"And?" she said, taking a bowl out of my hands.

"Well ... I think we both felt it more than we wanted to."

"But you seem fine."

"He's probably reading more into it. Did you know he is a Buddhist and meditates?"

"Yes, of course. I'll be sure to check in on him later. Hand me those glasses please," she said as she pulled out the top rack of the dishwasher. "About tomorrow, why don't we meet here and drive to Delray Beach together. You'll get a chance to ride in my new VW Tiguan."

"I thought you were getting another Beetle," I said, passing over the glasses.

"Red wanted me to get something a bit larger. It's like a mini SUV and drives like a dream."

"And color?" I said, using a towel to dry the items in the dish drain.

"They didn't have it in the pale-green so I went with wild-cherry. So about tomorrow?"

"I need to drive myself. I have plans later and I'm not sure at what time."

"Mason?" she asked, just as Kev and Stay walked through the swinging door to the kitchen.

I don't know why but I felt bad for Stay. It's not like I wanted to rub it in his face.

"Is there anything I can do?" Stay asked.

"Are they still working on the dessert?" Jacqs said.

"Yeah and talking mostly. Did you know Cat is considering giving up her place, but is dragging her feet?" Stay asked.

"I'm standing right here," Kev said.

"Yes, I can see that," Stay continued. "If I've learned anything recently, it's that you can't make someone be ready for something they're not. Just give her some time." He patted Kevin on the back.

"That's easy for you to say, brother. You have the patience of a saint."

"That's not true," Stay said, glancing in my direction.

"It really isn't," I concurred.

Both Kev and Stay stared at me.

"I'll just shut up," I said, going back to drying the

197

spatula in my hand.

"Let's go outside," Kev said to Stay as he threw his arm over his shoulder.

As soon as they traveled out the French doors, Jacqs said, "What the fuck?"

"I know. Please do talk to him if you get a chance."

"I will."

Overall the dinner was really great. I enjoyed seeing everyone and watching Red and Jacqs host and serve together. I vowed not to eat for three days after the meal. Still full by the time I crashed, it took me awhile to get comfortable. I figured the sooner I entered dreamland, the quicker I would be in Mason's arms again. Tomorrow would be another excellent day. Art and music, and then more love. I couldn't wait!

CHAPTER SEVENTEEN

My Blood

by Ellie Goulding

Jacqs, Blue, and I met in front of the main stage at eleven o'clock in the morning. The crowded streets belied the heat of the day. I had put my hair up in a ponytail and pulled it through the opening in the back of my House of Blues baseball cap. We all wore shorts and tank tops.

"Where do you want to start?" Jacqs asked.

"Why don't we start on this street and work our way over to Atlantic Boulevard?" I pointed behind Blue and said, "There's the information booth. Why don't we get a map? I'd also like to know when the different bands are playing."

"Okay," Blue said.

We each took a brochure and then strolled down the road filled with white, pop-up tents. The streets in downtown Delray had been closed off for pedestrian traffic only.

"I'd like to catch Daniel Wesley. He's playing at one o'clock at the Third Avenue beer tent."

"Sounds good," Jacqs said.

The three of us milled around, checking out all kinds of art from folk to fine. I perused the clothing tents but the prices were too steep for resale.

Jacqs and I shared a fresh fruit cup and paid way too

much for bottled water. By the time one o'clock rolled around, we were far from the concert tent.

"Why don't you guys keep going, and I'll text you after the show so we can hook back up."

"That works for me," Blue said, fanning herself with the brochure. "It's too hot for me to stay in one place."

"That's fine. See you soon," Jacqs said.

I waved and took off, heading toward Third Avenue.

By the time I arrived, the music had already started. Daniel Wesley sang out *Layde Maybe* while the crowd moved to the beat. I found a spot off to the side. I couldn't help but recall the concert experience Stay and I had shared. If we could ever find a place of normality between us, I would definitely love to go to a show with him again. Stay belted out the lyrics like everyone else in the crowd that night and really seemed to enjoy himself.

So Fine started up and I swayed to the beat, watching all the people who had showed up for the music.

Out of the corner of my eye I caught the sight of a recognizable walk. How did Jacqs put it? *Feline, but masculine.* My heart pounded uncomfortably in my chest—fast but shallow—I could feel it pulsing in my throat.

From the back, he looked strikingly similar to Mason. He held the hand of a petite woman, and two young children ran ahead of them. I'd never seen him in shorts or a T-shirt so I couldn't be sure it was him.

Barely able to breathe, I followed behind them. They entered a booth that contained stoneware. The woman held up a square plate with a coyote and trees painted on it. She appeared to be around Mason's age and was equally stunning with olive skin and dark hair. She said, "What do you think?"

I could tell by her expression that she was kidding.

They both laughed and then he reached out for her hand again, hugging her to his side.

And then he spoke, and I died, "Hey, Mason, wait up for us. You too, Valerie."

"Sorry," the children chimed, one taking Mason's hand and the other taking Victoria's.

I couldn't breathe—tears flowed freely—but I couldn't stop following them.

"Let's get out of the sun for a few minutes," Mason said, leading them to a grassy area under a tree.

I stepped out of sight, but could still see the scene playing out before me.

They all sat on the grass, the kids each placed a blade between their thumbs to try to make a whistle. Victoria leaned back into Mason as he circled his arm around her. She tilted her head toward him and they laughed. He kissed the side of her face and the top of her head as he had done to me on many occasions.

I jerked my cell phone out of my pocket and typed a text.

Me: DON'T COME!

I was so close to the edge of a massive breakdown that I shook uncontrollably. Even so, I wouldn't leave the spot until I watched him read my text.

His phone must have rung because he shifted to get it out of his pocket. He swiped the screen with his thumb and pressed in his code. The look on his face didn't help me feel the slightest better—his mouth open, the color rapidly draining from his face.

I angled my head so the brim of my hat hid my forehead, and fanned myself with the map to further obscure my cheeks.

He stood up abruptly, his mood completely altered. Scanning the area, he must have suspected I saw him, but then his shoulders relaxed just slightly. I could tell he had changed his mind.

"Is everything okay?" I imagined Victoria said when she touched his shoulder.

He nodded as they headed back toward me.

I dipped behind a tree before they reached me.

"It's too hot to stay," he said, leading his family away—his happy, beautiful family. His gorgeous, skinny wife, and adorable kids—leaving me with his lies and devastation.

"Oh god," I gasped out, grabbing my stomach and throwing up in the bushes. I couldn't call my father. If he'd been in town, I'd have asked him to come get me. I didn't want to lay this on Blue or Jacqs either.

I texted Jacqs.

> **Me:** The heat's getting to me. I'm going to take off. Bye to Blue. Love you, girl.
> **Jacqueline:** Okay. We will probably only make it another hour. There is a particular artist Blue is hoping to see. Love you too, girl.

Nausea sloshed in my gut. The only thing that propelled me from the spot I occupied was my utter disdain of crying in front of people. I ran down the street and continued until I reached the edge of the ocean. I found a spot void of people to the south behind a grouping of sea grass and crumbled down on the sand. Falling to the side, I cried like I never had before. I sobbed and wept for the love I thought I had, for who I thought Mason was, and who I'd become with him. If anyone could hear me, they'd most surely called the police because I wailed like a dying animal.

It probably would have continued on for days but between the heat and tidal wave of tears, I could hardly breathe my throat was so dry.

I wanted to die. Such acute, abject pain should automatically trigger self-implosion. Everyone would say, "That person there"—pointing to the pile of dust—"expired of a broken heart. It was ripped from her chest and pounced on."

Maybe if I lie here long enough lightning will be kind enough to strike me on the spot. Or the ocean. I could walk straight in and let the waves carry me away.

I've always been a coward for pain, which is why suicide wasn't really an option. That same fear was why I held people at such a distance before letting them in. Only I didn't do that with Mason and see what that got me. I'd never felt so stupid in my entire life. I could hear my mother's sharp voice saying, "For a smart girl, you really do dumb things." Thanks Mom.

I could have destroyed that family, those cute kids and his adoring wife, all because I believed his stupid fucking lies. Seeing his skinny, gorgeous wife made me think it was all some sadistic, cruel joke. *Why would he want someone like me? Find me sexy? Bull-fucking-shit!*

My phone chirped as I was trying to stand up and get my bearings. I saw that I had messages from two people.

> **Mason:** I hope everything is okay. Your message has me scared and confused. Please call me anytime between now and when my flight takes off. If I haven't heard from
> **Mason:** you, I'm going to drop by and check on you. Baby, I love you. Please call me.

Stayman: I'm sorry to intrude. I know you have plans with the girls but something keeps tugging at me to check in with you. I hope everything is okay. Call me either
Stayman: way when you get the chance.

Is he a witch or something? How could he possibly know?

Me: Your voodoo detection system is on target. I'm nowhere near fine and I'm certain that fine and I will never live on the same street again. How did you know?
Stayman: I don't know. Are you still at the fair?
Me: Yes and no. I'm on the beach nearby.

As if the universe was playing a cruel joke, the name of the event just hit me. *How apropos.*

Stayman: I'll come get you.
Me: My car is in paid parking. I can't just leave it there.
Stayman: We'll come back and get it later.
Me: I don't know.
Stayman: I do.
Me: That's just because you're a glutton for punishment. I think I'll just find some shade and sit until I stop shaking. Thank you though.
Stayman: I'm already on my way.
Me: You're so fucking stubborn and don't text and drive!

The phone rang in my hand, and I saw MM show up. I

hit ignore.

> **Stayman:** I have hands free. What street is still
> open up there?
> **Me:** Let's meet at 50 Ocean. I could use the walk
> and I'll get water at the bar.
> **Stayman:** Fifteen minutes.
> **Me:** Okay.

I guess the ocean will have to wait.

My phone rang again and I hit ignore. I had nothing to say. What could I say? I don't think words would suffice for how I felt. I wanted to punch and kick him like a punching bag, not stopping until I was too tired to stand.

In my current state, disheveled and sandy, I hoped 50 Ocean would let me in.

CHAPTER EIGHTEEN

Find a Way

by SafetySuit

The full bar at 50 Ocean shouldn't have surprised me. It was hotter than hell outside. I squeezed between two patrons and asked for a glass of water, placing a dollar on the bar. I drank the whole glass so fast it gave me brain freeze. The guy to my right got up and I took his stool. "Tequila with orange juice and cranberry, double the tequila," I said to a passing bartender.

"Gotcha," he said.

The guy beside me said, "Your phone is going off." I knew Mason's ring so I didn't bother to answer it. I thanked the bartender when he delivered my drink and refilled my water glass. To the guy next to me, I said, "Salute." Still so thirsty, I downed the entire cocktail.

"You okay?" Mr. Nosey Barfly asked. "You have sand on your cheek, and your hat is crooked."

"Will you save my seat and order me another drink while I go use the restroom?" I asked, deciding that if he was so inclined to be in my life he could help me out.

"Sure. Don't forget to take your phone with you," he said, holding it out to me.

I huffed and took it from him. Once Stay got to the restaurant, I could mute the damn thing. In the bathroom, I realized Barfly was being kind. I didn't look like myself at all and just seeing my reflection caused the tears to fall again. Sand covered my right cheek and tuffs of my hair hung out from around my baseball cap, which sat angled like a rapper would wear it. My eyes were red and puffy like I was ill or had some kind of disease.

I took off the hat and threw it in the trash, never wanting to be reminded of the day my life ended. I tried to smooth my hair as best as I could and retied it. Then I took a paper towel and brushed it against my cheek. Some of the sand fell into the sink but about half didn't. I tried to pick it off but I gave up. I used the toilet and then went back to the bar.

Another drink awaited me, and so did Stay. He wore a nice dress shirt and slacks.

"Stayman, Barfly. Barfly, Stayman."

"We've met. Can we go?" Stay pleaded with his eyes.

"Let me drink this first."

"He says you already threw back one like a shot."

I gave Barfly a dirty look and said, "He would be correct and I plan to do the same with this one."

Stay took my arm and pulled me toward him "Come on, Lainie, let's go. I think what you need is some food and some rest."

"When I'm asking you what you think, I'll let you know," I said, sitting down. "Don't look at me like that. Fuck, either of you."

"Is she your girlfriend?" Barfly asked.

Stay shook his head no.

Then I heard Barfly whisper, "Does she have a drinking problem?"

He shook his head again.

I took one long swallow of the cocktail and said, "Let's get the fuck out of here. Bye, Barfly."

We walked out and around the side of the restaurant to his car.

"You brought the Corvette?"

"I have ... had a date."

"You have a date? I thought you said you had a loyalty problem."

"I'm trying to get passed it. Want to tell me what happened?"

"Hasn't your voodoo, tantric powers clued you in?"

"I could take a guess given the state you're in, but I'd rather you tell me."

"I don't think I can. I—" My phone interrupted me. "I'm turning the sound off," I said and I did. "You have a date. I knew I should've finished that drink. Just drop me off at my—no, not my place..." I wondered if Jacqs still had her hidden key to the side of the front door of her apartment.

"I'm taking you to my place, Lainie."

"That's ridiculous, you have a date!"

"I cancelled it."

"Oh, Stay, you didn't. Call her back and apologize. Just explain ... explain that you had to rescue a friend and you have and now you're free."

"It's done, Lainie."

I turned in my seat, away from him, and started weeping again. Over my shoulder, he handed me a handkerchief. "Thank you," I said.

Although he had seen me cry before, he hadn't heard the pitiful sounds coming out of me. The torrent of emotion swept through me over and over like a never-ending tornado that lashed at my soul, ripping everything to shreds. I would never be a whole person again, never trust myself in any situation. Mason's deception wiped away any respect I held for myself.

Stay rubbed my back and his touch caused me to cry even harder. "It's going to be okay, Lane."

"It's never going to be okay again," I cried. "Not ever," I hiccupped. "I'm sorry about ... about being ... a bitch earlier. And your date..." Another wave of despair overtook me and I couldn't talk through the tears.

"We're almost there."

"Okay," I said in a shuddered breath. I felt cold down to my core, even with the sweltering heat outside. It pervaded my heart and soul. I gazed out the window seeing nothing.

My phone vibrated and I began to toss it out the window. Stay caught my hand as I drew back to throw it.

"Turn it off if you need to," he said as he made a right onto the road to his place. He parked, and came around to my side, lifting me out of the car.

"His wife is really skinny," I said, feeling like only half of me existed inside. The other part had left or gone into hiding.

"They were at the fair?"

"Yeah, with the kids."

"Did he see you?"

"No," I said. I started shaking again. "I feel cold."

"Let's get you inside."

I didn't start walking right away. "I'm so sorry, Stay. You were right about everything. Except about me. I'm not good enough for you or anyone. Please promise me you will call your date back."

Then he hugged me, and the anguish continued to rake at the fabric of my soul. He turned me toward the entrance, his arm holding me tightly against him.

"I'm so sorry," I cried again.

"Shh," he said. "You have no reason to apologize to me."

We rode the elevator to his floor, and once inside his apartment I started sliding down the wall by the door. Rusty greeted me, rubbing along my legs.

Stay kicked off his shoes and said, "No, Lainie. Come with me." He removed my sneakers and led me to his bedroom, the cat following behind. "Lay down. I'm going to get you some water."

I did as he told me to, and said, "I don't suppose you have any alcohol or other drugs in your place."

"You would be correct. I'll be right back," he said, placing a blanket over me. He returned quickly, setting the glass of water down on the end table. He climbed into bed and spooned me. Rusty tried to get between us, but Stay shooed him away. "Do you want to tell me what happened? Do Jacqs and Blue know?"

I shook my head and turned in his arms to face him. "I didn't tell them."

"Why?" he said, looping his arm around my waist.

"I don't know. Maybe because Blue was there, and I didn't want to ruin their day. If it had just been Jacqs and me, I might have. I would have called my dad, but he's out of town."

"If I hadn't texted?"

I felt Rusty snuggle against my back and didn't mind. "I had planned to find some shade and wait until I felt like I could drive. I didn't want to be home, and I wasn't sure where I would end up. Maybe I would have asked Jacqs if I could stay at her apartment. I can't believe you blew off your date."

"I had this recurring, crushing ache in my chest, and your name came to me along with the pain each time." His face winced as he recalled it.

"Did you ever consider it was a message to stay away from me, not rescue me?"

"I hadn't considered that. Huh, should I drive you back?" he asked, pretending to get up.

"Don't make me laugh, it hurts too much.

"I actually get that."

"You do?"

Rusty jumped in between us and I scratched behind his ears. He purred like a locomotive.

"Don't encourage him," Stay said but he petted him as well. "Yeah, Karen was unfaithful to me twice. The pain? There's really nothing like it. It's almost like possession, it takes over your whole body. I broke it off after the second time."

"And you were still my friend when you knew I was having an affair." I rocked my head back and forth.

"I don't judge, Lane. We all have our lessons to learn and I'm no expert at life."

I kept shaking my head. "Maybe Cat's right and a person can be too nice."

"Trust me, I'm not nice."

I stared at him, picking up his meaning. "Are you hard?"

"Rock-hard."

I sat up in the bed. "I'm flattered. I mean ... I think I am, but more amazed than anything. How could you possibly get hard with me in such a mess? That is ... I don't know what ... crazy."

He grabbed my hand and said, "I can show you."

"That's definitely not necessary."

He let go of my hand.

"Why are you unwilling to see that I'm a horrible choice for you? I'm not sure I'll ever trust myself, or anyone, again. I thought he loved me, really loved me. Since he met you, he's made all kinds of time for me and we were closer than ever."

He wiped the tears that began to spill again. "I'm sure he loves you, Lainie. How could he not? Some men will never be satisfied with one woman. Did he ever say he would leave his wife?"

I laid my head on his outstretched arm. "No, never. But he said their relationship was extremely strained and they were working on finding friendship to raise their kids together under the same roof. Jacqs tried to warn me that if he's lying to his family, he's probably lying to me too, but I wouldn't hear it."

"Love makes us blind sometimes. Let me make you feel better, Lainie." He started massaging my neck.

"I can't. I mean I could, but it wouldn't be fair. I'd be using you."

"What if I say I want you to?" he said, touching my cheek.

"I'd say you're being stupid, and I don't want to hurt you." I lifted my head to better see his eyes. "I have no idea how long it will take me to get over this or if I ever will."

"Then just let me be here for you. That's enough."

I stared at him in disbelief. "You are way too good for me. Way too nice. I don't deserve it." I rested my head on his arm again and closed my eyes.

"You deserve it and much more. Have you talked to Mason at all?"

Just hearing his name was like a knife twisting in my gut. "He was supposed to come by tonight before his flight. I texted him, 'Don't come' in capital letters, and with an exclamation point."

"Would you like me to send him a message for you? Or check what he said back?" He pulled out my hair tie and fanned out my light-brown hair above my head.

"No. Words? What the fuck are words? He'll tell me that when they're out they always pretend to like each other for the benefit of the kids. He'll say what I saw was acting."

"Could it have been?"

"Absolutely fucking not. They were laughing and touching each other even when the kids weren't looking."

"I've met him. I don't see him giving up easily," he said, running his finger over my eyebrow.

"Why do you say that?"

Then he massaged my head and it felt amazing. "Lane, I wouldn't give up."

I opened my eyes and said, "You also wouldn't cheat on your wife."

"That's true but that's not the point. I believe he loves you."

I sat up and pointed at his chest. "Are you trying to talk me back into seeing him?"

"No, but if you don't deal with him directly you'll be living in limbo without resolution."

"He's gone for the next two weeks for work. At least that's what he told me. I have no idea what's true anymore. Why did *you* give Karen another chance?"

"Because I believed she was sorry and understood how much pain she caused me."

"I'm sorry," I said, touching Stay's shoulder. "That sucks. Was it worse the second time?"

"Way worse. It's what ended our relationship."

"I hate that she hurt you like that, but I'm grateful to have you back with us. I've enjoyed getting to know you. I thought of you right before I saw Mason. Just before."

"In what context?"

"I was listening to Daniel Wesley live. Do you know his stuff?"

"I don't."

"I'll play my favorites for you some other time. Anyway,

I remembered how much fun the concert we went to was, and thought that I would like to do it again. Honestly, it was with the caveat that we sort out our friendship."

He held my hand between his two palms infusing his energy into me. "I know a perfect way to sort out our friendship."

"I have no doubt you do. You have a depressed woman in front of you and you're still flirting!"

"Lane, I can't help myself when you're around. I feel compelled to make you feel better."

"And merge our bodies."

"Yes, there is definitely that too."

"Will you spoon me again?"

"Come," he said, holding out his arms.

Back in his arms I sighed heavily. I bent my knees and he curled his legs behind mine. "Thank you. You are making the most horrendous experience of my life breathable."

We lay quietly for a bit while my heart continued to break and tears silently dripped from the corner of my eyes.

I broke the silence when I said, "I just don't understand why Mason would pick someone like me when he married a skinny, gorgeous, petite woman."

"I don't know. Maybe he likes variety and doesn't have a type."

"He probably picked me because I'm dumb and live alone."

"Lainie, turn around and face me. Come on, do it."

I complied.

"Mason is a very attractive man. He could easily have his pick. He's smart, worldly, and has an authority about him. If he picked you, it's because he sees what I see: a beautiful, accomplished, incredible human being. Was there an instant connection?"

"Well, yes."

"Those are the hardest to let go. In a way they seem fated because of their intensity." He lifted a tear off my check with his index finger.

"Karen?" I asked.

"Completely."

"I think you should take me back to my car." I moved to get up.

"Why? Where are you going to go?"

"I don't know. I'm just feeling like I need you, and I don't want to. For both our sakes."

"Come here," he said, holding out his arms.

"Stay, please."

"You need me and that's okay. I need you too. Let me hold you."

He scooted toward me on the bed and pulled me onto his lap. "Don't even say it. You're not too heavy for me."

"How do you do that?"

"I don't know. Rest your head—there you go."

"Why do I feel better when your energy is wrapped around me?"

"It's the same for me, and a first for me too. If I told you why I think, you'd just shake your head again. You do that a lot, you know."

"Do I?" Snuggling in closer, I took in his natural masculine scent and sighed. "Tell me anyway."

"I'm still a beginner in my studies of Buddhism. However, I do know that there is a lot of focus on different kinds of energy, and how those energies converge. I think we have bonded in a way that transcends logic and binds us in the heart chakra as well as the sex chakra. I believe that's why I felt your pain today."

"Well I have no explanation for any of it, so yours is

as good as any."

"Thank you, I think."

"I'm sorry. I don't know what I'm saying."

His mouth hovered near mine and I wanted him to kiss me. I wanted him to fix me and transport me away from my torturous agony.

"Do you mean it, Lainie? Because I will," he said as if he heard my thoughts.

I tilted my head and looked into his deep-blue eyes. "I'm not in my right mind."

"I understand."

I pulled away and rested my hands behind me. "A shower first would be good. Do you have mouthwash?"

With his hands still on my waist, he said, "Yes, and an extra tooth brush. I don't want to let you go because—"

"I might feel differently when I get out."

"Yes. Let me get you something to put on. Sweats or PJs?"

"Either is fine."

"Get started and I'll bring something in."

I got up and found myself incredibly dizzy. My hand caught the edge of the bed and I steadied myself. His bathroom turned out to be huge, with a bath big enough for two. I turned on the shower and placed a folded towel nearby. The clothes that I stripped off, I planned to throw away, including the socks. I washed my hair and body, running the water as hot as I could stand. Once clean, I sat on the floor of the shower and thought about what to do next.

I knew if I stayed at Stay's, I'd end up making out with him, or worse. I really wanted another drink, or five, to deaden the pain. I truly wanted to numb out. *Should I send a message to Mason?* I asked myself. *What the fuck would I say?*

A knock sounded on the door and I heard Stay ask, "Are you okay in there?"

"Yeah, I'm just getting out," I yelled so he could hear me.

CHAPTER NINETEEN

Fools in Love

by Inara George

I dried off and wrapped the towel around me. I then held my hand out through the door for the clothes. The gray, Timberland Company shirt went on first, and the navy, plaid PJ bottoms next. I hung up the wet towel and wrapped a smaller one around my hair. The toothbrush and mouthwash I found under the sink. After thoroughly cleansing my mouth, I gathered my clothes and stepped out the bathroom door. "Where can I throw these away?"

"You want to—I'll take them."

I sat on the edge of the bed and waited. When Stay returned I noticed he had changed into PJ bottoms and a T-shirt as well. "Do you really think I should send Mason a message?" I asked. "I have no idea what to write. I definitely don't want to see him now. I might pummel him."

"Want me to check your phone?"

"I think it's in my shorts."

He pulled it out of his pocket. "Here."

I turned the phone back on, punched in my code to unlock it, and handed it back.

He scrolled through the notifications and said, "You have twenty-three texts, and nine voicemails."

"Would you check if any of the calls are from anyone else? Or texts for that matter?"

"Um, no. Just MM."

"Okay. If you don't mind, you can read and listen, then just give me a summary."

"Okay," he said, sitting down on the edge of the bed next to me.

Rusty nudged my hand, so I resumed petting him as I waited. It seemed to take a long time.

"Well, he's very distraught. He bounced back and forth between being concerned that something horrible has happened to you, to you finding something out about him. He wrote and said, 'Whatever you're thinking it's not true. I love you completely and fully and always will.' He begged you to contact him, especially before he leaves. He still plans to go by your apartment."

"What do you suggest?"

"Be honest."

"And who does that help? I don't see how that helps me. It just opens the door for all his excuses."

"I can type up something for you and you can edit it, or just delete it."

I shrugged. "Okay."

Stay took a good ten minutes to craft the text and I watched him erase and continue several times. "Does he have any stuff at your place that he might want back?" he asked, glancing up at me.

"Yes," I said, thinking about his fraternity paddle. My gut roiled over the thought.

He typed a bit longer and then said, "Okay. Here you go. Keep what you'd like or ditch it all."

I looked down at the screen of my phone and read:

> **Me:** I'm sending this message solely so you don't have to worry if I've come to physical

harm. I am not in the hospital, and all of my bones are still in tacked.

Me: However, I'm not at all well. Don't bother to come by my place tonight. I won't be there. I was at the Delray art fair today, which I imagine you've already

Me: sorted out for yourself. I know what I saw so don't bother with your excuses. I don't want to hear them. When you get back to town, we can arrange for you to

Me: get your belongings from my apartment. Other than that, I have no wish to hear from you.

"Thank you. It's good, only it's way too nice," I said, and tinkered with it before sending.

Me: I'm sending this text so you can stop messaging with concerns that I've been physically hurt. I'm not in a hospital, and all of my bones are still intact. If you

Me: count my soul and my heart, then I've been hurt more than I ever thought possible. You have broken love for me, for my lifetime.

Me: Don't bother to come by my place tonight. I won't be there. If I saw you in person right now, I'd punch you and you'd have to go home to your beautiful, petite

Me: wife and lie to her again. "Honey, some guy attacked me out of nowhere."

Me: I was at the Delray Affair today, which I imagine you've already sorted out for yourself. I know what I saw so don't bother with your excuses. I don't want

Me: to hear them. When you get back to town, we can arrange for you to get your belongings from my apartment. Other than that, I have no wish to hear from you. I'm no

Me: longer your love, or baby girl. GO FUCK YOURSELF!!!

I handed the phone back to Stay and said, "Honestly, what do you think?"

He read through and said, "Wow, Lainie, that's intense."

"I thought you said I should send a clear message. So? Should I take out the part about his wife?"

"I'm not sure. Maybe you were right and you should wait until you're less angry."

"That will never happen. Here," I said, holding my hand out for the phone. I hit send on the combined texts and breathed out heavily. "That's done."

"I'd say. Are you hungry?"

"Not in the least but please go eat something. I can hear your stomach grumbling."

"I'll go order a pizza, and maybe you'll change your mind by the time it gets here."

"Okay." I lay down with Rusty, stroking his soft fur, wishing I could see Mason's expression while he read the text.

My phone vibrated in my hand. I stared at it as if it was a spider. I couldn't stop myself. I had to read his text.

MM: It is true that Victoria and I are in a better place, but that has nothing to do with you and my love for you. You have to understand that. I can't live

MM: without you. Baby, please don't do this. I know what you saw had to be hard and confusing but just give me the chance to explain. I have

never loved another
MM: the way I love you. Not even Victoria. Please
reconsider. Meet me at your place as soon as you can.

I texted back before I could change my mind.

Me: Everything that you've said to me has been a
lie. By the look of things, I have to assume you
are having sex with your wife. I thought you
should know that I'm
Me: spending the night at Stayman's. Call me
when you get back in town and I'll leave your stuff
outside the apartment for you to pick up.

"Was that him?" Stay asked when he re-entered the
bedroom.

"Yeah, here," I said, handing him the phone.

"Oh? Do you mean it?" he said, lifting his right eyebrow.

"How long until the pizza gets here?"

"Thirty minutes or so."

"On one condition."

"Anything." He sat down next to me and I could feel his
excited energy. Desire and love all wrapped up together.

"You won't hold this night against me. I have no idea
how I'll feel in the morning or weeks from now."

"I understand." He walked into the bathroom and
returned with a comb. The towel wrapped around my hair
fell quickly with a tug. Standing over me, he used the
comb to brush out my hair.

I stopped his hand and said, "You don't have to."

"Just let me."

I closed my eyes, tears threatening to seep out. His
attention felt so good, as if he could somehow stave off

the decimation I felt. Soon enough I would have to deal with it properly, but I didn't want to right then.

He gently detangled my hair and then pressed the towel against the ends to dry them.

"Thank you," I said, peering up at him.

He didn't say anything, but I felt his energy nonetheless. With my hand in his, he pulled me to my feet and directed me to lie on the bed.

Beside him, wrapped in his embrace, my heart still ached, but I welcomed anything that would take the pain away. "Don't say it," I said.

"I won't, but let me show you." Then he lowered his mouth to mine and I let him.

His kiss transported me away from the worst of the desolation, but I wasn't able to fully forget that I was dying inside. Wrapped up in his love, I let my body take over. I wanted his cock to fill me, and for him to fuck me hard. In a daze of desire, I snaked my hand under the elastic of his PJs and felt his silky erection.

Stay broke of the kiss and said, "Lainie, what are you doing?"

I rolled to the side of him and said, "I would think that would be obvious."

"I take these things slowly."

"Come on!" I said, rolling my eyes up to the ceiling. "What has all of this been about then?"

"Not just sex, I assure you. And I'm not against it, but you will not make me come until I've learnt your body and that takes time."

"What's there to learn? You stick your cock inside me and I come."

"That's really romantic, Lainie. I'm not your stud for hire."

"I knew this was a bad idea," I said, sitting up and propping my back against the headboard. I crossed my arms for good measure.

"Sweetheart, if you wanted a fuck, I'm not your guy. That's not to say we won't have full-on fuck sessions after a while. I like it hard and fast, your submission and me taking what I need, but that's down the road. That's after I know your limits and you trust me to push them."

"That's all well and good, but I need this pain to go away now."

"Fucking doesn't last that long so then what?"

"I don't know. I don't know anything anymore. I want to run but you can't run away from yourself because there is nowhere to hide."

"Give me a chance. We can—I think I heard the door."

"I heard it too," I said, following him out of the room.

He paid the pizza delivery guy and laid the box on bar next to the kitchen pass-thru. "Want a slice."

"No," I said, sitting on one of the two stools. I spun to the right and left and then leaned against the narrow wall behind me. "Did Karen drink?"

"Sometimes." He folded the slice of pizza and took a big bite.

The dough and cheese smelled great, but when your gut is filled with distress and anger, food just gets booted out.

"Did you consider living with her?"

He took a drink of his soda and held out the glass to me. "That's an interesting question. No, I didn't."

"Why not?" I took a sip and handed it back.

"We didn't care to spend our time the same way. It seemed easier to have our own places."

"You mean like watching *The Voice*?"

"Nah, I love anything with music and although I don't

have a TV or watch it much, I do have a computer and catch movies and shows on there. I'm somewhat addicted to Pandora and YouTube."

"I'm addicted to new music myself." We sat quietly for a few minutes. When he grabbed another slice of pizza, I asked, "Do you want a family?"

"I do. Red and I have that in common. Bond might get there someday, but if Kev and Cat stay together, I don't see them having kids."

"I have to agree with that," I said.

"What about you?"

"Definitely. I want to be a good mother, like my dad is a great father. I told him about you."

"Yeah? What did he say?" Stay asked between bites.

"Just that he understood that I'm already—well was—in a relationship and I can't just switch out one for the other."

"I agree with him, but that doesn't mean you should hold off letting one grow here." He held out his glass to me.

I shook my head. "How about all the stuff you hear lately about taking time between relationships to sort out what went wrong?"

"I think my last relationship applies more than yours."

I raised my eyebrows and said, "How do you figure?"

"According to you, you and Mason have had a wonderful affair, whether or not it was based on the truth. You weren't the one lying, he was."

"How is that any different from you and Karen?"

"I didn't like who I was with her. There were issues on both sides." He took another bite.

"Like?"

He chewed and swallowed. "I'm sensitive to rejection, or perceived rejection."

"Meaning you overreact?"

"Yes, and when I'm put second or fifth and feel I should be put first, it's not good." He sipped his soda and put it back on the counter.

"Not good for you, or for the people around you?"

"Both but mostly me."

"And you're pursuing me? Don't you see you're just hurting yourself?" I asked.

"This is different."

"How the hell is it different?" I said, throwing my hands in the air.

"Lainie, come on. At least admit there is something mystical going on between us. Not that I enjoy your repeated rebuffs, but at least I get why you keep rejecting me. Bad timing is part of it. You're otherwise occupied. But damn when we kiss. Come on, OCDC, don't lie to me. It's better with me than it is with Mason, isn't it?"

I shifted uncomfortably and said, "My kisses with Mason are perfectly fine. I'd go as far as saying excellent."

"And ours?" He moved his hand back and forth between us.

"I don't remember."

"Bullshit," he said, fiercely.

"Let's talk about something else."

"No way." He threw down the crust of his pizza and wiped his face and hands with a napkin. "Stand," he demanded.

"Why?"

"You know why." Not waiting for me to respond, he lifted me up under my arms, kicked the stool away, which went clattering against the tile, and pushed me up against the wall. His hard body pressed against mine, instantly arousing me.

Then his lips touched mine and I became pliant in his

arms. His soft lips caressed me, slowly at first, exploring my mouth with his tongue, seeking out mine. Once they collided he groaned and rubbed his hard, steely erection into my mound. I wanted to see his cock, touch it, taste it. Instead of lowering down in front of him, I grasped his ass with both hands and pulled him in tighter.

"Oh, Stayman," I mumbled against his lips.

"I won't stop," he whispered, the arousal clear in his declaration. Before I could protest, he swept me up and with my arms around his neck he carried me to his bed. His eyes stayed locked on me as he transported me with ease. He sat on the edge of the bed and resumed teaching me a lesson via his kiss. Bound and determined to prove himself right, he continued the odysseys of our abandon.

Something inside me opened up, and my heart expanded. At first, elation spilled out and eddied around us. Somehow his kiss fused vivid, sexual desire and tenderness into one incredible sensation, rendering me defenseless. He made me feel vulnerable and breached the door to all of my emotions.

In opening my soul, the pain caused by my recent revelations escaped. I gasped uncontrollably. Then a howl of hurt and betrayal erupted and I couldn't stop it.

"Oh, Lainie, I'm so sorry you're hurting," he said as he rocked me and held me close.

I lay my face against his chest as I purged the grief of my lost love affair. A part of me forever burnt in the wreckage. "I ... I'm ... getting your ... shirt—"

"Shh, It's okay," he said, moving my hair away from my face.

"I feel like ... like such a fool," I said, peering up at Stay.

His eyes were moist. He kissed my tear soaked cheeks and eyes. "There's nothing wrong with being a fool for love.

Us fools are the ones that ultimately find their true match."

Scanning his eyes for duplicity, I didn't find any there. "Don't let me go," I whispered.

"Never."

I started to wipe my tears on the back of my hand.

With me still in his lap, he reached over to the end table, took out a pale-green handkerchief and handed it to me.

Laughing through the tears, I said, "You weren't kidding about these things." I wiped my face and blew my nose.

"Abundant uses."

I sat up on his lap and saw the huge, wet spot on his shirt.

"Seriously, don't worry about," he said. "Is there anything I can get you? Anything you need?"

"Stay..."

"Yes, honey?"

"You."

"Me? Oh, I see. Come." He laid us out on the bed facing each other, his legs entangled with mine. "What can I do for you?"

"Kiss me again."

"Are you sure? I don't want—"

"Now you show some propriety?" I tugged his shirt toward me.

"Okay." His crooked smile shined bright.

Then, thankfully, he kissed me again. I finally got my wish and traveled away from myself, away from the pain and anguish, sparking a hope that I might really let go of the past and move on. It might take me weeks or months, but in Stay's arms, I believed I would make it.

His kisses were gentle and full of compassion and love. Even so, my body steamed with intense need.

I pulled back and said, "I want you."

"God, Lane, you have no idea. I just don't think—"

"Don't think. Please."

"You might regret—"

"I'll never regret spending this night in your arms. I can't make any promises about the future, but right now there is no other place I want to be. I want you Stay. Please make love to me. We'll do it your way."

"Lainie, I..."

I moved to sit up. "If you don't want to, then just say so. I won't be mad."

He pulled me back down and shoved my hand under the elastic of his PJs. "What do you think? Take your clothes off for me."

I hesitated and he seemed to sense why.

"I love your body. Trust me."

I sat up and pulled the shirt over my head and folded it to the side. I shimmied out of the bottoms and then lay with my arms in close, fighting off the impulse to cover my breast. My legs tightly shut.

"Relax," he said. "You're beautiful, Lainie." He ran his hand down the center of my chest and around my hip. "Womanly and soft."

"Thank you. Do I get to see?" I said, pointing down to his cock.

"If you're a good girl."

I harrumphed, and he laughed.

"Spreads your legs for me. Oh, yes. You have a beautiful pussy and she's already juicy." He ran his fingers through my cleft and then held them up observing all the wetness. "Oh, OC, our kisses are more than good. You smell incredible. I bet you taste good too." Laying his head near mine, he kissed my neck as his trailed his hand over the swell of my breast, grazing my nipples. "You have tiny nipples that really stand at attention. I like that."

"Ohhh," I said as he rolled and twisted my little buds between his fingers.

"Do you know how long I've wanted to see you, to have you just like this?"

"No." I shook my head.

"Way too long, OC, way too long. Your skin is so soft," he said, running both hands over my nipples to my shoulders around my collarbone and up my neck. His lips took mine, drowning out my moans. Sliding his hand down my stomach, he found my clit. "Already so wet *and* hard for me. I have to taste you now."

When he slid down the bed, I tensed up.

"What's wrong?" he asked, lifting his head. "Have you changed your mind?"

"It's not that."

"What is it?"

"I don't like men to do that."

He pulled his head back in surprise and confusion. "Are you telling me that M—I mean that none of your lovers have made you come with their tongue?"

I shook my head.

"Why don't you like it?"

"For one, I come easily from intercourse."

"It's a completely different kind of orgasm. Have you never had a clitoral orgasm?"

"I don't think so."

"Wow, okay. Why else?"

"My clit is very sensitive and the men I let try—not very many—hurt me. It didn't feel good."

A huge smile spread across his features.

"Why are you grinning?"

"I have so much to show you. It thrills me that we will

have a first together—starting now." He lowered back down and explored my labia with his fingers first, then his tongue. "Your smell and your taste are incredible. Poor guys, they so missed out." Slowly with soft caresses of his tongue, he worked his way around my opening, lightly sucking on my lips.

My back arched and my pussy flushed.

"There you go, she knows what she likes." He blew across my saturated labia, and then journeyed to my taut clit.

Feathering touches kissed my clit and I groaned.

He paused, peered up and smiled at me. Then he bent back down and continued. His slow, sensitive licks caused my hips to gyrate out of control. He wrapped his arms around the outside of my thighs and used his hands to spread me open. His dancing rhythm—never touching the same spot twice—had me vibrating on the edge of a tsunami. As if reading my body, he would taper off, dousing lower into my pussy, lapping up my come. Again, back to my most acute pleasure spot and down again.

He took me by surprise when he fingered my entrance, finding my danger spot just right inside. "Your G-spot is nice and swollen. Are you ready to come for me?"

"Yes, Stay, yes!"

"Good because it's going to be a doozy. Hang on."

I grabbed the comforter with both hands as he twirled around my clit and lightly massaged inside of me. My back arched again, guttural noises sounding. I felt high as if I'd already come, and yet the euphoria continued to grow. "Ohhh. Ohhh. Pleeease!"

And then I did. The explosive release fired off my first contraction. Every muscle clinched tightly and then relaxed over and over again. The climax lasted longer than I had ever experienced. I lay there spent, my pussy firing aftershocks repeatedly. "You've convinced me," I mumbled.

He scooped me up in his arms pulling me on top of him.

"You're still dressed," I whispered next to his throat.

"Just take your time and enjoy," he said, kissing my head and burying his nose in my hair.

"You're good at that," I sighed.

"That's just the beginning."

I grinned up at him, "That's a good start."

His still rigid cock pressed against my stomach.

"Does it hurt to be hard for so long?"

"For some men yes. For me, when I eventually come it's more intense if I've waited. Lately I've gotten used to walking around with an erection."

"Will you let me play with him? Will we have sex?" I asked.

"I haven't decided."

"Why?" I couldn't fathom why.

"If I tell you, I might have to kill you."

"Very funny. Tell me."

"Intercourse is a definite no, not until you're going to give us a real shot."

I thought about it for a second and then said, "I understand, I do. And if I return the favor?"

"Sex means something to me."

"Me too. Stop stalling, I want to see your body like you got to see mine."

He peeled off his shirt and threw it to the floor. "My nipples are sensitive."

"Really?" My eyes opened wide. "I didn't know that worked for some men." I brushed my fingers over his tiny nipples.

Stay's breathing became heavier.

I tugged at his bottoms. "Please," I said, dying to see

his cock.

He pushed off his PJs revealing his boxers with a large wet spot on the front.

"You *were* turned on. Does that happen a lot?" I ran my hand over the front of his shorts.

"When I'm super turned on, the pre-cum flows."

"That's sexy. Was it the kisses or going down on me?"

"Both," he groaned as I traced the outline of his cock.

"Huh. Did it happen at the club?" I wondered out loud.

"Yes. I'll never forget that kiss."

"Me either. Now stop making me wait," I said, tugging on the bottom of his boxers.

He pulled them down and kicked them to the side.

"Holy moly. I think you might be too big for me. I mean, wow, really."

"I promise you, we'll make it work."

The veiny shaft was significantly thicker than I'd ever seen. The full head covered a good portion of the top. In addition, the seven and a half inches or so were more than I usually liked.

When I realized that I was staring at it, I reached out and caught a pearl of his pre-cum on my finger and rubbed it around the tip.

His cock jumped and twitched and more pre-cum came to the surface.

I shifted to his side and lapped up the come. Leaning over, my breast grazed against his balls and shaft.

"Oh that feels amazing. Love your tits against me."

I danced my breast over and around his cock, lightly jostling his testicles with their weight.

He groaned and the sound turned me on even more.

Resting my upper body against his leg, I lowered my mouth over him. When I tasted his salty pre-cum, my nipples flared and my breathing accelerated. "Oh god," I murmured. He was so thick and long I thought I would never be able to take all of him in my mouth.

Mason never liked for me to go down on him and I realized at the moment, I never asked him why. It didn't matter anymore.

I licked around Stay's ridge and trailed my tongue to his balls. Breathing in, I could feel my pussy flush again. I glanced up and Stay could tell. "Wow," I said. He smelled divine.

"Would you kneel for me?" he said, swinging his legs to the side of the bed.

I hopped off the mattress, knelt down in front of him, my butt resting on my heels.

"Will you trust me?" He took my face in his hands.

"Yes."

"Scoot back just a bit and rise up on your knees." He stood in front of me, gazing down. His hand caressed my cheek right before he held his cock out to me. "I'm going to use your mouth how I like. Clasp your hands behind your back. Yes, just like that. You can stop me at any time, and I'll check in with you as well."

Peering up, I opened my mouth.

He painted my lips with his pre-cum and dribbled on my tongue, and then said, "Suck on the very tip."

I sucked the end of his hard shaft and savored his taste.

"Good, OC. I've often wondered if you would submit to me, and you're a natural. Keep your eyes glued to mine. I'm going to take your mouth now." He cupped my head in his hands and forced his cock deep into my mouth. The thrust hit the back of my throat.

Staring up at him, my eyes watering, I was dominated by his deep-blue eyes.

"So beautiful, Lane," he said as he slowly pulled back

and jabbed back in.

I swirled my tongue in mid stroke and licked down the length of him.

"Are you okay? Do you think you can take more?"

I nodded, scared and utterly turned on. He'd just started and I could already feel my wetness dripping down my thighs.

"Have you ever had a cock in your throat?"

I shook my head as much as I could with him in my mouth.

"Another first. If you need me to stop, just unlatch your hands and touch my leg. Thank you, OC, I've thought about this so often." He angled my chin all the way up and plunged down my throat, then he immediately pulled back out. "I won't push you too far this time. But soon ... take a deep breath for me."

I did and he immediately incurred back down my throat farther than before. "Yesss, that's so tight, so good." He stroked my hair as he drew out again. "These are the kind of tears I like to see. Again?" Staring down into my eyes, he knew. "Okay. This time a few strokes." He clutched my head tightly and rode my mouth in and out. The depth grew with each motion. "Jesus, woman, are you sure ... you never..."

At once I wanted him to stop and I didn't. He'd given me so much and I wanted to give it back. And the submission took me out of myself, a vessel for another's pleasure. Stay's pleasure. As I hovered away from myself, I clung to the place without thought. I continued to peer up at him.

He withdrew from my mouth again. "Can you take anymore? Between yoga and tantra my orgasms last a long time, and I'm so close. If I start—"

"Yes. I want to watch you come."

"Damn, woman." He knelt down in front of me and kissed me deeply.

I kept my arms behind me, pushing myself into him.

He intertwined the fingers of one hand in the base of my hair, kissing me harder than ever before. His free hand reached between my legs and I flushed with embarrassment. "Jesus," he groaned.

"I'm sorry. I think I might have leaked onto your carpet."

He bellowed a laugh. "Never apologize for getting turned on. Do you have any idea how wet you are? How hot that is?"

"I can feel it running down my legs."

"Touch yourself. Tell me, have you ever been this wet before, for any man?"

I reached down. "No," I admitted. And it was true. The blush remained on my face.

"You are by far the sexist woman I have ever known. This, you, is telling me everything. You may not realize it, but we are so well-suited sexually."

"Thank you," I said to his compliment, but I didn't want to acknowledge the other part. "How long can you stay hard like that?"

"Honey, with you? Forever. Once I come my cock takes a time out, but with you I don't imagine it will be a long one. Are you ready to continue?"

"One more kiss first?"

He obliged.

I fell into his kiss, not wanting to think about what any of it meant.

He again arrested me with his lips, and I no longer had to think. Then he stood and said, "Are you ready?" He grabbed my hair at the nape of my neck and tilted my head before gliding in. Up and down he used my throat, and I forgot myself. Lainie had fled the building and in her place a woman who wanted to give her body away.

"I'm almost there. Take a big breath for me. Okay, hold on." He pushed his cock into my throat one last time as he cradled my head in his hands.

Tears poured out of my eyes as we held eye contact. His orgasm contorted his features and he shook as he came and squirted down my throat. "Lainie," he yelled stretching out my name. And then he came for what felt like minutes. He pulled partially out while he continued to ejaculate into mouth.

Not only had I never been with a man who could orgasm for that long, I had never been with anyone who released so much come.

When he finally finished, he collapsed onto the bed and held out his arms to me.

"I'm really wet," I said.

"I don't care, come here."

I climbed on top of him and nuzzled into his neck.

"That was incredible. Beyond my imagination," he said.

"I'm not sure I should get credit for that," I said, circling my arms around his shoulders.

"Oh yes you do."

"Stay, I'm getting your leg all wet." I moved to get up.

He laughed and clutched me. "Stop worrying about it."

"I have a couple of questions."

"Shoot." He traced his finger down the contours of my spine.

"How far in my throat did you get?"

He held up his fingers about an inch and a half apart.

"Bullshit. That's all?"

"Honest to god, but that's great for the first time. Is your throat sore?" he asked.

"Not that I can tell. Also, what does this have to do with tantra?"

"Not a fucking thing." The wickedness in his deep-blue eyes made me feel more than I wanted to.

I laughed it off and said, "I thought so."

"However, at least for me, it was incredibly intimate."

"It was." I folded my hands over his chest and rested my head.

He played with my hair and said, "I think we need to take care of that sopping wet pussy of yours. Do you have a preference?"

"Yes, but you already said no," I said, looking up again.

"You want me inside."

"Badly." And I meant it.

"Me too, but not yet."

"I understand," I said.

"Do you?"

"No, not really," I admitted

"It's a different type of energy exchange, and one I don't take lightly. Mind you, I used to when I drank all the time. I no longer live like that, and haven't for years. You don't have to love me but you at least have to be healed and open to us."

"Okay."

"I have a suggestion. You have to be willing to put most of your weight on top of me though."

I bristled a bit and said, "What is it?"

"I was thinking we should take advantage of how wet you are. You can glide back and forth over my cock."

"Oh, I think I see what you mean." I sifted to the side and asked, "How will I come?"

"Your clit will rub against my cock."

"Show me."

He rolled me on top of him and lined up his semi-hard-on with my slit. "Use my chest for leverage."

I straddled him, my knees out wide, hips tilted back. As I slid forward clutching onto his firm, muscular chest, he grew underneath me. "Oh, I like this. You're expanding."

He used my hips to help with the motion. He smiled and grunted. "You're so silky and smooth. I'm getting so hard for you, Lane. And just for you."

I stroked across the underside of his cock, swiveling my hips up and back.

"That feels incredible. Make sure your clit hits against the head. Oh yeah, just like that."

"Oh, that *is* good." I felt so swollen and sensitive as I continued to move. "Can you feel my clit?"

"I can feel ... all of you. Come closer," he said, pulling me to him.

Dancing over his cock, I lowered down toward his chest and said, "Should I squeeze your nipples?"

"Not until I'm close. Let's pick up the pace." He lifted my right breast and sucked on my nipple.

I groaned still massaging myself on top of him. "I'm getting closer, oh that feels so good."

He moved to the other side, pulling and tugging with his mouth. Then his hands moved back to my hips and he helped me keep the fast rhythm. "Okay, Lainie, you're on."

I shifted my weight back slightly and, still leaning forward, I rolled his tiny nipples between my fingers. "You definitely like that. Oh, I felt you pulse ... and again ... you're twitching against my—" Loud groans escaped me, sounding my impending climax.

"Look down," he grunted.

When my orgasm hit, I watched the head of his cock become visible and then retract between my folds.

He moved us even faster, his hips jerking against me, and then I watched his come spurt out onto his chest. Once his release tapered off, I said, "I don't suppose you have another hanky for this."

He laughed and said, "I think we both need to head to the bathroom."

"Good idea."

He cupped his hand under the come on his chest and rushed to the bathroom.

I followed behind. "Washcloth?" I asked.

"Under the other sink."

I bent down and grabbed two, tossing him one.

"Thanks."

"Have you done that before?" I asked while running warm water over the washcloth.

"No, I've never been with a woman as wet as you were. The idea just came to me in the moment."

"Good," I said and I meant it. "Stayman, that was absolutely unbelievable. I never thought I could do that and the feeling, wow. I had two, count them, two clitoral orgasms today, and you were right, they are different."

"Seriously, it was definitely my pleasure."

I smiled at him and asked, "Do you have any idea what time it is?"

"None."

"Don't watch me while I clean up," I said.

"Have you never showered with a man?"

"No, I haven't. Now you're the one shaking your head. Just turn around."

"OCDC, I'm going to have to get you to loosen up about your body. You have a very, very sexy body."

"Fine, we can start tomorrow. Now turn around."

He chuckled and said, "Tomorrow," with a huge

smile. He left the bathroom to give me privacy.

When I entered the bedroom Stay lay in bed under the covers. He held the sheet and blanket up for me to climb in. I took a sip of the water on the nightstand and got into the bed.

"It's just after six," he said, folding me in his arms with my cheek on his chest. "Let's take a nap and then we can go get your car in Delray."

Stay saying Delray brought everything to the forefront. All that we had chased away while he and I played was a mere reprieve. He quickly drifted off to sleep as my gut twisted and turned. I knew I wouldn't nap.

I carefully extracted myself from under his arm and placed it down gently. Tiptoeing to the closet, I searched and found a pair of sweatpants I thought would fit me. I slipped into the pants and the gray shirt I wore before. I took my cell phone off the nightstand and left the bedroom, closing the door behind me.

My keys sat on the bar near the pizza box. I looked around for pen and paper and wandered into "the room" where I found both in the right drawer of his desk. Settling on the couch in the living room, Rusty purred next to me as I wrote Stay a note.

Dear Stayman,

    Once again, you've managed to rescue me from a horrible situation, and made it so much easier on me. Unfortunately, I can't just throw Mason up and feel better. Oh, if only I could.

    My time with you today ... there's so much to say. You are an incredible friend and lover. In the short time we played I enjoyed three entirely new experiences, which still have my head spinning.

I'm not sneaking out to get away as much as I couldn't relax and sleep with all the turmoil still running through me. The respite you offered me will never be forgotten. Never.

I'm not sure where we go from here. I'm heartbroken, and the last thing I want to do is hurt you in the process because you don't deserve that. I need time. I hope you understand.

With deepest affection,
OCDC

Using the powder room by the front door, I tied my messy hair into a knot. I wouldn't normally be caught dead in public in the state I was in, but there wasn't any other option. I slipped on my Keds, petted Rusty goodbye, and left. Outside the building, I called a cab and waited.

CHAPTER TWENTY

Fiction

by The xx

I managed not to cry on my way to my car. It seemed that grief not only surfaced for Mason, but also for Stay. As much as I enjoyed his company and sex, I couldn't be his girlfriend. It could take months for me to find myself in the rubble that my heart had become.

As I climbed the steps to my apartment, the last ounce of energy drained out of me. In front of my door sat flowers and an envelope. It only made my stomach broil more. The arrangement had pink roses and Gerber daisies. *Pink?* Knowing Mason, it had some significance. I left the flowers outside and took the card in with me.

Ridding myself of Stay's clothes, I then cleansed myself of his smell in the shower. Not that it was unpleasant in the least. Our smells had melded together in an intensely pleasurable way, but I didn't want be reminded of it.

In boy shorts and a T-shirt I sat on the balcony with a cigarette and Mason's card. It was still warm that evening, and I fanned myself with the envelope contemplating its contents. The man had a way with words so I imagined it would be an impassioned plea for forgiveness.

As much as I reveled in Stay's attention and affection, it further complicated matters. Sitting there, lighting a second cigarette, I felt selfish in regard to Stay. Whether I wanted to face it or not, Stay had strong feelings for me and I let our relationship to go to the next level, even though I wasn't available to live in it with him. *I'm sorry, Stay,* I thought.

When my tears fell, they were solely for Stayman.

I tamped out the cigarette and opened the envelope.

Dearest Lainie, the love of my life,

In every way I have mishandled our love. How could I have explained to you that things got better between Victoria and I, and not lose you in the process. If I could do this lifetime over, I'd wait until the night we met in GG's Waterfront Bar and Grill. But we both know I can't go back.

You must feel betrayed and lied to, but please, baby, I've never lied to you, ever. It was true when we met that my marriage was in a horrendous condition. I had little hope of finding resolution, but we both committed, for the sake of the children, to get counseling together. It helped us a lot. The relationship still isn't ideal but we are making it work.

For me, our time together is separate from the rest of my life. It's as if I live in two separate worlds. When I'm with you, it rejuvenates my soul and I can't live without it. If you make me choose, I will choose you, but I hope it doesn't come to that.

"Bullshit," I yelled. "What a load of crap!" *He knows I would never take him away from his kids, and how would that even work?* He would be sad and depressed, and would take it out on me. *Fuck you for even suggesting it.* I continued reading.

Please, baby, don't give up on us. I know I'm being selfish, but I can't, I won't, let you go. I know you mentioned Stayman just to hurt me and it worked. That boy isn't worth your time. He will never love you the way I do, with all of my heart and soul. You are the only woman I have ever felt this way about. No other relationship has felt close to what we have together.

What did we have? Sexual dalliances at his whim? I started to break down again, so I went back inside and plopped down on the bed. Resting my head on the pillow, holding the pages above me, I finished reading the letter.

I promise you, when the right MAN comes along I will give you my blessings and back away. It's not the boy, and now is not the time. More than anything in the world I want you to be happy, and, for as long as that can be, I want to be the one to make you happy. Please, baby, I'm begging you, let me back in to fix what I broke.

I love you so much, and I'm so sorry you're hurting. It hurts me to know I'm the cause.

Call me or text anytime. I waited as long as I could outside your place before I had to leave for the airport. My flight will land at ten o'clock, your time.

You have my heart,
Mason

"Jesus fucking Christ!" I yelled, throwing the letter to the floor. I pulled my journal onto my lap and started to write:

Mother fucker, goddamn everyone to hell! How I had let myself float in euphoria for the days leading up to the stab into my jugular? It just shows how delusional I was. Stupid, girl, so fucking stupid. I guess my mother was right—for a smart woman, I make dumb-ass choices.

Maybe I should run away to Canada like I used to dream about as a kid. Sell the boutique and start over somewhere else. Of course it's just a fantasy. I never would have left my father alone with my mother back then, and I would never abandon him or my friends now. The need to flee is overwhelming. At least in Stay's arms I didn't feel like I was dying. I feel it now, like death looms over me, following my each and every step.

I shot out of bed when the anxiety became too overwhelming. *How can I be this tensed up and tired at the same time?* I contemplated going for a walk or a swim, but instead crumbled on the couch in tears. The pain forced me under again, trapped in a tidal wave that wouldn't let me up for air.

A loud knock on the door snapped me out of it. *Who the fuck?* I decided not to answer it.

"Lainie, let me in," Mason said. "Your car is in your spot. I changed my flight till later. Open the door."

I didn't say anything or move. My stomach clinched, and the ocean of hurt held me down.

Then he pounded on the door repetitively, and I didn't want him to create a scene, drawing out the neighbors.

Through the door I said, "Give me a minute."

In the bedroom I threw on a pair of jeans and then grabbed the pack of smokes and the lighter. Without checking my appearance, I slipped on my flip-flops by the door and opened it.

He started to push in and I said, "No, you can't come in. We can go sit by the pool."

Not saying anything, I trudged down the middle set of stairs and around the back to the pool area. I sat in a redwood Adirondack chair in front of a circular, white, plastic table. I pulled the ashtray toward me and lit a cigarette.

Mason took the chair opposite from me. He was in a business suit I'd seen him in before. "You smoke? Since when?"

I shrugged not saying anything.

"I have an hour before I need to head back to the airport. I couldn't leave before we had a chance to talk."

"I guess I should have stayed over at *the boy's* place instead of coming home," I said tapping the end of the cigarette in the ashtray.

"Please don't do this."

I took another drag on my cigarette and said, "Do what exactly? Be a fool? Lay my heart out to be trampled on? Tell you I love you? I'm in full agreement. I should never have done any of those things."

"I don't see why my relationship with Victoria should alter what we have?"

"Then you're an idiot," I said, blowing out the smoke.

"Excuse me, Lainie, but that's not okay."

"I told you not to come by. I told you I didn't want to see you. Did you listen?" I swept my hand toward him. "And there you sit. Don't tell me how to fucking react or what the fuck to say. I'm no longer your weeping willow waiting for the next drop of rain you might send my way. I can't imagine what you want from me, what you expect from me? To pretend I didn't see your sweet family at the art show? Tell me how to do that? I will say this, the expression on your face when you got my message was priceless. I'll hold on to that." Anger felt oh-so much better than the pain that was pulling me down like quicksand.

He ran his hand over his hair and said, "What you saw was fear."

"I fucking bet it was. I have no doubt. 'Is Lainie going to walk out of the shadows and rip apart my perfect life like I ripped apart her heart?'" I stared at the end of the cigarette and tapped off the ash again.

"I never thought for one second you would do that. I was scared at first that something horrible had happened, and then that you saw me."

"You're lying even now," I said, pointing at him. "I saw you looking around for me and then you decided against it."

"If you say so. I was—I am—so scared of losing you. I love you so—"

I sigh and said, "Let's not, okay? You have lost me. If you have read my texts then you know I made myself abundantly clear. As much as you seem to despise Stayman, he said that he thought you genuinely love me and won't give up trying to get me back."

"He's right, I won't." He leaned forward and placed his arms on his thighs. His posture reminded me of the night he and Stay met.

"While I have you here," I said, "I might as well get all the questions answered I never asked. I was always too scared to push you away. It's freeing when you don't give a shit anymore. Am I your first?"

"First what?" he asked, cupping his forehead in his hand. When he raised his head, searching my face, his eyes filled with tears.

I felt no compassion. "Really, you're opting to play dumb. Here, I'll spell it out for you: Am I your first affair?"

"No, but I never fell in love with any of them." He

leaned back in the chair, knees out wide.

"Any of them? Great. How many?" I tamped out my cigarette, breathing out heavily.

"Lainie, I don't see—"

"Either answer my questions or leave for the airport." I pulled another out of the pack.

"Five."

That hit me straight in the gut like a sledge hammer. It took me a moment to catch my breath. "How long between me and the one before?"

"I broke it off when I met you."

I blinked my eyes a few times in shock. "How soon after?"

"After the first time we made love."

"Did you have sex with her one last time?"

"No. I couldn't. I wouldn't."

"Was she petite and beautiful like your wife?"

"Why does that matter?"

That would be a yes. Tears eked out but they didn't stop me. I lit the new cigarette and asked, "When did you start having sex with Victoria again?"

He didn't need to respond. His expression told me everything I needed to know.

At that moment I felt flattened as though a building had crashed down on my head, only it wasn't my body that was destroyed, it was my soul. Why did I have to know? I just did. I stood up and said, "I'd say it was a pleasure knowing you but in this moment it just feels like a big, fat waste of my time." Droplets fell freely from my eyes, but at least I was still standing.

As I passed by him, he caught my hand. "Baby, please," he pleaded, his cheeks wet.

"Do not call me baby. I'm not your baby, not ever again."

"Lainie, please don't do anything rash. Take time and remember what we're like together."

I glowered down at him. "What we were like? I was your beck and call girl, the latest in a long line of them. Don't fret," I said patting his cheek, "you'll find someone soon, on this trip maybe, to take your mind off of me. And, Mason…"

"What?"

"Good riddance." I stumbled up the middle steps and somehow made it back to my place.

CHAPTER TWENTY-ONE

Stay With You

by John Legend

After my conversation with Mason, I fell apart again on the couch, only this time there was no sound. The damage I felt lived so deep it quaked through me, and the rain from my eyes poured like an intense summer storm. I had no idea how much time passed, but another knock eventually sounded on the door, pulling me back to the surface. I tried to breathe normally but each breath came out in a shudder.

For a split second I thought maybe Mason came back for his stuff. *I'm such an idiot.* I should have shoved his stuff into his hands and made him leave, and forwent the heart-splitting revelations.

"OC, are you in there?"

Stay? I opened the door.

His arms hung at his sides, palms out. He didn't step inside. "I got scared when I couldn't reach you. I'm sorry to barge in when you need your space, but that feeling came back again."

I pulled him to me and hugged him like my life depended on it.

"He came here," Stay said as a statement.

I nodded.

"Have you eaten anything? Have you slept at all?"

I shook my head and the movement wouldn't stop.

Behind me, he put his hands on my shoulders, ushered me to my bed, and lay down with me.

Against his chest I wept as he held me close, smoothing my hair and caressing my back. He remained silent until the wave of angst and regret subsided.

He dried my eyes with his handkerchief, and it made me laugh. "So glad I can amuse you at a time like this," he said.

"You're lucky you caught me at my worst, it gives you more opportunities to use them."

"Someday you'll appreciate it," he said, handing the hanky to me.

"Oh, I already do."

"Tell me, Lainie, what I can do for you?" he asked, snuggling me close.

"You already are. Did you really feel it again?"

"Worse. I think it's because we are even more connected now. I paced back and forth, hoping you would call me back or text. Finally, I couldn't take it anymore. I had to know you were okay."

I touched his cheek. "I'm sorry. I'm putting you through so much."

"Oh, you've more than made up for it," he said and winked.

I playfully punched his shoulder and laughed until I thought I might cry again. Using the handkerchief, I dabbed at my eyes. "I can't cry anymore. I don't think I could eat or sleep either."

"How about this? I'll run to the store and make my Granny's famous chicken soup. If you can't eat any of it, at least you can drink the broth. It'll warm your stomach."

"Stay, you've done so much, too much already," I said, searching his eyes.

"That's for me to decide. I know how to take care of myself." And in the kindest voice possible, he said, "Please let me manage my own heart? Okay?"

"Okay," I said. "Today's your lucky day. I'm too spent to fight you."

"Good then let me call Sam to cover for you tomorrow."

"Now you are pushing it, Stay. No." I crossed my arms.

"You're grieving. Go look in the mirror."

I sat up and said, "I don't want to. I'll start crying again and I can't take anymore. I really can't. You might find this unbelievable but until recently, I hardly ever cried."

"No, OC, I believe it. Listen, I'm going to run to the store. Make a list of what else you need." He rose from the bed and held out his hand.

I let him pull me up. "Ten boxes of tissues or a supply of handkerchiefs evidently. Are you the kind of guy who won't pick up lady products?"

"What do you think?" he asked, giving me a look out of the corner of his eyes.

"I don't need any. Was just checking. Maybe an ice pack for my eyes," I said seriously.

When we entered the kitchen, Stay checked the cabinets and refrigerator. "Please think about taking tomorrow off while I'm gone."

"I'm going to see what movies I can find on the tube."

"Good idea. Come give me a hug before I leave," he said with his arms wide open.

In the comfort of his embrace I lifted my mouth to his and initiated a kiss. Although calling it a kiss was like calling tyrannosaurus rex a small pet. His energy infiltrated mine, making me feel weightless and somehow reborn. Unfortunately, when he pulled away all my heartache was still with me.

"Smoking is bad for your health," he said at the door.

"Oh, yeah, pick me up a pack of Natural American Spirit cigarettes, the yellow box please. And I insist on paying you back for all of it."

"Don't worry, OCDC, you will and then some," he said with his cheeky smile and a wink.

"What am I going to do with that boy?" I said, once alone again. Not dwelling on it or the ache in my stomach, I awoke the screen on my phone and dialed Samantha.

"Hey, Lane, what's up?" she said, chipper as ever.

"Sorry to bother you on a Sunday night, and for the last minute call—"

"Do you need me to open?"

"Only if it doesn't mess things up for you or your mom," I said, flipping on the TV and muting the sound.

"Nope, it should be doable. Will you be in later?"

"Yeah, but I'm not sure when. Sam?"

"Yes?"

"Thank you, I owe you."

"You don't, and I love to be able to help out. Have a good night and I'll see you tomorrow," she said.

"Thanks again and see you soon."

I turned the TV back off and decided on a quick smoke and a shower before Stay got back.

In sweatpants and a shirt I settled back onto the couch, letting my hair dry naturally. Scanning all the channels, I made note of five comedies. I needed something to distract me and cause me to laugh.

When Stay returned, I kept him company in the kitchen. "I called Sam and she can open for me but I will not have her open and close, so I do plan to go in."

"Good, that will give you time to rest up beforehand."

"Also, I found a few movies we could watch,

assuming you're staying."

"I'm staying," he said over his shoulder.

"Okay, your pick. *The Wedding Singer* is one."

He set a big pot on the stove and filled it a third of the way with chicken broth. "I'm not a huge fan of Adam Sandler."

I perched on the side of the counter, watching him work. "Okay, do you like Kevin Smith movies? I found *Chasing Amy* and *Dogma*."

"Yes, I think I've seen all of his movies. *Dogma* is more a comedy out of the two. What else?"

"*Groundhog Day*?"

He efficiently sliced carrots and celery, paused and said, "I feel like I've seen that movie over and over again."

I chuckled. "I see what you did there. Do you like old, black-and-white movies?"

"I'm a b and w buff."

"*The Apartment* or *Roman Holiday*?" I peeled the garlic while he prepped the chicken.

"Either of those is good. Both are classics."

"How many of these do you want?" I asked, holding up the garlic.

"Four or five big cloves."

"Okay. What did you think about *The Princess Bride*?" I asked, dropping the garlic into his palm.

"Never got next to that one."

"Me either," I said, marveling over our commonalities. "Everyone seems to love that movie and it makes me feel like I'm missing something. I've tried to watch it a few times and—"

"You get bored." He lowered the chicken into the pot

"Exactly," I said. "I do like the part with Billy Crystal and Carol Kane, but the rest of the movie is lost on me."

"I totally agree. They were a hoot. I think *The*

Apartment might be too close to home. I love Shirley MacLaine in that one though. How about *Dogma*?"

"Great. I'll set it to record," I said.

Stay joined me on the couch and said, "The soup is set, and now it just needs to cook for a few hours. If you crash before then, you'll have it for tomorrow. I also bought a variety of foods from the deli if you get hungry."

"I'm good, thank you," I said. "The movie starts in a few minutes."

He turned to face me, and asked, "How long have you been smoking? I noticed them on the balcony last time I was here."

"Too long, but until the last few days, I had cut back to one or two a day. Usually just one when I get home from work."

"So more when you're stressed," he said, touching my knee.

I nodded. "Is that a total turn off?"

"As long as I don't have to taste it or smell it on you, then no, however and I know you already know this, the costs are hardly worth the pleasure. Does anyone know?"

"Jacqs suspects that I'm smoking again, and now Mason knows." I rested back against the couch, rolling my head toward him.

"Oh?"

Then it all spilled out of me. "I smoked in front of him tonight. He seemed shocked and I enjoyed it. Just that one part, the rest—everything that I suspect you imagined turned out to be true. I'm his fifth affair. He broke it off with petite number four after he met me, but had no sex after we met, or so he said. Seems he was busy fucking his wife the whole time. I will say this, he is either the best actor in the universe or he really was desolated to lose me.

Maybe he doesn't like starting over. Honestly, Stay, I have no idea what to believe anymore. I feel numb, which I guess is a vast improvement from being one step away from hell."

"Do you give him any credit for being honest? It couldn't have been easy to answer those questions."

I stared at him in wonder and said, "He says he has never lied to me. Maybe he didn't outright lie but he certainly left me with impressions that weren't true. To answer your question, no, he gets no credit for it. So many times he told me he wished he could spend his life with me, and that his commitment to his marriage was just for his kids. I've been a colossal idiot, not seeing what I didn't want to see, not asking what I didn't really want to know, and deluding myself all the while.

"You know what hurts the most?" I asked.

"That there were others?"

"Yes, that I was one of many and not the only one. It's who he is and that certainly isn't who I hoped he was. Did he play the games like we did with other women? That thought makes me so nauseous I have to push away from it before I fall apart again.

"I'm as angry with myself as I am with him. I let him lead me to believe that what we had was special and like no other experience in his life."

"And you don't believe him?" he asked, taking my hand in his.

Stay's calm energy infused me and I sighed. I squeezed his hand and said, "How can I know? There's no way to know. I doubt he ever loved me. He probably says the same shit to all of us."

"It's hard to know. What games?" He grabbed my leg and arm and pulled me closer to him, draping my legs over his left thigh.

"Don't give me that look. I can already see what's churning in your mind. I hoped you would let that pass once it slipped out."

"It's up to you." He shrugged all innocent like.

"Fine. Role playing." My face and neck flushed hot.

"Like?" He put my hand in his lap and said, "I've never tried it, but I admit to being curious."

"Apparently," I said, feeling his hard erection through his jeans. "Professor and student, massage therapist and client, boss and employee, doctor and nurse, FBI Agent versus spy, and a few others."

He whistled out and said, "I can see the appeal. Your telling me about it turned me on. I'm not sure if it's the idea of it or that you shared it with me."

"Stay, you're like a teenager around me."

He adjusted himself in his pants and said, "You have no idea. If you could see inside my head you would kick me out of your place."

"How is it you're an absolute gentleman and a sexual deviant at the same time?"

"It's my most endearing quality." He laughed. "Stop shaking that head of yours. I'm not sure you even know you're doing it half the time."

"Nice way to segue the conversation," I said, tugging his ear.

"I'm more than happy to stay on the conversation of my hard cock, but I was trying to be sensitive. Since you so desperately want to talk about my bulge ... earlier today, wow, I mean I had high hopes, especially after the kiss in the club, but..."—he tapped his chin—"How can I say this so it comes out right? OC, you shocked me. I thought it would take you awhile to be so loose and receptive but—I'm struggling to be patient and wait to have you again."

"Maybe tomorrow," I said and watched his face transform in front of me into a brilliant smile.

He maneuvered me onto his lap and ravaged my mouth. His gift of mindless passion took me away from myself and allowed me moments of respite. Someday I hoped I could repay him for his friendship and kindness. I wouldn't even allow myself to think in terms of love. Love might never again be mine but thankfully desire still lived close by. And if I was to believe Stay, then I only had to worry about my heart and not his. I would have to trust him on it.

Our feral kiss became so explosive, so intense, I pushed away from him.

"Jesus, Lainie," he said, breathing heavily.

"Me? It's you. What the fuck do you do to me?"

"That, my dear, falls at least half on you."

I just stared at him, my body charged up and pulsating.

"You're shaking your head again."

"I am? I'm going to the bathroom. You, Stay, stay here."

He chuckled at me, and my lack of composure.

I'd clearly lost my mind and moved over to some strange alternate universe. "Clean up your wet pussy and go watch a movie. No more kissing for you, girl," I said to the stranger in the mirror. She didn't look like the Lainie of yesterday.

Back in the living room he said, "Were you talking to yourself?"

"Yes, but she ignored me."

He fell out in hysterical laughter. "I never realized how funny you are."

"Tragedy has a way of doing that to me. You need to keep your lips to yourself for the rest of the night."

"Yes, ma'am," he said, saluting me.

I sat on the couch with some distance between us.

"I know how to behave," he said, drawing me closer.

Pursing my lips, I said, "I call bullshit."

He laughed again. "OC, I love the natural wave of your hair," he said, playing with the ends.

"This is behaving?"

"That is known as a compliment. I also love your long, pale eyelashes that frame your eyes."

I turned his face toward the TV and started *Dogma*. My body melded with the side of his, and I felt grateful for the distraction of the movie.

"OC," I heard in a whisper. "You fell asleep."

"Huh?" I murmured cloudy with slumber.

"Throw your arms around my neck. There you go. Good girl."

I felt my pillow under my head and then blissful quiet.

CHAPTER TWENTY-TWO

Relax My Beloved

by Alex Clare

Sleep might have been my best friend, but the cold light of day was my brutal enemy. As I opened my eyes I had a brief window of reprieve until I realized the man next to me in bed with his arm draped across my waist, his hard cock enlarging and retreating against my thigh was Stay and not Mason. Everything that happened came flooding back and I lost my breath.

I scooted out of the bed and into the bathroom. After peeing and brushing my teeth, I sat on the edge of the sink, trying to decide what to do with Stay, but was not drawing any concrete conclusions, coffee became the priority.

Filling the filter with enough coffee for two and pouring in the allotted water, I flipped on the switch. I heard a noise come from the bathroom as I fought off a world of hurt inside. I zoned-out to the coffee dripping, focusing on the color, aroma, and sound.

"I'm approaching and I don't want to scare you," Stay said as he entered the kitchen sans clothes.

"You're naked," I said, straining not to stare at the semi-hard erection in front of me.

"That's how I sleep. Come back to bed, Lane, I have plans for you. It's still early."

"Did you carry me to bed last night?" I said,

pretending to look at something on the floor by his feet and then glancing up.

"Yeah, we didn't get far into the movie before you fell out." He rubbed his hand over the top of his head and said, "Mornings are hard, right? I'd hoped to make yours much better."

"Stop being so damn nice to me. And you cleaned my kitchen again," I said with an elevated voice. "I hardly merit it. I got what I deserved."

"Would you like me to go?" he asked, his arms held out in question. He looked incredibly adorable, naked in my kitchen, vulnerable and exposed. There was zero artifice with him.

"Yes ... no, I don't know."

"Don't do it, Lainie," he said, taking a step toward me.

"Do what?" I said, hugging the counter against my back.

"Bring up my heart again or hurting me. I take back what I said."

"About?" I curled my hands behind me and held onto the edge of the granite.

He came closer and said, "We can be whatever we are now. I won't pressure you for more."

"You can do friends with benefits?" I asked with real skepticism.

"I never have, but let's give it shot. I understand you need time and frankly if I don't get inside of you soon, I might blow a gasket."

Focusing on his face, I said, "It's amazing how our firmly held resolutions fly out the window with great chemistry."

"You think we have great chemistry?"

"I'm hurting, I'm not dead. I'd have to be blind not to have noticed. Not sure what that matters anyway. You yourself told me powerful chemistry doesn't necessarily mean a healthy match."

"I wasn't talking about us, OC," he whispered, standing way too close.

I cleared my throat and said, "Coffee's ready. Would you like a cup?"

"I'd rather have you first, and then take a shower together."

"I'm not sure I'm ready for that," I said, staring at his inflating cock.

"Which?" he asked, one eyebrow rose. He knew. "The shower can wait, but I hope to change your mind about that too." Closing the short distance between us, he kissed his way from my collarbone up the right side of neck, cradling my head in his hands.

"Do you ever take no for an answer?" I murmured, relaxing into him.

Mumbling against my throat, he said, "You didn't say no, OC."

"Didn't I?" I moaned.

His lips found my pulse and he nipped and sucked there. He tilted my head so he could savor the left side too.

When his lips finally reached mine, he owned me, leading me to his unique rhythm and guiding me through each step until the music became so frantic I had to part from the sensual dance to catch my breath.

"Oh ... give me a ... second," I panted.

And that's about all he gave me. When his mouth moved toward mine again, he escorted me through another melody, and it didn't take long for my natural juices to gather between my thighs.

I let him lead me back to the bedroom, my heart pounding from his near proximity.

"I dreamt of you last night," he said as he pulled my shirt over my head.

My nipples stood out for Stay to see, and his pre-cum beckoned me.

His hand brushed over my buds and I moaned. "I love how your body responds." He ran his hands down my sides, following the curve in at my waist and the flare of my hips. Hooking the elastic of the sweatpants, he slid them down my legs. "I adore every square inch of you and plan to get to know each spot intimately." He dipped down in front of me and kissed my mound and then my belly. With his arms he hugged me to him and sighed against my stomach.

I held his head in my hands, grazing them across his short hair.

"Oh, that feels so good," he said. He gazed up at me, his smile warming my heart. "Come"—he rose up and brought me into the center of the bed—"I have a request."

"Oh?"

"Be present with me," he said.

"That's not a challenge at all. Once you wrap me up in your energy—"

"Our energies," he corrected.

"Okay, our merged energies, I'm transported away from myself and acutely aware of every sensation."

"Perfect."

In the center of the bed, we sat facing each other, my legs over his, his cock resting against my mound. Once our kiss reignited, I left my mind, the world, and nothing mattered other than getting as close to Stay as humanly possible. I circled my legs behind his lower back, and he did the same, grasping me firmly, his hands buried in my hair and mine wrapped around his neck. If I could, I'd climb inside of him and stay there for months, allowing his love to repair the gaping hole in my heart. In his arms, I felt scared and saved, all joined into one strange concoction.

"You smell so good. I'm fighting with myself about where to go first," he said, dipping is fingers in my swollen labia. He licked them and we both groaned. "No one tastes like you, Lainie, so heady, musky, sweet, and salty all at once."

"I want you inside me," I said, raising my hips over his lap. "I don't know if I can take all of you so—"

"We'll go slowly," he said, helping me to lower down.

"Oh ... oh ... fuck," I said, my eyes opened wide.

He chuckled and said, "Damn, woman, you're so tight."

Gazing down between us, I said, "I'm thinking it's more that you're immense."

"Oh, Jesus. We might have to start all our sex with my cock down your throat first. Get you soaking wet."

"Very funny." I lifted my hips and settled back down again, but wasn't making much headway.

"The first time we make love, I want it to be phenomenal for us both. I have an idea." He maneuvered me onto my back and lowered me down onto the bed."

I reached and tapped him on the shoulder. "Your cock is too far away."

"Shh, OCDC, trust me." Once his tongue touched my pussy, I shut up. He licked around my entrance and then sucked gently on my labia. He pushed my thighs back and knees wide. His teases to my clit caused a flood of wetness. "There," he said. He moved up on the bed and positioned his cock at my entrance. "Are you ready to try again?"

I wanted him inside in the worst possible way and told him yes with my eyes.

"Me too," he said, slowly breaching my pussy.

"More," I moaned.

"Okay." He lowered his weight onto me and said, "There you go, relax for me. You'll get used to me in no time."

"I'll never get used to you."

"With all my heart, I hope that's true."

Our eyes locked in a different way and our breathing became synced. He rolled his hips going deeper with each down stroke.

"Can you take more? I'm almost there."

"Take it."

"Don't say if—"

I grasped his ass and he got the message.

He paused, once fully immersed, and said, "Jesus, Lane, I could stay here forever."

"I'd rather you start moving," I said with a cheeky smile of my own.

"Your wish, and all of that." He kissed the tip of my nose and then lightly bit my lower lip. Slowly and sensually he moved his shaft in, swiveling his hips, and eased out with equal precision.

My body better accommodated him with each stroke.

He took me by surprise when he manhandled me back onto his lap, facing him. He had slipped out slightly.

I lowered down onto him and had an easier time of it.

He wrapped his arms tightly around me and carried some of the weight of my up and down movement, controlling our pace. "This way ... I can easily—" He swept me up in another sweltering kiss.

I could finally touch his smooth, tan skin and I did. I caressed my hands down his back and then trailed up his neck. With one hand I stroked his head.

He broke off the kiss. "I love when you do that."

"I can tell. You can go harder."

"I don't want to hurt you. Lay down with me. Let me spoon you from behind, that way I can pound into you like we both need."

Side by side, my back to his, he entered me with a forceful thrust.

"Oh yes," I groaned.

"Kiss me, Lainie. I need to see those eyes."

I shifted my upper body and turned my face to him.

He curled his arms around my shoulders and gave me exactly what I need.

"Take me, Stay, please."

And he did, over and over again. I thought of nothing but the feel of his cock stretching me and the thick head of his shaft rubbing my G-spot on each stroke. "I'm close," I croaked through the breath I held.

"Connect with my breath again," he said as he slowed his incursion. "There, that's good. I want to take you really hard. Are you ready?"

"Pleeease!"

"Hang on." He pounded against me, gripping me tight, and I reveled in the force. "Look at me," he ordered.

I turned my body slightly, laying more of my weight against him. He lifted my top leg and penetrated even deeper. His body's energy permeated my back, his blue eyes captivating my soul, and his cock stretching me to new depths.

"Now," I screamed. I shot out of myself, away from all that reality had waiting for me. I sailed in the clouds above, praying, hoping, and begging never to come back down.

As soon as his orgasm began to fire, I was yanked back into my body for another stormy release.

"Lainie," he grunted. He jerked repeatedly until he finally stilled. Then he started laughing.

"What?" I demanded, spinning in his arms to face him.

"Relax, OCDC, I loved every damn second of it. You just continue to amaze me, is all."

"That's simply because you expected me to be different."

He gathered my hair behind my back and said, "That's definitely part of it and after we make love another twenty times this week, I'm sure I'll get over it."

"Twenty times?"

"Don't get bogged down with the details, OC. We can shoot for thirty if you'd like." He winked.

"The other part?"

"I'll tell you another time when I don't think it will send you running in the other direction. Friends with benefits, remember?" He twitched his eyebrows in mirth but then his expression transformed. He mesmerized me with another deep kiss and when he pulled back, he said, "Shower?"

My heart dropped when I realized what I really needed was time alone. "Stay," I started.

"Your expression says everything. I'll get going." He moved to get up and I caught his arm.

"Please don't be upset with me. Please. I ... I ... this time with you ... I would never trade it for the world. You have been so incredible to me in every way conceivable. If you truly think you can do friends with benefits, I want to. This isn't 'get lost' this is, I need time to myself."

He hugged me to him and said, "I understand. When can I see you again?"

"Can we play it by ear? I'd like to spend tonight alone but maybe Tuesday after work."

"I'd prefer my place. I have a few things I like to show you."

"Okay, your place, Tuesday night." I didn't know if I'd be ready by then but I also understood I couldn't put him off indefinitely.

He stood up and began to dress. "And on Wednesday? What do we say to everyone?"

"Um, I haven't thought about that. I haven't even had a chance to talk to Jacqs."

His energy shift became intensely apparent.

"How about we tell them the truth? I'd rather not share about Mason but more about us."

He smiled. "I'm good with that."

"Your energy has changed."

"It's going to take some getting used to for me. The on and off." He sat down on the bed and pulled on his socks.

"I don't understand. I thought you said that you and Karen spent plenty of time apart."

He looked up and said, "That's because I wanted to."

"Oh, I see."

"I'm not good at giving the control away."

I laughed. "I completely understand. We'll sort it out along the way. Please give me a hug before you go. I'm sure you understand that I need time to process everything."

"Yes, I do and that's what worries me."

My hand in his, we walked to the front door. We embraced and Stay rocked me back and forth just like my dad always did. When we separated, he said, "I won't reach out unless I hear from you. I'll miss you." He touched my cheek, and left.

Saying goodbye to Stay hurt way more than it should have. I poured myself a cup of coffee and used the bathroom. With my robe around me, I went out onto the balcony. Cigarette in hand and coffee set by my feet, I stared out at the table that Mason and I had sat at the night before. The last twenty-four hours felt more like a month had passed. Filled with such a jumble of emotions, I couldn't sort out how I really felt.

Back inside, I planned to climb into bed but decided to strip the sheets instead. It would be hard to concentrate with Stay's scent and the smell of sex in the room. Once I had remade the bed, I pulled my journal onto my lap.

The push and pull of emotions has successfully made me numb. I know Stay has helped. My heart has been shattered and there's no Mason to come back and glue the pieces together again. Stay is like a splint, which won't be able to hold it together forever.

Jacqs will tell me I need to grieve and move through all five steps. I'm pretty sure I've moved past the denial and isolation stage. It might be more accurate to say I was catapulted over them and into the anger stage. In my case, the denial had been going on for a long time. My first stage should be called, harsh reality and having your face smashed into it. There is nothing to bargain with, so stage three is a wash too. I guess I can look forward to stage four: depression. Oh joy!

Where is the devastation stage? I think I've already passed anger and am staunchly into self-pity. Why had I, how had I, deluded myself so effectively? I truly believed Mason loved me, which shows my utter stupidity. There is dumb and then there is dumb-ass dumb, and the latter would be me. How could a man like him love someone like me anyway? I was a convenient distraction from his life, and I guess he was the same for me.

Where the hell do I insert Stay into this mess? Aren't I a selfish bitch if I don't take his heart into account? He deserves far better than me, that's for sure. Seems like Blue and/or Sam would be a better choice for him.

I can't discount that he turned the worst day of my life into something incredible and memorable. But how flawed is that? So flawed. When I look back it's not like I can cut out the part of my shattered heart.

I still love Mason. How fucked up is that? I like Stay— and the man is sexy as hell. Who knew he had it in him. Apparently I've surprised him as well. His cock! I could go on about that for days. I never thought I could enjoy a man so endowed, but I'll be damned if he didn't show me otherwise. He's such a considerate lover, and a dominating one too. My pussy is twitching just thinking about his cock down my throat again. Maybe I should just be grateful for the distraction. It's hard not to feel guilty about it though.

When I'm not being dumb-ass dumb, I can be aware. Stay loves me. Like Mason said, no man does the things he has done for me, to me, and not love the one he's doing them for. Is it fair for me to continue forward with him when I doubt I will ever love him back?

He keeps telling me not to worry about him, but how do I do that?

I wonder if I'll hear from Mason again. I know I made it clear that I didn't want to but it doesn't keep me from wondering.

It's already so late and I need to jump in the shower and go to work. This is the first time that I'm not looking forward to it. I'd rather find a cave I can climb in and lick my wounds.

Don't forget to call dad. Consider checking your messages and checking in with Jacqs. Somehow talking about all that happened is the last thing I want to do. Another gift from Stayman: someone who already knows everything.

I got ready for work then heated up a small bowl of Stay's chicken soup. After a few spoonfuls I gave up. My stomach wasn't having anymore. I finished my coffee and checked my phone. I missed four calls: two from Stay from the night before, one from Jacqs, and one from my father. Also, I had seven texts: two from Stay, three from Mason, one from Bond, and one from Blue.

> **MM:** I hope at some point, when your anger has subsided, that you'll give me a chance to explain. I love you with all my heart and I'm so sorry for all the hurt and
> **MM:** anger you are going through because of me. You are the last person in the world I would ever want to hurt and I know I will never get over it or you.
> **MM:** For the rest of my life, no matter how much time passes, I will be here for you. You can call me or text me anytime, day or night. Miss you so desperately.

"Jesus H. Christ!" Reading those texts was a dumb-ass dumb thing to do. I deleted them so I wouldn't be inclined to reread them and obsesses over his words. "Fuck!" I screamed.

From Bond I received:

> **Bond:** Have you heard from Stay? Is he with you?

To Stay I texted:

> **Me:** Bond was looking for you. Have you touched base with him?
> **Stayman:** You miss me already? :D Yes and I told him all about how I ravaged your body. He asked for details and I declined. :P
> **Me:** You better not have!!!

Stayman: Not to worry, OCDC. I did however tell him that I stayed over at your place and wasn't paying attention to my phone.

Me: Good grief!

Stayman: I thought I wouldn't be hearing from you for a good thirty-six hours. That didn't take you long.

Me: Gloating again? I was just passing along a message!

Stayman: I miss you too.

Me: I've got to go.

Me: Wait

Stayman: What now, OC?

Me: Thank you so much for the soup. It's delicious. I think I'll be living on it for the next few days.

Stayman: My pleasure.

Me: Goodbye, Stayman.

Stayman: Goodbye, sweetheart. If you're pussy starts aching for me like my cock aches for you all the time, you know where to find me.

Me: You're incorrigible. Now leave me alone!

Stayman: Yes ma'am.

I shook my head and that time I was very aware of it. The last text from Blue said:

Blue: Sorry we ditched you for so long. See you Wednesday?

I texted her back:

Me: No worries. See you Wednesday.

I decided I would call Jacqs on the way to work and call my father later.

Once in my Saturn Sky, I hit dial on my speaker phone.

"Hey, girl," Jacqs said when she answered.

"You have a minute?"

"Yeah, I'm at my desk. I apologize that we got separated for so long yesterday. Next year just you and I can go."

I made a left turn and said, "I doubt I will ever go to that art fair again."

"Oh, you didn't enjoy it? Was the music bad?"

"Jacqs?"

"Yeah?"

"I have something to tell you, well a lot but I really don't have it in me to go into a lot of detail right now. Okay?" I stopped at a red light waiting to make a right turn.

"You're scaring me."

"I don't mean to. The Reader's Digest is that in Delray I saw Mason with his wife and family."

I heard her gasp and then she asked, "Shit! Did he see you?"

"No. To make a very long, godawful story short, I ended it with him yesterday."

I heard her blow air out, in relief maybe. "There's more, I can tell."

"Stay. Stay came and got me from the fair and well—"

"You're having sex with Stay? Get the fuck out of town. That's fantastic. How was it?"

"In some ways it's off-the-charts incredible but—" I pulled in behind the shop and turned off the car.

"But?"

"He has agreed to a friends with benefits arrangement. He is so nice to me, and I'm worried about hurting him.

He says that's for him to worry about."

"I agree with him. Hang on a second." I heard her cover the phone and say something. She continued, "Plus you never know, Lainie, you might just fall in love with him. Are you coming out to the get together on Wednesday?"

"Do you need to go?"

"You're not getting off the phone that easily. Finish!" she demanded.

"I have to assume it will be fairly obvious that Stay and I are together. Letting people know then is the plan."

"Whoop, whoop! I can't be happier for you! Please, can I tell Aidan?"

Shaking my head again, I realized Stay was right. I did it a lot. "Yes, you can tell him. Listen, I'm at the shop and need to go inside. I'll see you Wednesday if we don't talk before."

"Love you, girl. I'm going to barge into Aidan's office and tell him now."

I chuckled and said, "Love you too."

I placed my bag down in the office and walked out into the shop.

"Hey, Lainie, I love your hair like that. Did you put waves in it?" Sam asked, walking over to me.

"This is my natural hair. I usually blow it straight. I didn't feel like taking the time today. Same for the casual dress and no makeup."

"You look great. I hope you were late because you were getting the good stuff in bed."

That I could possibly look good had to be some sort of magic. "My lips are sealed."

"Come on! You're so secretive. I'm trying to live vicarious through you. Jacqs tells me nothing."

"Lucky you. Jacqs often wants to tell me too much."

Samantha laughed.

"I'll tell you one, well two things, but no questions afterwards."

She pretended to turn a key over her lips.

"No more MM, and Stay and I are ... casually dating."

"Oh, lucky you. He is one hot man and so into you. Plus, he's one of the good guys."

"He's ... I don't know what he is other than extremely persistent."

We laughed together and then the air got caught in my throat. I wanted, needed, to be alone.

"Why don't you take the rest of the day off? You have been filling in for me so often lately, you deserve it."

"Are you sure? I could surprise Sarah and take her to the park for a picnic. Thankfully it's not hot like it was yesterday."

"Go for it. Enjoy."

She stepped toward me tentatively and I met her halfway for a hug. "Thank you, Lainie, and not just for the time off," she said as she stepped back.

Once she left, I sighed out and breathed a little easier. Samantha was great but I didn't feel up to engaging in idle chitchat. The store had little traffic after lunch, and I spent my time on mindless tasks. I sorted through the inventory in the back, refolded shelf after shelf in the shop although it really didn't need it, and I scrubbed out the bathroom even though I have cleaners come in twice a week. With my ear out for the door, I straightened and wiped down my office too.

Bella Boutique looked great by the time I got ready to leave. After entering the numbers for the night, I headed home.

Nothing earth shattering happened that night, thankfully. I smoked a couple of cigarettes, ate a bowl of Stay's chicken soup, and watched *The Voice*. I didn't even feel like journaling. For a moment, as I was falling asleep, I wished I could be one of those people who climbed into bed and didn't get out for days.

My mother didn't tolerate such nonsense. To her catching a cold and giving into it was a major weakness. The walking wounded I had down to a science.

Just before the edge of oblivion overtook me, I thought of Stay and wondered if I'd feel the same about him when I saw him at his place tomorrow.

CHAPTER TWENTY-THREE

Dark Paradise

by Lana Del Rey

At work on Tuesday I felt on edge the entire day. I hadn't contacted Stay and even with all that had happened, part of me was waiting to hear from Mason. Stay said that Mason wouldn't give up easily and yet it felt like he had. His lack of communication felt like further rejection. Rationally I understood that hearing from Mason would make matters worse but that didn't keep me from craving any kind of sign that he was still thinking of me.

I missed him and the idea of us. The Lainie from the days of Mason had perished and I missed her too. In some ways Stay felt like a Band-Aid, a sweet, sexy, considerate, masculine kind of first aid. Almost like candy that was slightly too sweet. I certainly didn't have the willpower to resist because in his arms I enjoyed orgasmic abatement from my anguish.

When my phone chimed I ran to the back to check it.

> **Stayman:** You've exhausted my patience so please forgive the intrusion. What time will you be here?
> **Me:** Around eight. I'm not exactly sure how to get there. Should I pick up some food on the way?
> **Stayman:** Why don't I pick you up? Got food

covered.

Me: That's silly. Why pick me up?

Stayman: Did you pack clothes for tomorrow?

Me: Yes.

Stayman: Then I'll come get you and I can drive you back in the morning.

Me: Why?

Stayman: Then you are my captive and can't run off in the middle of the night. You're shaking your head, right?

Me: I am. You've conveniently forgotten that I took a cab from your place last time.

Stayman: Well then, I'll just tie you to the bed. And STOP shaking that pretty head of yours.

Me: Fine. Seven thirty and thanks.

Stayman: Oh, and OC…

Me: Yes…

Stayman: I have plans for you.

Me: You'll have to catch me first.

Stayman: The trap is already set.

Me: Let me finish up so I'm ready by the time you get here.

Stayman: I'm on my way.

Damn the man for being so darn charming and cunning. With him I felt sure I'd experience something new. That potential already had me turned on and hungering for his touch. The perils of emotional involvement had me dreading it in equal measure.

I turned off the lights in the shop and headed back into the office to grab my bag and purse.

The bell rang on the back door.

"Coming," I yelled. I flipped off the computer screen

and then the office light.

After locking the door behind me, I took in Stay's appearance. He wore jeans and had on a very nice sateen turquoise dress shirt.

"You let your hair dry naturally," he said, fingering the ends of my light-brown hair.

"Don't let it go to your head."

"You're beautiful, Lainie, and it always goes to my head."

I couldn't help myself. I glanced at the front of his jeans.

"Come on, OC, it's already getting late and there's still lots to do."

"To do?"

"Plus I ran you a steaming hot bath and I don't want the water to get too cold. Let's go." He took my hand and opened the passenger door to the Corvette. "You're chariot awaits." He waved me in.

We rode with the top down, music blasting, my hair flying in every direction, and I was able to relax into the wind. I rarely put the top down on my own car and it was nice to experience it with another.

"You don't have to dress up for me, Stay," I said as he pulled into the garage under his building.

"Do you like this shirt?"

"Well, yes," I said, touching the fabric.

"Do you like me in this shirt?"

"Of course. It makes your eye color even more intense."

"Just because we're casual dating, doesn't mean we shouldn't make an effort. Just like you leaving your hair wavy for me." He came around to my side of the car and helped me out. "I can't wait any longer," he said, taking me into his arms.

His kiss bore into me, ferrying me away from my problems and into his energy field. In his arms he at once infused me with strength and weakened my resolve. Breaking away from me, he said, "We need to stop or I'm going to take you on top of my car. Jesus, woman, it's like you cast this spell over me and my need to take you roughly surfaces with such force that I have to fight against it."

"Who asked you to fight it?" I said, stepping back and straightening my shirt.

"Don't say shit you don't mean, OC. I mean it."

I stared at him. Neither of us smiled. Truth be told, I wanted him to fuck me and fuck me hard. It was far easier to take than being made love to. His domination allowed me to escape to a safe place, away from the realties I had to face. The sweet stuff just left me feeling guilty as if I were cheating on Mason and deliberately hurting Stay.

"I mean it," I said.

He opened his mouth and then shook his head. "You're bath awaits."

Inside, I heard soft music playing. After removing my shoes, Stay brought me into his bedroom. He unbuttoned my top and stepped behind me to remove my bra. With his hands he caressed the surface of my back and neck. He flipped me around and tickled up my stomach to my breast.

I had to push away from his intense expression. On my knees, I unbuttoned his jeans and pulled them off.

"Lainie," he said, looking down on me.

"I need to taste you," I said, tugging on the boxer shorts that were in my way. Once I sucked his cock into my mouth, I risked peering up at him again.

"I know what you're doing. Oh Jesus, it's working. Lainie, come on, let's bathe together."

I rested down on my heels and said, "As sweet as that sounds, can we please fuck first and clean up later. I promise I'll be more relaxed by then."

"Why, Lainie?"

"You're asking a question you really don't want the answer to. Now take me and take me hard."

His chest moved up and down rapidly. I could see him struggle between what his body wanted and what he thought was right. He clinched my hair in his hands yanking my head back. I opened my mouth, staring up at him. He forcefully sluiced in and out of my throat a few times and I groaned around him. Still holding onto my hair, he pulled me to my feet and led me over to the couch. "Goddamn it, Lainie, I wanted to introduce you to the tantric chair in a different way." He roughly bent me over the high end of the chair, my hips over the top, just barely on my tiptoes.

He plunged into my wetness without mercy and I cried out, "Yesss ... don't stop." His cock banged against my cervix and I welcomed the pain. "More, harder," I yelled.

My hair in one fist, my shoulder gripped in the other, he thrust rapidly and I could tell he was angry. Wholly turned on, but pissed off too.

I didn't care. I lifted my feet off the ground, the chair holding my weight and spread my knees wider apart.

He grunted when he finally hit all the way home.

My orgasm threatened as he split me wide with his girth and speared me with his length. "Don't stop. Stay, don't stop. Oh please ... I'm ... going to come!"

He pounded through my release and then pushed off of me. His hand rubbed across his short hair as he paced away from me and then back. His engorged cock stood at attention, not lessening in the least. "Goddamn it!"

"Would you please relax?" I said, reaching out to touch his leg as he paced by again. I stood up and faced him.

"I feel like..." he started.

"Like?"

"I could hurt you with my intense need," he confessed.

"If you mean your pulsing cock, I can handle it. If you mean your emotions, then I'm at a loss."

"My way this time," he said, sitting on the couch, his back against the high end, and his legs on the floor on either side. He drew me to him and I straddled his lap. "This position is going to be deeper so let me know if it's too much."

He was right. The angle of the chair slanted my hips in perfect alignment with his cock. As much as I fought the sensuality before, it felt exquisite having his hands softly caressing my ass and back, through my hair and over my shoulders, while the front of me lay atop of his. The chair allowed us to kiss with ease, my hands fondling his head and neck.

Then he flipped us around so my back was against the chair. In an elevated missionary, with his feet on the ground, the position gave him leverage to grind his hips into me. Resting my head on the top of the chair arch, I swiveled my pelvis into his thrusts. I watched as Stay tugged on my hard nipples. He then folded my legs under his arms as he continued to penetrate my pussy in a slow, sultry rhythm. I held the back of his head, our eye contact absolute.

"You feel so good, Lane. Thank you for letting me take my time."

"This ... time, oh yes ... this time."

"I could do this forever ... just like this. Can you feel—you're so wet."

"Don't stop," I said, kissing him deeply, circling my arms around his back.

He laid his hands on the top of the chair on either side of my head and increased his propulsion.

"Stay."

"What, sweetheart?"

"Ohhh!"

"I feel it. Look at me."

And I did. I cried out staring deeply into his eyes, tears blurring my vision.

He demanded that I open myself to him in a way that scared the hell out of me, but oh, it felt so damn good too.

I convulsed around his shaft again and groaned, feeling so utterly full. "I've never felt—"

"Me either." With one arm around my waist and another around my back, he helped me to move up and down on him until he came, and came, and came. His face contorted in extreme ecstasy as he grunted out, "Lainie." When his orgasm subsided, he fell against me, his lips to mine.

We kissed and caressed until we both settled back to earth.

"Shall we bathe?" he asked.

"Sure. I can see why you like this chair."

"You haven't seen much yet. There are several other interesting positions we can try." He got up and held out his hand to me.

I let him pull me up and usher me to the bathroom.

"I'll let some of the water out and turn on the hot water."

"Candles?" he asked. Three large candles sat on the outer ledge of the tub.

"Sure," I said. "I rarely take the time for a bath. This is a special treat." I lit the candles and once the water temperature was right, we got in.

I leaned against him as he leisurely washed my skin with a washcloth.

"What was going on when you first got here?" he asked casually.

"Do we have to talk about that?" I glanced at him over

my shoulder and then turned back around.

"Yes we do. I believe in honesty and transparency and whether we are friends or more, we should be able to talk about anything or ask each other anything. Holding it back just leads to lack of authenticity in a relationship."

"You mean like me and Mason."

"No, OC, I wasn't referring to you but speaking generally."

"Okay. You asked for it." I took a deep breath and spit it out, "Sex with you, you demand so much. Too much. When we fuck, and it feels incredible by the way, I can get lost in the fierce sensation without involving my heart. When we..."

"Make love?"

"Yes, that. You rip my heart open and strip me bare," I said.

"I do what?"

"At least that's how it feels to me," I said, watching my hand as I swirled it in the water.

"Interesting."

"Interesting? All you're going to say is interesting?" I spun around in the tub and rested back on the opposite end.

"I wasn't finished. It feels the same for me and different than it has with anyone else. The major difference is that I can't get enough of it, and you want to run away from the feeling."

"Do you blame me?"

He lifted my foot into his lap and massaged it. "Given what you've recently been through, not at all. But you should know, I don't know how to do things part way. If you really want a fucking, after tonight you're going to get it. Just be sure you know what you're bargaining for."

"And what would that be?" My heart beat a bit faster.

"Your submission, Lainie. I will take you how I want. I'm not into pain so I will never intentionally hurt you, but when things get rough, it can happen."

"Your words are making my pussy pulse," I blatantly admitted.

"I've never known anyone like you," he said, working his thumbs into my arch.

"How do you mean?"

"For one, I don't think you realize how passionate you are. You have this innocence about you and yet when you're lost in sex, you lose it entirely. It's sexy as hell."

"Thank you," I said, embarrassed by his words.

"That's exactly what I mean. You're blushing."

"I don't mean too," I said.

"That's that beauty in it." He switched to my other foot and said, "If you're serious about submitting to me, then we need to talk about a few things."

"Why did my stomach just drop?"

He massaged between my toes and said, "Maybe you know what I'm going to ask. Have you submitted to Mason?"

"I'm not sure." I shrugged.

"Have you let him spank you?"

"Yes." That was an easy one, I thought.

"Whip you?"

"No, but he has used a paddle." I worried that my answer would upset him but he still seemed calm.

"Okay. Has he tied you up?"

"Once during one of our games." I felt the pulse in my neck.

"How?"

"You want me to tell you how?" My respiration increased.

"Yes."

I eyed him and then said, "My arms were handcuffed

behind my back and over a chair and my ankles were tied to the legs."

"Do you feel they were tied securely?"

"My feet?"

He nodded.

"No."

"Did you have anal sex with Mason?"

My eyes widened. "I've never had anal sex."

"Anal play?"

I shook my head and said, "No."

"How does your pussy feel now?"

"Very hot."

"Good."

"Are we done?" I asked.

"No. Did you have rough sex with Mason?" He used my foot to drag me to him, situating me onto his lap, his legs straight out underneath me. His hard cock bobbed behind my back.

"Maybe during two role playing scenarios, but I don't know if you would think so."

He spread my thighs and dipped his fingers past my labia. He whispered into my ear, "You're already mine. You just haven't accepted it yet."

His assertion caused my nipples to flare, and my clit to twitch.

"I'm going to let some of the water out so I can better play with your pussy. Tell me about the two scenes."

"The first, professor/student, he held my head down against the desk as he paddled me and then fucked me from behind."

Stay lightly pinched his way up one thigh and down the other, making me squirm. "Did it make you come?"

"Yesss," I said.

"And the other?" He bit my shoulder and continued to pinch closer to my pussy.

"Um, spy versus FBI agent. That's the one where he tied me up. He spanked me and fucked me hard from behind. He was mad about you."

"Interesting. Did you come?" he asked as he tugged on my labia.

"Ahhh ... yes."

"Was I on your mind too?" He yanked on the other side.

"Yes, but I didn't want you there."

He abandoned my pussy and began working on my nipples. "And now?" He squeezed harder than before.

"I want you inside me over and over again."

"Oh, I will be and more, Lainie. I'll penetrate you in every way known to man." One hand twisted my nipple until I cried out and the other snaked down to my saturated pussy. "See how wet you get for me."

"Yesss."

"Think this over. If you submit to me, I'm going to take your ass. Do you know what that means?" He plunged two fingers into my entrance, his thumb making a trail around my pussy.

"Yes, I think I do."

"Your clit is so hard, it's poking out and pulsing under my thumb. Tell me what I mean."

"You're going to fuck my ass with your cock."

"Yes, that's exactly what I'll do." He circled around my bud and I moaned as I thrashed about in his lap.

"Will you tie me up?"

"No, because your submission will be so much sweeter when you give it to me without restraint. It's a gift of immense trust and you will find it has its own kind of intimacy."

"Oh, Stay, that feels so good."

He teased my clit and said, "I want to hear you say that you've never gotten this wet for another. Never so hot."

Over my shoulder, I said, "Never, Stay. I'm so aroused by you I'm shaking."

"Stand up," he ordered.

I stood in what was left of the bath water. He dried me off and helped me out of the tub. After drying himself, he grabbed a towel, and circled his arms around me. He walked me over to the bed.

"Are you hungry?" he asked.

"No."

"Lay down for me and put your ass on the towel, all the way to the edge of the mattress. There, that's good." He opened the drawer and retrieved a bottle of oil. "Spread your legs wide and to the sides. Nice. Your pussy is beautiful and still shiny from your juices.

"What are you going to do to me?"

"Give you a small taste of what you will get if you decide to submit to me." He lowered down on the carpet on the side of the bed.

I piled two fluffy pillows under my head so I could see what he planned to do to me.

He coated two fingers in oil and lowered his mouth to my pussy, licking up my juices. His coated fingers rubbed around my anus but didn't penetrate. "You taste so good, OC." He climbed over me, his hard cock hanging down, and kissed me deeply. His tongue grazed below my bottom lip, catching some of my essence that his mouth had lay there. After nipping my bottom lip, he said, "You continually challenge my restraint."

He knelt back down and resumed his oral and tactile treatments. As he continued to pass back and forth over my anal opening it relaxed and then reflexively tightened up again. Then he lightly sucked on my clit and wiggled a finger into my bum.

"Ohhh..."

"Do you like it?" he asked, holding his finger still.

"I don't know," I said honestly.

"Well, Lane, hang on because we're about to find out." He forced more of his finger inside and moved it around. With his head raised, he said, "Oh you like it. Your pussy just spurted come on my face. So hot."

Then I lost myself in the sensations eddying through me, gripping the comforter beneath me with both fists. The one finger in my anus shifted and pressed while the other caressed around the rim. His tongue, his blessed tongue, choreographed its soft sensuous dance around my clit and into my wetness. The duel sensations had me at the edge of a riotous climax.

He stopped and said. "I know you're close. You will take another finger first."

I rapidly shook my head back and forth.

"Oh, OCDC, but you will. Breathe out slowly for me. There you go." And then he inserted another finger.

I felt so stretched and full, I had no idea how I would ever take his cock inside of me. "Ohhh ... ahhh ... oh, oh, oh." My whole body arched, every muscle stretched and as he continued to penetrate my ass with his fingers, I screamed, "Fuuuck!" The shocking intensity had me panting and twisting as my release clutched and racked me over and over again.

"That was spectacular. It will take all of my willpower to take you slowly when the time comes."

He held me as I hummed in the afterglow.

"You're turn," I said with a yawn.

"You will pay me back tomorrow when I ask."

"Okay," I mumbled.

"I'm going to eat something and be right back to snuggle you close."

I must have dozed off.

When Stay came back, he spooned me to him and I struggled to fall back asleep.

I lay there, trying to let sleep find me again, but visions of Mason's face felt branded on my brain: the tears in his eyes, his desperate expression, and his attempt to get me to stop and listen to him. Quietly, I lifted the covers and rummaged into my bag for my T-shirt and boy shorts. I set and plugged in my phone and then slipped out of the room.

In Stay's office/meditation room, I found an unused notebook and a pen. In the living room, I settled on the couch facing the windows and started to journal with Rusty purring at my side.

I was so angry at Mason that I couldn't get past the hurt to hear what he wanted to say. I couldn't get past my own hurt to see that he was hurting too. Maybe I should have listened to him. Maybe he really did love me.

Each time I feel Stay pulling me closer to him, I feel my heart reaching back for Mason. The horrible mental tug-of-war is leaving me completely off-kilter.

I can see what's going on here, the bargaining stage, and yet I can't stop it. And if I am bargaining, that means depression is still to come. What the fuck? If I'm not depressed yet, I can't even imagine. I know Mason didn't die but it sure feels like a death. He's dead and gone from my life, and I'm the one who chose it.

Here I'm contemplating submitting to Stay while my heart is still so wrapped up with Mason. How do I heal and reconcile the past when I'm so caught up in something new. How do I move onto something new while I'm so caught up in the past? How can I possibly still want Mason, need his touch, when what Stay offers me is far more intense and captivating? And he's not married, is kind, sexy as hell, desires me, and his cock—wow. I thought I would never enjoy one so large, but I was so wrong.

I don't hold my breath with Stay. What does that mean? I think it's more like our breathing gets in sync so don't end up holding it in. Still, it seems odd.

I can't believe I let him play with my ass but I have to admit—

"What are you doing?" Stay said, squinting at the light coming from the floor lamp.

I was startled, and felt like I was caught doing something wrong. "Journaling. I tried not to wake you."

"I rolled over to pull you toward me and you weren't there. I became concerned you left again."

"I'm still here."

"As I see." He flashed me a sleepy grin. "Come to bed and I'll massage your back until you fall asleep."

Leaving the journal on the coffee table, I let him lead me back to bed.

CHAPTER TWENTY-FOUR

Love Love Love

by Of Monsters and Men

I awoke to the sun shining in from the wall of windows. The empty bed beside me took me by surprise. Tiptoeing through the apartment, I found Stay meditating naked in front of his altar. Backing out slowly, I headed to the bathroom for a shower.

Once dressed, I wandered to the kitchen in search of food. I finally felt hungry. "Oh, that smells good."

"Sit at the table and I'll bring the food over." He wore a short plaid robe, and I guessed nothing else underneath. "Would you like some orange juice with your coffee?"

"Just some water please. Are you sure I can't help?"

"Be right there." He carried a tray over to the table and deposited our plates and beverages.

"I'm starving," I said.

"That's a good sign." He leaned over, gave me a quick kiss, and sat down beside me, facing the windows.

"Thank you so much for last night and this meal. Is this turkey bacon?" I asked.

"Yes. I don't eat any mammal," he said, sticking a piece of bacon into his mouth.

"I haven't heard that one before. So you're not a vegetarian, but won't eat mammals. Clearly you eat eggs and cheese. Is that Gouda in the eggs? Yummy and smoky."

"Yes it is. Good sense of taste. I also eat seafood and poultry."

"Of course you do." I chuckled slightly, remembering our dinner out.

"How are you feeling this morning?" He rested his elbow on the back of my chair and held the nape of my neck.

My nipples responded to his touch. Trying to ignore it, I said, "My pussy feels well used, which I like, and I'm okay over all."

"Can I read your journal from last night?"

I practically spit out the coffee in my mouth. "I don't let anyone read my journal."

"You leave it out on your nightstand. You don't think Mason ever had a look?" He took a sip of coffee.

"It's called privacy, something I think you and I value differently."

"So I won't like what you wrote?" he asked.

"No," I said, my lips pursed in annoyance. Why did he have to keep bringing Mason up? In anger, I said, "Fine, go read it."

"You're mad," he stated.

I looked up at him and took another bite of the bacon.

He brought the journal over and read the passage. "So I'm sexy as hell and what we have is more intense. I can live with that. There goes your head shaking again. Just say what you're thinking."

"And the rest of what I wrote?"

He caressed my knee. "OC, sweetheart, I know you still need to grieve Mason, which is why I agreed to keep things casual."

"This doesn't feel casual."

"It's whatever we make it. If you need space, just tell me."

I tried to assess the truth in his words. "Okay. Tonight

I plan to sleep at home alone. We can meet up at Red's in our own cars."

"Sounds good." He continued eating as if my request was perfectly fine. When he swallowed, he said, "But I will fondle you at Red's in front of everyone."

"That didn't sound like a question."

"It wasn't. Have you thought about submitting to me? I can't think of much else myself. Especially the way your ass took to my fingers. I want inside there." His comments sent my heart racing.

"I ... what if I change my mind?" I noticed my hand trembling and placed my fork down.

"We can always revisit it."

"Okay." I nodded.

"Okay? Are you saying, 'Stay, I want you to use me and take me to places I've never considered'?"

"Yes, Stay, I want you to fuck and use me every way to Sunday. If I didn't have to get to the shop... I'm already wet sitting here."

"How much time do we have?" he asked, opening his robe revealing his straining erection. He didn't wait for my response and gathered all the items on the table back onto the tray and set it on the floor.

I stood and removed my jeans and lace panties. "Not long."

"Lie down and bring your hips to the edge."

I arrived at work fifteen minutes later than usual, but I wasn't the least bit bothered by it. My pussy still felt a bit swollen from our romp on the dining table. The two orgasms he sparked in me still hummed under the surface of my skin. I could get used to regular morning sex.

In the office I checked the mail, email, and paid a few bills. Once I opened the shop, the day flew by.

Over lunch Samantha asked me, "What time are you heading over to Red's?"

"I'll leave here around five or so. Jacqs and I are meeting early to catch up."

She touched my arm and said, "I know you're very private but I'm dying to know. Will you tell the group about you and Stay?"

"I have a feeling he plans to make it very obvious. You're coming right?"

She wrapped up the other half of her sandwich and said, "That sounds like him. Yes, after I put Sarah to bed."

"Great. I might need the support."

She smiled. "You can count on me."

❀ ❀ ❀ ❀ ❀

When I arrived at Red's, I didn't see Jacqs car.

"She's running a bit behind," Red said, pulling the last clean plate out of the dishwasher. His hand made the dinner plate seem like a saucer. His big frame loomed over most things in the space, even me, though we were fairly close in height.

He and Jacqs made quite the pair, her so petite and him so tall and broad.

"Is it just us?" I said, glancing out back.

"Yes. Can I get you something to drink?"

"I'm good. So how are things going with the triad?" I asked.

"Let's go outside and dunk our feet. It's gorgeous out."

"Okay." I slipped off my sandals by the French doors

leading out to the pool and rolled up the bottoms of my jeans.

Red didn't need to worry, his casual attire of khaki shorts and rust-colored T-shirt were perfect for the warm, spring day, and allowed him to sit right down at the edge of the pool without any fuss.

Bordered by palm trees, a large stone deck surrounded the Jacuzzi and pool. His two-story home sat on the Intracoastal Waterway, allowing him to keep his small yacht right behind the house.

We both sat on the edge of the pool, enjoying the sun and slight breeze.

"Everything is going well," Red said, inclining with his arms behind him. "I believe we are all waiting for it to come to a head. Between us, I want to ask Jacqs to marry me. I can't do that until Jacqs and Bond have moved on."

"Good thing you're a patient man." I shuffled my feet in the water.

"I heard Stay stopped being patient."

"Does everyone know?" I felt that I was about to shake my head and stopped myself.

"I think that's a safe assumption. How's that going?"

I slanted my head in his direction and said, "It's a complicated answer to an easy question. I'm not over my previous relationship and—"

"Jacqs told me what happened. Sorry, Lane."

I stared down at my feet in the water. "Yeah, thanks. Does she tell you everything?"

"Another safe assumption. Does it bother you?"

I rocked my head back and forth, deciding. "Not really. I trust it stays with you."

"Always. So Stay? You know Jacqs will grill me later."

"He's an incredible man but sometimes I feel like I'm moving forward in a relationship that I'm not fully in yet.

That didn't make any sense." I made eye contact with Red to see if he got it.

"It makes perfect sense. I've known Stay a long time. When he wants something, he throws his whole self into it."

I kicked my feet and said, "I know. I'm just not in the place where I can do the same."

"You're worried about hurting him."

"Shouldn't I be?" I asked.

"Just be exactly where you are. That's all you can really do, and be honest about it. I believe these things have a way of sorting out. I've never been happier in my life since Jacqs. It wasn't ideal timing but we're managing. Plus you can always trust Stay to be upfront."

"Yeah." I nodded. "To a fault sometimes."

"Agreed. So it's your coming out tonight."

"Apparently it's not necessary since everyone already knows. I'm certain he plans to make it abundantly obvious."

Red touched my arm and said, "Grant him that. He's liked you for a long time."

"You've all turned pining into a fine art," I said.

Red had loved Jacqs for years before he finally made his feelings known.

"Want to help me put the food out? I'd like to check in with Jacqs too." Red stood and grabbed each of us a towel to dry off our legs.

"Sure."

Red and I set up the house for the gathering in companionable silence. The love that he shared with Jacqs was highly enviable, and I wondered if I could love like that or even allow myself to be loved that way. I never had before.

After laying out the spinach dip and veggie platter, I went to the bathroom to check my appearance. I wished Stay would show so I could stop feeling so anxious about being with him with all our friends.

Jacqs finally made it home and after making out with Red while I stared at the floor and ceiling, she waved to me to follow her upstairs.

"I'm going to quickly change," she said, stripping off her work clothes. She threw on a flowery, short, halter dress. "Sit"—she patted the bed beside her—"Have you changed your hair? I really like it."

"I didn't blow it dry this morning. I think I heard the door," I said, sitting down next to her.

"Give me the scoop."

"Ask Red," I said, lying back on the bed and folding my arms underneath my head.

"I'm sure you didn't tell him about the sex. How's the sex?"

I raised an eyebrow and said, "Too good. It's all too much."

She patted me on the thigh and said, "I'm happy for you. Red is too much too, and I love every minute of it. Give it time."

"Uh-huh."

"That sounded like Stay's laugh." She stood up and checked her hair in the mirror.

"Can I hide up here?" I asked, sitting up.

"Buck up, girl, and face the music."

Stay watched me walk down the steps, and before I reached the bottom he swept me up in his arms. "It's good to see you. I missed you today." He then kissed me and I let him. It was no mere peck but a sweltering kiss. He accomplished what he intended—to make me hot and bothered.

"You're a naughty man," I whispered into his ear.

"Just remember you said yes, and you'll get a taste of how naughty I can be."

"Stop that," I said.

"Which part?" He bit my ear lobe and whispered back, "The part that made your nipples hard or the part that caused your neck to flush and your breathing to accelerate?"

"Break it up," Cat said. "Are you going to be all over each other like Red and Jacqs? I'm certain he has an extra room. Use it."

"Cat, I'm *certain* you don't want to use up one of your lives," Stay teased. "I plan to kiss and grope her often."

Cat hung her arm around my waist and said, "Lainie, if you don't put your man in his place early on, trust me, you'll regret it."

"Excuse me. I'm standing right here," Kev said and he didn't look happy. "Just remember whose night it is."

I had a feeling she was to be topped and he planned to show her who was boss.

The evening breeze beckoned us all, so we settled outside with the food and drinks. Stay sat right by my side and was the perfect gentleman. He gave me plenty of space and I didn't feel smothered like I thought I might.

I sat back watching our friends shift from one conversation to another. I really loved all of them, even Bond now too.

"Let's go for a walk," Stay said after we had finished laughing at Bond and his ridiculous impersonation of a dancer at his club.

"Sure."

We walked away from the group, down the short yard, and onto the dark dock that extended out over the Intracoastal Waterway.

He led me to the end of the pier and we sat down, our legs hanging over the edge but not touching the water. He scooted me closer to him, draping my right leg over his left. In his arms, he swept me up in his kiss, seizing my mouth and making me dizzy with lust. He slid my hand into his jeans over his cock. His penetrative stare told me what he wanted.

"Anyone could walk out here. I can hear them laughing."

"Unbutton my pants and take my cock out."

I glanced at his bulge and back at his face. He meant it. So titillated, I did as he asked. I unbuttoned his pants, pushed down the elastic on his boxers, and freed his erection. Scanning around us, I didn't think the people across the water or the house to the right of us could see us in the light reflected from Red's house.

He gathered my hair in his fist and moved my mouth up and down over his shaft. His scent filled my nostrils turning me on and making me light headed. He used my mouth, and I gave myself over to it. In his seated position, he couldn't penetrate my throat like before and I missed it.

He pulled my head off his cock and slammed his lips against mine. Once apart, he said, "I can't get enough of you."

"Your smell, it does something to me," I moaned.

His deep-blue eyes told me he loved me and that he wanted me to know.

"Please don't say it," I silently begged. I needed it to be about sex and not love. "Do you think I will be able to take more of you down my throat next time?"

"Do you want to?"

"I want you to make me wet like you did before. Yes and I want it to feel better for you."

"It couldn't have felt any better. Next time we'll try with some lube. We'll practice now a bit before I fuck you from behind. On your knees." He stood and with my hair still in his hand, he helped me to kneel in front of him. "Are you ready?"

I nodded and swallowed a few times. With my head tilted up, I opened my mouth like a bird.

"You look so sexy like that," he said and then doused into my throat. He held the back of my head and bent his knees down, forcing his cock deeper.

When he pulled out, I said, "More please." The heat in my pussy continued to burn, my lips swollen from the aggression. My saturated panties would have to be removed and stuffed in my bag once I was back inside.

"Just a few more strokes, because I want to explode in your pussy, knowing you're going to carry my come around for the rest of the night. Then he thrust into my throat repeatedly and I felt the gush in my panties. "Stand and bend over," he said. "This won't take long."

I unbuttoned my jeans and exposed my ass to Stay.

He turned me around so we faced the house and bent me at the waist. "Spread your legs wider," he said.

It wasn't easy to accomplish with my jeans down around my calves, but I did my best.

He plunged into me from behind, grasping my hips.

I dropped down, my hands on the dock, exposing and spreading myself fully. The wind whirled around us as my excitement grew. It felt dangerous, and naughty, and highly stimulating to have sex twenty feet away from our friends. "I can't believe I'm doing this," I muttered.

He rode me hard, pushing me closer to the edge of release. He then tapered off. Groaning, he said, "OC, damn you feel too good. I want you to come first."

"Don't stop, please, I'm right there with you."

Listening to me, he continued to pound into me. I reveled in his ability to skyrocket my arousal with his aggression and circumstance. He carried us both further into our excitement until we both erupted.

I strangled the sound in my throat, trying to catch my breath.

His body lay over mine until I gently pushed him off once I felt our come dripping down my legs.

"Shit," I said, struggling out of my jeans and hopping on one foot to catch my balance.

He held my arm to help me remain standing.

"You don't happen to have—" I sighed in relief when he retrieved a handkerchief from his pocket. "Have I told you how much I love these?" I wiped up all the wetness and leaving my panties off, I pulled my pants back on. "How do I look?" I asked after I buttoned my jeans and straightened my shirt.

"Well fucked," he said, adjusting himself and smoothing out his jeans down his legs.

"Great," I said sarcastically.

"They will all be jealous," he said, taking my hand.

"Hang on," I said, holding up my panties and the hanky.

"I'll take them both," he said with a wicked grin and shoved them into his pockets.

I laughed and thanked him.

When we re-entered the pool area, the entire surface of my skin blushed, so if they hadn't figured it out already I was sure my stupid body would tip them off.

"Have fun?" Cat asked.

"It's beautiful out by the water," I said, trying to pull off nonchalance.

Jacqs gave me a knowing glanced, which I ignored. The men seemed to either not notice or more likely didn't give a rat's ass.

Me? I didn't recognize myself anymore. It definitely started with Mason. Me doing all sort of things I'd never considered, enjoying aspects of sex that until recently were foreign to me. Stay, on the other hand, was an unfolding anomaly that surprised me all the time. Such a mix of gentleman and sexual deviant—it made my head spin. My heart? It was staying out of it. My body on the other hand was moving full speed ahead.

I really didn't want to spend the night alone, but for Stay's benefit, I thought I should. If I really wanted a casual relationship, it was up to me to keep it that way.

We sat on the glider couch together, Stay's arm around me. Bond sat on the edge of the pool with Jacqs inclining against him. Sam, Red, Blue, Kev, and Cat sat in wrought iron chairs around two tables covered with food and beverages.

"Can I get you something to drink?" Stay asked me. "Anyone else?"

"Water would be great, thanks."

Everyone else declined.

Cat continued telling her story about a client. "She wanted this huge tattoo on her ribs. The design idea was pretty cool, but she had never gotten a tattoo before and that's the most painful area on the body. Granted, I could do it in small installments but it seemed like a disaster waiting to happen. I tried to talk her into a different location or a smaller piece but she wouldn't listen. Tracy said she would take it and I let her. Boy, is she regretting it now. From what I heard, the woman only sat for thirty minutes and was moving the entire time."

"Is she still giving you shit for not having any tattoos?" Bond asked. "I could rough her up for you."

We all cracked up.

"Yes, but since the new manager is there, it doesn't bother me anymore."

"That's good," Jacqs said.

"You ready to tattoo Bond and Red on either butt cheek," Cat asked Jacqs.

"Very funny, and absolutely not."

"Blue's almost settled on something, right?" Cat said.

"I'm still debating between three of your drawings. I love them all. Soon though."

After I drank some of the water Stay brought over, I yawned. "I didn't sleep well last night so I think I'm going to shove off."

They all looked from me to Stay as if they knew why.

"Cut it out," I said, standing to go.

They chuckled.

"I'll walk you out," Stay said, standing next to me and holding my hand.

"Thank you Red for hosting again, and Jacqs ... and Bond," I said.

"Of course," Red said.

Jacqs rose to hug me and whispered, "I hope it was good. I haven't ever done it on the dock. Something to think about."

"Red, Jacqs needs a good spanking," I said, giving her a dirty look.

"I'm on it," he said.

"Can I clear any of this away before I leave?" I asked.

"We'll take care of it," Jacqs said.

"Bye all," I said and walked through the French doors into the house. I collected my purse from the kitchen. "They all knew."

"And none of them cared. Seriously, they're only speculating anyway." He swung his arm over my shoulder and walked me toward the front door. "I'd love to house sit here for a few days. So many rooms, so little time."

I playfully shoved him. "My first choice would be

305

there," I said, pointing to the fireplace alcove off the sitting area. "We haven't yet explored your place thoroughly."

"Or yours," he said, opening the door for me.

"True."

"Will you stay over tomorrow night?" he asked, my hand swinging in his.

"Maybe. Damn, it's a gorgeous night. See all the stars?"

"I hadn't noticed," he said, staring straight at me.

With my hands I turned his face up to the moon and stars.

"Still doesn't even come close."

"Stop it," I said, standing in front of my vehicle.

"Stop what?" he said, forcing me up against the side of my car.

"Stop being so nice to me," I said. Chills rushed over my body as he nibbled his way up my neck.

"Come over tomorrow night and I'll be as mean as you can take."

My clit jumped over his remark.

He pinned me, holding my arms above my head, roughly rubbing his hard cock against my pelvis. "I could take you again right here."

My body screamed for my submission but my mind said, 'No fucking way!' "We're in the middle of a street with a bright streetlamp above us."

He rested his full body against me and kissed me with zeal. By the time our lips parted, I was panting and wet.

"Say yes," he said as he stepped back.

"Yes," I groaned, already missing the heat of his body on mine.

"I know why you're not taking me home tonight."

So close to changing my mind, I didn't say anything.

"Do you have plans for Saturday?" he asked, angling my head up.

"No, why?"

"I want us to go out on a proper date. We can discuss the details tomorrow."

"Okay." I stood there not moving, not really wanting to leave.

"Be ready for me. I'll be at the shop by seven-thirty. Make sure to eat something beforehand." He gave me a light kiss and opened the car door for me. After he shut it, I watched him walk away.

Back at my place, it almost seemed foreign for me to be there alone. The past week reinserted itself into my thoughts and my gut clinched. So much had happened in such a short time, I had a hard time processing it all. After my nightly cigarette, I heated a bowl of Stay's chicken soup and ate it while I watched the elimination round on *The Voice* from Tuesday. I enjoyed the distraction.

Genuinely tired, I dragged myself to bed wondering what Stay had in store for me tomorrow. I had an idea and it both thrilled and scared me. My thoughts drifted away as I feel asleep.

CHAPTER TWENTY-FIVE

Comes and Goes (In Waves)

by Greg Laswell

Waking up alone hurt more than I could have imagined. Stayman had become such a wonderful relief from the grief, allowing me to hold it at bay. Alone with myself, the pain gripped me and tried it's best to force me to the ground. Shaking, I went out on my balcony in my robe and lit a cigarette. I couldn't sit down. I paced back and forth across the short distance. Mason's face, his unique smell, the sex, the laughter, and the horrible, life changing rejection bounced around in my head.

The next stage of grief must have begun because all I wanted to do was climb back into bed and sleep, pulling the covers over me to hide.

I could see my mother shaking her head at me, and I had to acknowledge another way I was like her. That broke the damn. I tapped out my cigarette, climbed back into bed and hugged a pillow to me.

After a few minutes I tossed myself out of bed and took a shower. I hadn't spoken to my father since his trip and I really needed him. Throwing on a dress we were selling at Bella at the time, I didn't bother blow-drying my hair or applying makeup. I figured the tears would just wash away the eyeliner and mascara. I gathered breakfast and the clothes I needed for the next day.

On my way into work, I called my father.

"Hi, baby girl. I've been thinking about you," he said when he picked up.

"Hi, Daddy."

"What is it, Lainie?" His tone immediately changed to one of concern.

"My life is a mess," I said, when I stopped at a red light. I didn't feel like taking the highway and drove the back streets instead.

"Tell me."

"I saw Mason with his family at an art fair and they seemed very happy, and in love."

"That must have been a shock. When did this happen?"

"Sunday."

"I'm very sorry, sweetheart. What did you do?" His voice and concern calmed me.

"I ended it that night."

"And how are you doing now? Hold on a second." I heard a door close. "Are you having second thoughts?"

I made a left turn and joined the flow of traffic. "Second, third, and fourth. I was so angry that night and he looked so distraught, but I was so hurt..."

"I'm sure you were."

"Then there is Stay. He came to my rescue again and we are sort of seeing each other."

"Sort of?"

"Friends with benefits," I said, speeding up to pass a car.

"Interesting term. How is that working out?"

"He says he understands I need time to get over Mason. I'm pretty sure he loves me already."

I heard him cover the phone and say, "Just a minute." To me he said, "Baby, I'm sure he does. How could he not?"

"You're biased. Do you have to go?"

"No, I have a few more minutes. Your mother is just impatient. How do you feel about Steadman?"

"Stayman, and I don't know. I like him a lot. He's a great man. He kind of reminds me of you at times. He is patient, and surprises me all the time." I pulled into the shop complex.

"But you don't love him?"

I parked in my usual spot and said, "I do not."

"Can you love him?"

"I don't know. I find myself feeling guilty for being with him because of Mason, and because of him too."

"Stayman knows how you feel?" he asked.

"Yes, Dad."

"Let him worry about him. Hang on a second." A door opened and he said something to my mother although I couldn't tell what.

"That's what Stay said. Should you go?"

"In a minute. Mason on the other hand, I'm not sure why you still feel loyal to him given what he's put you through."

I turned off the car, got out, and held the cell phone to my ear. "Because I still love him. I miss him. When I'm with Stay I forget about it all, but as soon as I'm alone, Mason's front and center in my mind."

"Baby, do you want some advice."

"Yes, please!"

"Stop avoiding the pain of your breakup. Until you deal with that, you won't be able to give your heart to another, whether it's to Stay or another man."

"I'm not sure I want to fall in love again," I said as I unlocked the back door to the shop.

"But you will, sweetie. I promise you."

I heard my mother's voice again in the background.

"Right," my father said. "Your mother wants me to

remind you that her party is going to be a week from Saturday."

Once inside, I said, "Okay. Are we still on for walking this Sunday?"

"Can we shoot for the following week? Your mother wants me to go with her to pick out new blinds and curtains for the house. It could be an all day ordeal. Let me know if you can get away during the week instead."

"Okay. I love you lots."

"I love you more. Call me anytime."

"Bye-bye, daddio."

Diving into my work at the shop provided a great distraction. Although Mason and Stay managed to weasel their way into my thoughts, the steady flow of customers helped me to shake away the images.

"That new sale really generated some business," Sam said after the rush left.

"Yes, it's turning out better than most. I think the hot weather is helping. Do you mind covering while I eat the rest of my lunch?"

Folding the discards, she asked, "No. Hot date with Stay?"

"He'll be by later and said I should eat first."

"Oh, I'm so jealous," she said, placing a dress on a hanger. "He'll probably ravish you the moment you get through the door. I don't miss the men in my life, but I sure do miss the sex."

"That's what vibrators are for."

"You know it's not the same."

"Yeah, I do. What do you think of this dress on me?" I asked, showing her the front and the back.

Holding out a sleeveless, navy and turquoise color block, lace sheath dress she had just hung up, she said, "Try this one on."

"I'll do that after I eat. Be right back."

I decided to save the new dress for our date on Saturday. I added a bit of eye makeup and then closed up the shop. Stay drove up moments later in his Prius.

"Hi," I said, feeling nervous.

He didn't give me a second to wallow in it. "Damn, woman it's good to see you. I'm already so hard I can barely stand it."

My body immediately responded leaving my mind far behind. Pressing up against him, I held his head in my hands and kissed him, tasting him and breathing him in.

"I need to get you home." His eyes had the same wild look I witnessed at the club after our first kiss. He opened the car door for me.

Still vibrating from the kiss and his proximity, I got in. Looking around, I said, "You cleaned her."

"I did, for you."

"That wasn't necessary," I said, staring at him as he drove.

Glancing over at me, he said, "I enjoy making the extra effort." He took my hand in his and tucked it in his lap.

We rode in silence the rest of the way, my heart pounding uncontrollably. He parked the car and came around to let me out. Without a word, he led me to the elevator and unlocked the door to his condo.

"I put Rusty in the guest room so he wouldn't interfere," he said.

I stood waiting, my nerves and titillation in overdrive.

Once in his bedroom he spoke, the deeper register of his voice took me by surprise. "Get undressed and kneel by the door."

The charged energy between us had me hanging off a luscious precipice. I quickly shed my dress, panties, and bra. I knelt down where he indicated, already high on the unexpected.

Still dressed, he climbed onto the bed and slung a strap over the center of the headboard. I then watched him retrieve a towel from the bathroom. Folding it in half, he laid it down in the center of the bed. From the nightstand he gathered oil, and a small, ribbed, glass dildo.

He stalked toward me and lifted me to my feet. Pulling me along with him, we entered his office. Seated in his chair, he pulled me down onto his lap, holding me tightly to him. After turning on the screen to his desk top computer, he whispered, "I want you to see what you've gotten yourself into. We'll start slow."

He hit play on a video and the screen filled with a full-figured woman tied down onto a table, with her legs over her head and her ass right to the edge.

Stay's hands roamed my body, tweaking my nipples, kneading my breasts, caressing my belly and thighs. He pushed my legs out wide and felt my growing wetness. He groaned in my ear.

In the scene before us, the man knelt down before the woman, a bowl of oil directly under her. He drew his hand through the liquid and coated her pussy and ass with it. It slowly dripped off the edge of the table back into the bowl. Using a finger from each hand he penetrated her ass, stretching her hole. After dipping back into the oil, he shoved two fingers of each hand, pulling and tugging at her anal entrance.

Stay delved two fingers in my pussy and rubbed my juices all around, coating my clit and opening. In his other hand, he twisted and pulled my right nipple as his mouth bit and kissed his way up my neck.

I turned my head to kiss him.

"No, Lainie, watch."

My body pulsed from all of his manipulations. Turning to watch the screen, my breath caught.

The man saturated his hand again with the oil and that time he forced four fingers of one hand into her tight hole. The woman cried out in pleasure and the man told her she would have to take his whole fist.

"I don't think—"

"Shh. Just watch." He tugged on my labia and then gathered more wetness. "Tilt your hips forward," he ordered.

I did what he demanded.

He used my juices to cover my anus and fingered around my hole.

In the video, the man swiveled his hand in circles, stretching her even more. When he pulled his hand out, her anus stayed open. He captured more oil and dripped it into her ass. After rubbing it around her opening, he plunged back in getting more of his hand inside her.

Stay lightly stuck his finger in my bum and said, "I'm going to have to stretch you so you can take my cock. Do you understand?"

"Oh god, I'm not sure. I mean ... I get it."

"Trust your body. Feel your pussy."

I dipped my fingers into my slick opening.

"You're dripping like the naughty submissive you are. Let me know when you're ready." He continued to work his finger into my ass as his other hand pinched and pulled my hard buds.

The man on the screen continued to work his fist in her ass and with his other hand he rubbed and squeezed the woman's clit. She thrashed as much as her bindings would allow, groaning and crying out the entire time. When he pushed all the way in she squirted several times and screamed out her climax. He wasn't done with her, but I'd seen enough.

"I'm ready," I said but had no idea if I really meant it. "I'm scared."

"Good. I won't take you like that. Not tonight anyway. Let's go." He flipped off the screen and led me back into his bedroom. "Lay down in the middle of the bed. There's a strap hanging from the headboard. There are loops on either side for your wrists. Place your hands in them and hang on. Your butt should be centered on the towel. Your arms will be stretched up. Tilt your hips knees out wide."

I stared at him and hesitated.

"Do you need some coaxing?" he asked as he undressed. His cock and as well as the tiny nipples on his defined chest both strained for attention.

"Oh, uh, no." I climbed up on the bed and followed his instruction.

"Butt down farther."

Once I did, my whole upper body was stretched upward and I could see my lower body. My rapid breathing had my chest and stomach rising and falling quickly.

"Such a sexy sub." He hopped onto the bed and starting at my stretched arms, he caressed each, stopping to kiss my arm pit. Moving down, he straddled my stomach and kissed me deeply.

I had to work to keep my head up to meet his kiss.

His hands trailed down my neck, fondling my shoulders and breast. He intoxicated me with his touch, every nerve ending on fire. Wetness dripped down my ass as he continued to pet every inch of me. He settled at the end of the bed with his legs on either side of me.

Before he even began playing with my ass again, I

315

was panting in extreme fervor. I felt certain I would never allow him to fist me, but felt crazed from the anticipation of having his cock fill me.

He poured a copious amount of oil over my pussy and ass, spreading it around the area, between my folds. "You are damn sexy, so exposed like that." My knees up and out, left me nowhere to hide.

His fingers played across my anus as his other hand soothed across my swollen clit. "Relax, OC. I don't want you to hyperventilate. I'll go slowly."

"Okaaay," I breathed out.

He poured more oil over his fingers, and used one on each hand to stretch me like the man in the video had done.

"Ohhh," I groaned. It still felt foreign and oh so naughty too. I pulled on my restraint, my hips bucking at the sensation.

Then he inserted three, working them in and around, pulling at the sides of my opening. "You're so tight. I can't wait to slide my hard cock into your virgin ass." After my anus relaxed a bit he held up the small, five-inch, glass dildo and poured oil over it. "This will be cold," he warned.

Oh and it was. It sent chills up my back when he forced the head past my sphincter. "Oh ... oh ... oh. That's so ... so ... potent."

"I'll hold still until you acclimate." He massaged my clit as my ass clutched around the violation.

My hips started to roll as my orgasm built and I tightened my grip on the strap.

"I'm starting again," he said, pushing more into me.

"Uh, uh. Oh, I don't know."

"You're gushing pussy does. It's almost all the way in. Good, Lane, take it for me."

"Yes, Stay, I want to." The sensation made me dizzy with lust and the ferocity of stimulation had me flying high.

"Now I'm going to stroke it. This will help you loosen up for me." In and out he slowly glided the glass invader as he continued to roll my clit. "I'm so hard I think I might spontaneously combust," he groaned

"I'm so close," I cried.

He stopped moving. "No, Lainie. Hold it back for me, and only let go when I say. I want to feel you come around my cock—clutching and pulling." He continued to thrust into my ass, pulling it all the way out and popping the head back in.

My head rocked back and forth in an effort to stave off the orgasm that threatened to erupt. My ass and clit throbbed and I didn't know how much longer I could hold out. "Stay, oh please."

"Tell me. I need to hear you beg."

"I want you to take me. Please, Stayman, please."

"Please what, Lainie?"

"Please fuck my ass."

"And stretch you out?"

"Yes, pleassse!"

"And make you come harder than you ever have before?"

"Oh ... Stay ... yes. Take me."

"Oh, I'm going to, and fuck you hard too." He got up on his knees and coated his large cock with oil. The head touched my clit first. He rolled it around my arousal and then ran it down my labia. He bucked into my wet pussy and stroked a few times.

Stayman's trim, hard body knelt at my entrance, his knees out wide. He drew out of my pussy and lined his cock up to my anal opening. "Getting the head inside is the hardest part. When I thrust, bear down. His hand pushed on my lower abdomen and then he rocked forward.

My eyes opened wide and I started panting again. "Stay?" I cried.

"Push out. There you go. You can take it. I'm in. Jesus." Not moving, he said, "Lainie, look at me. Make your breathing slower."

"Oh god, I'm trying! That's..." I shook my head. "What the hell means more than intense?"

Stay chuckled and smiled his wicked grin. "I promise you, your orgasm will be more than intense too. Are you ready?"

"Slowly."

"I plan to go very slowly until I'm all the way in. At that point you will have to hold on." He withdrew slightly and thrust forward. "So good. We're half way there."

My body started trembling and heat shot across the surface of my skin. I stared directly at him and said, "More."

"Damn, Lainie," he said as he pulled back. "I'm never letting you go." He lunged deeper. "One more inch." Then he began a steady rhythm and I thought I might expire from the force of my depravity.

"Oh god. It's ... it's so good," I moaned.

"I'm there, OC, can you take more?"

"Take me."

And he did. He grabbed the straps above my wrist and pounded into me. The forced from his pelvis rubbed up and down on my clit with each incursion and retreat. He placed his hands on the bed under me and wildly kissed me, possessing me in a way I had never allowed another.

I grunted against his lips allowing him to take me fully.

Grasping the straps again, he watched my face as he rolled his hips against me. "You can come now as many times as you like."

My eyes fluttered and my heart pounded as I lost

myself in the rapture of our coupling. "Stay," I mumbled. "Oh, Stay."

"Yes, honey?"

"Now. Ohhh, holy ... mother ... of ... god! Ahhh."

He rode out my climax and then paused. He unhooked my hands from the straps and lowered my head down onto the pillow.

Swimming in the sea of my orgasm, I floated on my back through each wave as I rose and fell over the crests. "Damn, damn, damn," I mumbled. I opened my eyes to find Stayman staring down on me. "Wow."

He smiled his crooked grin and I felt a slight crack in my sealed up heart.

"Now that's a high worth getting addicted to," I said.

"It's not over. Turn over and place a pillow under your hips."

"You need to pull out of me first."

"Of course." He laughed. "It just feels so good." Once he slid out, I felt so empty.

I flipped over and shoved one of his fluffy pillows right above my pelvis.

"Damn, woman, you have a fine ass and I love to see your pussy peeking out." He drew his finger through my copious juices and said, "A close second to fucking your throat."

I chuckled.

"Reach your hand underneath so you can play with your clit. I want you to come again before I do." He positioned himself between my legs and spread my butt wide. "Here we go." With strength, he plunged into me.

With my left cheek against the mattress, I used my right hand to circle my swelled bud. "I grunted each time he pulled out and forcibly re-entered.

Propped up on his arms along my side, he continued

his hard sensual salutation. "You feel ... so good. I never knew—never hoped," he mumbled.

"My clit is so hard. So ... oh ... soon!"

"I'm going to take you hard." He lowered his weight down and forced my legs farther apart. He circled his arms under and around my shoulders and using them as leverage, he smashed against me.

"Oh, make me ... yes ... don't stop!" I cried as my release began.

A growl started deep in Stay's throat as he grunted out his orgasm. I felt his warm release fill me. We flew together through the most decadent liberation, soaring higher than I ever had before. His weight rested against me and I loved the feel of him.

I pulled my arm out from under me and disappeared into bliss. I don't know how much time past until he rolled off me.

"I'll be right back." I heard the water run in the bathroom and I assumed Stay was cleaning his cock.

When he came back, he said, "Damn, Lainie. You continue to surprise me."

"Me?" I muttered.

"Yes you," he said, moving me onto his chest.

"What did you mean?" I said softly.

"When?" He tickled down my back.

"Never knew? And you said something else." I breathed out a contented sigh.

"Never hoped." He gathered my hair and draped it over my shoulder.

"Yes, that. What did you mean?"

"I've never met anyone who suited me as well as you do and I've never been so sexually satisfied." He hugged me to him, breathing against my hair.

"I'm at a loss."

"I know, OC, but you'll get there." He kissed my head.

"Why are you so sure?" I asked, peering up.

"There are so many reasons but you're not ready to hear them."

"I hope you're right." And I meant it.

"Me too."

As much as I enjoyed my time with Stayman, I didn't know if I could love him. I adored him as friend, and as a lover he rocked my world but when it came to love, it was another beast entirely.

"Are you hungry?" he asked.

"Mmmhmm," I said into his chest.

"You're not moving."

"I'm too comfortable," I said, snuggling in tighter.

He stroked my hair and said, "Thank you."

"I'm positive I should be thanking you. That was ... I don't even know how to put it in words."

"It was for me too. Will you submit again?"

I folded my arms on his chest and rested my chin on top. "Are you worried I might decline?"

"Or run away, yes."

"No, I won't."

"Submit?"

"No. Run away, I won't. Submit? Whenever you take me again."

"Jesus, woman." His cock hardened next to my thigh.

"You're insatiable."

"I promise you, I've never been like this before," he said, looking dead serious.

"I call bullshit. You're a very sexual man. I don't believe you."

"You'll get there," he said again.

We noshed on left over pizza and crashed soon thereafter.

When we woke in the morning, I checked the clock and screamed, "Shit."

"What?" Stay asked, groggily.

"I'm late. The store opens in forty-five minutes. I'm getting into the shower and we have to leave right after."

"Okay. Breakfast?" He got out of bed and pulled on sweats and a T-shirt.

"No time," I said heading into the bathroom.

"I'll throw something together for you."

"Thanks."

CHAPTER TWENTY-SIX

Use Me

by Bill Withers

After frantically rushing to shower, gathering my stuff, and impatiently waiting as Stay drove me to work, I still had fifteen minutes to spare before I had to open Bella Boutique.

Once we arrived at the shop, Stay handed me a paper bag and kissed me goodbye. "Thanks again for last night," he said.

I paused and took a deep breath. I took a minute to take in the wonderful man in front of me. With my hand, I brushed over his hair and along his cheek where his bristle had started to grow. "You are a truly great person. I'm grateful to have you in my life."

We hugged and rocked together for a moment, and I allowed myself to thoroughly enjoy it. I took in his smell and carried it with me to work. I waved goodbye as he drove away.

In the office, I opened the bag Stay had given to me. Inside I found a vanilla yogurt, the very brand I ate, and a banana. Damn him for being so amazing.

Halfway through the day I received a text from him.

> **Stayman:** I miss your body next to mine. Thank you for spending the night. I'll miss you until tomorrow.
> **Me:** I miss you too. What time on Saturday?

Stayman: Are you driving or should I come get you?
Me: I'm flexible.
Stayman: I'll be at your condo at two o'clock.
Me: See you then.

When I got home from work that night, the menagerie of thoughts left me mildly nauseous. Collecting my journal and pen, I sat on the balcony and lit a cigarette.

Do people really expect me to just turn off all my feelings for Mason? I truly wish it were that easy. Screw the faucet tightly off. I know if Mason wasn't a married man no one would have that expectation of me.

How do I grieve and let him go like Dad said I should? Mason and I had gotten to the absolute best place in our relationship. With one hundred percent of my being, I believed he loved me. That's why seeing him in love with his wife hurt so much. How could he love us both? He hasn't texted or called again. Maybe I wasn't as important to him as I thought I was, or maybe he believed me when I said I never ever wanted to hear from him again.

I'm battling myself constantly not to text him and the only thing keeping me from doing so is Stay. Is it fair that Stay is my stalwart support against reaching out to the man I love. I don't care what anyone else says, I know I'm using Stay. I also know we both are having a lot of fun with it but that leaves me feeling no less guilty. It would be so easy if I could let go of Mason. I can see it. I'm not an idiot. Part of me even wants to. I love him. I still love him. I need him and want him too.

Parting in anger didn't come close to the closure I need. I want to hear from him. I need to know it wasn't all in my imagination. DON'T DO IT, LAINIE.

I went inside and picked up my phone. I did something worse than texting Mason. I texted Stay instead.

> **Me:** Whatcha doing?
>
> **Stayman:** Waiting for you to breakdown and text me.
>
> **Me:** You know I'm not being nice.
>
> **Stayman:** And you know I don't care. I can be there in fifteen minutes.
>
> **Me:** Want to go for a swim?
>
> **Stayman:** Amongst other things. Am I spending the night?
>
> **Me:** Why?
>
> **Stayman:** So I know what to pack.
>
> **Me:** This was a bad idea. I was feeling...
>
> **Stayman:** Lonely and missing Mason.

My eyes filled with tears.

> **Me:** I'm sorry, yes.
>
> **Stayman:** I'm sending you an MP3. Listen to it and text me back.
>
> **Stayman:** UseMe.mp3 *download media content*

I downloaded the familiar Bill Wither's song and listened. The words caused me to laugh. Stay wanted me to use him up.

> **Me:** For a smart man, I have to say, you don't make great decisions for yourself.
>
> **Stayman:** I'm perfectly fine with you reaching out to me instead of Mason.

Me: How do you do that?

Stayman: What did you call it? Voodoo, tantric magic? It's simply a connection between us. Use me, OCDC, I can take it.

Me: Geez Louise! What am I going to do with you?

Stayman: Eight more minutes and we'll find out.

Me: Damn you!

I laughed, giddy for the distraction in the form of a very sexy man. Hurriedly I scanned around the apartment and put everything in order. I dumped the ashtray and rinsed it out. In the bathroom I gargled and brushed my teeth. I changed into my sexy, black, one-piece bathing suit, and tied a wrap around my waist. Then I settled on the couch as if I was casually waiting. My heart pounded from all the rushing around and the relief from my angst. I popped up and unlocked the latch and then sat back down.

A knock sounded on the door shortly after and I said, "Come in."

He walked in and kicked off his shoes. In his hands he carried a shirt and pants on hangers and a black overnight bag. "I'll put these in the bedroom."

I watched his cute ass stroll down the hall. "I hope you brought a bathing suit."

"Got it," he called from my room. When he came out, he had on swimming trunks that hung down to mid-thigh. He was already hard, the bulge apparent. He saw me looking. "Since you texted me." He pulled me to my feet and held my hair back on either side of my head. "I've missed you." His eyes searched my face as if he was committing each detail to memory.

Overwhelmed with need and the passion he inspired in me, I crashed my body against him. We grinded into one another as our lips locked. I hooked my right foot around his calf, trying to get closer.

When we broke apart, he said, "If you keep that up, we won't make it to the pool." His smooth, tan chest rose and fell.

"I invited you over for a swim," I said, trying to gather my wits about me.

"Yes you did."

"Can I smell you before we get all chlorinated?" I asked.

"Jesus, Lainie, you make it hard to keep a modicum of control." He tugged his shorts down and step forward as I knelt before him.

I buried my face against his cock, breathing in his heady masculine scent.

He stroked my hair as I kissed around his shaft and balls. "You're testing my resolve, woman."

"Pre-cum? I'm sorry, I can't resist." I lapped the tip of his cock and sucked gently on the head. "You smell too good," I said.

"We can shower after the pool."

"Yes, I realize that but then you'll smell like soap." I ran my fingers up the length of him.

"How do I smell now?"

"Oh so uniquely you Stay: masculine ... salty ... musky, and it drives me crazy."

"My favorite is when your pussy juices are covering it."

After unknotting the wrap I wore, I stood, bent over the side of the couch and pulled the bottom of my suit to the side. "Let's see."

He groaned and moved in behind me. His cock filled me, knocking out any anxiety I held over my relationships.

I reveled in the firm grip on my shoulders and the velocity of his aggression. My pussy clutched, so close to being driven over the edge.

"You're already so close. Shall I make you wait?" he asked, not slowing in the least.

"No. Harder please. Just don't come."

He obliged me, letting me surge into a freefall.

"Ohhh ... I'm ... yesss," I cried out. My orgasm shattered around his cock giving me the high I so craved.

He held himself tightly against me as I slowly recovered.

I negotiated myself on shaky legs over to sit on the couch, my wrap under me. "Come," I beckoned.

His erection still stood at attention. He stepped forward, holding his cock out.

I twirled my tongue around the head, riding the rim. "You and me together, I have to agree. Yummy." With one hand I caressed his balls and swallowed his cock as deeply as I could. I moved to kneel in front of him, using my fist on the lower half of his shaft and my mouth on the upper.

He twisted his nipples as he gazed down on me, looking so sexy.

"That feels incredible. Are you ready for me to fill your mouth?"

I nodded.

His balls tightened up in my hand and his warm, creamy come fired into my mouth shot after shot. "Jesus," he grunted, bucking his hips in and out. He held my head as his eyes bored into my eyes.

I struggled to keep up with the volume, swallowing several times. The contortions of pleasure that flashed across his face turned me on even more. I licked my lips and lapped up the last drops from his flared head.

He yanked up his shorts and collapsed on the couch, pulling me along with him. In his arms, I rested my head on his chest, hearing the pounding of his heart. He mumbled against my head, "I thought you invited me over for a swim."

"So did I, but..."

"But?"

"Well it's your fault," I said, sitting up on his lap.

He made a sound that could have been both a choke and a laugh, then said, "Come again?"

"Maybe later."

"Huh? Oh, very funny. How is it my fault?"

"Who asked you to walk around with a hard on all the time?"

"My silly sweetheart, that's entirely your fault. Once you stop being so damn sexy, which I'm certain will never happen, then my cock will behave. Otherwise, it's a cross we both must bear and I don't mind it a bit. It keeps my creative juices flowing..." He twitched his eyebrows.

I smacked his arm and said, "Let's go swimming. I'll get the towels."

Once at the pool, Stay dove into the deep end. We had the place to ourselves. I worked my way into the pool from the shallow end steps.

I thought about the one other time Stay and I were in a pool together. It was at Red's house one night when we all decided to go skinny-dipping. I had consumed a few drinks, which made exposing my body to the group far easier. Stay may have noticed me, but he wasn't yet in my sphere of attention.

"You ignored me that night," he said when he swam up to me.

I shoved off the bottom step and began to swim away.

He caught me by my calf and turned me over, cradling me in his arms. Back and forth, he swayed me in the water as if orchestrating a dance.

It was so relaxing as I drifted in the comfort of his arms

and stared up at the stars above. Addressing his earlier statement, I said, "I told you before, I was otherwise occupied."

"You were flirting your ass off with Dawg."

"I was mad," I said, stretching my arms out wide.

"Oh, I think I see. Well you could have taken it out on me."

"I didn't really know you then." The direction of the conversation drained away my loose state.

"And you knew Dawg?" he asked, pausing the water waltz.

"Well no, but I knew enough to know he wouldn't confuse sex with anything else. Jacqs was completely against it and I quickly changed my mind anyway."

"Why?" He started moving me around again.

"I was hurt, and angry, and that's a really bad time to have sex with—oh fuck." I kicked out of his hold and went to sit on the top step. I folded my arms across my chest.

"Stop it, OC."

"Everything is like this crazy mine field. I get it, I get it, I get it! You can decide for yourself. It doesn't stop me from feeling like it's wrong half the time. I don't want to talk about it again. Everyone keeps telling me to let you decide, but they're all hoping for something I'm not sure I'm capable of."

"What's wrong with what we have now? It's all still so new and we need time. Both of us. You were willing not to think about the future with Mason, give me the same consideration."

I cocked my head and contemplated his words. I had known there was no future with Mason, but it didn't keep me from falling in love with him, enjoying the time we had. Not that I had planned to fall in love with Stayman, but I couldn't ignore he had a point. "You're right," I said. "I won't mention it again."

"Good. The wind's picking up out here. Want to go in and snuggle up to the movie you slept through?"

"I'd love too."

We watched *Dogma* late into the night. Once in bed, Stay spooned me to sleep and I slept soundly.

Sometime in the morning I felt a shake on my shoulder that woke me.

"It's supposed to be another hot one today," Stay said, sitting on the edge of the bed beside me. "Let's eat breakfast and then do the first part of the date early. We can reconvene at my place later for the rest of the date."

"That's too much for my brain to take in first thing in the morning."

He reached over to my nightstand and held out a cup of coffee.

I smiled and yawned, stretching my arms above my head. "Thank you," I said as I took the mug from him. I drank a sip. "Perfect. Did you shower?"

"Yes, I've been up for a while," he said as he caressed my leg.

"Where are we going? What shall I wear? I have a new dress—" My body began to respond to his touch. "If you keep doing that we won't get out of the house."

"Sorry, it's hard for me to keep my hands to myself. Wear shorts, a T-shirt, and comfortable shoes. The place is a surprise. I'm certain you'll love it."

"It's already ten-thirty? Give me twenty minutes and I'll be ready."

"Okay. I cut up the fruit in the fridge and there's yogurt and cottage cheese." He gave me room to get up.

"Great," I pushed myself out of bed and gathered the

clothes I needed. "I love surprises," I said over my shoulder on the way to the bathroom.

CHAPTER TWENTY-SEVEN

Blue Skies

by Noah & The Whale

In Stayman's convertible, my ponytail waved in the wind. I turned on the stereo and we sang along with the Red Hot Chili Peppers to *Scar Tissue*. My body hummed with what felt strikingly similar to joy. Without censoring myself I said, "I like you Stay."

He flashed me his adorable smile and said, "I like you too, OC. You're a lot of fun to be around."

Me fun? I've thought of myself in many different ways, but fun never topped the list. I liked that he thought so. "Are you going to tell me where we're going?"

"No," he said with his devious expression.

"How much longer?" I asked.

"Not much."

I couldn't imagine what he might have in store.

He drove north on I-95 and exited the highway onto Sample Road. We traveled west until we reached Tradewinds Park. After driving for a bit, he parked near a sign that read Butterfly World in orange.

"Have you ever been?" he asked as he helped me out of the car. He retrieved a Nikon 3000 digital camera from the trunk and hung it around his neck.

"No."

"Awesome," he said, taking my hand. The ultra-modern entrance had palm trees and flowering bushes on either side. We entered a roped off line where Stay paid for us. We strolled through the butterfly farm and then the museum. Through two large doors we entered an open-air hallway. On the right wall hung pinned butterflies.

I found it fascinating that butterflies had such a short life—mere days. Stay shot pictures of me as I perused all the information.

When we accessed the next section, I gasped, "Wow!" The butterfly wonderland lay out before me. Trees filled the space and a vast variety of butterflies flew about. Classical music mixed with the sound of cascading waterfalls and streams provided the backdrop.

"Oh, Stay." I threw my arms around him. "I love it!"

He moved the camera from between us and hugged me back.

"I feel like a little kid on a new adventure," I said. The same feeling I had at the concert re-emerged. "I didn't know you were into photography."

"It's an old hobby. I've been inspired to pick it up again." He winked at me.

Two paths diverged in either direction and we went to the right. A black and yellow tiger butterfly lit on my arm and we watched it flap its wings. Stay shot pictures of it from different angles, a few with my smiling face in them.

My eyes filled as I pushed back the emotion. It wasn't sadness so much as awe because of the beauty of the place, and the fact that Stay thought to take me there.

The butterfly flew away as we walked deeper into the environment. We crossed a bridge, and next to a small waterfall we found a bench and sat on it. Across from us several butterflies ate fruit from a hanging plate.

"This place is amazing. Thank you so much for taking me here. Have you been here before?"

"I haven't. I found it while I was searching for something fun to do. Lainie, watching your face light up, there's nothing like it." With his arm around me, he drew me in for a kiss.

His lips touching mine felt different. The chemistry still simmered but instead of flaring, it tugged on my emotions, pulling me into him in a new way. It was as if he influenced my resolve with the love he felt for me. His feelings called me to open up and terrified me too.

When we disengaged, he held my face and I rested my head in his hand and closed my eyes. He didn't have to say the words. They floated all around on the wings of the butterflies. When I looked into his intense, blue eyes, the tears fell. He kissed my eyes, my cheeks, and then my lips again. We held each other tightly as if something on the horizon might force us apart.

Other people milled around, but I hardly took notice.

Stay stopped a father and daughter passing by. "Would you mind taking a shot of us?"

"Sure," the man said.

Stay showed him how to use the camera and we posed for a picture.

"Smile," the father said. He fired off a few shots. "You guys are a good looking couple."

"Thank you so much," I said as the man handed the camera back to Stay.

When another kind of butterfly landed on Stay's knee, neither of us moved not wanting to disturb it. The Blue Morpho had iridescent, blue wings with black trim and white dots lining the outside of the top of the wing and red dots on the bottom. After it flew away, Stay and I explored the rest of the ecology hand in hand.

We exited from the back and he said, "There's more."

He led me through the gardens and across a suspension bridge that crossed a body of water.

He showed me to the Lorikeets pavilion where we were able to hold and feed the colorful, medium-sized birds. We took turns taking pictures of each other.

Then we went to enjoy the hummingbirds. Entering the environment, we had to be very careful not to let any of the birds fly out. We sat on a bench and watched their antics. So fast, they would fly and dip into the water and soar away again. Stay focused his lens to get a good shot.

After we sat there for a while, a humming bird decided that it liked my hair and kept buzzing around my ponytail and the side of my face. The odd sensation caused me to laugh. I tried to stay still as a crowd gathered to take shots, Stay included. Laughing and staying still didn't go so well together. When the humming bird decided to try to steal one of my long hairs, chills took over. Between shaking and laughing, I doubt anyone got a really good shot but it amused me to know I could potentially be a part of so many photo albums.

Once the bird gave up on my hair, the crowd dispersed.

"Did you get any good ones?" I asked.

Stay shuffled through the photos and said, "A bunch. Check this one out."

In the photo, I'm laughing, my eyes wide, and somehow Stay managed to get the bird in mid flap.

"Wow, Stay, that's very cool. I mean other than I look totally ridiculous."

"Not at all, OC, you look totally adorable. Look at the light in your eyes. I might have to frame this one. Are you ready?"

"Sure," I said, taking his hand.

We went to the gift shop and Stay bought me a

butterfly calendar. I planned to hang it in my office at the shop. "I love it. Thank you!" I spontaneously kissed him.

After returning the kiss, he took a stray hair of mine and placed it behind my ear. He kissed my forehead and held the car door open for me. We both smiled from ear to ear.

On the way back to my place, before he dropped me off, I said, "That was so much fun. I could totally do that again."

"Me too," he said, taking my hand in his.

"What time do you want me to come over?" I pulled my ponytail holder out and let the wind blow my hair.

"I can come get you," he said, driving down the street to my place.

"No, I need to drive. I have brunch with Jacqs tomorrow morning."

"Right. Five o'clock, and bring a jacket in case it cools off." He parked in front of my building and came around to open my door.

Butterflies from the day attempted to swarm in my stomach. Again I felt the shift to the next level in our relationship, and I felt even less prepared for it than the last.

"Come on, Lane, it's all good." He ran his fingers over my clenched eyebrows and smoothed them across my forehead. "Don't do too much thinking before you get to my place. Promise me."

"I promise."

He gave me a light kiss goodbye and I waved to him as he drove out.

Inside my apartment, I combed my refrigerator for something to eat. I picked one of the items Stay had previously purchased for me. Standing by the island, I ate a few bites of curry chicken salad.

In my bedroom, I placed my phone on speaker and called Jacqs.

"What's up, girl?" she said. "How was the date?"

"How did you know?" I could feel myself shaking my head.

"Stay told Bond, who told me. So?"

"Amazing. He took me to Butterfly World. Have you ever been?"

"No but I've wanted to. Maybe we could get the gang to go."

"Maybe you should just take Red, it's very romantic. Did you know Stay's into photography?"

"Yeah, some of the framed art photographs at Red's are his."

Stay was like unwrapping a package only to find inside another box. "I had no idea."

"That's what I've been trying to tell you all along. He's a very interesting guy."

"Yeah, you were right. So tomorrow? Here or there?" I straightened the sheet on the bed, tucking the bottom and sides.

"Can we meet at your place? It'll give us more privacy to chat."

"Good thinking." Holding onto the ends, I whipped up the comforter and let it float down in place.

"I thought you had an all-day date."

"I'm heading over to his place at five. Do you know what he has in store for me?" I asked.

"Nope, sorry, girl, but I want to hear all about it tomorrow."

I aligned the pillows and asked, "See you at ten?"

"See you then. Love you."

"Love you too."

In the bathroom, I scrubbed the bottom of the tub and then filled it with warm water and lavender oil for a bath.

It felt decadent and I vowed not to let my mother's voice into my head. After relaxing for a while, I used the time I had left to shave my legs, vagina, and arm pits. I showered as the bathwater ran out.

I scoured my clothes for just the right jacket to compliment the blue and turquoise, color block, sheath dress I planned to wear. A navy bolero dressed up the look, but the short-cropped jean jacket made the outfit more casual. I chose sandals and the jean jacket.

Downstairs, I unlatched the top on my Saturn Sky and let my hair dry on the way. A mantra played in my head the whole way over to Stay's. *Have fun. Have fun. Have fun. No one is pressuring you. You can enjoy yourself without having to make promises or commitments. Have fun. Let the past stay there. Have fun. You can pick it apart again tomorrow. Shut up and just have fun.* "Ahhh," I yelled and that seemed to turn off the chant.

Once at Stay's I texted him.

> **Me:** Where should I park?
> **Stayman:** I'll meet you downstairs and you can pull into my spot once I back out.
> **Me:** Are we going somewhere?

For some reason I had assumed we were staying in.

> **Stay:** Yes. I'll be right down.

He entered the garage wearing brown slacks and an Asian style, cream, open-necked shirt. He looked incredibly sexy. Once he backed out his car, he came and opened the door of my Saturn after I parked in his spot.

"Wow, look at you," he said as I exited the car.

"I was thinking the very same thing. You look incurably handsome." I stepped up to him and put my arms around his neck.

He kissed my shoulder and murmured, "You smell so good. Another dress from the shop?"

"Yes," I said, lifting my chin as he kissed up my neck. "Sam suggested I try it on."

He pushed me up against his car, my face in his hands and he inflamed me with his plundering.

"Stay," I said.

"Yes, sweetheart."

"We're blocking the way." I pointed to the car waiting behind his Corvette. I gathered my purse and coat and with a click of a button the convertible closed and the doors locked.

He held the passenger door open for me and then jogged around to his side of the car. As he drove out of the garage, he said, "You're legs look incredible in that dress, and I love what you've done with your hair."

I had twisted the top sides of my hair and pulled it back into a barrette. "Thank you. I'm glad you like it. Where are we going?"

"Downtown Fort Lauderdale but that's all I'm saying."

"Two surprises in one day? I love it." I relaxed into the seat and watched the scenery pass by.

Stay drove into a parking garage at Las Olas Riverfront. We walked to the water and down the boardwalk. People had gathered to board a water taxi. Stay walked up to the booth and purchased two tickets.

"We're going on there?" I asked, pointing at the yellow, twenty-six passenger water taxi with a yellow and blue awning.

"You're not afraid of the water, are you?"

I laughed and said, "No, this is great! So where are we going?"

"That's the next surprise."

"Woohoo," I called out. "I sure do hope it includes food because I'm getting hungry."

"You won't be disappointed," he said as he assisted me into the boat.

"I don't see how I possibly could with you along."

"You flatter me, and please don't feel like you need to stop on my account," he said and then patted my rump.

"You better behave," I said, taking a seat near the back of the vessel.

"Never."

I hoped he meant it.

He held my jacket out for me once the taxi started down New River.

"Thanks," I said, snuggling back against him. "You're spoiling me."

"That's my master plan. I told you, Lainie, my new goal in life is to see you as happy as you were at the concert, as often as possible."

"You're brilliant at it," I said, laying my arms across his, which circled my stomach. "I have no idea why you think I deserve it. Don't worry, I have no plans to try to talk you out of it."

"That's good because there's no chance of that happening."

Downtown Fort Lauderdale sped by on either side of the river. After going under a railroad bridge, a large, blue, two-story restaurant with a cupola on top loomed in front of us. Dark-brown, shellacked picnic tables with large, green umbrellas overhead lined the dock along the perimeter of The Pirate Republic Seafood & Grill.

"Are we getting out? That was short," I said, hoping we would though. The aromas from the restaurant were torturing my stomach.

"Yes, I thought we would take a longer ride after dinner," he said, giving me his hand as I stepped out of the taxi.

"Oh, I hope we get a table along the water," I said, turning around and taking in the view of the big, lush trees across the way.

"Come," he said.

I curled my arm around his and we approached the hostess stand. She helped two other couples first and then directed us to a table along the water's edge.

We sat on opposite sides of the large picnic table, which held condiments and napkins.

"What's good?" I asked, perusing the menu.

"Your guess is as good as mine. I've never been here."

"Well it sure looks interesting. If I may?" I asked.

"Go for it."

"I'm a huge garlic fan but I won't eat it unless you do so we cancel each other out."

He looked up and said, "So you want to get the garlic spiced shrimp appetizer?"

"And the calamari."

"Which sauce?"

"Do you think they'll bring them all for us to try?" I asked, searching around for a server.

"Let's find out. Is there anything else?" He touched my arm.

His question sparked a whole myriad of images in my mind, all of which had nothing to do with food. I rubbed my lips together and said, "Let's start with that and see if we're still hungry."

"Perfect. I have dessert waiting back at home."

The electricity in his look had me wondering if he meant an actual sweet dessert or what he planned to do to me later.

"It kills me when you look at me that way," Stay said.

"And what way would that be?" I asked, angling my head.

"A look that tells me you want me to take you right here, on this table."

The server came over to take our order, and as she did, I kicked off my sandal and did something completely bold, especially for me. With my foot I fondled the front of Stay's pants. After she walked away, I said, "I thought so. Just checking." I slid my foot back into my shoe and folded my hands in front of me like a steeple.

He furrowed his brow and said, "You're going to pay for that, Lane."

"Uh-huh. You're a big talker."

"Go to the bathroom and take off your underwear. Make sure to dip your fingers into your honeypot for me to taste when you get back."

"You're kidding, right?"

His expression said otherwise.

"You don't think I will," I said, sitting up straighter.

"I guess we're about to find out."

I took my purse and sauntered away. My nipples hardened further on my walk to find the restroom. I not only took off my panties, I removed my bra as well. If he wanted to play, I had no plans to lose. In the stall I penetrated my wetness and coated two fingers. With my other hand, I tweaked my nipples so they would be obvious through my dress.

As I approached the table, Stay whistled. Apparently he noticed. "Put your foot back," he ordered.

I held out my fingers to him and fulfilled his request. I

wiggled my toes against his zipper.

He breathed in my scent. "You were already wet, as I expected. You should wear a bra less often, but only with me."

"How do you mean?"

He licked the tip of my finger and then sucked it into his mouth.

I groaned.

We abruptly parted when our drinks and the calamari were delivered.

"We need to eat quickly and head back," he said, his head down and looking at me through the top of his eyes.

"We can have them wrap up the other dish," I said, desperately wanting to be alone with Stay again.

"Are you serious?"

I held up my arm and our server came over. "Can you wrap up the shrimp dish to go? And what time is the next taxi going back?"

"Sure. It should be here in ten minutes or so."

"Thank you." When she walked away I said, "I'm sorry to cut our water taxi ride short."

"No you're not and neither am I. We'll just do it another time."

We ate the calamari, trying the different sauces, and kept an eye out for the taxi returning for the short ride back to Stay's car.

Once back to the parking garage, neither of us spoke. The frenzied energy between us hadn't lessened with food or the water taxi ride. Inside the car, we met in the center, his hand up my dress our tongues meeting in a duel of savage aggression.

"Have you christened this—oh that feels good—this car?" I panted.

"No. Jesus, Lane, you're already so wet."

I tugged on his pants, working his zipper down.

He said, "What are you doing?"

I ignored the inane question and freed his cock.

He quickly got on board and kicked opened the passenger side door. With his legs out the side, he lay down across the bucket seats and held his arms out to me.

I shimmied the bottom of my dress up around my hips and lowered over him.

"Oh Jesus," he grunted.

Our frantic pace felt like we couldn't find relief fast enough. The intense friction brought me right up to the brim until we heard a car door shut. We froze, both of us breathing heavily.

I giggled against his chest, shaking on top of him.

"Let's get home," he said, helping me off his lap.

"Good idea," I said, shocked by my own behavior. "You're dangerous."

"Me? Honey, I think it's a joint effort." He fastened his pants and started the car.

I smoothed down my skirt and checked my hair on the mirror on the visor. "Yeah, I don't know. Don't speed but get us back there quickly."

He drove out of the parking garage. "I'm on it. I had plans to go slow tonight. Give you a tantric orgasm."

"I'm not sure our chemistry will allow for it. Maybe after we've thoroughly exhausted ourselves."

"Lainie?"

"Yes, Stay?"

"I've never—"

"Me too," I said. He glanced over at me and I squeezed his hand. I needed him back inside me, and soon.

"Can I see you tomorrow after your brunch with Jacqs?"

"We haven't even finished tonight," I said.

"We've barely started. That's not the point. I already know I want to see you tomorrow."

"Stayman?"

"Yes, OC."

"My place after Jacqs leaves." I no longer felt like fighting with myself over Stay, our chemistry or any of it. I planned to let sex happen as often as possible.

"And I'll spend the night," he said as he made a right turn.

"That wasn't a question," I said, shifting in my seat to better face him.

"No, it wasn't." He glanced at me and then straight ahead. "We have a lot of rooms and surfaces to explore and we still haven't showered together. Plus—"

"Plus?" I asked, playing along.

"I don't plan to go another day without penetrating your body or having you beside me in bed."

"Well then it's a good thing I've decided to stop fighting it."

"A very good thing." He pulled the Corvette into a spot outside of the garage.

"We can swap out our cars so yours is in the garage."

"No we can't. Grab your stuff."

We scurried to the elevator and then quickly removed our shoes when entering his condo.

In the bedroom, he unzipped the back of my dress and let it fall to the floor. I stood naked in front of him. He brushed across my nipples while I unbuttoned his shirt and then worked on his pants. Once naked, skin on skin, we shared an ardent kiss until he led me to the tantric chair.

"Lay on your back over the high side, legs over the end."

My body arched over the chair, my butt on the downward slope. Stay stepped between my legs and slid home. He held my upper back in his arms as he sensuously rolled his hips into mine, rocking me forward and back. My legs curled around Stay's butt, my toes pointed in pleasure.

After several sultry strokes, he said, "I need to take you harder."

"Oh, yes. Please."

"Kneel on the lower end and reach across to the other side."

I balanced on my knees using the chair for support as he fucked me hard from behind. "More," I cried.

"Are you sure?"

"Give it to me. I'm so close."

He clutched my hair, causing my back to bow as he rammed into me. His fingers found my clit and he accelerated my climb.

I loved every second of it, and just before my climax began I felt his cock expand inside my pussy. "Oh ... Stay!"

"Now, Lainie," he called out.

Blessed relief flooded my bloodstream. I knew it would be short-lived with Stayman and the crazy effect he had on my libido, but I no longer minded it a bit. Living in the moment offered me such profound ease.

"I'll be right back," I said and stole myself away to the bathroom.

After cleaning up, I found Stay sprawled across the tantric chair. He held his arms out to me and I lay on top of him, nestling my nose against his neck. He played with my hair and traced his fingers down my back. "Lainie, I..."

"Yes?" I looked up into his intense, blue eyes.

"I'm really happy. More than I've ever been." He kissed my forehead.

I threaded my fingers into his short hair. "Me too. I sometimes don't recognize myself with you."

"How so?" He kissed me gently and then let me answer.

"Well besides my crazy, sexual behavior, it's hard to explain. Looser ... freer ... less OCDC." I rested my head against his chest.

"You're always cute and adorable, amongst other adjectives, but I understand." He massaged my earlobe as his heart thumped in my other ear.

"I'm sorry I didn't see it sooner," I said and I meant it.

"Timing is everything as they say."

"Yeah, I guess, but Jacqs tried to get me to see you. I just didn't think—"

"You didn't think we would fit together nor have anything in common."

I looked up again and said, "Yes, sorry, that's true. Plus I had no reference for a relationship like ours."

He sat up in the chair and pulled me into is lap. "How do you mean?"

"The voodoo, tantric connection."

He laughed, his eyes shining bright. "You know that's not what it is."

"I do but I've never had this with anyone else. The closest I have come to it is with Jacqs. Occasionally we'll call each other at the same time, or I'll pick up the phone to call her and she's already on the other end. But it's different with us, you feeling what I'm feeling. You knowing what I'm thinking. Are you like this with everyone?"

He shifted me up a bit higher and said, "Not like with us. As I've mentioned, I know when people are lying, even if they are just lying to themselves. But how we are together—that's new."

"Karen?" I asked.

"Not at all," he said, holding me close.

"Good. Did you mean at the restaurant you didn't

want me going without a bra unless we are together?"

"You caught that, did you? I'd rather not add to the docket of men I need to compete with."

"There's not much competition," I said, sitting up.

"Until you get the closure you need, there always will be."

"Let's not bring him into it." I stood and said, "I'm hungry. Shall we eat the shrimp?"

"And the Godiva chocolate cheesecake."

"Oh, let's start with that!"

"We can eat on the balcony. I have an extra robe."

"I'd love that."

Stay held out a long, blue, terrycloth robe and I stepped into it. "Thank you," I said, touching his hand, which rested on my shoulder.

He threw on boxers and a T-shirt and gathered the cheesecake and two forks.

Once on the balcony, I said, "This is ridiculously yummy and rich. I can feel my thighs expanding with each bite."

"We'll work it off together."

I laughed and said, "What do you have in mind?"

"I've always wanted to have sex out here. I couldn't talk Karen into it. She thought I was a pervert."

"Well you are, but fortunately I find it an endearing quality."

"Hey you," he said, yanking me into his lap.

"You brought it up, not me!" I said, still laughing.

He stood me up and removed my robe, laying it over the chair. Off went his boxers and T-shirt, and then he sat back on top of the robe. He positioned me on his legs, facing away from him.

The night chill had my nipples rock-hard and Stay's love bites along my neck and shoulder didn't help. Bright lights, buildings, and the waterway sparkled around us.

When he bit down on my shoulder I wiggled in his lap.

He abruptly stood me up and said, "I'll be right back."

My gut told me the simple fuck on the balcony was gone.

"What are you up to?" I asked as he came back out with a towel and oil.

"I'm taking you again. Your ass took so well to my cock last time..." He placed the folded towel down in front of me and ordered, "Kneel on the towel and bend over, your butt facing me."

My pulse raced as I did as told.

He massaged my buttocks and lower back before he drizzled oil down the crack of my ass. His fingers stroked and coaxed over my anal opening and when his finger penetrated me, I began to pant. "You'll have control this time," he said.

I didn't know what he meant but felt sure I would find out soon enough.

He pulled and stretched my anus, causing my clit to bulge with heat. "Come sit on my lap facing out." With his hand, he held his oiled cock up for me to slide down on.

"I don't know," I said.

"Try. If you don't enjoy it, we'll do something else."

"Okay," I said, feeling turned on, and incredibly slutty, I held onto Stay's thighs as I lowered my ass down onto his erection. My hips gyrated, allowing the head of his cock to pop in. "Oh my god. Oh ... oh ... oh." The intense feeling stole my breath. I tried to settle my breathing before I descended farther.

"You're doing great," Stay said, his deep voice dripping with lust. He held onto my hips to steady me.

Slowly and incrementally, I rose and fell until I became fully seated on his cock.

He spread my legs farther apart, his between mine.

One hand roamed my neck, shoulders, breast, and stomach while the other found my clit.

I used his knees as leverage to grind my ass against him.

"Jesus, woman that feels incredible." He moved his hips under me as we continued to thrash our bodies together.

I then lay my head back on his shoulder and we shared a smoldering kiss as he caressed my clit and held me tightly against him. I moved my hands to his hips and propelled myself up and down. My clit throbbed dangerously close to the tipoff. "Stay ... I'm close."

"Come for me, OC. I want to feel your ass tighten around my cock." He continued to massage my clit as I fucked him. He squeezed my nipple as I felt my release explode around his shaft. He held me as I drifted in the high of my climax. "Are you ready? I'm almost there myself. Close your legs."

Now my legs were sandwiched between his. He wrapped one arm around my chest and the other around my stomach. I no longer had control of the fuck. "Damn, Lane, I can't stop," he grunted in a whisper. He pumped me up and down on his lap.

I felt dizzy with desire as he owned and used me in a new way.

"Lainie," he groaned into my ear as he shot his hot come into my ass.

My back rested on Stay, both of us struggling to come back to earth and the balcony where we sat.

"Do you think it will lessen?" I asked after a few minutes passed.

"What?"

"The intense chemistry we feel for one another?"

"Not if I can help it." He scooped up a piece of cheesecake and said, "You deserve another bite after that workout. How does your ass feel?"

"Like it still has a semi-hard cock in it."

We both cracked up and then I ate the cake held out to me.

"Would you like to move over to your seat?" he asked, still holding onto me.

"No."

"Good."

CHAPTER TWENTY-EIGHT

I Will Possess Your Heart

by Death Cab for Cutie

The following morning after snuggling in bed, Stay followed me downstairs to move his car and say goodbye. As we embraced, I gave myself over to the safety I felt in his arms. It was far easier to focus on the explosive alchemy between us than my growing feelings. I could hear the three words coming from him even though he never once uttered them. They wrapped around me like a warm blanket, and instilled panic that I wouldn't be able to get out if I wanted to. I had just recently said I love you to Mason and regretted it every moment of everyday when Stay wasn't busy distracting me with his love and sex.

"I'll see you later," he said as we broke apart.

"Not if I see you first," I said, skipping away laughing. He caught up to me, flipped me against the front of my car and spanked me with force. "Hey!" I yelled playfully.

He let me up, but he looked upset.

"What is it?" I asked, feeling acute concern that I had somehow hurt him.

"Nothing, Lane. I'm sorry."

"It turned me on but I'm very concerned I upset you. I was just kidding around."

"I know. It's something my father used to say to me. He thought it was hysterical, only I knew he meant it.

Karen managed to find my weak spot often. I'm sorry for over reacting. I know you didn't mean anything by it."

He looked so young standing in front of me. My sexy, confident lover had a vulnerability that I hoped I never again stepped on.

"Come here," I said, holding my arms out to him. As soon as he moved into my embrace, I held his head in my hands. I nuzzled his neck and then kissed his eyes before I found his mouth. He melted into me just before our inferno of lust took over.

"I really have to go," I said against his throat.

He lifted my chin and said, "Thank you."

"Anytime," I said and then gave him a quick kiss goodbye.

On my way home, my carefree attitude toward Stay morphed back into regret and concern. The last thing I ever wanted to do was hurt him, the one man who had been there for me like no other male in my life other than my father.

I found Jacqs waiting for me on the bottom step of the stairs. "Hey, girl," I said.

"Are you okay?" she asked as she followed me into my apartment.

"I'm a huge mix of emotions."

"I know exactly what that feels like," she said, sitting on one of the stools next to the island.

"I bought cinnamon buns on the way here. There's some fresh fruit and other stuff in the fridge. I'll start a pot of coffee."

"Sounds good," she said and yawned. "I'm too tired to cook."

"Was last night a threesome night?"

Jacqs sighed and smiled, "Bond got home late and

woke us up. Neither Red nor I complained. I love sleeping between them both at night."

"Sleeping, uh-huh. Spare me the details." I measured out the coffee and added the necessary water.

"Don't spare a word on my account. How are things going with Stay?"

"That all depends," I said, getting two plates from the cabinet.

"On?"

"Whether or not you're going to feed everything I say to Red. Some of it is too personal." From the fridge I got the leftover sliced fruit and set it down between us.

"If you tell me not to, I won't. You know that."

"Okay," I said, handing her a plate and a fork. "Things with Stay have been going great. He's an amazing man. The sex is off the charts, mind-blowing really. Not that there was anything wrong or lacking with Mason at all, but with Stay it's like we're explosive together. It's hard for us to be together without ... you know what I mean."

"Yes, I do." She opened the box of cinnamon rolls, took one out for herself, and placed one on my plate. "So what's the problem? Mason? Have you heard from him?"

"Sort of Mason, sort of not. I haven't heard from him since the day after the fiasco. It's been about a week. I still miss him. Not when I'm with Stay, but when I'm alone. I think that Stay thinks if he's always with me I won't have the chance to miss Mason. Do you want some coffee?"

"Yes, keep going."

I poured each of us a mug of coffee, and placed the cream in front of Jacqs. "I keep thinking about how he looked Sunday night. I was so devastated, I didn't care that he was hurting. His expression, his tears, I can't get them out of my mind."

She added cream and said, "He cried?"

"Yes."

"And Stay?"

I mixed the cream into my coffee with a spoon and said, "I found out we have so much in common and we have a lot of fun together. For the most part he is incredibly easy going. Now don't share this with anyone, Jacqs."

"That he's great?"

"No, what I'm about to say."

"Okay."

After taking a sip of coffee, I explained what happened earlier with Stay.

"I sometimes forget that he had such a shitty childhood," Jacqs said. "Were you scared?"

I could feel myself blush. "No, it turned me on."

She giggled and said, "I see. *That* kind of sex. Good for you. I didn't think you had it in you."

"I didn't either, honestly." I peeled off a piece of the cinnamon bun, ate it, and chased it down with some coffee. "I had stopped giving myself a hard time over our friendship because he seemed to really understand that I'm limited in what I'm capable of right now."

"But?"

"He told me he doesn't deal with rejection well, and I believe him now." I massaged my head, feeling a headache coming on.

"Maybe after you get over Mason you can love Stayman."

"I don't know." I spooned some fruit on my plate and picked at it. "Enough about me. I'm bored with myself and my drama. How's it going with you and the boys?"

"Very well actually. I do get the feeling sometimes that Aidan is ready for Bond to move on, but you know him, he has patience of steel."

"Are you ready to let Bond go? Is he ready to let you go?" I asked and then tossed a grape into my mouth.

"Those are tricky questions." She paused and ate some of her breakfast. "If you had asked me if I could be happy with Aidan alone, that would be easy to answer: yes. Are Bond and I ready to let go? No, not yet."

"Jacqs, you must realize that if you wait long enough, Bond will find someone else to be serious about."

"Yes, that's what I'm hoping for," she said, looking completely serious.

"What the fuck are you talking about? You just flipped out when you found out he was seeing someone regularly."

"I didn't say it would be easy for me. I'm sure it will fuck me up, but I'll get over it. I have Aidan, and I love him more than I could imagine loving anyone. Here's the thing—and mind you, I'm not ready—if I end it, it will be bad for all of us. If Bond ends it, it will only be bad for me. That's the way I want it."

"Jesus, Jacqs. That's some fucked up shit, but even crazier—I understand."

"I knew you would," she said, smiling at me. "I love you, girl. I'm so glad we have each other."

"Me too. Which reminds me, my mother's shindig is Saturday evening. Please say you are still coming."

"Why not take Stay?" she asked casually.

I shot her a look.

"Okay, okay! Just promise me we won't have to stay late."

"We'll slip out as soon as possible."

"It'll be nice to see your dad," she said, her elbow on the counter, her chin resting in her hand. "How's Samantha doing?"

"She's incredible—so reliable and always available

when I need her. She's been doing an amazing job on the window displays. She's neat, organized, and fantastic with the customers."

"I'm happy for you both. Sam loves the job and says working for you is a breeze. She mentioned the time you both were singing so loudly when the store was empty that you didn't notice a customer coming until they walked up. She said you both nearly died laughing and that you managed to get it together to greet the customer but she had to run into the back."

I wiped my mouth on a napkin. "She's really easy to work with. Did she tell you she's pushing for lingerie in the shop?"

"Nope, sounds like it's time for me to drop by Bella." Jacqs ate more of her bun. "What are your plans for the rest of the day?"

"Stay's coming over." I filled my coffee cup and topped off Jacqs's.

"Are you changing your mind?"

"I don't know, Jacqs. I feel like I'm moving forward in a relationship I'm not ready for. I honestly don't know what the right thing to do is. I mean I like him. I really like him. I enjoy his company, but where I'm using him to survive my breakup, I think he is falling more in love with me."

"You're using him? Fuck, Lainie," she said, pointing right at me.

"Don't get mad at me. He told me to use him. He said that it's too early for us to be thinking about the future and if I could be involved with Mason knowing there was no future, I could certainly do so with him."

"So you're being honest." Her shoulders relaxed.

"Completely."

Her eyes went wide with genuine concern. "He's being a complete moron."

358

"I'll tell him you think so. You're forbidden to share any of this. I don't want Bond getting involved."

"Can I talk to Stay?" she asked.

"I'd really rather you not. I'll tell him what we talked about and let him decide." I stood and circled around the island to Jacqs.

"Okay. Let me help you straighten up and I'll head out."

"Don't worry about it." I walked her to the door and said, "Please send my love to Red and Bond."

We hugged tightly and then she said, "Please tell Stay I'm here if he needs to talk."

"I will. Love you, girl."

"Love you too."

I locked the door behind her and cleaned up the kitchen.

Out on the balcony, I had a smoke and journaled.

I'm so glad Jacqs is in my life. It's nice to have a friend that gets my certain kind of insanity.

Should I or shouldn't I? That's the real question. I shouldn't have said Stay could come over ahead of time. Ahhh! I feel like I need space, and yet I don't really want any. I wish Monday was here already and I could be busy at work.

I need to stop making this complicated and just be honest.

In my bedroom, perched on the end of the bed, I called Stay.

"Hey, gorgeous. How was brunch?" he asked.

"Hi, Stay. It's always great to catch up with Jacqs," I said as I lay back onto the mattress.

"What is it?"

"Jacqs said, and I quote, 'You are being a moron.' She wants you to know she's available to talk." I twirled my hair around my finger and tapped my foot, still not comfortable with being that blatantly honest.

"It sounds like you two had a fairly intense conversation, care to fill me in?" he asked.

"Well I mentioned that you gave me permission to use you and—"

"Oh, I see. Yes, well, she doesn't know what it's like between us. Do you still want to see me today?"

I didn't care for his tone of voice. "You're angry."

"No, Lane, I'm not. I just can feel a brush off when it's coming. If you need space, I completely understand, but if this is you trying to decide for me—"

"No, I want you to come," I said and I meant it.

"See you soon."

I greeted Stay at the door in my robe. "I thought we could shower together."

"Perfect, and then I have other plans for you."

"Oh? Another surprise for me?" In his embrace, I couldn't fathom that I might have chosen to spend the day alone without him.

"Yes, a good one. Let's shower first."

I had never showered with a man before, and after basking under the flow of water I found out that Stay had very specific ideas about it.

"Turn around and angle your head back." He washed my hair and massaged my scalp. Under the water, he rinsed my hair too.

The highly sensual experience had my nipples standing at attention. His cock was equally engaged. However, when I tried to kneel down in front of him, he said, "Later." He washed my whole body, slowly and erotically, and then quickly washed himself.

"If your intention was to leave me hot and bothered, you did a great job," I said as we dried off.

"And now I'm going to make you come like crazy," he said. His devious expression and the twitch of his eyebrows caused me to laugh.

In the bedroom, he set up a pillow at the head of the bed, two stacked to the left, and one on the right. "Do you have lubricant?" he asked.

"No, I usually don't—"

"Right. Olive oil?"

"Sure." I ran out to the kitchen, found it, and returned. "Is this the tantric thingy?"

"A small taste."

"Oh, yay."

"Lay down at the head of the bed."

Just the positioning had me turned on. I felt so exposed and instead of shying away from it, my arousal spiked. My left knee rested on the two pillows beside me and my right hung over Stay's right leg. His left leg curved around my stomach. His right foot and my left lined up against each other, almost like creating a circuit connection of energy.

He massaged my body slowly and sensuously, teasing my nipples and working closer and closer to my epicenter. He kneaded my thighs and then flirted around the folds of my pussy.

"I don't think you're going to need the lube," I moaned.

"I was thinking that myself. You're already glistening."

His fingers trailed around my inner and outer lips. Deep into my wetness, he used my essence to coat my clit. "All you need to do is relax and breathe steadily."

"Okaaay," I sighed out.

He gently rubbed the top of my clit in repetitive strokes. "Is this working for you?"

"Oh yes," I groaned.

"You're responding well. Your clit is already so hard." He pressed down on either sides of my opening, shifting the hood back, exposing more of my arousal."

"Oh ... ohhh."

"Just breathe and relax."

He gathered more wetness and continued the sashay of his fingers. "You're almost there," he said, his voice gravely with desire. With his free hand, he pressed down between my breasts.

A grounded energy coursed within me. Then starting at my feet a tingling sensation rose up my legs, and spread out to encompass my whole being. Just before my release took hold my body shook like a rag doll. The electric current weaved internally and then sparked out of my extremities sending me on a new voyage of emancipation.

"Holy hell," I groaned once all the tension in my body left and I melted into the bed.

He lay down next to me and whispered, "That was phenomenal."

"It was," I said, my eyes still closed. The aftershocks fired their pulsing tremors in my core and out my limbs. "Wow."

We spent the rest of the day making love, cuddling, napping, noshing, and laughing a lot. He made it easy for me to relax with him and not worry about the future. At night he spooned me and I sighed against him completely contented.

CHAPTER TWENTY-NINE

A Sadness Runs Through Him

by The Hoosiers

At work on Monday, I helped Samantha move the wire mannequin over to the window. She used it in the center of a colorful beach display. Several wraps hung like fringe around the bottom half creating a skirt.

"I love it," I said once she finished setting it all up. "Love the beach ball, buckets, and shovels too. Nice job."

"Thanks, Lainie. I'm very happy you like it."

The bell on the door jingled and a woman walked in who seemed out of place. She looked around and not just at the clothes, which was the first thing that struck me about her. She seemed to be checking out the ceiling, flooring, and walls as well. In addition, she wore expensive clothes, which were a very different style than I offered at the shop. Her turquoise, corded, shimmering, knit jacket and corset-seamed dress were tailored to perfection.

"What's up with her?" Sam whispered in my ear.

"I'm about to find out." I walked toward the customer and said, "Can I help you?"

Then her assessing gaze landed on me. Looking me up and down, she said, "You're not at all what I'd expected."

"Excuse me?"

"It's Lainie, right?"

"Yes, and you are?"

She held out her hand and said, "Victoria Mason."

"Oh," I said, clearing my throat and trying to catch the breath that fled out of me. On automatic pilot, I shook her hand.

With her hair down and little or no makeup on she looked nothing like the woman I saw at the fair. The woman before me had her dark hair pulled back in a drastic bun and her face was fully made up. "Relax," she said. "I'm not here to yell or scream. I have a favor to ask."

"How did you find me?" I asked, shifting uncomfortably.

"Let's just say I keep track of things." Her attention shifted to Sam who walked over to us, out of curiosity I'm sure.

"Can you give us a minute?" I asked her.

"Right, okay," she said.

Once Sam walked away, Victoria said, "You've done a nice job with the place."

"Thank you," I said, swallowing with difficulty.

"I guess I should start. You can't be married to Mason and not know what he gets up to. As much as he thinks otherwise, he has very little capacity for subterfuge. I won't lie, the first affair nearly cost us our marriage until I realized he was a much better husband when he had a lover. He has extra pep in his step and is generally happier and calmer. I don't normally get involved or interfere, but I felt like I had to do something in this case.

"Maybe I should have realized the extent of his feelings for you, because somehow we found a better place in our marriage than we ever have before." She paused and made direct eye contact. "I'm sure you're ready for me to get to the point—I want you to take him back. Since you ended the relationship, he hasn't gotten out of bed. I have never known Mason to be depressed. I can't get him engaged in anything, including the kids. I don't know how much longer I can tell the children that he's ill.

"He cancelled the job he was flying off to that Sunday and hasn't worked since. I have to assume you loved him, and probably still do. Since you helped create this mess, I'm asking you to clean it up."

"Wow. I'm sorry I don't know what to say. I had assumed what he said he felt for me was a lie especially after ... anyway, I'm sort of seeing someone now and ... the others? Did he love them?"

"No, I don't believe so. If he told you he loved you, I have to assume that he meant it."

"You're being very civil about all of this."

"Lainie, I want my life back and I'm asking you to get it for me. I think we can agree you owe me that." She opened her white clutch and then held out a card to me. "If you ever need to reach me."

I took the card from her and stared at it. Once I looked up, she was on her way toward the front of the store. *Holy fucking hell! He wasn't lying to me.* My heart felt like it was breaking all over again.

"Are you okay?" Sam asked, touching my elbow.

I couldn't speak. I just shook my head and said, "Can you close up tonight? I need to take off."

"Yes, of course. Are you going to be okay?"

"I need some time to think. Thanks, Sam," I said and reached out to give her a hug.

She seemed incredibly grateful for my demonstration of affection. She hugged me back tight and said, "If you need an ear, I'm always here."

"Thank you, Samantha."

On my way home from the shop Stayman called me. I

almost hit ignore but guilt made me answer it.

"Is everything okay?" he said.

I had no privacy with him. "I need some space right now."

"Mason?"

"I just need some time."

"You're lying."

"I haven't seen or talked to Mason and I don't want to talk right now. I'm sorry I can't get together tonight. I ... I ... please... I'll call soon."

"I think if you go back to him, you will regret it for the rest of your life. I love you, Lainie, don't forget to factor that in," he said and hung up.

I sat in my car, not being able to breathe. My eyes darted around while my mind tried to make sense of what I just heard. Stay finally confessed his love, and Mason really loved me all along. His wife actually wanted me to take him back. The thoughts in my head were swimming around too fast. Frozen, I couldn't decide what to do. I felt paralyzed. I knew if I called Jacqs or my father they would both tell me that Stay was the only sensible choice.

It killed me to think I could hurt Stay. I should be overjoyed, right? Instead I bounced around in a rapid river of confusion. I gave in and texted:

> **Me:** Can you talk?
> **Stay:** Only if you intend on being honest.
> **Me:** Okay. Maybe it would be easier to text?
> **Stay:** You heard from Mason. I felt it.
> **Me:** Not exactly. His wife came by Bella.

I waited for his text back but my phone rang instead.

"His wife?" Stay asked.

"She wants me to take him back. She says I owe it to

her to clean up the mess I made. According to her, Mason hasn't gotten out of bed since last Sunday."

"Jesus, Lainie. I can't imagine what you must be going through, although I feel it twisting in my gut. You must be incredibly confused. I'm sorry I just blurted out that I love you that way. I've wanted to say it to you a hundred different times but I knew you weren't ready to hear it. You probably still aren't, but I can't let you go back to Mason without knowing."

"The last thing I want to do is hurt you."

"It's already hurting, Lainie. If you loved me back there would be no question. Do what you need to do. I release you."

"Oh god, my heart feels like its breaking."

"I have to go. Take care of yourself," he said and hung up.

I banged my fist against the steering wheel and howled out my pain. With tears still running down my face, I started my car and drove out. I stayed off the highway and made it back to my apartment safely.

Out on my balcony, I paced back and forth with a cigarette in hand. The broken pieces of my heart no longer knew how to form back on their own and I couldn't decipher the ache in my core. I wanted to go hide in the safety of Stay's arms and wanted to see Mason at the same time. In my hysteria, laughter bubbled to the surface when I envisioned Stay going with me to see Mason.

My mind was close to shattering just like my heart. My insides where jumping for joy and hurling me over a cliff to my death. *How the fuck do I reconcile that?*

I imagined Stay feeling all my pain and it made me feel even worse. "Tell me what to do!" I yelled at no one.

I stared at the phone in my hand, not really seeing it. Setting my phone to the side, I pulled my journal onto my lap.

Breathe. Stop being hysterical. Let's not make this more ridiculous than it needs to be. Do I want to see Mason? Yes, of course I do. Do I want Mason back? I don't know. And Stay? It kills me that I'm hurting him. I don't want to hurt him. He really is the last person I would want to cause pain. He has been my savior in so many ways. It's just so fucking messy.

Breathe, Breathe, Breathe.

Mason's wife showed up at work! What the fuck? Can I assume she is telling me the truth? Why would she lie? I know what I need to do. Yes, but it's like drawing this invisible line in the sand that separates me from Stay.

Stay knew this might happen, right? I don't even know if Mason wants to hear from me. Maybe he doesn't. UGH! Fuck me. Okay. I'm going to get this over with.

Me: Mason?

I lit another cigarette and paced back and forth. My phone rang and it startled the crap out of me.

"Lainie?" Jacqs said.

Oh god, I breathed out. "Hi, Jacqs."

"Sam called me. She was worried about you. She said some woman came into the shop and you took off just after. She said you looked like you were in shock."

"It was Victoria," I said, blowing out smoke.

"Who?"

"Mason's wife," I said, sitting down in the chair and bouncing my knees.

"Holy hell. What did she want?"

My phone vibrated in my hand. "Listen, Jacqs, I need to go. She wanted me to get in touch with Mason. It's a long story and I promise to fill you in soon. Please call

Stay, or have Bond call and check in on him."

"You told him?" she asked, her voice strident.

"I didn't have to, but yes, I did."

"I don't understand."

I closed my eyes and said, "Let him explain it. I have to deal with this. I'll call you soon."

"I love you, girl, and you can reach me anytime."

"You too."

I pulled up my texts and found:

> **MM:** I thought I would never hear from you again. Please tell me you want to see me. Please, Lainie. I'm so sorry. Please give me the chance to explain.
> **Me:** I'm home, can you come here?
> **MM:** Right after a shower. Don't go anywhere.
> **Me:** I won't.

I felt suffocated by my work outfit and stripped out of it. The shower beckoned to me and I set the water as hot as I could stand it. I quickly washed off, and dried, and then gargled and brushed my teeth. In sweatpants and a T-shirt, I sat on the couch and waited.

Fear seemed to overwhelm every other emotion. I kept rearranging myself on the couch, not finding a comfortable position. In the kitchen I found a hard apple cider and thought about drinking it but put it back instead. I grabbed my cigarettes and journal from the balcony and placed them in the draw of my nightstand and then I emptied the ashtray. After rinsing it, I put it in the dishwasher.

A knock sounded on the door and I felt slightly dizzy, my heart was beating so fast.

I opened the door and I hardly recognized the man before me. He looked ten pounds thinner, his face gaunt.

His energy was marinated in sadness.

"Thank you for reaching out to me. I really thought I'd lost you forever."

"Come sit on the couch," I said, taking his hand and leading him there.

"You look beautiful, Lainie, as radiant as ever. Have you been well?"

I had no idea how to address his comment so I said, "Your wife came by my clothing store today."

"She what?" He looked completely stunned.

"Yes. She asked me to take you back."

He stared at me, dumbfounded.

I shared what she said and gave him a minute to digest it.

"Would you have contacted me otherwise?" he asked, running his fingers through his salt and pepper hair.

"I honestly don't know."

"Baby, I'm so sorry. I never ever wanted to hurt you. You are the love of my life, and my life makes no sense without you in it." His eyes filled with tears. "I wish we had met years ago."

I could feel all the pieces of my rejected heart, amassing back together.

We stared at each other and I didn't know what to do. I still—even with him right in front of me—didn't know what I wanted.

He gathered me in his arms and I let him. He held me as I cried, his tears joining mine. We held on tight as if gravity might pull us apart. He stood and said, "Please let me show you how much I love you."

Standing up next to him we kissed and I closed my eyes hoping to find the love that once lived there. What I felt was a mixture of sadness and confusion.

He led me to my bedroom and reached to undress me.

I held his hand against me and said, "Mason, I can't have sex with you. There's too much that's unresolved."

"You're right. Let's talk."

I started, "Is it true that you've canceled jobs and not gotten out of bed?"

"I couldn't live with myself, knowing how much I hurt you."

My eyes filled with tears again but I continued, "You led me to believe your relationship with Victoria was incredibly strained."

"It was when we met. That was all true but somehow my love for you spilled over into my marriage."

"You plan to stay married then," I said.

"Yes," he said, touching my thigh.

"So nothing has really changed other than we know your wife knows about me, has always known about me."

"Her knowledge will allow us to have more time together." He pleaded with his clear, blue eyes but I didn't feel their impact anymore.

"Or less. Regardless, what are you offering me?" My anger began to resurface.

"My love."

"I'm sorry, Mason, that's not enough anymore."

"Why not?"

"I'm in love with someone else." I finally admitted it to myself.

"In a week? The boy?"

"His name is Stayman, and he's offering me a full life not bits and pieces of one."

"You're still angry."

"Only with myself. I hurt someone very important to me so I could see you again. I forgive you Mason. Maybe if you channel the energy you funneled to me into your marriage you might find you have everything you need. I can't wait around for you anymore."

"Lainie, please think about this. We haven't had the chance to spend time and reconnect."

"Mason, I need to go. I need to find 'the boy' as you call him. Please stop hiding in your bed and take care of your family. They need you." I glanced at Mason and then woke up my phone.

Me: Stay are you home? Can I come over?

Mason didn't move off the bed, his expression dejected.

I went to the second bedroom and gathered his belongs. Handing them to him, I said, "Maybe someday you and I can be friends. I care about you deeply but it's time for me to have a real life for myself. Come on." I held out my hand to him.

In front of the door, we hugged one last time and said goodbye.

I hoped he would find his way back to his wife for good.

When I received nothing back from Stay, I called him.

"You've reached me. Well my voicemail anyway. Leave a message, I'll call you back."

"Hi Stay. Where are you? Can I come by? We need to talk. Please call me back as soon as you get this."

I thought about driving over to Stay's. Instead, I texted Bond.

Me: Have you heard from Stay? Is he with you?

To Jacqs I texted:

Me: Did you talk to Stay? He isn't responding to me.

The waiting drove me crazy. All I wanted to do was tell Stay how I felt about him and no one was texting me back.

Finally I got something from Jacqs.

> **Jacqueline:** I haven't spoken to Stay but I know Bond has.
> **Me:** Bond isn't responding either.
> **Jacqueline:** I think they went to an AA meeting. They might have their phones turned off.
> **Me:** Because of me? Do you know where?
> **Jacqueline:** No, I don't know where. What happened with Mason?
> **Me:** I said goodbye.
> **Jacqueline:** Oh fuck, I'm so relieved. Don't worry, I'm sure you'll hear back from Stayman soon.

Only, I didn't. A few hours later I heard back from Bond.

> **Bond:** Stay needs some time. I'm sure you'll hear from him soon.
> **Me:** I need to talk to him, tell him how I feel. Can you help me?
> **Bond:** Lainie, all I can tell you is to give him space.
> **Me:** He hasn't asked me for space, he just hasn't responded.
> **Bond:** Look, Lane, I can't tell you his business. I know you understand that. He's hurting and needs to work it through himself.
> **Me:** But he doesn't need to be hurting.
> **Bond:** My suggestion is to email him.
> **Me:** I can't say this stuff over email. Okay, thanks for getting back to me.

Bond: Hang in there.
Me: I'll try.

CHAPTER THIRTY

Say Something

by A Great Big Word & Christina Aguilera

The next few days moved by painfully slow. Most of the time I felt like I was trudging through sludge, forcing myself to put each foot in front of the other. The irony wasn't lost on me. Before I would wait and wait to hear from Mason and now it was as if I sat at a bus stop where my bus never passed through.

I finally broke down on Wednesday and texted two songs to Stay.

> **Me:** David Gray pleaseforgiveme.mp3
> **Me:** Incubus imissyou.mp3

I figured out that I had never experienced depression over Mason because I had new perspective with Stay. If he didn't contact me soon, I planned to bang down his door.

I hadn't decided if I would go to the get together at Red's. Would it be worse for Stay not to show at all or be there and ignore me? Of course I couldn't imagine Stay ignoring me in person. He clearly was a master at avoidance over the phone though.

Samantha had to be sick of my dark funk, I know I surely was. I texted Jacqs to find out the lay of the land.

Me: Is Stay coming tonight?
Jacqueline: I haven't heard, I can ask Bond.
Me: I'll text him.
Jacqueline: Are you coming?
Me: I haven't made up my mind.
Jacqueline: Let me know.
Me: K. Later

Me: Do you know if Stay's going tonight? Will you be there?
Bond: Yes for me and I think for Stay too. We're going to hit a meeting first.
Me: If I go, will he talk to me?
Bond: Lane, I don't see him ignoring you.
Me: That's not very encouraging.
Bond: I have your back. See you soon.
Me: Thanks.

As I started to get ready to leave for the day, Sam said, "Will I see you at Red's?"

"Yeah, I'm going. It's a chance to see Stay. If he won't talk to me, I can always shove him into the pool."

"That sounds like a good tactic," she said, laughing. "Sure to endear you to him."

"I'm desperate."

"I'll keep my fingers crossed."

"Thanks. And thanks for closing up."

"Of course."

We hugged and I went out through the back.

At my apartment, I showered and spent way too much time trying to decide what to wear. I let my hair dry naturally and finally decided on a twisted, mint-green, halter, chiffon dress. I couldn't wear a bra with it because the straps crossed in front leaving a sexy keyhole between my breasts. I chose beige, strap heals and a wide, clip on bracelet I situated halfway up my forearm. Dangling earrings peeked out under my hair. I applied a little eye makeup and then grabbed my bag.

When I arrived at Red's, Bond and Stay hadn't showed yet. Most of the group was busy playing pool. I sat on the couch glider outside, wishing I had decided to wear jeans and T-shirt. *I look like I'm trying too hard*, I thought.

The French door opened and Bond came out.

"Hi," I said, expecting Bond to tell me Stay chose not to come.

"Hi, Lane."

I stood up and met him halfway.

"You look incredible in that dress. Stay will have a hard time denying you."

"Is that his plan?" I said feeling defeated before I even had a chance.

"He's out front and wants to talk to you."

Fear and apprehension accompanied me as I stepped forward. "If Jacqs comes out, please tell her where I went."

"Yes, of course," Bond said and lifted my hand. "I'm rooting for you."

"Thank you. It means a lot to me."

Bond held the door for me and I plodded through the house, not in a hurry to get to my destination. When I stepped outside, I saw Stay leaning against his antique Corvette. I took it as a good sign. His dress also indicated he'd made an effort, black slacks and a dark-gray button-down shirt.

He turned when he heard the door shut.

My throat felt blocked and I didn't know if I could speak. I had no idea what to say anyway. I stood awkwardly in front of him, staring down at my heels.

"I got your songs," Stay said. "You look amazing tonight."

I nodded, peeking up.

"Do you want to tell me what happened with Mason?"

"I said goodbye. I told him he should put the energy he was putting into me back into his marriage." *Don't cry, don't cry, don't cry,* ran through my head before I said, "Why have you cut me off?"

"I told you about me and rejection. We aren't the best of friends," he said as he stood up straight.

"If you had given me half a chance you would have found out otherwise. Why is it you only feel the bad stuff?"

He stared at me, and I didn't care for the emotion I felt.

"So just like that"—I snapped my fingers—"you stop loving me?"

"It's not that simple."

"Why do I continue to allow myself to love the wrong men? If you don't want me anymore, fine, I'll leave. Have fun tonight." I started to walk away.

"Lainie, wait."

"I've been through enough already Stayman."

"Did you say you love me?" he said, clutching my arm and not letting me go.

"If you hadn't been such an ass, you would have known that on Monday. Please let go of my arm," I said, trying to tug it free.

He let me go. "When you said you were going back to Mason—"

"I never said I was going back to him. I had to see him. I found out that what I felt for him was gone. I told him that I love you."

"You told him that?" His eyes opened wide in surprise.

"Yes, and if you would have given me even one moment you would know that what I felt for you was completely different."

"Felt?"

"Did you drink alcohol?"

"No, but for the first time in years I wanted to. I called Bond instead." He touched my arm again and I shrugged it away.

"This is such a mess," I said. "I understand that this stirred up some old, dark stuff for you but I'm not sure I can be with a man who will shut me out when it gets tough."

"I thought we were over," he said, holding his palms out in front of him.

"Did you get my text? Did you listen to my message?"

"Yes."

"Did I sound like I was ending our relationship?"

"In my mind you already had."

"If I keep standing here, I'm going to start crying or hit you and I don't want to do either. I'm mad at you Stayman. I've been so desperate to hear from you, all I could think about was being with you, in your arms again and yet you greet me like some kind of stranger."

"I need some time."

"Yeah and I'm always the one that gets to wait. Sort it out. I'll either be here waiting or not. Why the car and the clothes?"

"I ... I'm scared."

"And I'm not? You woo me, make me fall in love with you and now you're not sure. How am I supposed to take that? Why are you dressed up? Oh god. You have a date. That's why you were waiting out here for me. You're not even planning to go in." I punched his chest with the sides of my fist, my tears flowing freely.

He grabbed my wrist and pulled me to him. "Don't,

Lainie. There's no one else," he said as he held me tight.

"Don't do this, Stay," I cried. "Please. If you send me away, I don't think my heart will survive it."

"I need to get myself under control again."

"Let me help. I love you," I pleaded.

"I don't know if I can."

I stepped back and said, "Okay." I blinked my eyes several times. "Take care of yourself. Tell Jacqs I decided to go home."

"Lainie," he said.

I didn't turn around. I barely made it to my car. The dark haze that filled in around me felt so oppressive that the angst became trapped inside, tearing me to shreds. Never again, I vowed. Never!

CHAPTER THIRTY-ONE

Start of the Breakdown

by Tears for Fears

The dark funk turned me into a hollow version of myself, functioning at work, putting on a smile when necessary, and breaking down at home. I hated Stay with a passion I had never felt toward another, not even when I saw Mason with his wife. Stay had promised me the moon and then took the stars away along with it. At least Mason was honest from the beginning about what he had to offer. Stayman was a fucking liar.

Everyone other than Stay kept texting me. I even received some from Mason. He asked if I had really taken the time to think, et cetera. The only one I responded to was Jacqs, letting her know we were still on for my mother's party on Saturday and asking her to tell everyone else I was fine.

Fine is a funny word when you think about it. Telling someone I'm fine, in dictionary terms means being satisfactory or in a satisfactory condition. However when our group used it, we tended to mean agreement, or that we aren't so bad off we're going to kill ourselves. It didn't really mean that how we felt was acceptable but just that we would make it through. I would make it through, of that I had no doubt, but I thought I might have to find a new circle of friends.

Maybe someday I'd be capable of being friendly with Stayman but it would take a long time.

Over that Thursday and Friday the only positive thing that happened was that I gave Samantha a substantial raise.

"Here's your check for April," I said.

"Why so much? I mean I'm not complaining."

"I've given you a raise and changed your job title to assistant manager."

"Get the fuck out of town!" She glanced to the check, then to me, then back to the check. She danced around a bit and then threw her arms around my neck and gave me a big hug. "I can't wait to tell Mom. She'll be so thrilled."

"I don't want you sneaking off and working for someone else," I said with a smile I actually felt.

"Not a chance."

I dreaded Saturday night like the plague. My mother had a keen sense of my vulnerabilities and tended to exploit them for her amusement. If I didn't feel like I'd totally be letting my father down, I would have blown off her party.

CHAPTER THIRTY-TWO

Heart Skipped a Beat

by The xx

O n Saturday, staring into my closet, I wished I hadn't worn the green dress on Wednesday. I liked it and knew I could never wear it again. Instead I slipped into a navy, sleeveless, sequin and lace dress with a sweetheart neckline. The hem came down to about mid-thigh. I wore black pumps and took my time with my makeup. My mother wouldn't leave the house without a full-face on.

She hated my hair down with natural waves but I figured I needed to give her something to gripe about. Frankly I didn't have the energy to blow-dry my hair straight.

Jacqs planned to meet me at my parent's house so she could make her escape when she'd had enough. I didn't blame her at all. My mother had a knack for spreading her venom around when she wanted to.

I gathered all the red wine I still had in the apartment for Mason and brought it with me to the party along with my clutch. Cars lined either side of the street adjacent to my parent's place.

My father took the bag filled with wine bottles out of my hand and scooped me up into a big hug. "Hi, baby girl. Thank you so much for coming."

"Is Aunt Sue here yet?"

"No but most of your mother's friends are. A friend of

yours is waiting in the den."

"Thanks, Dad," I said, wondering why he didn't just say Jacqs.

The door to the den stood closed and I had to assume my mother didn't want her friends going in there. My father mostly used the wood-paneled room anyway. I shoved open the door, which tended to get stuck on the thick carpet below. Stay sat on the couch and not Jacqs.

"She's not coming is she?" I asked, crossing my arms in front of me.

"No."

"I'm going to kill her," I said through gritted teeth. "Why are you here?"

"I wanted to talk to you."

"Phone, email, or coming by the store were all viable options and you chose this? It's bad enough I have to contend with my mother," I said, which made me think I should probably close the door. I pushed it shut behind me and locked it. I turned and placed my back against it. "Let's get this over with and then you can go."

He stood and started toward me. His snug, black jeans and his white dress shirt clung to the firm planes of his physique.

I held my palm out in a halting gesture. His sexual energy hit me like a battering ram and I felt his crystal clear intention. "Don't," I said.

"I'm sorry, OC."

"Fine, I accept your apology. You can leave now." I turned to open the door and he descended upon me.

"No, Lainie. Please stop for a minute and listen." He held my face in his hands and pressed his body into me.

"Pushing your hard cock against me isn't fighting fair."

With a devilish expression, he said, "I've never fought fair where you were concerned. I'm asking you to hear me out."

"I can't think straight with you on top of me," I said but didn't struggle to get out from under him.

"Then I'll consider it an advantage. I'm not moving."

I crushed my palms against the door, not allowing myself to touch him back.

"I'm sorry I spooked. Never in my life have I felt what I feel for you. How we are together, the connection we share. When I thought you went back to Mason, I realized how much I had been lying to myself. I had long since passed casual with you. You had my heart and it felt like you just dropped it on the ground and left it unguarded. And you were right that it triggered abandonment and being cast aside like I had been in the past.

"I went to see my grandmother yesterday and she knocked some needed sense into me. She said I was treating myself just like my parents did. That it was me alone causing my pain. That if you loved me, why wasn't I reaching out to you to help me through. That I was treating myself as if I didn't deserve your love. That I wasn't worth it."

"I know what that feels like." I broke down and touched his cheek.

"I love you so much that it's hard to know what to do with all the emotion." He started kissing up my neck and then said, "I promise, if you give me another chance, I'll never walk away again."

"You really hurt me, Stay," I said, still in pain.

"I know I did. I will spend the rest of my days making it up to you." He kissed my head and held me tight. "I love you."

"I hate you," I said.

Stay crowded me, his lips an inch from mine. "No you don't, you're just angry."

"I should be angrier with you." I felt myself giving in.

"Yes, you should be. Lane, I was so dumb." He nodded.

"Yes you were. Dumb-ass dumb."

"You're absolutely right."

"If we try again, I'm never letting you go," I said, a sob catching in my throat.

"Don't cry, honey. I've got you." He took me in his arms and carried me to the couch, rocking me in his lap.

We sat that way for several minutes, not letting go of each other. I held on so tight as if he might be a dream that could go up in a cloud of smoke.

"I'm here, Lainie," he said as if he heard my thoughts. "Damn I missed you. Everything about you, but your smell especially." He buried his nose in my hair and breathed. "Listen, OC, I want us to live together. I can move in with you or you can live with me. Either way."

"When?" I asked, brushing my hand over his head.

"Oh, don't stop," he said, closing his eyes. "We can start packing up tomorrow."

"Your place definitely," I said, holding his head in my hands.

"You're saying yes?"

"Yes, Stay. I love you and I can't wait to wake up with you every day."

"And make love to me every night?"

"Yes, that too. What are we going to do about that?" I asked, pointing down at his erection.

"I have an idea." He lowered me down in front of him.

Kneeling, I unbuttoned his pants and freed his cock, tasting the wet tip. "Hmmmm," I moaned. I opened my mouth and took him in as deep as I could. I wanted my nose buried against the base of his shaft but I couldn't manage it on my own. Tilting my head up, I said, "Help me."

And he did. He shifted to the edge of the couch and

thrust down into my throat, riding in and out. "Lainie," he called out. "Oh, you're taking more ... Jesus ... it feels..." He withdrew and said, "That feels incredible."

"More."

He penetrated several more times and said, "As amazing as that feels, I need to be inside you." He helped me up to my feet. "Have you ever done it in your parent's house?"

"No, never." I shimmed up my dress and removed my silk panties.

Over his lap, he guided my hips down. Then our frantic quest for fulfillment raged and with our mouths locked in a steamy kiss, our hips collided into one another.

So lost in our coupling, it took me a moment to recognize the sound of a knock on the door.

"Lainie, is everything okay?" my father asked. "Your mother keeps asking for you."

I giggled against Stay's mouth, trying to hold in the sound. "Just another minute or two and we'll be out."

Stay continued to grind his hard cock into my pussy and I continued to silently laugh until we both quietly uttered our release, lips still pressed together.

Every muscle in my body contracted and convulsed in the ecstasy of our reunion. I wanted to languish in the bliss but knew we had to get moving. I held out my hand and he placed a handkerchief in it. As I wiped up our come, I asked, "Did you tell Granny that I love your hankies?"

"As a matter of fact, I did. She wants to meet you. What she really said was, when you get off your ass and win her back, come bring her to me."

"I think I'm going to like her," I said as I pulled on my panties.

"I know she's going to love you." He zipped up his pants.

"How deep in my throat this time?" I asked,

straightening the bottom of my dress.

"This far," he said, holding his fingers about two and a half inches apart.

"Well that's progress I guess."

"We'll keep practicing." He winked and said, "You look amazing in that dress, Lane. I really loved the green one too, and you weren't wearing a bra."

"I didn't think you noticed," I said, handing him back the cloth.

"How could I not? Please wear it on our next date. No panties either," he said, smoothing his black jeans.

"Damn you for making me hot again."

"Let's meet your people and then get out of here. I already need you again." He held my hand as we walked to the door.

"Is my hair okay?" I said, smoothing down the sides.

"You look positively radiant." His quick, carnal kiss stole my breath again.

"Enough or we'll never get home," I said, backing away and unlocking the door.

My father hovered a few feet away.

"Dad, I'm assuming you've met Stayman?" I said, walking forward.

"Briefly. Thank you for putting a smile on Lainie's face. She, more than anyone, deserves it."

"Sir, it's my goal in life to keep it there." Stay kissed the top of my hand.

"Then I like you already."

"Dad, before we go in, I wanted to tell you, I'm moving in with Stay."

He patted Stay's back and said, "You're a lucky man, although she's not much of a cook."

"Daddy!" I groaned.

"I've got it covered," Stay said. "She makes up for it in so many other ways."

My father actually winked at Stay and I almost died of embarrassment. "He's a keeper," my dad whispered into my ear.

We found my mother in the kitchen, checking on the progress of the help she hired.

"Hi, Mom," I said, getting her attention.

She scanned me up and down and said, "That's a gorgeous dress but you cheapen it with your hair down."

Stay didn't give me a chance to respond. He held out his hand and said, "Stayman Stills, Lainie's boyfriend."

She looked up in shock.

"Boyfriend?" she muttered.

"Yes, and she is wearing her hair my favorite way. Wearing her hair up with that dress would just prematurely age her. She has beautiful waves she should be proud of, which I'm sure you agree?"

"Well ... I ... you're really her boyfriend?"

I rolled my eyes and said, "Yes, Mother and we're moving in together."

"Well, I don't know what to say. It's surprising."

"Do you need any assistance?" Stay asked her. "I used to help my grandmother in the kitchen a lot."

"Lainie's useless in the kitchen," she said.

"That hasn't been my experience," Stay said and winked at me.

Sex on the dinner table flashed in my mind and I could have sworn Stay sent the image to my brain.

"Did you know I used to have a dancer's figure until I had Lainie?" My mother said.

"You're still a very shapely and attractive woman, Mrs. Simmons," he said.

I rolled my eyes and on the way out of the kitchen I heard her say, "You're a very nice young man. I hope Lainie can hold on to you." I wandered over to my Dad who was perched on the sideline watching the gathering. "Stay's busy schmoozing Mother."

He held my hand and said, "I'm happy for you, baby girl. Does he rock your world like Mason did?"

"Better, much better." I snuggled against his arm and listened to him make up stories of what the people around us were saying.

When Stay finally made his way back to me, Dad and I were hysterically laughing.

"I think I missed the fun part," Stay said. "You were right, Lane, your mother is not a fan."

"Fortunately her father is," Dad said.

"Yes it is," I said, reaching up for a hug. "I love you, Dad. We're going to head out."

"I understand. I love you more, baby girl."

"Bye-bye, daddio."

He held out his hand to Stay and said, "It's been a pleasure meeting you, son. I do hope to see a lot more of you. Baby, drag him along on one of our walks."

"I will."

Outside, I said, "We both have our cars, but I don't want to be apart for a second."

"Neither do I. I can drive you back here on Monday morning before work." Stay and I strolled to his car down the street.

"Did you park this far so I wouldn't see your Corvette?"

"Yes. Lainie?"

"Yes, love?" I said, hugging his arm to me as we walked.

"I love you so much."

We stopped moving and I said, "I love you too, Stay.

When I was with Mason, I realized that I had started loving you the night you took care of me."

"So did I. That mother of yours," he said, shaking his head. "Phew, I know you warned me but she is—"

"A bitch. Did she try to change your mind?"

"She actually said I must be blind or stupid."

I cracked up, I couldn't help myself.

We continued down the sidewalk to Stay's car.

He opened the door for me and said, "You father on the other hand is great. I would love to spend more time with him."

"We will. Now take me to your place and take me hard and fast."

"It's our place now," he said as he started the engine.

"Damn that sounds good."

CHAPTER THIRTY-THREE

Lifetime

by Maxwell

When Wednesday rolled around, I couldn't wait for our get together at Red's. No one knew of our plans to move in together, which was a minor miracle amongst our chatty group. I was excited to let them know. Stay seemed to be up to something and I could sense another surprise on the horizon.

I left work early to go with Stay to visit his grandmother.

Once in the Prius, I said, "Let's stop and get some flowers. You said she has her own apartment, right?"

"Yes. That's a great idea." He made a right turn onto the main drag.

"Do you know her favorites?"

"Roses and lilies."

"That just reminded me of the card you left for me at work. I laughed so hard."

"I love making you laugh. Do you still have it?"

"I do."

"We should frame it."

"That's a great idea." I loved that we were creating memories together. "I'll search for a flower shop along the way," I said, waking up my phone.

After we picked up a bouquet with a vase, Stay drove us to meet Granny.

"I'm a bit nervous," I said to him when he opened the door to the assisted living complex.

"I understand. I'm sure you'll hit it off with her."

He knocked on her apartment door and she let us in. I stood in shock for a minute. For some reason I had envisioned a tiny, elderly woman with white hair, maybe even stooped over a bit. Granny was a vital woman, life brimming in her blue eyes just like Stay. She stood almost as tall as me and hugged me immediately.

"Gorgeous, just like I imagined," she said to me as she accepted the flowers. "Very nice bouquet."

"Thank you. You're nothing like I expected," I said with a laugh. "The name Granny threw me off."

She laughed with me. "You can call me Edith."

"It's very nice to meet you, Edith. I hear I owe you a huge debt of thanks."

"I think it's the other way around, honey. My Stayman is happier than I have ever seen him." She patted his leg.

Edith showed us around the complex and I understood why she chose to live there. It was like a vacation resort with apartments.

Both Edith and Stay went into the back bedroom for a bit, leaving me to look at all the pictures on the wall. Some were photographs that Stay had taken and many were pictures of him as a kid. I didn't see any pictures of his parents or baby pictures of him.

We had a wonderful visit, and while spending time with Edith it was easy to see how Stay turned out to be the wonderful man I knew.

"Please come back and see me again," she said as we hugged goodbye.

"You can count on it." Once we were back in the car I said, "I had no idea."

"She's amazing, right?" he said as he drove out of the complex parking lot.

"Totally. A force of nature."

"Like you." He glanced at me and smiled.

"Like me? You're crazy."

"Not at all. You'll make a great mom, just like her."

I shook my head and asked, "Do you think of her as your mother?"

"I do."

By the time we made it to Red's I was busting out with excitement.

"What is it?" Jacqs said as soon as she saw me.

"We are going to move in together. We're telling the gang tonight."

"Whoop, whoop," she shouted, dancing around. "I hate to gloat but I knew it. You guys are perfect for each other." She patted her own back.

"You told her," Stay said as he joined us outside.

"I couldn't keep it from her."

Jacqs jumped up and hugged Stay. "I'm so happy for you guys."

After hugging Jacqs, he straightened up, "Is everyone here yet?"

"I'm not sure about Bond," she started.

"I'm here," he said, "So is the rest of the group." He picked up Jacqs and gave her a quick kiss.

Stay threw his arm over Bond's shoulder and led him back inside.

"Jacqs, I'm so in love," I said. "It's feels completely different than my love for Mason did."

"I can tell. You look really happy."

"I am."

Bond returned a moment later and asked us to come back in.

Everyone had gathered on the couches in the front sitting area. Sam, Cat, and I sat on the right couch, Red, Jacqs, and Bond sat on the left. Kev and Blue sat in the loveseat, and Stay stood before us.

"Lainie and I have some news," Stay said.

Sam clapped before he even finished.

"Lainie and I are moving into my place together."

Everyone cheered and my silly eyes watered over their support.

Bond rose and slid the coffee table away from the couch I sat upon and sat back down.

I looked up and Stay caught my eyes. "You're everything and so much more than I ever hoped to find in a lover, a friend, and soul mate. There is no doubt in my mind that I want to spend the rest of my life with you." He knelt down before me and opened up a box. Inside nestled an oval opal ring with ruby petals lining the perimeter. "Lainie, would you do me the great honor of becoming my wife."

I scanned his face and the smiles of my friends, and I knew there would never be another man for me. "Yes, definitely, but on one condition."

Everyone in the room held their breath, or so it seemed.

"Which is?" His smile lit up his face giving me the idea he might know.

I tugged on his shoulder so I could whisper in his ear. I quietly said, "No fisting."

He laughed so hard he nearly fell over. "Deal," he said aloud.

Everyone cheered as Stay slipped the ring on my finger. As he hugged me he said, "It's not my grandmother's engagement ring, but a family heirloom her mother passed on to her. If you don't like—"

"I love it. It's perfect. Thank you so much." I put my arms around his neck and kissed him, not at all caring about the audience surrounding us.

"Thank you, Lainie, for saying yes." He sat in my spot and shifted me onto his lap.

I watched our friends chatter about the news. Reclining back on Stay I asked, "Is this because we're moving in together?"

"Partly yes, you know I'm old fashioned. But mostly it's that you're mine and I want everyone to know it. We can set the date when we're ready."

I whispered into his ear, "I'm ready."

"Sorry folks for the short visit but I need to get Lainie home."

The group laughed as we hugged everyone goodbye.

We managed to get very little packing done over the next few days. We couldn't get enough of each other. With Stay I found a joy I hadn't thought possible.

I never responded to Mason's texts and emails. Internally, I thanked him for his love. I learned a lot about myself with him and he helped me release some of the hang ups I had about my body. He also opened my mind to trying new sexual experiences, which Stay benefited from.

I thought that when all the drama of my life passed by I would go back to being less emotional. Somehow Stay had opened my heart and now my emotions lived at the surface. I was getting used to getting teary eyed over a moving show, or a song that really touched me, or even the joys of my friends.

Sometimes the very worst experiences in life have a

way of transforming into exactly what you need at the time. I felt grateful every day for the wonderful people in my life. I even found a true place of love for Bond, which I never thought could happen.

Stay and I decided to wait a year to get married and planned to do it at Butterfly World.

Thank you so much for reading *Bittersweet Deceit* (book 2 of the Bound by Your Love series). If you enjoyed my writing style, I have other books available on Amazon.

My latest stand-alone romantic comedy
The Second First Chance
Bound by Your Love Series (erotic romance)
Stuck in Between
Blue Persuasion
My Body Trilogy (dark, erotic, suspense)
My Body-His
My Body-His (Marcello)
My Body-Mine

Co-Authored with Dana Bennett (romance)
The Demarcation of Jack

Blakely Bennett grew up in Southeast Florida and has been residing in the great Northwest for over nine years. She graduated from Nova Southeastern University with a degree in psychology, which accounts for her particular interest in crafting the personalities, struggles, and motivations of her characters. She is an avid reader of many genres of fiction, but especially enjoys erotica and romance. Writing has always been her bliss.

Blakely is married to a wonderful, loving, and supportive husband, who is also a writer, and who helps to keep her grounded. She is a mother, a communitarian, a lover of music (it is always on while she is writing thanks to Pandora), and a good friend. An advocate of love and female empowerment, she is also a facilitator for a women's group. She loves to walk and hike for exercise, and finds that, since moving to Seattle, Washington, she is now one of those crazy people who walk in the rain.

Bittersweet Deceit is her sixth novel. She is also the author of the dark erotic suspense My Body Trilogy *(My Body-His, My Body-His (Marcello) and My Body-Mine*) and the co-author of the contemporary romance, *The Demarcation of Jack,* which she wrote with her husband, Dana Bennett.

You can find Blakely on the web at:
www.blakelybennett.com